More Praise f
Merivel

"Tremain contrasts beauty and coarseness, melancholy and slapstick, tenderness and pageantry. Wonderfully rich."
—*Publishers Weekly*

"A richly painted setting enlivened by an intriguingly empathetic portrait of Charles II and an all-too-human hero—passionate, paradoxical, self-destructive, and infinitely sympathetic."
—*Library Journal*

"Richly marbled with intelligence, compassion and compelling characters, leavened with flourishes of lyricism and an attractive tolerance towards human frailties." —*Times* (London)

"What ultimately makes the book such a joy is simply being in Merivel's company. His narration is by turns rueful, comic, despairing and joyful; but it's always bursting with life, always good-hearted—and always entirely loveable." —*Daily Mail*

"Robert Merivel is one of the great imaginative creations in English literature of the past 50 years. . . . [*Merivel* is] as rich and as dazzling as its predecessor—steeped in wise and witty reflection on the great Mysteries of Life, and the timeless, futile Hopes and Follies." —*Daily Telegraph*

"When he appeared in 1989, Merivel was truly the man of the Thatcherite moment, an individualistic, hedonistic creature who held up a mirror to his audience. So does he still have something to say to us in 2012? Resoundingly, yes." —*Observer*

"Tremain's control of her character and her reflective but often dramatic unfolding of events are impressive acts of authorial ventriloquism, in which she gives a nod to the great diarists of that era but carries off her own man's story with wit, grace and originality. . . . [S]he not only effortlessly sustains momentum and mood, but brings the novel to as near a perfect ending as one could wish." —*Herald*

Novels

Sadler's Birthday
Letter to Sister Benedicta
The Cupboard
The Swimming Pool Season
Restoration
Sacred Country
The Way I Found Her
Music and Silence
The Colour
The Road Home
Trespass

Short Story Collections

The Colonel's Daughter
The Garden of the Villa Mollini
Evangelista's Fan
The Darkness of Wallis Simpson

For Children

Journey to the Volcano

MERIVEL
A MAN of HIS TIME

ROSE
TREMAIN

W. W. Norton & Company
New York • London

For information about permission to reproduce selections from this book,
write to Permissions, W. W. Norton & Company, Inc.
500 Fifth Avenue, New York, NY 10110

For information about special discounts for bulk purchases, please contact
W. W. Norton Special Sales at specialsales@wwnorton.com or 800-233-4830

Manufacturing by RR Donnelley, Harrisonburg
Production manager: Devon Zahn

Library of Congress Cataloging-in-Publication Data

Tremain, Rose.
Merivel : a man of his time / Rose Tremain. — First American edition.
pages cm
ISBN 978-0-393-07957-9 (hardcover)
1. Great Britain—History—Charles II, 1660–1685—Fiction. 2. Physicians—
Great Britain—Fiction. 3. France—History—Louis XIV, 1643–1715—Fiction.
4. Switzerland—History—1648–1789—Fiction. 5. Historical fiction. I. Title.
PR6070.R364M47 2013
823'.914—dc23
2012047744

ISBN 978-0-393-34893-4 pbk.

W. W. Norton & Company, Inc.
500 Fifth Avenue, New York, N.Y. 10110
www.wwnorton.com

W. W. Norton & Company Ltd.
Castle House, 75/76 Wells Street, London W1T 3QT

1 2 3 4 5 6 7 8 9 0

For Penny, of course,
with love

Contents

Part One
The Great Enormity

I

On this day, which is the Ninth day of November in the year 1683, a most singular thing has occurred.

I was taking my habitual midday dinner (of boiled chicken with carrots and small ale) when my Manservant, Will, came into my Dining Room at Bidnold Manor, bearing in his gnarled old hands a package, wrapped in torn paper and bound with faded ribbon. He placed this object at my right hand, thus causing a cloud of dust to puff onto my plate of food.

'Take care, Will,' said I, feeling all my breath drawn in and then expelled in such an almighty sneeze that it flecked the tablecloth with tiny morsels of carrot. 'What is this Relic?'

'I do not know, Sir Robert,' said Will, attempting a dispersal of the dust, by waving his misshapen fingers back and forth.

'You do not know? But how has it arrived in the house?'

'Chambermaid, Sir.'

'You got it from one of the maids?'

'Found under your mattress.'

I wiped my mouth and blew my nose (with a striped, very faded dinner napkin once given to me by the King) and laid my hands upon the parcel, which, in truth, appeared like a thing purloined from some Pharaoh's Tomb, far down in the dry earth. I would have questioned Will further about its unlikely provenance and the reason of its sudden discovery on this particular day, but Will had already turned and was embarked on his slow and limp-

3

ing return journey from the dining table to the door, and to have called him back might well have occasioned some physical Catastrophe, which I had no heart to risk.

Alone once more, I tugged at the ribbon, noting some stains upon it, as of Mouse or Fly droppings, and the notion that some creature might have had its whole lowly existence beneath my mattress caused me a brief moment of amusement.

Then I had the package open and saw before me a thing so long forgotten by me, I think it would never have come back into my mind of its own accord by any means.

It was a Book. Rather, it had once aspired to the immortal status of a Book, but never did acquire any such immortality, but only remained a collation of pages, written in my inky, looping hand. Long ago, in the year 1668, when I returned here at last to Bidnold Manor, I contemplated destroying this Book, but I did not. I gave it to Will – with the instruction to consign it in some hiding-place of his own choosing and to contrive to forget where that hiding-place might be.

The pages contained the story of my Former Life. I had set down this story at a time of great confusion in the last years of my fourth decade, when I felt for the first time the radiance of King Charles II fall upon my insignificant shoulders.

I had hoped the writing of it would enable me to understand what role I might play in my profession as a Physician, in my country and in the world. But though in all my frenzied Scribblings I believed myself to be moving towards some kind of Wisdom, I cannot now recall that I ever arrived there. I was driven from place to place like a hungry dog. It was a time of marvels and glories, crammed with sorrows. And now, to read my own words and see this Life again unfold before me, brought to my heart an almost unbearable overload of Feeling.

I take up the Book and go to my Library. I lay the Book on my escritoire and attend to the feebly burning fire, placing more logs upon it and exhorting it to remember why it was lit – and that reason was to warm me. But I am still shivering. I wonder whether I shall send again for Will who, from long and weary habit, has a knack for coaxing flames into life. But in these late times of the 1680s, when I am approaching my fifty-seventh birthday, I am more and more reluctant to assign to Will any task whatsoever, owing to his extreme age (seventy-four years) and his many Infirmities.

Indeed, the whole Question of Will is one which hugely vexes me, for I do clearly see that, in regard to this faithful Servant of mine, I am caught in a very painful Trap.

I have known William Gates (ever and always called 'Will' by me) since the year 1664 when the King gifted to me the Order of the Garter, together with my Norfolk Estates. These Rewards I got for an important service I had rendered His Majesty, which changed utterly the course of my life.

Will came into my household, along with my cook, Cattlebury, in that same year and, in all my many joys and tribulations, never for one moment showed me anything but loyalty and consideration of the most touching order.

Though my interior Decorations were, at one time, very loud and vulgar, Will pretended his admiration for them. Though I myself behaved towards my young wife Celia in ways loathsome to her and to the world, never at any moment did Will throw me the least glance of sorrow or reproach. And when I and my beloved house had, for some years, to part company, on account of my innumerable follies, Will became its de facto guardian, faithfully writing to me with News of the comings and goings within it, and of the changing colours in the park, as some several seasons passed. In short, no man could have had by his side for almost twenty years a more admirable, loyal, honest and hardworking Servant.

Now, however, Will's body and mind are much decayed. Though I pay him handsomely, he is no longer able to perform to any satisfactory degree the Tasks about my house and person for which he receives his money. He cannot walk without his knees bend outwards and his spine curves over, like the spine of a little rat, so that his progress across any room is most painful and slow. When attempting to carry any Article, whether a tureen of soup or a tankard of ale, he is like to let it fall and smash or spill, for that his hands have some Disease of Curvature and cannot fasten themselves securely round an object. Other afflictions are come upon him, viz. Forgetfulness, near-Blindness and a Deafness, which I fancy may be dictated more by Whim than by any true loss of hearing. For if I give Will an order that he does not relish, such as that of accompanying me on one of my visits to my Patients, he affects not to hear a word that I have uttered, whereas any command that is to his liking he obeys without question or hesitation.

He has become very fearful of the world beyond the gates of Bidnold. Where, once upon a memorable time, he came with me by fast coach to London and waited patiently in the gardens at Whitehall while I endured an encounter with the King which almost broke my heart, and Will's too, now he keeps close within the house and is barely to be seen taking the air of the park, 'lest,' he says to me one day, 'it give me a bitter Winter Ague, Sir Robert, or that I might trip upon a grassy tussock and break my Shin and fall, and be not able to raise myself up and lie undiscovered till night come, or morning, when frost or snow obliterate me quite.'

'Ah, is that what you think of me, Will,' say I to this, 'that I would leave you lying alone and wounded under the stars or out in the snow?'

'Well, I do, Sir,' says he, 'for the reason that you would not *know* of my falling, for I am a Servant, Sir Robert, and have practised the Art of Invisibility for these twenty years, so that the sight of me, whether upright or lying down, be never troubling to you.'

I wanted to remark that, in recent years, the Sight of Will causes me *nothing but trouble*, but I did not. For to say anything wounding to Will appears to be quite beyond my powers. And when I think of what I should rightly do, which is to dismiss him from my service, I feel in my heart a terrible Ache. For the truth is that

I feel for Will a most profound affection, as though he might be a sort of Father to me, a Father who, in his goodness, has chosen to overlook my many imperfections and to see me as an Honourable Man.

What am I do, then?

If I take from Will his seniority in the Servants' Hierarchy at Bidnold Manor and assign to him lighter duties, such as those a mere Footman might easily perform, I know that he will feel the pain of this demotion through to his heart's core. He will deduce that I no longer value him. The sweetness of his nature will turn sour towards those who would now be above him in rank.

If I call him to me and tell him that I wish him to Take his Ease henceforth and do no more work, but live in honourable Retirement here in my house, with all his pecuniary needs accommodated by me, it is possible that – such being the intensity of the bodily pain he suffers – he might fall at my feet and bless me and shed tears of gratitude and tell me that no kinder being than I, Sir Robert Merivel, lives and breathes in the world.

But though I admit I do like to imagine this scene, with my poor old Servant prostrate at my feet as though I were the King Himself, with all his inestimable power, I do also foresee, alas, great perturbation coming from another source, namely the rest of my Household, including Cattlebury, who is not far behind Will in age and Mental Confusion, and who has alarmed me with his occasional bouts of violent, seditious Agitation, during which he is fond of blaspheming against the Monarch and the Stuart dynasty and all their works.

Indeed, I dread that I might find myself the butt of a jealous Mutiny, upbraided for my unfairness and for my lack of consideration towards Cattlebury, but also towards the housemaids, footmen, washerwomen, woodcutters, grooms, and kitchen maids et cetera et cetera. And then I see in my mind a terrible Cavalcade of all my servants (without whose presence this household would soon enough fall into chaos) disappearing down the drive, and I left alone but for Will, to whom, in time, I would become a Nurse . . . thus performing a neat but vexing turn upon the Wheel of Fortune.

Better, say I to myself, to harden my heart and let Will perform his solitary Exit, with the destination 'Workhouse' writ upon his retreating back. But a Trap closes even upon this notion. For I have seen the Workhouses. Indeed I have. Not only are they cold and inhospitable places, and full of vermin and noise and stench, they must also, by law, live up to their name and so demand of their inhabitants that they *work*. Thus we return by a dread circle to the one thing of which Will Gates is well-nigh incapable: labour.

I ask again, what am I to do?

I cannot put Will out, to beg in the lanes and fields of Norfolk. He has no Family anywhere (nor ever has had, as far as I can ascertain) to take him in.

And so I conclude that – as with very many vexing things in this life – the only course is to *do nothing*, in the vain hope that the Question of Will may somehow be resolved by Nature.

But no sooner has it entered my head that Will might soon *die*, than a feeling of the utmost Panic seizes upon me and I ask for Will to be sent to me in the Library straight away, so that I may verify that he is *not dead yet*.

Some time lapses between my command and Will's arrival at my door. As it lengthens – by virtue of the Slowness with which Will moves – I find myself drawn again to the sight of the Book lying on my escritoire and remembering that within its pages are numerous accounts of Will's kindnesses to me, as when I was commanded to ride in haste to London for an Audience with the King, without my supper, and Will thrust two Roasted Quail into the pocket of my riding coat and tied a flask of Alicante to the saddle of my mare, Danseuse, without which repast I might have fallen down in a faint when at last summoned into The Presence.

It has been, indeed, as though, for almost twenty years, Will's mind had kept a vigil upon mine, anticipating its many vacancies and shortcomings, and attempting to remedy these before I had become aware of them. And this realisation moves me to sudden tears, so that when at last Will enters the Library, he finds me blubbing by the fire. Though his sight is poor, he can tell at once that I am crying and says: 'Oh, not again, Sir Robert! Upon my soul, I think you will wear out all your handkerchiefs before the year is gone.'

'Luckily,' I say, 'it is November, Will. So there is not much more of the year in which to wear them out.'

'True, Sir,' he says, 'but I do not know, and nor does any of us here at Bidnold know why you must always be weeping.'

'No,' say I, blowing my nose on a silk foulard once given to me by my former Amour, Lady Bathurst, and now worn to a gossamer thinness. 'I do not know either. Now, Will, I have sent for you to ask you about this Book. It is the same Book, written by me in the years 1664 to 1667, which I gave into your possession when this House was restored to me in 1668. Was it then that you placed it under my mattress?'

Will's eyes go wandering about the space before him, as though it might be some dark cave where no light entered. His gaze falls at last upon the package containing the Book.

'1668?' he says. 'That was long ago, Sir Robert.'

'I know it was. It was fifteen years ago to be precise. Was it then that you laid the parcel under my mattress?'

'Must have been, Sir.'

'But you cannot be certain?'

'Of what thing in the world can a man be certain, Sir Robert?'

'Well. There is such a thing as Memory. Do you have any recollection of placing this object in my bed?'

'Yes, Sir.'

'You do?'

'Yes. I took it and laid it under your mattress, where you would not see it.'

I leave the fireside and begin to pace about the room, stuffing away my foulard and, in a general way, trying to assert in my person some semblance of Dignity and mastery of the moment. Then I turn and stare accusingly at Will.

'Do you mean to say, therefore,' I say, 'that my mattress has not been turned in *sixteen years?*'

Will does not move, but stands by the escritoire, holding fast to its edge, as though he might be about to fall. At length he says: 'It is not my job to turn mattresses, Sir Robert.'

'I know. But all the same, Will. Sixteen years! Do you not think that you, as head of the staff at Bidnold, should take some responsibility? Could not fleas and bedbugs have clustered there and done me harm?'

'Done you harm?'

'Yes.'

'I would never do you harm, Sir Robert.'

'I know, Will. All I am asking—'

'But there is another thing.'

'Yes?'

'A person does not always see a thing when it is there.'

'What d'you mean?'

'I mean . . . this Book of yours, it is so faded and snowed with dust and time, it might have looked – to the chambermaid – as a mere Wedge, to hold fast the corners of the bedstead.'

A Wedge to hold fast the corners of the bedstead.

I will freely admit, this last utterance of Will's does make me smile. My smile turns quickly to laughter, at which Will looks mightily relieved. I suppose it is not very agreeable to work for a Master who is so frequently overcome by Melancholy and childish tears, and I know that I must devise some way to become more buoyant in my existence. For the moment, however, I am at a loss to know how to go about this task.

I send Will away. I once again open the Book (which I shall henceforth refer to as *The Wedge*) and begin to read.

I read so long that the November Darkness begins to fall. No servant appears in the Library to light a lamp, so that the room becomes very blue with shadows.

And one darker shadow creeps out of the Story and seems to stand in silence beside me. I fancy I can smell the fustian of his clothes and see his white hands folded round an object I know to be a blue-and-white china soup ladle. His name is John Pearce.

2

I cannot think about John Pearce without a feeling, almost, of Suffocation coming into me. For this reason I endeavour not to think about him at all. But I am not always successful.

He was once my friend and fellow student of medicine at Cambridge. All his life he held to the Quaker religion, about which I used to tease him very frequently, hoping to engrave on the sombre map of his features the small indentation of a Smile, or even to hear his laughter, which was a singular croaking sound, like the mutterings of a bullfrog.

Though Pearce showed me much kindness, I know now that the Person I am, with all my uncontainable appetites, my mockery of the World and my failure to overcome my abiding Melancholy, was never truly loved by him.

When he visited me here at Bidnold, he looked about him at all my scarlet and gold Furnishings, at my gilded mirrors, my tapestries and marble statuettes and collections of pewter, and told me that Luxury was 'snuffing out my Vital Flame'. And when – after his being struck down with fever – Will and I kept Vigil at Pearce's bedside for thirty-seven hours, he gave neither of us any thanks whatsoever.

It was to Pearce that I went, however, when the King saw fit to cast me out of the Paradise into which he had put me.

I strove to be of use in the Quaker Bedlam at Whittlesea where Pearce and his Friends offered care to some of those who had collapsed into madness beneath the burden of the world. But the follies I committed there were very great and, as if in sorrow at all that I was capable of by way of Debauchery and Stupidity, Pearce's frail body brewed up a very violent Consumption, from which he died.

We laid branches of pear blossom in his coffin. Into his hands I placed the blue-and-white china soup ladle, to which he had been passionately attached, for it was the only Thing he possessed from his Mother. The dark Fenland earth was heaped upon him.

From time to time I return to Pearce's grave. When she was nine or ten years old, I took my beloved daughter, Margaret, with me, so that I might present her to the Quaker Friends who had been so kind to me. (She is and always was a very beautiful child, with soft white skin and an abundance of fiery curls, and a dimpled smile of great sweetness.) I am immoderately proud of her.

When we came to the causeway known as Earls Bride, leading to the place where the Bedlam Hospital once stood, I saw at once that the buildings were deserted and the land about them overgrown, and that not one soul remained there. As we dismounted from the coach, a freezing wind howled round about us. I took Margaret's hand and led her forward into the first of the Houses, where, still, some straw sleeping pallets lay, and I saw her eyes very wide with wonder and confusion, and she said to me: 'Oh, Papa, where are all the people? Are they drowned?'

'Margaret,' said I, 'I do not know. But it seems certain that they are gone.'

And then I found myself in a Quandary. I had planned to leave Margaret in the care of the Quaker Keepers for a little moment, in order to walk out and stand beside Pearce's grave. I did not wish her to look upon his sad mound, (for so far Death had not made any imprint upon her innocent mind) and yet, having made this long journey, I was reluctant to drive away without standing for a moment under the sky, to commune with my dead friend.

Margaret and I stumbled together about the place, where weeds grew tall and rank, and I showed her the gnarled and twisted oak tree in the courtyard, where once I played my oboe and my young friend Daniel played his fiddle and we – the Keepers and the mad people all together – danced a Tarantella – but I did not tell her that her Mother was one among the mad.

'What is a Tarantella?' said Margaret.

'Oh,' said I, 'it is a wild whirling jig, like this . . .' And I held her, two hands and began to prance about with her and she hopped and skipped with joy, and her laughter was like a cluster of bells, shaken under the vast, vaulting sky. And then I lifted her up and carried her to the coach and said to her: 'Rest here a moment, while I make one last tour of the houses, to be certain no one has been left behind, and I shall be back in a trice.'

I had brought with us a bag of dried currants and I gave her a handful of these, and she began to eat them obediently as I told the Coachman to wait for me, and I strode away towards the place where Pearce lies.

The grave, marked by a plain wooden cross (for that everything, with the Quakers, has to be Plain) was very choked with Elder and rough Briars, and I could not help myself from trying to get these away. And so, tearing the skin of my hands in my haste, I heard in my mind Pearce's disdain for what I was doing, saying to me: 'Merivel, tell me what purpose your actions serve. For, in all truth, I see none.'

'No,' I said. 'None at all. Except that these things Offend me.' And then I burst out with a cry, saying: 'Where has everybody gone, Pearce? Tell me where they have gone!'

But of course there was no answer from beneath the neglected mound. I cleared all the weeds away and bound my hand with a handkerchief, and touched the black clay with my fingers.

'John Pearce,' I said, 'you are with me always.'

Margaret has now reached the age of seventeen. She has lived here with me at Bidnold all her life and I have striven to be both

Father and Mother to her, and, to my joy and relief, I observe – without any boasting or paternal Blindness – that she is a most beautiful, chaste and affectionate young girl, with a trusting nature not unlike my own, but miraculously devoid of her father's Silliness.

She loves me, I know, as much as any father could ask of a child, but as she has grown up, she has become more and more fond of spending time in the House of my near Neighbour in Norfolk, Sir James Prideaux, Baronet, who is a man most venerated and learned in the Law and who presides at the Sessions House in Norwich three times a week.

This house of Prideaux's, Shottesbrooke Hall, is a very lively place, on account of the presence of his admirable wife, Arabella, and their four daughters, Jane, Mary, Virginia and Penelope. And I do see that Margaret has more to make her joyful there than here at Bidnold with me.

That Prideaux has no son must be, to a man of his stature and ambition, a disappointment, but he never speaks of it. To his girls he shows nothing but affectionate kindness, endeavouring to get for them all that they could possibly want. Music masters, dancing teachers, young professors of Mathematics and Geography, no less than Pattern-makers, Seamstresses and Haberdashers (such as my dear parents once were), come and go from Shottesbrooke, and the Prideaux girls demonstrate, each one, a fine curiosity about the world.

Towards Margaret, who is the same age as Mary, all the family shows a most touching care – just as though she might be a true part of the household. They recognise that although I, too, have taken some pains with Margaret's education – to the end that she plays the harpsichord admirably well and can speak French quite fluently, and dances like a beautiful Sprite of the Woods – she must often find her days with me a little dull. She is now studying Geography with Mary and over this is in rhapsodies, saying to me: 'Oh, Papa, never until now did I see that the world was so wide and vast. And never did I know that Great Rivers began as little Springs in the bosom of the mountains, and did you know that there are more than two hundred languages spoken on the Earth?'

'No,' say I, 'God be praised that I did not. The mastery of French is quite difficult enough for me.'

Margaret is staying at Shottesbrooke Hall now, in this grey November, when *The Wedge* has suddenly come into my possession.

I note that when I first set down my Story, I speculated that there may have been more than one Beginning to it. I suggested indeed Five Beginnings. For I understood then that no life begins only when it begins, but has many additional inceptions, and each of these determines the course of what is to come.

And I now see with equal clarity that a man's life may have more than one Ending. But alas, the endings I may have earned present themselves to me, each and every one, in a sombre light. If there are five, as there were Five Beginnings, then these must surely be they.

An Ending through Loneliness. I cling to Margaret. She it is who stands between Myself and a very paramount feeling of the Void round about me. Whatever is good or noble in me, I see only in her. But I know that Margaret must soon enough marry. She will leave Bidnold for some other (and better) life.

Already, I am colluding with this Future, conferring with Prideaux and other Norfolk acquaintances about the suitability of certain young sons of the County Squires – or even of the Aristocracy – as husband to the daughter of a Knight of the Garter and Close Confidant of the King.

Hugo Mulholland, the son and heir of Sir Gerald Mulholland, a handsome youth, but with a strange stuttering speech, has called upon Margaret more than once. I can tell that she thinks Nothing of him and, when he is gone, laughs at his stutter and imitates it to perfection.

The last time this poor Hugo called, when he was safely in his Departing Carriage, Margaret folds her arms round my neck and says: 'Papa, do not cast me off to some stammering husband, I beg you!' And I kiss her hair and reassure her that she will only marry when she herself desires it and that, as far as it concerns myself, I would keep her with me at Bidnold to the end of time. But I know that I must not do this. Margaret will marry one day and that is that.

An Ending through Poverty. Though I am still practising Medicine, attending to the sores and sufferings of my neighbours in Norfolk as best I can, I seem to be one of those individuals to whom others prefer to become Indebted, rather than to pay him what they have contracted to pay.

From time to time I make up Accounts of what is owed to me and these sums are always large, and for a short time I endeavour to pursue my debtors with Firmness and Resolution. Some have the goodness to settle my bills, but little by little, in the absence of the rest of the money appearing, my Firmness and Resolution in regard to it die away, and I weary absolutely of my pursuit, as though it might be of some Unicorn, lost in the forests of Legend, which I am never going to find.

Thus, in time, my income may fall to almost nothing, and – unless the King keeps up the very generous Stipend or *loyer* that he allotted me when he returned my house to me in 1668, to ensure that I would always be ready at any moment in Time to receive him at Bidnold Manor – I may pass into a State of Destitution for which there will be no remedy. Without the *loyer* I would certainly be a discomfited man.

An Ending from Poisoning. My cook, Cattlebury – as already mentioned – is not so far behind Will in human Muddle that he can any longer be trusted to perform his culinary tasks with any real skill or competence. Last week, Cattlebury sugared a meat pie and fried a herring in molasses. When I returned these concoctions to the kitchen, Cattlebury appeared like an Ogre in my Dining Room, all awash with sweat and steam and holding in his hands not a cudgel, but a wooden Colander, through the holes of which his brains seemed to have slithered away, and asked me why, when he has taken so much trouble to Invent new dishes for me, I was so scornful of them.

'Cattlebury,' said I, 'if these are Inventions, pray return to what has already been invented.'

Will stood at his side, half bent in two and looking mournful. 'He did not mean any harm, Sir Robert,' said Will.

'He may have *meant* no harm,' said I, 'but harm there was, nevertheless. A good herring and a quantity of beef have been wasted.'

'He did not mean it,' repeated Will.

'If he did not mean it,' said I, 'then he did it through inattention or confusion, neither of which Commodity do I wish to find in abundance in a kitchen.'

The two men appeared at a Loss, the one leaning at a right-angle to himself, the other looking as though he had been boiled in a vat of broth, and I looked at them and thought, you will be the Death of me. I shall not survive the Chaos that you bring.

An Ending from Suicide. I learn from Sir James Prideaux, who has attended many an Execution at the scaffold on Mouse Hill, behind Norwich, that among all the robbers, counterfeiters, pickpockets, debtors, pirates and murderers who pass along the thronged way to their Ends, few go there without what he calls 'some element of Pride'. It seems that the Condemned Man sees his last journey on this earth as a veritable Moment of Glory, as though he were raised, suddenly, to be celebrated for his wondrous deeds, instead of hanged for his knavery and deceit.

He will wear the best coat that he has, and his wig, if he has one, will be powdered, and the buckles of his shoes polished, and upon his face – so says Prideaux – resides invariably a beatific smile. Then he waves, even like a Royal Prince, to the crowds, and when the moment comes for him to mount the scaffold he swaggers up there, still waving and showing off the dirty lace at his cuff or the bedraggled plume of his hat.

And I do truly marvel at this and think to myself, why, Merivel, if such men do not fear Death, are you so craven before the thought of it? And so I now instruct myself to cast off this terror and steel my cowardly soul to outdistance my own predestined end by running like a Highwayman into the arms of my Maker. My only difficulty is in trying to imagine that Maker. I see him always and only as my poor Father, who died in a fire in 1662, burning with the feathers and ribbons of his humble Haberdasher's trade.

An Ending through Meaninglessness. This, I think, is the prospective ending that most dismays me. Despite a most almighty Struggle with God and with my Vocation, endeavouring always (as once exhorted by the King) to discover my own Usefulness and Purpose, I arrive very frequently at the suspicion that my life is a trifling thing, ill-lived, full of Misjudgement, Indulgence and Sloth, leading me only deeper and deeper into an abyss of Confusion and Emptiness, in which I no longer recall why I am alive. And a man who has lost this particular recall must surely be destined soon to Ultimate Oblivion.

Today, Margaret is returning to Bidnold.

Fittingly, a pathway discovers itself among the clouds, and in my park the sun shines copper and golden on the beeches and oaks. I take a turn about the gardens, where I have recently established an alley of pleached Hornbeams, with which I am mightily pleased, and watch the Deer contentedly grazing, untroubled by the winds of November, flicking their tails in the pretty light. And I note, as I have noted a hundred times before, what beauty is here.

When the carriage containing Margaret begins to make its way down the drive, I hasten back to the house, where I find Will already trying to assemble himself to greet his young Mistress. Margaret's maid, Tabitha, comes out also, and smooths her apron and pats her hair to rearrange what the wind has disturbed, and I see on both these faces expressions of great gladness.

Margaret steps down, wearing a new brown Cape, which I think must be a gift from Lady Prideaux, and I hasten to her and fold my arms about her and tell her how glad is all of Bidnold to see her. Though she is my own child, I am struck afresh, each time I see her, by the Glory that she brings with her. She is like a rainbow, or like some dazzle of light, where before there was none.

At supper Margaret says to me: 'Papa, I have some news to tell you: Sir James and his family are going to his mother's estates in the County of Cornwall for all of December and onwards past Twelfth Night. And they have invited me to go with them.'

We are eating a Carbonado, which is one of the few dishes seldom adulterated or burned by Cattlebury. I had been enjoying its excellence until this moment, but now, at once, I feel my appetite fade.

'Cornwall?' I say helplessly.

'Yes,' says Margaret. 'Mary says there are warm winds in that part of the country that blow all year round, and flowers that bloom at Christmas, and pathways of sand and camomile, leading from the house to the sea . . .'

I say nothing. In my mind's eye I see Margaret descending these scented pathways to the sea, wearing her new brown Cape, and walking onwards and onwards, always further and further away from me, until she is out of sight.

'Papa,' says Margaret. 'I hope that you will give me leave to go. There is an island, to which we may sail in a little barque, and on the island are Puffins, and I have never seen a Puffin.'

'Ah,' say I. 'Nor have I.'

I think I have gone pale, for Margaret stares at me and says: 'Are you well, Father? What's the matter?'

'Non . . . nothing . . .' I stammer (like Hugo Mulholland). 'I was merely trying to recall the colours of Puffins and what tail feathers they possess.'

'Their colours are black-and-white, with a yellow or orange bill, according to Penelope, but as to tail feathers, I will, if you let me travel to Cornwall, try to make some drawings or paintings of the birds for you, and then we will both be certain about Puffins.'

I take a gulp of wine. 'That will be a Great Relief,' I say, 'to have all uncertainty about Puffins cast aside!'

We laugh and I try to resume my consumption of the Carbonado, while I tell Margaret that of course she must go to Cornwall, which, in all of England, is one of the kindest places. And so it is accepted. Margaret will be away for some two months. And I hear myself promise to give her money for new clothes and a new fur muffler, in case it be a little breezy aboard the barque. But all the while I am thinking, not about Margaret, but about myself and I see come towards me the spectre of my Death through Loneliness, and I cannot help but feel the sadness of it and its slow chill.

The morning before she left for Shottesbrooke – a day of cold winds and a perturbation of hail, which spattered all the parkland with its white stones – I sat with Margaret beside the Library fire, trying to fortify my spirits with a continuous sip-sipping of some fine Alicante, yet knowing how horribly visible my Melancholy appeared. (I have lately acquired the habit, from the reading of the French philosopher Michel de Montaigne, of trying to see myself *de près*, or 'close up', not looking only outwards, but inwards upon my own demeanour and my own responses, with the eternal aim of acquiring some wisdom about the Person that I am, or might become.)

Trying to cheer me a little, Margaret began promising she would send me frequent letters from Cornwall, describing the beauty of the secret coves where the sea washes in and ebbs out in its perpetual restlessness, and the intricacy of the shells that she and Mary might discover there.

'Ah,' said I, 'and the intricacy of all the Wrecked Ships attacked by Pirates, then torn apart upon the rocks, and of all the Dead washed ashore . . .'

Margaret regarded me with sorrow, as a mother disappointed by the behaviour of her child. 'Father,' she said, after a moment of silence, 'I have been thinking about something.'

'I am glad of that,' I said, 'for a mind empty of thought is prone to terrible Error.'

'Hush and do not mock, for once.'

'Puffins again, I suppose? You have been thinking of those?'

'No. I have been thinking of a thing Sir James said to me when I was last at Shottesbrooke, and that was the Importance – in a man's brief time on the earth – of embarking on some Life's Work.'

'I agree with him. But do not look at your father in that accusatory way, Margaret. You know that I have a great deal of *work* already, and—'

'He was talking about writing, Papa: the composition of a treatise upon some subject of Importance. He himself is embarked upon a very long and substantial Work he has entitled *Observations upon the Poor and upon the Prevalence of Crime in England*. And he told me that this labour of his gives him much satisfaction, for it takes him quite out of his own world . . .'

'You cannot say entirely out,' I snapped. 'Sir James is a magistrate, as you know, and his dealings with the Criminal Poor are therefore very frequent.'

'Indeed. But he is not one of them. He does not have to try to make his way in the world by selling oysters or by petty thievery. He is not shuffled onwards and always onwards from one parish to another, because no one wishes to have the expense of his care . . .'

'True. However—'

'The proposition I am trying to make, Father, is that I think, were *you* to embark upon some great enterprise of Writing, you might be less sunk into yourself and more contented with the world.'

I gaped at my daughter. It is true that I have brought her up to perfect a certain Independence of Thought, but when that same Independence appears directed, like a barbed Arrow, against myself, I feel . . . well, what do I feel? I suppose that I simply feel

Foolish. Yet it is a Foolishness mixed with Fear. (Was not the life of old King Lear brought all to naught by the Independence of Thought of his most beloved daughter?)

I drew nearer the fire, stretching out my hands to warm them. I was within a whisper of relating to Margaret – as some pitiful Defence of what she sees as my idleness and absence of cheer – my earlier attempts to set down the Story of my Life in *The Wedge*, but I remembered in the Nick of Time that this Life reveals, in all their naked horror, many of my Follies and Wickednesses, including the Wickedness I showed towards her own mother. I thus drew back from presenting it to her.

I resumed my sipping of the Alicante. Warmed a little by this, I said: 'It is very kind of you to be devoting your thoughts to my Welfare and do not think that I am not touched by this. And you are right that we are held to the world by our Endeavours in it, and yet . . .'

'And yet what?'

'Oh, Margaret,' I said, 'you did not know me when I was young! For then I was All Endeavour. For every minute of my Existence I was composing some great and Marvellous Plan. I even tried to become an Artist – until some vainglorious portraitist told me I had no talent. There were not hours in the day, nor days in the year, sufficient for all my Schemes. But after you were born and when Bidnold was restored to me, I resolved that I would calm my restless ways and settle down here in Norfolk to take care of you and pursue my profession, and to think no more of Glory or Preferment, or any worldly thing.'

Margaret rose from her chair and came to kneel by my feet, and rested her arms on my knees. 'Papa,' she said gently, 'I was not speaking about Glory.'

I lingered long in my chair after Margaret had gone to bed. 'Merivel,' said I to myself, 'to sit alone like this, day after day, while Margaret is gone to Cornwall, will assuredly bring you to a dark despondency. You must rise up and look about you, in some new place.'

Perhaps it was Margaret's mention of the word 'Glory' that brought to my mind the idea of travelling to France, to the Court of Louis XIV? I knew that what I longed for in these, my declining years, was to be dazzled by Wonders. At Versailles I would surely find them.

3

I have come to London.

I am attired in a very smart Russet Coat and brown Breeks, with a Cascade of lace at my neck and upon my head a very Lively Hat, which seems to shift its own warm weight from time to time as though it might be some tame, nesting Pheasant I had reared in Norfolk.

My wig is full and shiny and new. And I am wearing the Sword – a thing I have not done for some while, so that it keeps dragging upon my coat and threatening to make me stumble and topple me into the gutter. Luckily, I have also brought with me one of my ebony walking Canes and, with this to steady me, I am able to make a reasonably elegant progress down Birdcage Walk.

I am on my way to visit the King, having secured my Audience most easily by messenger and receiving from His Majesty a most delightful short Response, which reads as follows:

Ah, my dear Merivel,
You cannot know, in these sombre and Difficult Times, how much it cheers Us to have word of you. You may come to the Apartments of the Duchess of Portsmouth (our sweet 'Fubbs') at Noon, where you will find Us more Grey and Grave than when last we met, but not lacking in Gladness to see you. And I hope that we may coax Laughter from our hearts.
                                                    Charles Rex

In the Walk, so called for its many airy Birdcages installed by the path, I am jostled by a great quantity of people, who perambulate up and down within that vast shadow still cast by the Palace of Whitehall upon the nation's heart.

I know that the King, who seems to have wearied of every one of his Parliaments and now rules without them Absolutely, is less admired and revered than at his Coming In, when he appeared to us like a god. Indeed, there is a restless or even seditious spirit abroad in the Coffee Houses – or so I am told – and the country would much prefer England to be steered towards war with Catholic France by a Parliament, than to behold in the King's chambers a French mistress planted in splendour, and no Parliament anywhere to be seen. But yet I think there are many men (and women) who still suffer, as I suffer, from an old Disease and that is the Disease of Loving the King.

Though John Pearce, in his Quaker hatred of Monarchy and the Hierarchy of the so-called Nobility that it begets, tried to his dying moment to cure me of this malady, and though I struggled always to be the person that Pearce wanted me to be, I find, still, that the sight of the King – or even the mere *thought* of his arrival at Bidnold – wakes in my heart an extraordinary gladness that I am not able to suppress. And I think it may now be true that I no longer care to suppress it. The King's nature is very like mine, a composite of yearning appetite and sullen hypochondria, so we console each other, and this Consolation is very well understood by both of us.

I go on, without tripping or stumbling, into St James's Park, my heavy Sword making a vexing clicking noise as it bounces against my thighs, and come to a stop by the canal there, where a group of fops are gawping at a Crocodile, which is paddling itself out of the water.

'*Mon dieu! Mon dieu!*' yelp the fops, pointing at the creature and clutching at each other's shoulders in mock terror. 'What a

Brute! Oh, but imagine that great Jaw opening and closing upon one's leg!'

'Or upon one's torso!'

'Oh, horror! Or upon one's *parts*!'

And they scuttle away at a jaunty run, laughing like Choirboys, with all their Swords clicking together and the silk of their stockings catching little glints of sunlight as their legs skip up.

I stand and stare at the Crocodile. It lies upon the grass in an attitude of boredom, as though asking itself how it came here, to London, to be an entertainment for fops and visitors from Norfolk, and I note the seeming thickness of its skin, as though it were a thing born in armour, and valiant always in its readiness for war.

And I remind myself that almost every animal on earth has something about it that calls forth my Respect. Even a Mouse or a horned Beetle: by the softness and silence of the Mouse and the hard shine of the Beetle I am caught in momentary wonder. I have no idea why this should be so, but yet it is. For the beautiful chestnut mare, Danseuse, given to me by the King, I felt an admiration that bordered upon worship. At the death of this animal, I wept for many days.

King Charles receives me in the *petit salon* of his Mistress's apartments, which, I am told, possess more grandeur even than the Queen's, and where, indeed, the King appears very content, lying among furs on a Chaise longue, with an amused smile upon his face.

I kneel at his feet. My knees creak and my Sword clanks upon the floor.

'Ah, Merivel,' says His Majesty, 'I am glad to hear you are just as noisy as you ever were!'

A laugh bursts out of me.

The King claps his hand upon my shoulder. 'Excellent!' he says. 'I have not heard your laughter for far too long! I am drinking Sack. Will you join me?'

'I never find myself capable of refusing Sack, Your Majesty,' I say.

Then I endeavour to raise myself up from my fawning position, but the sheath of my pesky Sword lodges itself behind one of the legs of the Chaise and I tilt forward, only saving myself from falling into the King's lap by reaching out the hand holding my Pheasant Hat and pressing it against the Royal Leg.

I murmur my apologies as I rise at last and am relieved to find that the King is still smiling. It is at that moment that I first take note of how – in the year or more that I have not seen him – he has aged.

Then I am settled comfortably on a chair and given a tumbler of Sack, and the King begins a melancholy discourse upon his state of mind, which, he tells me, 'is becoming prone to irrational Fear and only longs for Peace and Quiet'.

'That I can comprehend,' I say. 'Indeed, Sir, I have no doubt I would long for it too, were it not already a little too peaceful and quiet at Bidnold.'

'Ah, Bidnold. A singular and very lovely place. We shall come there when the winter is past. How is Gates?'

'Well. I must admit he is causing me . . . some moderate anguish, Your Majesty,' I say, and proceed to lay out for the King my Great Dilemma with regard to Will – ending with the conceit that I, in due time, am destined to become Will's Nurse.

Though this entertains the King for a moment (in particular my account of how long it takes Will to walk across my Withdrawing Room, viz. three or four, or even *five* minutes), his features soon enough become grave and he says to me: 'We must never cast away the few who have been loyal, Merivel. Some close to me want me to get rid of my Queen, because she has given me no Heir. But I say to them, "wherefore should I cast her out, she, who has such goodness of heart and abides in her love for me through all my Amours?" I say to them, "You, too, should bow down before the Queen, as I bow down, because there is no one in the Kingdom as noble as she."'

I nod very vigorously, remembering how Queen Catherine once saved me from casting up my dinner onto the Royal Tennis Court by the bringing out of oranges from her native Portugal at a moment when I was faint and sick with running about after the King's balls. Then the King says: 'But we should get to the Main Business of your visit, Merivel. You have come to ask something of me. Or am I mistaken?'

I take a gulp of the Sack. The King's ability to read what is in my mind has always disconcerted me. I cannot suppress a sigh before I say: 'I do not know precisely how to explain why I am here.'

'Perhaps that is because you do not precisely know?'

I look about me at the room and cannot help but notice that the colours with which it has been decorated recall, albeit in tasteful measure, the scarlets, crimsons, magentas and golds I once scattered around the interiors of Bidnold, and I conclude that the Duchess of Portsmouth (born in Paris, Louise de Kéroüalle and known by the King as 'Fubbs' or 'Fubbsy', for reason of her succulent fatness) may have about her some lingering vulgarity of Taste.

Then I turn to the King and say: 'My daughter is going into Cornwall and I shall thus be all alone at Bidnold. And I have it in mind, Sire, to travel to France, to bring about some change of mood in me . . .'

'What mood do you wish to change?'

'Well, I know that I am becoming self-pitying. Gates sees it all too well. I find myself very often sunk in memories of the Past . . .'

'Ah. The Past is always with us. Our lives fill up with it, till there is a brimming-over. How can France help you?'

'It can help me, I believe, because I have never been there. I imagine that the very air is altered, and the weather, and the shape of things . . .'

'Most true. But what will you do there?'

'Well, Sir,' I stammer, 'I do not know exactly, but I had rather not go there as some poor wanderer, knowing no one. And I had begun to wonder whether, in the weeks that I am there, my medical skills might somehow be of service . . . if I might be introduced to—'

'I see. You wish to be received at the Court of my Cousin King Louis?'

'I know that is a very great presumption. Yet my mind has merely begun to meander on the idea of being of some use to His Majesty *le Roi* . . .'

'Do you remember when you first came to me, I gave you the care of my dogs?'

'I remember it very well, Sir.'

'You saved my little Lou-Lou from death and I rewarded you. You might perform the same task for Louis, but alas, he does not like dogs. The French have not our sentimental love of animals. On the other hand my cousin is surrounded by a great Multitude of fawning *supplicants*. Such is their anxiety to be recognised or rewarded by their King, who is regarded as a demi-god, we can well imagine that their poor hearts might be in some distress. So perhaps, you – of all people – might be of use there, devising physic for the hearts of the *plaideurs?*'

Though a little disconcerted by the King's emphasis upon the phrase 'you, of all people', I force myself to nod and bow my assent.

'You must understand, Merivel, that Louis's Court at Versailles is so vast that it eclipses all that surrounds it. It is France itself. This poor Whitehall of mine and these curtailed powers I have as King of England are as naught in comparison with the universe that is Louis's. It is a Wonder of the World. Did you know that thirty-six thousand people worked upon its construction?'

'No, I did not, Sir.'

'Thirty-six thousand men! And as for the gardens, entire Forests were uprooted in Normandy and dragged there, tree by tree. I fancy Versailles may be greater in its ambition than Ancient

Rome. I think you must go there and feel its beauty and its burning.'

I am about to stammer how full of joy I would be to be received at Versailles when the King sets aside his tumbler of Sack and rises suddenly to his feet. I am obliged to follow suit, scrabbling out of my chair and knocking my Pheasant to the floor.

'I will consider how it might be for you at Versailles,' he says. 'The immediate problem I foresee is that nobody will laugh at your Jokes. The French have a much graver and more cruel kind of wit, and Louis has no sense of humour at all. But now there is something that I want to show you. Follow me.'

Servants rush to the King's side, but he waves them away. I note, then, that, as he walks, he limps very slightly, favouring his right leg, yet he strides on and leads me by fast turns out of the Duchess's apartments and on to a narrow stairway, heading upwards.

It becomes colder as we ascend and when we reach the topmost floor I can hear the wind sighing in the slates of the roof. And I am put in mind, just for a moment, of the West Tower at Bidnold, which Space was the only Space restored to me when I returned in 1667, and in whose confines I had to make my entire existence for many months. The sound of the wind that keened always, just above my waking and my sleeping, is something I have not been able to forget.

We go in at last to a low Room, lit with lamps and in which a small fire is burning. Seated on a chair and surrounded by bits and ends of half-completed embroidery is a middle-aged woman. Her hair, once brown, is streaked with grey. She wears a grey gown.

She looks up when we enter and a wan smile crosses her features. She does not stand up or curtsey to the King. It is as though she does not know that this person *is* the King. Instead, she holds out towards us the piece of embroidery on which she is working, with threads of blue and gold, and says: 'I have completed all the flowers of the Ground. Will you note? All save a few small things of no consequence.'

'Very pretty,' says the King. 'Do you not think so, Merivel?'

'Indeed,' I say. 'Admirable work.'

'You note its neatness? No stitch too loose, nor any pulled too tight.'

'Yes, I do note. A marvellous Neatness.'

'The Patterns are already upon the material,' says the King to me in a low voice. 'They are put there in Advance by the Artists' stamps and dyes, so all she has to do is to follow them. Where the Artists have put blue, there she will sew with blue thread, and I have noted that she never transgresses this. She will never introduce green where there is no green. Because she is following a Pattern and the Pattern gives her days their purpose and their calm.'

I cannot find any reply to this. I am gazing at the woman in a rapt kind of way, for the reason that she reminds me of someone. There is something in the way her head tilts towards her work and in her stillness upon the chair, which I know I have seen before, but I can by no means recall when or where.

'You see how content she is?' the King whispers to me.

'She does appear to be . . .'

'No. She *is*. This I know to be true and beyond question. I believe the Stoics used to term this state *ataraxia*, or "freedom from Anxiety". And how dearly one wishes for this state. Truly, I would relinquish my Kingdom to come upon such marvellous peace of mind. Would not you?'

'I would, except that I have no Kingdom, Sir.'

'Yes, you do. For you are a Kingdom Entire unto yourself, Merivel! You are you, with all your chaos of heart and all your great Fears. Would you not prefer to spend your days upon that chair?'

I am about to say that by no means would I like to spend my days upon a chair, looping thread in and out of linen weft, when I find myself suddenly unable to speak. For I know – all at once – who this woman is: it is my former wife, Celia.

I feel very cold. I turn to the King, as if wanting the shelter of his arms. 'Sir,' I say. 'It is Celia!'

He stays aloof from me, plucking idly upon his moustache, watching Celia as she returns to her sewing.

'Yes,' he says at last. 'It is Celia.'

'And yet . . .'

'Not as you and I knew her. No. She is quite mad and has been so for many years.'

'Ah,' I say. 'What Calamity brought her to madness?'

'My dear Merivel, you surely know the answer to this as well as I. Celia was unable to recover from the disappointment of finding her bed empty of the King of England.'

I am silent, looking intently at the woman, whose beauty once brought my life very close to ruin. Now there is no vestige of that beauty remaining.

'Her parents sheltered her for many long years,' the King continues. 'But when they died I arranged for her to be brought here. It was the least I could do. She does not recognise me, of course – nor you. But hers is not a Boiling Madness, such as you once described encountering at your Fenland Bedlam. It is an Insanity of Unknowing. Therefore she is at peace.'

Behind Celia, in the depths of the room where the lamplight and the firelight does not reach, sits an old woman, also mute upon a chair, whom I take to be Celia's guardian, or Nurse. I think about the blazing light that had once shone upon Celia's existence. And it does appear to me to be a most wretched thing that she now resides here, not yet old, but living the life of an elderly Crone, with a true Crone as her only companion, both of them mired in Darkness and forgotten.

'How can you know that she is at peace, Sir?' I ask.

'Well, look at her, Merivel,' says the King. 'Regard her concentration. Nothing disturbs the moment-to-moment tranquil onflow of her mind.'

'Would she not *like* it to be disturbed – by a visit to the Duke's Playhouse, or by some games of Cribbage, or by—'

'No. On the contrary. She would be entirely confused by these things, for she can no longer remember their Laws.'

I walk away from the Palace in the early afternoon. I am in such a state of Perturbation after my encounter with Celia that I unbuckle my Sword and carry it over my shoulder like a Blunderbuss until I come to a vacant iron bench, where I let it fall upon the ground with a terrible clatter, then sit down and mop my brow, and try to calm the beating of my heart.

Why does it beat so? Because the name 'Celia Clemence' will, to the day of my death, catch at my heart . . .

As *The Wedge* relates in great detail, in 1664 I entered into a most extraordinary and unlooked-for Pact with the King. Till then a lowly Doctor to the Royal Dogs at Whitehall, I was, upon the King's strange whim, taken from this Veterinary work and offered an Estate in Norfolk and a Knighthood.

In return. for these bounties I was ordered to become the bridegroom of Celia Clemence, the King's youngest mistress, so that his liaison with her might be camouflaged from the world and, in particular, from his première amour, Lady Castlemaine. But there was a Condition put upon the Bargain: I was forbidden by His Majesty to touch my wife. I was to be her husband in name only – a Paper Groom, a Professional Cuckold. In effect, I was invited to trade my Honour for worldly riches and preferment – and I agreed.

And so I was married to Celia. On my Wedding Night the King, not I, made love to my bride.

For some long while, being caught up with other diversions and very fervent in my mad revels at Bidnold with my own mistress, Lady Bathurst, I was able to remain true to my promise. Celia resided most often in London. Though she was a very pretty woman, I seldom thought of her.

But one day, after the King had sent her to Bidnold for a space, I heard her singing in my Music Room. I sat myself down upon a chair outside the room and listened. Celia Clemence sang with extraordinary musicality and passion. And alas, alas, I was so moved by the sound of this sweet, perfected voice, that not only did it lead me swiftly to one of my bouts of Blubbing, it began, from that moment, to alter all my feelings towards my wife and led me very swiftly to the notion that I was in love with her.

This delusion grew very strong in me as the succeeding days and weeks passed. I longed to possess Celia as a true bride. I knew that I should have tried to quell my inclination, that my Bargain with the King was unbreakable, but I did not seem able to supress my feelings of desire.

On a starry night, taking Celia with me to the Leads of my roof, with the pretended promise of finding for her the planet Jupiter in the sky, I turned to her and, in an unseemly scramble, seized her in my arms and attempted to kiss her. I had thought, because she had recently been very civil and kindly towards me, that she might find it in herself to return my ardour, but I was deluded. She resisted me as fiercely as an angry Ostrich and pushed me away so violently that I almost fell sixty feet into the garden. Then she ran from me, screaming for her maid, and I understood what I had already helplessly known: that my wife felt nothing for me but contempt and detestation.

And now, in terror, alone upon the freezing roof, I saw what was going to befall me. I had transgressed the King's Law. Like Adam, I had done the one and only thing I had been forbidden to do. When word of my behaviour reached the King's ears, as I knew it would soon enough, His Majesty would banish me from the Paradise I had imagined would be mine for ever.

And I was indeed summoned to Whitehall. In the space of a brief audience the King took away from me everything he had given me, including my title and my house. All that remained to me were a few clothes, a few shillings and my chestnut mare, Danseuse.

In terrible sorrow I rode back to Bidnold for the last time, packed the few possessions remaining to me, said goodbye to Will Gates and Cattlebury and my other Servants, and began my long, lonely journey to the Fens, where Pearce and his Quaker Friends had founded their Bedlam. I did not wish to go there, to work among the Mad, but I did not know where else I might find shelter. When Pearce saw me arrive, he ran to me and called my name, and the Quakers took me in.

And it was here, in time, that I was seduced by Margaret's mother, Katharine.

All this, in its fiery Frenzy and confusion, *The Wedge* sets down . . .

To cheer myself now, and to try to banish all memories of Celia, and all memories of Katharine and the Bedlam, I take out of the pocket of my Russet Coat a very valuable Document given to me by the King. This is a Letter addressed to his cousin, King Louis XIV of France, asking that: '*Sir Robert Merivel be made welcome at the Court of Versailles and given, if he should request it, a temporary position as Physician of the Second or Third Rank.*'

Despite the somewhat condescending mention of 'Second or Third Rank', I realise that I am nevertheless, at this moment, one of the most Favoured of men and that I have got this favour, in a single afternoon, without Travail or Deceit, but only by being Myself.

I know, too, that I should now bend all my thoughts towards travelling to France. 'Woe to you, Merivel,' I say to myself, 'if you do not *move onwards in your life* and resume you search for Meaning. You must make haste to reach the land of the inimitable Montaigne. If you do not strive to do this now, you will surely end upon a chair in some attic, stitching rags with green thread. And that destiny is to be strenuously avoided!'

But I am tired. I am not yet capable of travelling even as far as Dover. My head still boils with the cruelties of the Past. I yearn for rest and consolation.

⊰ ⊱

I go where I always go when my body and mind are troubled.

She lives now in a very bright and clean apartment above her Premises, *Mrs Pierpoint's Superior Laundry* on London Bridge. The great River boils eternally about the elm stanchions beneath her.

Being older now, she does not get many visitors of the kind that I am, but makes a Living Entire from her Laundry, with two girls, Marie and Mabel, working under her guidance, lathering and scrubbing and rinsing and ironing, all in a perpetual cumulus of steam. She tells me that her Laundry is now 'famed throughout London' and that people trudge many miles through the mud and the rain to bring their washing here.

I find her at her Ironing Table, her arms and face cherubically pink, as they were always wont to be, and her hair, greying a little now, tied up rather fetchingly in a pink scarf.

'Rosie!' I call out. 'Rosie Pierpoint!'

She looks up and sees me, all smart in my Russet Coat and shining wig, and she sets down her Iron and comes to me straight away and puts her arms round me and kisses my lips. 'Sir Rob,' she says, 'I am full of joy to see you.'

Her body, always fleshy, is now categorically fat and the skin of her face is not smooth as it once was, but these changes to her have not lessened my Desire for her, but only tempered it with a sweet Sadness, which mysteriously adds to its intensity.

We retire to Rosie's Bedchamber, hung with Muslin at the window and seeming to be a kind of airy receptacle for all the music of the river, its churning and shouting and lamenting and laughter. In this way all that we whisper to each other and all that we do is taken in and gathered by the world, and we become as one with it, minute specks of moving flesh, yet alive still, swimming and breathing in the Cauldron of Time.

4

I boarded the Night Coach at Deptford.

It was conducted by an elderly Coachman, with a swarthy Guard, standing behind. Both men appeared weathered by the seasons and by all that they had undergone upon the dark Dover Road.

Inside the coach I found myself with five companions of assorted fortunes. One of these was a Minister of God and he (putting me much in mind of Pearce's way of conducting himself in the world) chose to bless our little company as the horses began to struggle forth and the wheels of the coach to turn. Nobody asked him to do this, but he did it anyway, and this I find I do dislike among the very pious, that they must always *assume* a man's soul requires their Intervention, without first politely enquiring whether that soul wishes it or not.

Another of our number, a Landowner of some corpulence, thanked him after this blessing was given and said: 'I am much at peace now, Reverend. I had been prey to imagining Highwaymen coming down upon us, but henceforth I shall fear no such thing.'

The year was running down into December and the night was frosty. Clean straw had been strewn upon the coach floor and we all, in time, reached for this straw and began to heap it about our legs, to try to warm them.

I attempted to doze, but I was seated between the Reverend's lank bones and the Landowner's greasy rump, and could find no way to balance myself between these two disparate nubs of flesh, and so felt forced to hold myself upright, as though about to rise from my seat. And then what did the Man of God and the Man of Substance do but fall towards each other in their noisy sleep *behind me*, so cutting off absolutely my body's contact with the seat's back.

Opposite me were three women, in their middle years and so much resembling each other that I took them for sisters, or even triplets, born in the same hour. What preoccupied them chiefly was the enormous basket of provisions they had brought with them for the journey, and they passed between them legs of Chicken and spiced Meat Patties and salted Radishes and a flask of Ale, consuming everything as though indeed they were never going to eat again.

After a while of their identical gobbling, drinking and munching, I found myself in the grip of a most frightful hunger, and I took the liberty to remind them that, in France, the food was said to be most abundant, diverse and excellently prepared. But they merely reminded me with identical sniffs of disdain that it was 'as well to be furnished with our own good larder'.

'True,' I said, 'and alas, I myself did not bend my thoughts towards any larder whatsoever for this journey to Dover', hoping to get from them a small Patty or at least a chicken wing, but they chose to ignore my evident distress. All they offered me was a Radish, which, being bitter, brought to my stomach an unwelcome excess of bile, and I found myself disliking the triplets intensely and feeling sorry for the woman who had borne them.

Some long time after midnight, I (being the only person still awake inside the coach) heard the sound of hooves approaching fast from behind us, and our conveyance began to judder and tremble as the Coachman cracked the whip over the poor nags labouring through the dark, spurring them to something like a gallop. Still the other rider came on, nearer and nearer, and then I heard a shout: 'Put up! Put up! Or I shall take your lives!' And I knew that, despite the blessing given out to us by the Reverend, we were now about to lose our lives or our limbs or our *livres* to a Kentish Highwayman.

With much whinnying of the horses, and tearing and grinding of the wheels on the flinty road, the coach was pulled up. This terrifying, lurching stop woke my fellow passengers, who looked about them like children, all damp from their dreaming, and searching in vain for their mothers or their nurses.

'Do not fear,' said I with a smile. ''Tis assuredly only a Highwayman!'

And I must admit it did amuse me to see, by the guttering light of the coach lamps, the Shock on all the faces, and to witness their sudden scrabbling, as they attempted to shovel their possessions further under the seats. One of the triplets thrust her shawl over the food basket, and the Landowner took a stuffed purse from his pocket and tried to slither it down into his boot, but his leg was a mite too fat and the neck of the purse stuck out at the top. The Priest snatched up the cross he wore round his neck, not to kiss it or to beg of it any Divine Help, but only to hide it beneath his robe, because it was made of silver.

I now bethought myself of what I might do, to save what I had taken with me, but I had nothing much concealed about me, all my possessions (which included some fine new clothes I had had made in London) being inside two Valises mounted with all the other baggage on the roof of the coach. And I did not think that Highwaymen, needing to make swift their escapes, could often burden themselves with trunks and boxes. Their prime currency was Currency.

The King's Letter to Louis XIV, however, in the pocket of my coat, did cause me some concern, for without this I had no entrée into France – and I know that the King's Signature and Seal may always fetch a goodly price, regardless of the document to which they are attached. I put my hand on the letter, as though putting my hand on my heart, yet at the same time found myself thinking, 'if I cannot get to France, then I cannot, and there's an end to it. And nothing matters to me in my life but the safety and happiness of Margaret, and to hear, from time to time, the approving laughter of my Sovereign.' And, knowing that these thoughts were true beyond all doubt, I suddenly understood why I was not in the least afraid.

Soon enough, the door of the coach was tugged open and a strange visage appeared, with a hat pulled low over its eyes and some foulard or muffler tied about its face, so that it seemed to be All Nose and nothing else.

This Nose sniffed the noisome air of the interior where we sat, its helpless victims, then a gloved Hand reached in and the Hand held a Flintlock Pistol, which it pointed first at me, then at the Priest and lastly at the triplets, who, well-fortified with Ale and Pasties, strove to be brave and stifle their screams.

Then a low Voice spoke: 'I do humbly beg your pardons, Gents. Ladies, please accept my Apologies. But I am come to a bad pass and have no means to live and pay my debts, except to rob you. I trust you will pardon me.'

'Ah,' whispered I to the Priest, whose trembling I could feel all through my being, 'a very polite and courteous Highwayman.'

'What's that? What's that?' said the Voice. 'Who speaks? Is it you, Sir?'

I said nothing, but saw the Flintlock pointed again at me.

''Tis no use to think you can escape me,' said the Voice, and the Nose sniffed back and forth, perhaps smelling the roast Chicken or the fragrant pies. 'Life deals its cards. I regret the inconvenience. Just give me all your money. That is all I ask. Then I shall be on my way. And you may carry on to Dover.'

Nobody moved. I could still see the purse sticking out of the Landowner's boot and, as my eyes went to it, so did the Nose move itself downwards and then another Hand appeared and snatched the purse away. The Landowner uttered a little cry of rage and the Priest, seeing that our Highwayman was in Earnest of his Profession, began to babble about being a Poor Man of God, who owned nothing.

'I am sorry, Reverend,' said the Voice, 'I dislike drawing a man's attention to any Error he may utter. I do not doubt that you strive to be honest in what you say, but I cannot admit that you own *nothing*. Have you not, for instance, a Cross hanging about your neck? And would you not prefer for me to take that Cross than for me to wind the chain on which it hangs about your throat and pull upon it till you breathe no more?'

The Priest's body, at my side, was now shaking so terribly, I could hear his bones rattling in their sockets and perhaps it was pity for him that caused me to announce: 'I have a ring, Highwayman! It is a Sapphire and was given to me by His Majesty King Charles, to atone for the frequency with which he used to beat me at Tennis. I vouch it is worth more than any other thing in this coach, so why do you not take this jewel, which may get you a hundred *livres*, or ten *pistoles*, which is a deal more than your own *pistol* is worth. Then you may be gone in peace?'

I removed the glove of my right hand and was just about to prise the sapphire ring from my finger when a very vast Noise, as of the Thunder of Jupiter, filled all the air around us and I saw the Nose and the Head on which it sat disappear sideways, followed instantly by the Hand and the Flintlock, and I smelled the stench of sulphur, and in through the open door of the coach came the acrid smoke, which was the smoke of a fired Blunderbuss.

The triplets then gave way to their screaming and the Priest fell forward into the straw. I scrambled to my feet, stepped over the Priest's recumbent form and went out into the dark. The bitter cold night clamped itself around me and the smoke from the Blunderbuss clouded all vision. But in a very little time it cleared and I could see the Coachman trying to hold the horses to stop them from rearing up and, at my feet, the body of the Highwayman with his head shot clean away. The Guard, holding the Blunderbuss pointed at the Robber's body, as though wondering whether shooting a man's head off might not kill him sufficiently, stood there, shaking his head. Then he kicked out at the corpse.

'I cannot abide them,' said he. 'Highwaymen are Vermin. There is not one of them that I do not despatch, whenever I can.'

I am on the Seas now.

In my little cabin (which is so small, it reminds me of the room I inhabited when I worked at Whittlesea – which, in turn, reminded me of my broom cupboard at Bidnold) I am endeavouring to write to Margaret, but after my adventures on the Night Coach, I find myself overcome with weariness, and set aside my letter and lay my head down on my mattress of sacking and fall into a deep sleep.

It is late morning when I wake. The day is very cold, yet the Channel is calm and the rocking of the Ship, which is a Brig taking English Wool to the port of Dieppe, is so gentle that all my fears about the sea travel have vanished. Indeed, I suddenly find myself most enamoured of this means of transportation and wonder why I have never attempted it before.

I go up and walk about the deck, and marvel at how the lazy wind is just enough to fill our sails and push us onwards, and I feel glad to be alive and not dead on the Dover Road, with my head shot off. I have seen many deaths in my life as a Physician: death by Consumption, death by Convulsion, death by Wasting, death in Childbed, death by Plague and death by Fire. But I have never before seen a man's head catapulted from his body by a Blunderbuss and I do not think I shall forget it very quickly.

Yet now I am calm. Out here, on the great ocean, all seems to rejoice at itself: sunlight silvers the wavelets and the wings of the white gulls that follow us, just as they follow the plough, diving for fish in the turning of our wake. The bright pennants flying from the mastheads seem to proclaim a pride in our cargo of wool and in us and in England. And I find my heart to be filled with a ridiculous patriotic joy.

I strut about like a fat pigeon (I am wearing grey) conversing about this or that thing with the Sailors, uncaring if they think me foolish or mad, and regret only that Margaret is not with me, to feel what I feel and be cheered to see that my Melancholy has, for the time being, departed and been replaced with a sudden zeal for living.

All the way to France I am a-dazzle with unexpected happiness. But when the French coast at last appears I feel an onrush of disappointment. It is not that the little port of Dieppe appears uninviting, for it does not. It is merely that I have been held in an embrace so strong by the journey that I find I have relinquished the will to arrive.

My plan had been to hire a carriage and be driven to Versailles without more delay. But as I disembark from the ship I sense that clouding of the air, which always feels to me like the gradual fading of my sight, but which is only the slow coming of the dusk.

And I know that – cold, now, and parted from my mood of joy – I have not the heart to bargain for a carriage, nor to endure the long ride to my destination without some hours of sleep. To excuse myself this frailty I think once again of the words of Montaigne, who insists that a man's happiness may be determined by his knowledge, acquired only by slow Degree, of *his own capabilities.*

I ask about me for the whereabouts of any hostelry in Dieppe, where I might find food and a bed, and I am directed to what the French call an Auberge, a superior kind of Inn, where I am shown to a handsome room. A fire is lit for me by a Chambermaid, with her hair all a-curl beneath her white cap, and I feel glad that I was not robbed of all my money on the Dover Road, so that I can give her a few grateful *sous.*

The room is like a gallery, long and thin, and inhabiting the topmost storey of the building. It is big enough to sleep four or five people, but contains only one bed, curtained with chenille, and having at its foot a quantity of books piled up in a precarious stack. I note within the pile the admirable *Commentarius* upon the way human speech distinguishes us from the Animals by

Théodore Bibliander and, on the top of the stack, a copy of the *Fables* of Aesop.

There is also a heavy wooden bureau, set in the middle of the room, as though on an invisible island. On the bureau has been placed an Inkstand and a dozen quills and some pieces of parchment and a painted Globe, showing all that is known of the world. Near the door is a basket of Walking Sticks and a leather cloak, hanging on a nail.

I walk first to the fire and warm myself, till I feel the chill depart from my hands, and I take a covering off the bed and wrap it round me to comfort me. Then I sit down at the bureau and, finding that my rump fits the chair very snugly, say to myself that surely some Ghost of a Scribe resides here, as though he might be a man who, like me, once wrote the Story of his Life and placed it under his mattress, finding it to be a thing of no value. And this notion, no less than the bedcovering, warms my body and my heart.

I send down for some wine and a plate of Oysters. In the distance I can hear the sea, breaking on the shores of France.

My most dear Margaret, I write,
   Now I am truly embarked upon this great and exotic journey of mine. Yet do not imagine that because I am far Away, I am not thinking about Puffins . . .

5

My journey by coach to Versailles was long and, as I travelled the grey road unlit by any sun, with here and there a scattering of poor villages and hovels, it was difficult to believe, seeing much misery around me, that I was moving towards the Great Enormity the King had described to me. But then I remembered that within the word 'enormity' lie two meanings: the first being 'vastness' and the second being 'error'.

His Majesty had requested in his letter that I be given Board and Lodging in the Château, but I reflected, as the weary hours passed, that all depended upon depositing my letter into the hands of King Louis, and my knowledge of the workings of Whitehall was sufficient to remind me that Supplicants for favours, bearing letters to which they cling as to little rafts on a wind-dragged ocean, often find themselves waiting many days without food or sleep in the Royal Corridors. (It is related, though I have not seen this, that some waited so long that they *died* there and this, I think, is so pathetic as to wake in a man no other reaction than helpless mirth.)

I tried to put all pessimistic thought out of my mind when at last I sensed that we were approaching the Palace. The first sign that drew my attention to this was a great noise of hammering and pounding. I opened the window of the coach and this noise grew very loud, and I smelled that the air was clotted with dust and this clotting mingled with a marshy Stench. Then we came upon the source of these things: a widening plain on which a great quantity of Stonecutters were toiling upon blocks of granite and white marble, and Carpenters hewing wood, and all the heavy material of their labours being loaded into carts, drawn by horses and mules.

This plain extended far to the east and west horizons, and was altogether filled up with this arduous labour. There must have been five hundred men and a hundred horses spread over the earth, which appeared very damp, so that the wheels of the carts were sometimes sunk into it, and the straining of the animals to move the carts pitiful to behold. God be praised that I have never seen a Battlefield, but this is how the scene suggested itself to me, as though blood had mingled with the soil, to make it heavy. And everywhere there were things broken and cast away: ladders and wheels and shafts, and horses themselves, appearing to lie still and dead in the mud.

I gaped stupidly at this panorama. It seemed to me that, in truth, what lay before me were the workings of the mind of King Louis. Though Versailles stood already garlanded with universal glory, he evidently desired it to be greater yet. He had not finished with Nature but, like the Emperors of Rome, was still tearing at it, to conjure from it wonders never before imagined.

I remembered the thirty-six thousand souls who had already given their labour to the enterprise, and asked myself how great that number might be now and how great it would become, and how many had perished. And I thought how fortunate I was to be living my life of relative ease in England and not breaking my sinews as a stonecutter, here on a black and malodorous plain, as winter came on.

I turned my head away. I examined my Letter once again. Beyond the plain was a steep incline, up which my carriage toiled, and then, lo, it was there before me, the Great and Marvellous Palace.

I admit that it caught at my breath. In an instant, the sufferings of the stonecutters vanished away. Everything vanished away. For here was a disposition of buildings unlike any that I'd ever beheld. I am at pains to describe it with simple words. The best I can set down is to say that the whole seemed, almost, to *flow* in its wondrous horizontal order, and its colours of pink brick and cream stone to rise up in one harmonious chord, as though it had been conjured there, not by any architect but by a composer of Music. Even the sun colluded with this Song of Magnificence and Beauty by breaking through the grey clouds and etching the buildings with soft winter light, so that the slate roofs gleamed like pewter and the glass of a thousand windows was touched with a diamond brightness, like the high notes from a flute.

I could have wished it to be deserted, so that I might hear its music played for me alone, or even to be some Picture of itself at which I might pause and gaze in rapt silence. But as we came on, I found my coach surrounded by a throng of people, mostly of the poorer kind, who dared not try to enter at the outer gate and contented themselves by hawking their wares or by performing little feats, such as walking on stilts or turning somersaults, to get a few *sous* from the Courtiers, as they passed by.

My coachman drove through this little crowd impatiently, as though they might have been a troupe of geese, sending one man flying off his stilts into the dust, and we entered into the first of the two vast courtyards, built upon ramparts, called the Place des Armes, which lends to the Palace additional space and grandeur.

Once entered here, it is as though you have come into a *city*, for everything folds in around you. All you can absorb is the march upon march of ornamented façades, seeming to stretch almost to infinity. The world beyond these façades ceases, on the moment, to exist. Lined up in two great ranks, guarding the *portail*, beyond which lie the King's *Appartements*, are the uniformed Swiss Guards, their ranks moving slowly and in unimpeachable step to the soft beating of twenty or thirty drums.

The coach drove on to the *portail*, where our way was barred by Sentries carrying halberds, who had been chosen, no doubt,

for their furious dark eyes and their largeness of form. I descended
from the coach, a little stiff and bent-over, and dusty and smelling
of straw, and took out my Letter. This document – already somewhat creased and dirtied by the journey it had endured (and with
a small crack in the sealing wax now horribly visible to me) –
was examined by the Sentries with disinclination, as though it
might have been the corpse of a mouse, and handed back to me.
I was informed peremptorily that my coach could not proceed
beyond this point.

'Messieurs,' said I, in the best French I could muster after all my
hours upon the road. '*Regardez-bien*. This is the Great Seal of His
Majesty King Charles II of England. This Letter contains his
express wish that I be granted an immediate audience with His
Majesty King Louis, to whom I am come to offer my services . . .'

'The King,' replied the tallest of the sentries, 'does not grant
"Immediate Audiences". Please make your way to the *Grand Commun*, over there, where the Correct Formalities for Foreign Supplicants will be explained to you by one of the *Surintendents*.'

The *Grand Commun* was revealed to be the very substantial
three-storeyed building to the right of the courtyard, with a great
quantity of windows and a press of people coming and going
through two doorways. I had no choice but to obey the Sentry,
clambering back into the coach, so that I could be driven to one
of the doors with my Valises, and here I was set down at last.

I paid the Coachman and thanked him. As he turned the horses
and made to drive away, I put up my hand and waved to him
sadly, as though I might have been a Pauper's child deposited on
the steps of an orphanage. And when he had quite gone, I felt all
around me the great World of Versailles pressing upon me, as
though to sweep me up and lead me on into its thousand wonders, but then pushing past me and buffeting me and showing
me a very vast Indifference, and I really did not know, in that
sudden instant, what to do or where to turn. I only wished myself
younger and more lithe, and with a heart beating more strongly
than mine for the great Adventure upon which I had embarked.

Abandoning my heavy Valises to temporary chance of theft, I entered the *Grand Commun*, turned left down a passageway and was relieved to find myself, upon opening the first door that I came to, in an enormous kitchen, where fifteen or twenty chefs were preparing some imminent feast. The air was steamy from two great cauldrons of soup upon a blackened range, fragrant with the smell of boiling leeks and onions, and noisy with the shouting and badinage of the chefs as they worked.

Not having eaten for many hours, I stared about me with longing, noting now a quantity of chickens and rabbits being turned on a roasting spit, and some delectable soft pastries set out to cool upon a marble slab.

Doffing my hat, I saluted the chefs and said in my inelegant French: 'Good day to you, Messieurs. I am come out from England, an emissary of my King.'

One or two of the cooks raised their heads and stared at me. The others merely carried on with their work. Nobody spoke.

'Please forgive the intrusion upon your labours,' I continued. 'But I confess I am a little lost. And somewhat hungry.'

At this, one of the chefs threw a muslin cloth over the pastries, towards which he could see my eyes (if not yet my hand) straying; then he wiped his brow with a corner of his apron and said to me: 'Please go away, Monsieur. We have no time to talk to strangers.'

'Ah,' I said, 'I understand. But if one of you might direct me . . . I was advised to ask for the *Surintendents du Grand Commun* . . .'

Taking hold of my arm with his damp, meaty hand, this chef manoeuvred me towards the door through which I had arrived and pointed to a staircase at the far end of the passageway. '*Surintendents* up above,' he said. 'Not in the kitchens.'

For the next hour I walked the corridors of the *Grand Commun*, where the stone of the ground floor was replaced, on the First *étage*, by polished wood and great tapestries hung between the windows and marble busts, and statues were everywhere to be

seen in a state of such magnificent whiteness, it was as though
they had been brought this very day from the studio of the
sculptor.

But it was difficult to look closely at anything, because every
great space was choked with people: men and women wearing
what I took to be the latest fashions from Paris and vitiating the
air with their strong perfumes and their wig powder, and those
strange chemicals the women use to paint black moles on their
faces.

I walked among them with a smile on my lips, just as though
I were an old habitué of the building, when in truth I had no idea
where I was going, or whom, precisely, I was seeking, nor in
what direction my orphaned Valises any longer resided.

I noted, after a while, that some of the Courtiers looked at me
strangely and one man, wearing a coat of coral-coloured satin,
flicked at my shoulder lightly with his thumb and forefinger, and
laughed, before scampering away. And then the others in his
company turned and regarded me, and joined in the laughter. I
looked down at myself, to see whether mud or straw still clung
to my coat, but it appeared clean enough, so I walked on,
unknowing. And this is a thing I do detest, that others laugh at
me for no reason that I can understand. I am happy to be the butt
of a jest, as I frequently was at Whitehall, but to enjoy myself I
must know what the jest is about.

Hunger persecuted me. I was almost ready to go down again
to the kitchen and beg a bowl of soup from the chefs, when I
was at last shown into the company of one of the *Surintendents*
of the building by a kindly crone, walking in a slow and stately
step, under a peculiar coiffure of black lace.

I felt, by this time, exhausted and teetering on the edge of some
kind of madness. I clutched at this *Surintendent* with a desperate
grip. For it seemed to me that the exquisite Order of the façades at
Versailles was matched, once one entered the buildings, by a
corresponding Chaos. I could make no sense of anything, so I held
tightly to this man, like a desperado about to carry him off, guess-

ing that only someone calling himself a *Surintendent* might possess the means to lighten for me my heavy burden of confusion.

'Monsieur!' I cried, reaching yet again for my Letter, and holding it out to him, 'I am counting upon you to help me.'

'Who are you?' said the man, extricating himself deftly from my
hold upon his arm.

I told him my name as calmly as I could, styling myself *Chevalier* Robert Merivel in the case that 'Sir' had no meaning for him,
and drew his attention to the Great Seal on the Letter, which, to
my vast consternation, he immediately broke.

'*Ah, non!*' I cried out. '*Non, Monsieur!* That Letter is intended
for the King alone!'

The *Surintendent* paid no heed whatever to my distress, but
only brought the Letter close to his face in order to read it. The
Letter is brief, but his reading of it seemed to take him many long
minutes. The he looked up and regarded me with a disbelieving
air. 'A Doctor?' he said. 'You are a Doctor?'

'Yes,' said I, 'and it has been my good fortune to be of service
to my most Beloved Majesty, King Charles. Thus, he recommends
me for some service here . . .'

'You do not appear like a Doctor.'

'Nevertheless, that is what I am. I have held this profession for
many years. I trained in Anatomy at Cambridge . . .'

At that moment a distant bell chimed the hour of five o'clock
and the *Surintendent* hastily thrust my Letter back into my hands,
with no apology for having broken its seal, and made as if to
depart. But I reached out and again held fast to his arm. 'Please,
Monsieur,' I said, 'I beg of you, tell me where I am to lodge. My
journey has been a long one and I am very tired.'

'I am sorry,' said the *Surintendent*, 'but I must leave you, Sir. I
am needed elsewhere. Indeed, I am already late, as I know by
the five o'clock bell. As to *logements*, you will have to take your
chance on the upper floors. Versailles is very crowded at the
moment, as you can see. Your best chance is to offer to pay
money to someone willing to share some little corner with you.'

'What? What do you mean, "some little corner"?'

The man shrugged his thin shoulders. 'It's the best you will come by,' he said. 'Here, even a Marquis must sometimes sleep in a passageway.'

It is night now.

I am lying on a tilting cot in a cold upper room. A screen made of linen gives me a little privacy, but the rest of the room is occupied by a Dutch Clockmaker, to whom I have given three English shillings to share his room and his pisspot. He lies in a narrow bed, snoring like a hog.

I have opened my Valises – found at last where I had left them – so far as to procure a nightshirt and a nightcap, which I have put on, but there is nowhere to hang my clothes or set out my few possessions, but only this Portion of space in a very small room under the leads of the *Grand Commun*.

I fall into a shifting kind of sleep and am awoken almost immediately, or so it seems to me, by the gnawing hunger in my belly, which has passed from a State of Longing to a State of Agony so fierce as to make me cry out. And I think, on the sudden, that this is the kind of hunger Will Gates would suffer, were I to cast him out of Bidnold and I know that – at all or any cost to myself – I must never do this. And I swear that I will not.

My mind returns once more to the kitchens down beneath me. The Clockmaker has informed me that the food prepared there goes all to the *Grands Appartements*, where the King and his entourage consume it in great quantities. Nobody, I am told, who inhabits the *Grand Commun* is ever fed, for the reason that the King believes the expense of this to be too great.

'How are we to survive?' I ask.

For answer, the Dutchman (whose skin is very pink and healthy but whose jaw appears occupied perpetually by the grinding of his Lower Molars upon the Upper) opens a wooden box he has brought with him and shows me what it contains, which is a quantity of pots of Jam and bags of Oatmeal. On this, he tells me, he lives. He drinks water from the garden fountains. For ten successive days he has attempted to procure an audience with Madame de Maintenon, the King's Mistress and Confidante, for that he is a distant cousin of her dead husband, the poet Scarron, and she, allegedly, a great admirer of Dutch Clocks, but so far she has not been 'at leisure' to see him.

'I will try again tomorrow,' he says. 'And the day after that.'

I have no Jam or Oatmeal and I really cannot steal from the Dutchman. But added to my hunger, now, is a terrible thirst and I know that I cannot lie here a moment longer. I must attempt to find some sustenance and some water.

I take off my nightcap and put on my wig. I tug on my stained breeches and my dusty coat and my shoes, much worn down by trying to hold my feet on the ground in the jolting and tilting coach.

Taking a Tallow candle, I go out into the passage, which is blocked, here and there, by men asleep on pallets of straw, such as those upon which the mad people used to rest at Whittlesea. I step over these and, by long searching and some wrong turnings, find myself once again on the ground floor opposite the door to the kitchens.

I turn the handle. A delicious odour of roasted meat still lingers here and I feel sure that, within moments, I will have procured some cold limb of rabbit to plug the pain in my stomach. But the kitchen door is locked.

I sit down where I am, in the cold stone passage. I rub my eyes. I reflect that only at Whittlesea did I ever feel a comparable hunger and, even there, it was usually possible to procure a bowl of gruel or Frumenty on which to make a poor feast.

Thoughts of Whittlesea bring to my mind images of my dead friend. Though, from childhood, I was always greedy, Pearce lived his short life on so little food that I often wondered how his flesh held itself to his bones. I once asked him, indeed, in a mocking vein, how it did so and he replied simply: 'Do not be so stupid, Merivel.'

As ever, this Memory of Pearce calms me a little and I whisper to him: 'What am I to do, Pearce? Surely, I shall be dead by morning . . .'

I hear in my mind his croaking laugh. He frequently scolded me for being a Great Exaggerator and for pretending my lot to be always and ever worse than it was. Now, I imagine him saying: 'Consider the people at the outer gate, Merivel. Consider the man who fell from his Stilts as your coach came rampaging in. For perhaps he broke his arm or his collar bone, and who is to give him help and where is he to lay his head? You have a room and a cot, but where will he sleep tonight but out on the cold earth?'

And then I see that this thought has done me a great Favour. For I remember that, among this gathering of the poor, were sellers of bread and Peas bottled in Brine. And I tell myself that perhaps, even though it is the dead of night, they are still there and can be roused from sleep to sell me some meagre victuals.

But the great Expanse that is the Place des Armes lies between me and this one hope of sustenance, and the thought of traversing this in the cold and dark, only to find that the Hawkers have all vanished away, fills me with misery. 'I am wretched,' say I to myself, 'and I will have to stay this way till morning, and that is that.'

Unexpectedly, however, as though urged on by the ghost of Pearce, I rise up and go out. Lines of Swiss Guards, motionless in the moonlight, with their serried shadows falling upon the flints of the Place, like fallen statues, endure their freezing Watch. And I wonder, as I make my shivering way towards the gate, how much of life is endurance and nothing more. And I think of Margaret in Cornwall and pray that she is asleep in a warm bed.

At the gate, all is deserted and silent. I take hold of the railings and peer out, wondering if there is somebody asleep on the ground that I cannot see. I call softly and jingle the few coins I have found in my coat pocket. But nothing stirs.

I am about to turn and make my way back to my cot – if, indeed, I am able to locate the room where it is – when I hear the rattle of wheels and the snort of a horse. I wait and watch. At length appears a slow cart, pulled by a big mare and I see two huddled female figures, wrapped in shawls, riding in the cart.

And then I recognise what this is, the heavy conveyance that comes long before dawn to the Palace gates: it is a Milk Cart.

Never did I imagine that Milk could become such a thing of Beauty and Wonder to me. I pay for a brimming tankard from the hands of the Milkmaids. The milk is creamy and fresh, cooled by the night air, and I drink it down with all the joy and satisfaction of a baby suckling from its mother's breast. Then, I buy a second tankard and gulp this too, and the Milkmaids in their woollen cloaks stare at me and smile.

6

I have arranged my portion of the Dutchman's room sufficiently well, by moving my cot six inches to the left, so that some of my clothes can be hung on makeshift wooden pegs and my boots laid out to air.

I live on Peas in Brine, bread and milk, got from the poor Tradesmen at the gate and, like the Dutchman, whose name is Jan Hollers, drink water from the fountains. Hollers has generously loaned to me a wooden plate and spoon, and we sit side by side on Hollers's bed, spooning Peas and Oatmeal into our ravening mouths.

And I reflect that, in the middle of the richest Court in the world (and despite a Letter from the King of England in my possession) I am living like a Pauper, which paradox both weighs me down and makes me laugh. And I try to hold to this laughter, as a weapon against melancholy. For I do not see any imminent chance of my fortunes being turned round and the thought of returning to Norfolk with a terrible burden of Failure upon me feels somewhat difficult to contemplate.

I have been advised by Hollers as to the Only Means of presenting my Letter to King Louis. It seems there are but three:

1. I am to seek out, if I can, one Monsieur Bontemps, who is the
   King's chief *Valet de Chambre*. 'If,' says Hollers, 'you have the

Ear of Bontemps, then you will get the Ear of the King.' But though I have been told what Bontemps looks like and that he stands out in the crush of people surrounding the Monarch because that his wig is small and fluffy, I have never yet managed to set my eyes definitively upon him.

2. At eight in the morning, when the King leaves his *Appartements* to attend Mass in the Chapel, I am to contrive to position myself in the corner of the *Salle des Gardes* nearest to the *Appartements* doors. For here, King Louis is in the habit of pausing and, from among the press of Courtiers, receiving one or two Petitions.

'I have heard,' says Hollers, 'that he is gracious. And whatsoever thing he promises, this will he do, or cause to be done.'

I told Hollers I would attempt this and he ground his molars in approval. However, on the first morning that I was due to do so I overslept. And on subsequent mornings, after endeavouring to brush my wig and shake the creases from my Best Coat and shine with spit the Buckles of my shoes and hasten to the *Salle des Gardes*, all before the striking of the Eight o'clock bell, what did I find already there but a vast crush of People, all pressed like animals in a cage into the corner and pushing vilely at each other the moment the doors opened and the King stepped forth. He then walked on, without glancing in my direction.

I was, however, able to observe him at last. He is not as tall nor as handsome as my Master, King Charles. Yet his bearing has great dignity and he holds himself straight and composed, as though about to begin upon a formal Gavotte. His nose is very long.

3. Near to Dinner Time, which is to say at about eleven-thirty in the morning, King Louis very often (but not invariably) likes to walk up and down in the *Galerie des Glaces*, one of the most sumptuous rooms at Versailles, having within it seventeen windows and more than one hundred Mirrors. Here, it

seems, he may sometimes be approached. So, in due time, I will try this. Yet it seems that, for the moment, I lack the courage. For if I were to be rebuffed here, this rejection would be a most public and horrible thing, and I would have no alternative but to pack my Valises and take the road back to Dieppe.

Many days have now passed. I myself have made no Progress in my attempts to catch the attention of King Louis, but I am happy to relate that today Madame de Maintenon sent for Mr Hollers.

Hollers dressed himself in his best Cambric coat and, in his hands, held tenderly like a child, wrapped in a cloth of baize, was the small but very beautiful clock he had brought out from Holland as a Sampling of his work.

I asked him if I might examine this object before he left on his Great Errand. I am no connoisseur of clocks, but I could nevertheless judge that the Facework was extremely delicate and the Brass Pointers fabricated with great simplicity and beauty. Yet I could not prevent images of Hollers, snoring on his bed, gobbling Jam, delousing his wig, grinding his teeth and farting and shitting into our shared pisspot, from coming into my mind and obliterating the lovely symmetry of the clock.

And I reflected upon how one should strive to avoid judging a man's sensibility by his daily habits, or the state of his clothes. To atone for my grosser thoughts I said to Hollers: 'I do not understand, my good Friend, why, with work of this quality, you had any need to come into France. Do not your Countrymen command sufficient clocks from you already?'

Hollers began to wrap the Timepiece once more in the baize, folding it over and over countless times. 'It is perhaps,' he said, 'the Curse of our Age, but to get a little Name in Holland has not felt sufficient to me. I seem to live to *desire more*. If Madame de Maintenon will be my Patron, then I will move my Enterprise to Paris and I will become famous.'

I wished him well and he went off, and my heart began suddenly to be afraid for him. To endure a life of Jam and Oatmeal for so long and then, at the end of it, to come away with nothing did strike me as a lamentable thing and I found myself praying that this would not happen.

In my mind I followed Hollers as he made his anxious way to Madame de Maintenon's Rooms. I had caught sight of her only once: a stout woman of mature years, of no particular beauty, dressed all in black Velvet. But Reputation told me that she was extremely clever and full of Wit, and it was these things that held the King to her. Nothing indicated to me whether or not she might be moved by a delicate Dutch clock.

I sat down on Hollers's bed, where I could still see the impress of his body. I tried to imagine his dreams become reality: the sign above his Premises in Paris, situated near the Seine, with the light from the river flickering in upon the shining brass of innumerable Pointers and Pendulums.

And as the seconds and minutes moved on, I pondered Man's efforts at the representation or 'capture' of Time, and I thought how, for Clockmakers like Hollers, the very Commodity with which they were trying to work was a heartless and capricious Enemy, who stole from them all the while and never rested.

When Hollers returned it was almost dark in our little room. He came in, and sat down upon my cot and rubbed his eyes.

'Well, Hollers?' said I, rising up, 'how did it unfold? Did Madame take the Clock to her bosom? Is your future assured?'

Hollers let escape a long sigh and reached for the box that contained the Oatmeal and the Jam. He began spooning jam into his mouth, shaking his head as he did so. 'I do not know if I shall survive, Merivel,' he said at length.

'What d'you mean?' said I.

'Look at this Jam. It is running low.'

'That is my fault. I have eaten too much of it.'

'No, no. You have shared your Peas with me. But how long can either of us survive?'

'So Madame de Maintenon did not admire the Clock?'

'She said she considered the *Facework* of the Clock "very pretty". But she insisted that she judged nothing on earth by its Face and that I should wait out a period of Time (she did not say how long) during which she would see whether the *Workings* of the Clock were accurate. She wishes the Time shown by it to deviate by no more than one minute per day, whether fast or slow, from the time told by the Great Clock of the Chapel. She said, if it did not keep "God's Time" it was no use to her.'

'I see,' said I, 'but surely I see some flaw here, my friend. For supposing your Timepiece is *more accurate* than the cumbersome Chapel Clock, with all its mighty Cogs and Escapements? How would she be able to ascertain this?'

'She would not be able to ascertain it. She believes the Chapel Clock to be the infallible Arbiter of Time and would never admit to any fault in its workings. My Clock must chime with it, or I am lost.'

We had no choice but to let yet more days go by, during which Hollers's agitation grew into a very palpable thing, only relieved a little by our fortunate discovery, early one morning, of a Bathhouse behind the Swiss Guards' *Pavillon*, into whose steaming waters we plunged our filthy and stinking bodies, and lathered and rinsed them with childlike joy.

I tried to persuade Hollers that this sudden cleanliness would signal a change in our fortunes, but the Dutchman's anguish diminished only as long as our bath lasted and, as we came out into the cold air, he hunched himself over in an attitude of despair.

I, by contrast, chose this as my moment to dress myself in the finest Suit I had brought with me (of a flatteringly soft Taupe colour, ornamented with expensive silver Frogging) and try my luck walking up and down in the *Galerie des Glaces*. I gave my wig a sincere and tender brushing (as though it might have been a pet Spaniel returned from a truffling expedition in Bidnold park), pressed a little discreet Rouge into my cheeks, took my Cane and set forth.

In the *Galerie des Glaces* the sun was shining through every one of the seventeen windows and bouncing off the hundred mirrors, so that one had the impression of being imprisoned inside a colossal Diamond, whose brightness made my eyes drip. I attempted to walk with elegance, mimicking the long stride of King Charles (albeit with somewhat shorter legs and a fatter stomach) but only getting for myself successive mirthful glances from the other Courtiers promenading there.

Holding my stomach in, and alert at every moment for any Commotion that might herald the appearance of King Louis, I sauntered on, but in due course found my way definitively barred by a gaggle of Fops, who surrounded me and, in complex harmony with each other, began laughing at me.

One of the Gallants made that flicking gesture at my shoulder that I had experienced before, while another made so bold as to stoop down and take hold of my knee.

'Messieurs,' said I. 'Why are you detaining me in this ungracious way? Pray tell me what is wrong.'

'Ah,' said one, 'you mean you do not know?'

'No. I'm afraid I do not know.'

'He does not know!' shrieked the man who had hold of my leg. 'He must be from another land! Perhaps he is from the Moon!'

More laughter echoed round the Diamond and bounced off its thousand facets.

I held up my hands in a gesture of Surrender. 'Pray do enlighten me,' I said. 'What faux pas have I committed?'

The Fops then herded me unceremoniously towards one of the Mirrors, where they positioned themselves around me. 'We do beg you to look at yourself,' they chorused. 'And then look at us. Do you not see the *grave* enormity of which you are guilty?'

I looked at myself, as instructed. Despite my recent ablutions, I could at once see that I did not appear as a man in the very picture of health. My skin was sallow, my eyes somewhat red and my wig lacklustre, in spite of my grooming efforts. But it immediately became apparent that it was not my visage with which these Gentlemen were concerned, but rather with my Shoulders and my Knees.

With much renewal of their mirth they declared that my Shoulders were *bare*. (The French word they used was *nues*, meaning naked.) And it was only then that I noticed, on their own gorgeous apparel, great clusters of ribbons, sewn into the shoulder seam and falling in elegant cascades to their elbows. My coat had no ribbons at all. Though I had commanded it to be made by a High-Class Tailor in St James's Street in London, before my departure from England, this excellent man had had no thought of putting ribbons where the French Fops decreed that ribbons should be. Indeed, the word 'ribbon' had not entered into my discourse with the Tailor at any moment.

As to my knees: I was now made aware that round the leg of every Courtier within my sight in the *Galerie des Glaces*, between the cutting off of the Breek and the appearance of the silk stocking, was entwined a kind of satin Ruff, apparently known as a *canon*. And my poor legs were again *nues*, with no *canons* anywhere, and with my knees suddenly resembling, to my smarting eyes, the knobbly, outward-turning joints of my servant Gates.

'I am sorry,' said one of the laughing Courtiers. 'You are from England, judging by your vexatious accent. We do sympathise. But here in France, everybody knows that one just cannot be seen in Society, let alone *at court*, without *canons*. We strongly advise you to consult your Tailor.'

Tailor? I wanted to protest, 'Where am I to find a Tailor in this hurly-burly, when I cannot even find adequate food to sustain the body on which my clothes must hang?' But I only saw how pitiable this remark would make me appear in the eyes of these well-fed Gallants, so I chose, instead to say: 'Ah! How foolish of me. Only yesterday, a pair of *canons* was delivered to me – of a marvellous Aquamarine colour, as it happens, to go very nicely with this Taupe coat of mine – but I forgot to put them on.'

'Well, if I were you,' said another, 'I would not promenade here again until you have adjusted yourself, as to both *canons* and sleeve-ribbons. And Taupe, of course, is not *à la mode* this Season. Versailles is the Centre of the World, Monsieur "Eeenglishman". The King wishes us all to maintain the Honour of France, at all times, in our outward appearances – and that includes Foreigners.'

They walked away from me.

I was left alone, staring at my own inadequate reflection, which seemed to show me, in this pitiless light, every single one of my fifty-seven years and a few more besides, and yet – despite this and despite the sartorial humbling I had just received – I could still notice an obstinate Jauntiness in my demeanour which gave me some small cause for gladness.

It was then that I became aware – in the mirror – of a woman standing behind me. She held up a fan, so that I could not see all of her face, but I could nevertheless tell that she was smiling.

Before I could turn round she approached me and said, in mellifluous but accented English: 'Forgive me, Monsieur, but I could not help but overhear what has just occurred here. People at Court are very, very rude. They feel obliged to be so, I think. They see rudeness as one of their many duties on the Road to Advancement. Please let me apologise on their behalf.'

I turned and bowed to the stranger, who wore a very becoming yet modest gown of dark-blue silk and whose age I put at perhaps forty-five. Her smile, I saw at once, was a thing of quiet beauty.

'Thank you, Madame,' I said. 'It is extremely kind of you to interest yourself in my shortcomings! I will proceed to remedy them, if I can. But please let me introduce myself. My name is Sir Robert Merivel, from the County of Norfolk in the East of England.'

She dipped a little curtsey to me, her fan fluttering all the while against her cheek. 'I am delighted to make your acquaintance, Sir Robert,' she said. 'I am Madame de Flamanville. My husband is a Colonel in the Regiment of Swiss Guards.'

'Ah, the Swiss Guards! What an unforgettable impression they do create. Such discipline in the ranks. Such stoicism in the cold nights. And the way the Drums are played so delicately . . .'

'Yes. I find the Drums moving, too: so many Drums to make such a hushed sound. Yet few people notice. I shall tell my husband what you said.'

I bowed again. Madame de Flamanville had now removed her fan from her face and I was struck by how clear and animated were her hazel eyes.

'On the question of ribbons and *canons* . . .' she said hesitantly, 'I personally consider emphasis upon such Artefacts to be a kind of insanity. But if, on reflection, their absence from your otherwise admirable attire begins to vex you, I do know a very able Tailor in Paris who would adjust your coat and manufacture the *canons*, at very reasonable cost.'

'Thank you, Madame,' I said. 'Thank you for your concern . . .'

My words faltered here, for I did not know what more to say to the offer of a Parisian Tailor. Into my mind came the desolate picture of the room I shared with Hollers and of the Pauper's fare with which we kept ourselves alive, and I saw how far removed I had fallen – in the small space of Time in which I had been at Versailles – from the kind of normality that could include a visit to a Paris Couturier.

Perhaps my face became clouded by the onrush of these thoughts, for Madame de Flamanville approached nearer to me and laid a gentle hand upon my arm. 'My coach goes to Paris on Wednesday,' she said. 'Though I am at Versailles to be beside my husband, I confess I find the Court absolutely without intellectual stimulation. You may be aware by now that nobody here talks of anything but Royal Gossip – and that, usually, as bearing on their own Preferment. So I escape to Paris, where we have a house, as often as I can. And I would be delighted to offer you a place in the coach.'

I looked into the clear hazel eyes. I tried to read what was in Madame's mind, but her gaze was so steady that I found myself at a loss. However, the touch of her hand on my sleeve was, I now realised, so wonderfully pleasing to me that the thought of riding the eleven miles to Paris with her made me suddenly crazed with happiness. Yet, I found myself stupidly answering: 'Oh, Madame, that is more than kind of you, but I could not possibly accept.'

At this moment there was a Stir in the room and it became clear, from everybody within it suddenly turning in the same direction, that the King had entered the *Galerie*. Madame de Flamanville also turned and we both saw, to my great astonishment, King Louis striding with his entourage directly towards the place where we stood.

He wore a magnificent coat of Scarlet and Gold. His wig, above the long-nosed, fleshy face, was also golden and audaciously high. His bearing was entirely that of a contained and beautiful dancer, his feet (shod in heels a little raised, to procure for him more height) turning outwards as he moved and his spine held sublimely straight.

He stopped in front of us and Madame de Flamanville fell into a low curtsey, while I hinged myself at the waist into the kind of bow long ago perfected at Whitehall, but which I now find a little difficult to execute, my kidneys seeming to gripe at it.

'Our dear Madame de Flamanville,' said King Louis. 'We are always glad to see you at Court. Madame de Maintenon is very fond of your discourse. She says she is surrounded by Ignoramuses! Please do visit her this evening at six o'clock. Bring your embroidery. As you know, she likes to stitch while she talks.'

'I will, Sire,' said Madame de Flamanville. 'With great pleasure. Please tell Madame that I will much look forward to it. Meanwhile, may I present to you Sir Robert Merivel from England . . .'

I prepared myself to utter some suitable humble words of appreciation of the Sovereign's willingness to cast his glance upon me, but by the time I had unhinged my body from its painful Obeisance, I saw that the King had passed on beyond me and was now engaged by the very band of Fops who had caused me my earlier distress.

Though inwardly disappointed, I wanted to reassure Madame de Flamanville that this peremptory passing on did not signify, that in my earlier concern for my wig and my clothes et cetera, I had in any case forgotten to put King Charles's Letter into my pocket. But even as I opened my mouth, I was aware that the whole vast *Galerie des Glaces* had fallen silent and the only sound to be heard was the voice of King Louis, who talked in the seductive whisper of one who would always and ever be heard.

We endured this silence for a goodly while, as though Time itself had stopped, and this notion suddenly reminded me once more of the Dilemma in which Hollers found himself. I determined on the instant to try to help him and, once the King had moved out of the *Galerie* and Normal Time resumed, I ventured to say to Madame de Flamanville: 'As you are going to visit Madame de Maintenon tonight, Madame, might I ask of you a small favour, on behalf of a friend?'

'Ah,' said Madame de Flamanville, turning away her head with a sigh, '*Favours*. In these times, here is a word I have come to dislike.'

'Indeed . . .' I stammered. 'No, indeed. Or perhaps I mean "yes, indeed". In any case you are quite right. Please think no more of it.'

'The discomfort with Favours, you see,' she said, turning back her glance in my direction, 'is that they must almost always be repaid. If I am to do you a Favour, how are you to repay me?'

The look she gave me was defiant, yet I now detected, at the corners of her mouth, the beginnings of a smile she was endeavouring to suppress.

'I do not know, Madame,' said I lamely. 'But repay you I would. Ask of me what you will. And perhaps I may permit myself to tell you that I have learned a strenuous lesson about the Keeping of my Word from His Majesty King Charles. I once broke a promise to him and the price I paid was most horribly high and of long duration. Since which time I have always tried to be honest and true in all my dealings.'

'Have you? "Honest and True"? How extraordinary! For look around you, Sir Robert. How many 'honest and true' people do we see here in the *Galerie*, I wonder?'

My eye reluctantly quitted the gentle face of Madame de Flamanville and took in the great crowd of pomaded Courtiers and beauty-spotted Ladies scintillating in the glassy light. 'Well,' I said, 'to their own Aspirations and Desires I would presume an absolute fidelity.'

The smile now broke free of its confines and Madame de Flamanville touched me provocatively on the chin with her fan. 'I like you, Sir Robert,' she said. 'So now do please tell me what this Favour is. I have the ear of Madame de Maintenon and she is that rarity at Versailles, a Woman of her Word.'

I related the story of Hollers's Clock. I did not describe the squalor in which he and I lived at present, but only mentioned his anguish at the long wait to know whether his work had found favour or no. I further said that, to my unpractised eye, the Clock was a work of great beauty and distinction, and prayed that Madame de Maintenon might find it so.

'I understand perfectly,' said Madame de Flamanville. 'Let us hope that the Dutch Clock has kept time with God and that your

Mr Hollers will come by the Patronage he desires. I will enquire on his behalf.'

'Thank you, Madame,' I said, once more executing a somewhat ridiculous bow. 'I am most grateful.'

'Well,' said Madame de Flamanville, 'gratitude is an admirable Sentiment, of course, but *tiens*, now that I come to think of it, I have found the perfect means of your Repayment for this favour.'

'Tell me what it might be and I will do my best—'

'My carriage will leave for Paris from the Places des Armes at nine o'clock on Wednesday morning. I shall expect you to be in it.'

7

The de Flamanvilles inhabited an exquisite stone mansion in Paris, known here as an *hôtel*, in the Faubourg Saint-Victor, very near the entrance to the Botanical Gardens (or *Jardin du Roi*) founded by the father of the French Monarch, King Louis XIII.

'The house is large,' said Madame de Flamanville, as the coach entered a circular driveway and I saw smartly clad servants standing in line to greet us, 'so of course you will stay here, Sir Robert.'

I did not argue. One thing I had learned, on the very agreeable journey from Versailles, was that Madame de Flamanville, whose Given Name was Louise, (putting me rather deliciously in mind of the King's mistress, 'Fubbsy', also Christened Louise) was a woman well used to getting her own way. From this I surmised that she may have been the child of a Doting Father (such as Margaret is) or that Colonel de Flamanville was likewise a Doting Husband, or else a weak man – or, indeed, both of these things.

But I saw, too, that Madame de Flamanville wanted her way because her mind was infinitely lively and interested itself in everything around her. Her education, mainly got in Switzerland where she was born, had been what she called 'sufficient', but it struck me, as the journey progressed, as having been far superior to that.

She spoke four languages, including Latin. She composed music. She knew the Scriptures 'well enough to hold up my head in a Convent, if that Fate ever fell upon me'. Like Margaret, she was set aflame by the Geography of the world. But she told me that the thing which gave her the greatest satisfaction was the study of Medicinal Plants and their properties, and in the *hôtel* in the Faubourg Saint-Victor she had furnished for herself 'a small Laboratory – with wide-opening windows in case of explosions! – in which I practise an amateurish kind of Chemistry'.

You may imagine the delight this admission gave to me. It allowed me to speak of my intimate knowledge of King Charles's Laboratory at Whitehall and my own interest, as a physician, in Nature's cures – even so far as to mention my departed friend, John Pearce, and his Buttercup Root Prophylactic against the Plague and the use that I made of it, which saved me from Death in 1666. And, just as I hoped, these revelations of our shared interest and our shared knowledge created a bond between us such as I declare I had never felt with any woman before.

In all the long miles to Paris, with a cold December rain making mournful the flat countryside around us, we kept up a most bracing Discourse, so that by the time we arrived, I was aware that my cheeks were fiercely overheated and my heart beating to a galloping rhythm.

In the *hôtel* I was shown into a large and comfortable Bedchamber with, behind a curtain, its own commodious close-stool. The sight of this object, no less than the appearance in my room of a large jug of hot water, almost brought tears of gratitude to my eyes.

The same servant who brought the water then informed me supper would be taken at seven o'clock. And this too – the delicious imaginings of a meal that did not consist of Peas and Jam – brought a constriction to my throat, so that I almost burst into one of those fits of Blubbing that so discommoded Will Gates and which had worn out innumerable handkerchiefs over the swiftly passing years.

When I had cleaned myself and chosen the Suit I would wear for supper, and washed and shaken and scolded and brushed my wig until it had miraculously resumed something of its former liveliness and sheen, I sat down at a little Cherrywood table and began the following letter:

To: Miss Margaret Merivel,
In the Care of Sir James Prideaux, Baronet,
Mevagissey,
Cornwall

My dear Margaret,
Your Neglectful Papa sends you his fondest love and greet-ings, and apologises for the absence of any Letter since his arrival at Dieppe.

His sojourn at the Court of Versailles has been somewhat Difficult, owing to the great Press of People there and I have not yet had any Success in obtaining a Position among the King's Doctors.

But fear nothing on my account. I have, of late, been very for-tunate to meet some enchanting Friends, Colonel and Madame de Flamanville, and I am now arrived in Paris as their Guest.

All that I can see of the City is most Orderly and Beautiful, with, laid out at my feet as it were, the allées *and parterres of the* Jardin du Roi, *where I hope to walk tomorrow and where, I have been told, there is a captive Bear, waiting for Trans-portation to the King's Menagerie at Versailles.*

So you see, I am among Wonders. The Melancholy, from which I suffered recently and which so distressed you, my dear Margaret, is, I believe, quite gone. I only wish that you were with me and that we might go together to visit the Bear, and I could hold your hand in mine.

Meanwhile, I think of you and Mary and the others taking your Scented Paths to the Sea and making for yourselves little Collections of Cowrie Shells, as sweet as babies' fingers . . .

I had imagined that at supper Madame de Flamanville and I would be alone together, to continue our animated conversations, but this was not to be and I had a moment's difficulty stifling my disappointment.

We were joined by the Colonel's unmarried sister, Mademoiselle Corinne de Flamanville, who lived permanently in the house, under the care of her brother, and who, it transpired, did not like to move from Paris 'owing to my great fear of becoming lost'.

She was a very thin woman of about my age, dressed all in black and having no teeth whatsoever, so that to eat a meal in her company was a dangerous pastime, with food flying from her mouth in wondrously far directions and her conversation all but impossible to follow. (My own table manners, about which my wife used to complain very strenuously, appeared, I must believe, impeccably co-ordinated by comparison.)

I wished to try to make myself agreeable to Mademoiselle, nevertheless. Spinster Women create in my heart a kind of terrible anguish, for I know that their lives are bitter. They are the possessors of nothing but their own souls.

Not really knowing on what kind of topic to begin, I told her I was most interested in her agitation about losing her bearings, for that I sometimes suffered the very same thing and had found Versailles, for instance, to be a confusing place.

Mademoiselle Corinne stared at me in stupefaction. 'What did he say?' she enquired of Madame de Flamanville. 'What language is he speaking?'

I could not restrain a burst of mirth from breaking from me at this. I was unable to look at Mademoiselle Corinne, from whose pendulous bottom lip a morsel of soft Parsnip was dangling like a worm, but I looked over at Louise (for such I will call her from now on) and saw that she was laughing too.

'I apologise,' I managed to say to Mademoiselle Corinne, suppressing, as best I could, the Riot inside me, 'for my horrible French. I know it is most inelegant. Would you prefer me to speak English? I have been very impressed by how many of your countrymen understand the English tongue.'

'I have absolutely no idea,' said Corinne, 'what he is talking about. Is he Flemish? Has he got a Flemish name? The Flemish are always impossible to comprehend.'

'He was only enquiring about your reluctance to leave Paris,' said Louise. 'He sympathises with your fears. He says that there are many places in which one may feel lost.'

'Many places in which one may feel lost? But what a stupid thing to say! I told him, I don't *go* to those places. I stay in the Faubourg Saint-Victor. What city is he from?'

'He is from England,' said Louise. 'He is a Doctor of Medicine, residing in England.'

'Doctor? Did you say Doctor? He doesn't look like a Doctor.'

'Ah, that is very interesting,' I ventured to interject. 'How do you imagine a Doctor to look?'

Mademoiselle Corinne wiped her mouth, at last removing from our sight the parsnip worm, which fell into her lap, took up her Lorgnette and looked me up and down through its pearly lenses. 'Thinner,' she said.

At this I felt another attack of mirth coming on, which I was unable to supress. Reluctantly I rested my knife and fork from their exertions with an admirable roast Grouse, and buried my face in my table napkin and my helpless gurgling filled the air of the *Salle à Manger*. And, alas for Mademoiselle Corinne de Fla-manville, my laughter was such a wondrously contagious thing, it followed that Louise was soon enough overcome with hectic and unstoppable mirth of the kind that almost unseated us from our chairs.

Mademoiselle Corinne stared at us, looking from one to the other in pure dismay. To the Maître d'hôtel, standing by Louise's chair, she snapped: 'It is the wine, Bertrand. The wine has turned them into Hyenas. Do not serve them another *drop*!'

The wine, perhaps, no less than the stimulating journey and the excellent Grouse and the sight of a clean bed, had all contrived, by nightfall, to exhaust me. I had intended to finish my letter to Margaret, but had no will to do anything more than put on my night attire, climb between the linen sheets and surrender myself to the sweet sleep I felt approaching. As I closed my eyes, I reflected that I had not felt as happy as I was at this moment for many years.

All night long, I had a very marvellous Epicureanism of Rest and, when I woke at some time after eight o'clock, found my heart filled with an instantaneous joy.

After breakfast Louise asked me whether I would like to visit her Laboratory and I willingly agreed.

The Laboratory was set out on marble-topped tables, along two sides of a narrow room. Above the tables were stacked, on neat wooden shelving, a great quantity of small Apothecaries' Jars, carefully labelled and containing, I instantly saw, properties as strong and precarious as Arsenic, Calomel and Ceruse.

'My word!' I said. 'You have poisons here a-plenty. Does your knowledge match their exigencies?'

'By no means,' said Louise at once. 'But I am learning. I am allowed, sometimes, to watch the experiments done in the Laboratory of the *Jardin du Roi*, on our very doorstep, beyond the gates there. At first the Chemists did not wish me to come there because I am a woman. But I said to them: "Women are kept from all Experimentation in the World. Even our *feelings* are supposed to follow a Pattern Ordained and never altering. But why should I not at least bear witness to *your* Experiments? What danger is there in that – only that my admiration for you shall increase!"

'And though some grumbled that to observe what they did could be "bad for my mind" and one said he thought it might "turn me into a Witch like the infamous La Voisin", they did not in the end deny me, provided only that I made no comments and never attempted to participate in anything. But they could not prevent me from hastening back here and setting down Notes on what I had witnessed. And so I have begun to learn . . .'

As she spoke, Louise's hands were passing tenderly, yet restlessly, along the table, examining jars and Alembics and baskets of herbs set to dry, and a glass tank crawling with snails. I watched her with great attention, reflecting that I had surely never met any woman like her, who was so delightfully compounded of Wit and Seriousness. And I realised that every moment spent in her company had become enthralling to me.

'Now,' she said, pausing at the end of one of the tables where a cluster of identical jars were arranged in a little pyramid. 'Let me show you my only small success.'

She uncorked one of the jars and held it out to me. I pressed it to my nose and the smell reminded me, on the instant, of that muddled time in my Former Life, when I tried my hand as an artist, before giving up in despair.

'A Salve for sores,' said Louise. 'Efficacious also for burns. My chef burned his hand and my Salve restored it within two days!'

'Bravo,' I said. 'I must take some home to England for my cook, Cattlebury, who is so covered in burns, it is as though he had only just escaped a roasting at the stake.'

Louise smiled and went on: 'I had some difficulty, for a long while, with the proportions of the Ingredients, but they are correct now. Sheep's tallow, Beeswax, Oil of Turpentine, Plantain leaves boiled for one hour on a soft fire of coals until you have the Reduction you desire. The wax melted very slowly and the Reduction and the Oil stirred in over a very timid heat. The difficulty seemed to lie in getting a Salve that was soft enough to apply, once it cools. But it is soft now. Put your finger in.'

I sampled the Salve and rubbed a little of it onto the back of my hand.

'What d'you think?' she asked. 'You as a Doctor know, many Salves smell rancid, but this does not, does it?'

'No. It smells very fresh. The Turpentine . . .'

'Yes. That I added almost as a perfume. The cure is in the wax and the Plantain, but to me the scent of things is important. Let me make you a present of this jar.'

Offering my thanks, I looked up at Louise, with all my admiration for her surely evident upon my face, for though she held my gaze for a second, she quickly looked away. A woman like Louise de Flamanville, I thought, surely acts like a Salve on a man's life. By slow degrees, life inflicts its wounds upon him and she heals them.

She showed me other preparations on which she was at work. These included a Lotion 'to mask or reduce the Stench of the Armpit'.

'Ah,' said I, 'that is much needed at Versailles!'

'Quite so, Sir Robert. You know, by the way, that Madame de Montespan had a terrible Stink to her person?'

'No, I did not.'

'Perhaps my lotion would have prevented her from falling out of favour. There is a thought. But I have not got it right yet. I am using white wine, Rose-water and seed of wild Rocket. I boiled them first in a glass Alembic, so that I could observe their clarity or their cloudiness, but my fire was too hot and my Alembic exploded, and I was cut with shards of burning glass!'

'*Oh, mon dieu!*' I said. 'It might have blinded you.'

'Yes, it might, but it did not. And, strangely, I did not really suffer at all. Indeed, I rather enjoyed myself. For I was struck by the thought that this is what *real Chemists* undergo, these Shocks and Reversals, and that I could now count myself among their number.'

She handed me a vial, which contained all that she had made of this preparation, and I sniffed it carefully, as connoisseurs of wine sniff their beloved libations.

'Is it right, d'you think?' she enquired. 'It needs to be strong, but not so strong that the lotion itself smells worse than the sweating and engrimed flesh. The Rocket seed will lessen Perspiration, that is proven, and the wine and Rose-water will cleanse, but . . .'

'Lemon Grass,' I said. 'No more than a few leaves, boiled and added. And you would have a longer-lasting tincture.'

'Ah,' said Louise. 'Lemon Grass. I had not thought of that. What a delight it is to have so able a Laboratory Assistant.'

≒ ⊨

Though cold, the December day had dawned very fine and when we left the Laboratory to walk into the *Jardin du Roi*, the sun gave to the neat walks and Knot Gardens an air of shining, wintry beauty.

Louise and I were almost alone in the gardens, they being prohibited to all but a few chosen people.

'The Royal Chemists allow me to take a few leaves or sprigs from time to time, for my own little experiments,' said Louise and when we came upon a bed of Lemon Grass, its freshness long past with the onset of the dark season, she leaned down and picked a few ragged stalks and handed them to me.

As she picked she said: 'I understand very little of Newton, from the few papers of his circulating in France, but his Separation of light into a Spectrum by means of a Prism was explained to me and is, I think, quite wondrous. And I am attracted by his differentiation between Hypothesis, which he says is "pure speculation" and Theory, which has undergone proof. As soon as I took this in, I knew that I must follow his example and make no claim for any of my compounds until I know – for certain – that they are efficacious. Healing must be my only proof.'

'Quite so,' I agreed. 'My friend, John Pearce, was very, very determined upon this question, following his hero, William Harvey, who based everything upon Dissection and Observation, rather than upon Ancient authority. Pearce once said that my tendency to hypothesise made him feel sick.'

'Ah. Your "tendency to hypothesise". Is this still with you?'

'Less with me than at any time. My mind still boils, occasionally, with suppositions and wonderings, for without some of these no new thing will be tried. But I believe I am growing more and more like Harvey in every respect.'

'Yes? What respects might these be?'

'Well,' I said, 'to name one: Harvey loved the dark. He had caves made in the earth near his house in Surrey, where he delighted to sit and meditate. I have not gone as far as to dig caves, for I am not very enamoured of the creatures who live in them – Bats and Snakes and so forth. But when I am alone in my house in Norfolk, I like to endure the dusk, without lighting a lamp or Tallow. In the Almost-Darkness I can sometimes feel my mind becoming very still, so that I can see with clarity what was indistinct to me before.'

Louise pressed more Lemon Grass into my hand and regarded me closely. The winter sunlight glanced upon her cheek, which in spite of her forty-five years was very smooth and of a very pale olive colour, and I had to restrain myself from leaning forward and placing my lips upon it. Instead, I lifted my bunch of Grass stems to my nose and inhaled their lingering Perfume.

'There is still a little Lemon freshness in it,' I said.

'Good. We will boil the stems and see what the Reduction will add to my tincture. Do you live alone in your Norfolk house, Sir Robert, when your daughter is staying with her Friends, or do you have a wife?'

I fell silent. So congenial did I find the companionship of Louise de Flamanville that I was tempted, there and then, in the cold light of the *Jardin du Roi*, to relate to her the whole story of my marriage to Celia and its Annulment some years later, after I had been restored to the King's favour. But I also knew that this piece of my history served mainly to make me appear importunate and foolish, so I drew back.

'I have no wife,' I said. 'She departed from this world long ago. From time to time the King arrives, with some of his retinue and very many dogs, and then I am whirled into fine company once more. But for much of each year I am alone.'

'I see,' said Louise quietly and we walked on. We crossed into an *allée* of Planes, whose great leaves had fallen, to reveal their branches decked with dangling seed-heads, like tarnished jewellery. And it was at this moment that we both became aware of a strange sound, a pitiful howling noise, which spoke to us of great distress. Following the *allée* to its end, we turned left into a grassy meadow and saw before us a very sorrowful sight.

In a square cage made from branches of elm a great Brown Bear was standing on its hind legs and clawing at the wood, and crying like a wolf. Its jaw was open, to show a tongue foaming and parched, and the sound that came from its throat was as desolate as any sound I have heard in my life.

We stopped and stared. Louise reached out and touched my arm, and I took her hand in mine.

'I know where its end is to be,' she said.

'I, too. The Menagerie at Versailles.'

We stood very still, the misery of the animal choking our senses, so that all we could smell was its terror, and all we could breathe was its woe, and all we could feel in our throats was its thirst.

I could feel Louise's hand trembling in mine. I held her more tightly to me and, to try to soothe her, began very quietly on a story about a neighbour of mine in Norfolk, one Squire Sands, who whipped the Shire horse that pulled his plough so relentlessly that it died of its wounds.

'Squire Sands had no money,' I continued, 'with which to buy another nag. For a whole season his fields were left to the weeds. But when he saw that he was going to starve if he did not plant his corn and his vegetables, he had no choice but to yoke himself to the plough. And I saw him in his Condition of Horse, straining his heart and lungs to till his own soil. And for a moment I pitied him. But then I remembered what he had done to the Shire mare, and in an instant my heart emptied itself of pity.'

Louise was still and silent for a moment. Then she turned and faced me, and put her arms round me and kissed my mouth.

8

Twenty-four hours have passed: hours very choked with incident and strong feeling.

Eating oysters at lunchtime in an admirable Auberge, as Louise and I licked and wiped our fingers and cooled our salt throats with a delicate wine from the Loire Valley, she leaned near to me and said: 'I want to tell you about my life, Sir Robert. Or shall you think this very forward?'

'No,' I replied. 'I would be honoured to hear about your life . . .'

Louise sipped her wine, wiped her mouth and whispered: 'I would like to explain to you – in the strictest confidence of course – that my marriage with Colonel Jacques-Adolphe de Flamanville, for all that he is a very courageous Soldier, and worthy of my respect, is as arid as an empty lake.'

'Ah. I am sad to hear—'

'We have no children. I would have liked to be a Mother, but de Flamanville always and ever said: "You cannot be a Mother, Madame, unless I consent to be a Father, and this I will not do."'

I touched Louise's hand. 'I am sorry for this,' I said. 'For I know how precious a child can be . . .'

'I think I would have been a loving mother, Sir Robert, but it is too late now. My Chemistry work, amateurish though it is, gives a little Meaning to my life, but I am growing tired of the way each passing year is arranged. Paris I like; Versailles I cannot abide. But I think I may soon leave both Paris and Versailles and return to Switzerland, to care for my father, who is old and lonely. I am his only living child and I am very fond of him, and I would not wish him to die alone. Jacques-Adolphe will protest, but I shall not be missed by him, except only as his Camouflage in Society.'

'His Camouflage?'

'He is very particular about this, though I scarcely see why. There is a Society at Versailles called the *Fraternité*. You may guess what kind of Society this is. Its members love only men and de Fla-manville is one of their number. Madame de Maintenon would have the King denounce them, but what can he do when his own brother, the Duc d'Orléans, is one of its founders?'

'Ah. I understand.'

Louise drank more wine. Her hazel eyes were bright and her gaze intense.

'Perhaps I should not be telling you these things, Sir Robert, except that in you, I seem to find a Spirit very kindred to mine. My life, you see, has been a somewhat solitary thing and I fear this makes me too bold. I have had lovers . . .'

'Louise,' I said, 'for so shall I call you from now on – and you must call me Merivel, which is the name that I prefer – I rejoice that you have had lovers. I hope they were as rampageous as leopards and as tender as puppy-dogs.'

Louise smiled. 'I can scarcely remember,' she said, 'it was so long ago.'

I took a sip of my wine, the taste of which had never seemed to me as marvellous as it did at this moment. 'I would like you to say my name,' I said. 'Say "Merivel".'

'Merivel,' she repeated quietly. And this saying of my name tugged at my heart.

I took hold of Louise's hand. 'Say "Merivel, will you be my lover?"'

I expected her response to come without hesitation. She was a daring woman who appeared shocked by nothing and who, by her recent revelations about her husband and her lovers, had seemed to be leading me closer to her bed. But, to my great Discomfort, she suddenly withdrew her hand and blushed and said she could not say what I had asked. And now I was the one to wonder if, remembering the passion with which I had kissed her in the *Jardin du Roi*, I had been too ardent and too calculating.

In the afternoon we visited a High-Class Tailor, Monsieur Durand, in the rue de l'Oiseau near the Porte Saint Antoine, to take in hand the alterations to my clothes, decreed by my sojourn at Versailles.

While I cast my eye upon Shoulder-Ribbons and tried on *canons* of different styles and colours, I reflected mournfully that if Louise had in no way decided to let me become her lover, I could not for long trespass upon her hospitality in Paris, and would soon enough have to return to Versailles and resume my Pauper's life there.

Into my bitter remembrance came an image of my cot-bed and of the smell of Peas in Brine, and the sight of Hollers sitting on the pisspot.

'Hey-ho!' said I suddenly, 'but assuredly life is all contrast and contradiction!'

I breathed out a long sigh. A pair of scarlet *canons* were pinching my legs infernally and I cast them off. I could feel rising in me a mood of immoderate frustration and anger, such as I suffered so frequently in my Former Life, and I knew that I had to force myself to contain it, or lose all possibility of obtaining the thing I wanted above all others.

'Of what are you thinking?' asked Louise sternly, as the Tailor picked up the *canons* I had petulantly flung across the room.

'I was thinking of Hollers,' I said. 'While Time, here, goes by so swiftly, in such a pleasing way for me, for him it crawls, no doubt. And I know that such a Crawling of Time is very painful to endure.'

'It is,' said Louise. 'But your friend must learn patience. Madame de Maintenon is correct: you cannot make up your mind about a clock until you see how it behaves over many days and nights.'

Nights.

I wished the night to come and I wished it not to come.

We sat at supper dutifully, watching Mademoiselle Corinne's chin dripping with Leek Soup and her black silk gown becoming spattered with morsels of Duck. I attempted to talk to her about the myriad wares to be bought in the rue de l'Oiseau. But all she would say was: 'Yes, yes, I know that street, but I do not go there now. For why should one go there? To buy brooms or birdcages or toys? Why ever would one want them? Why ever should one go anywhere?'

I had no reply to make to this. I looked helplessly towards Louise, but she would not catch my eye. We shared no laughter.

After supper, we all retired to the *Salon* and Mademoiselle amused herself by drawing profiles of faces upon black paper and laboriously cutting them out to make Silhouettes. For her sad sake I admired them, in the clearest French I could muster, but she did not thank me. She merely remarked that in the winter evenings there was nothing else to do but this, the cutting out of Silhouettes on black paper and that over the years she had completed more than five hundred.

'You therefore comprehend, Monsieur,' she said, 'that I am not idle.'

'I comprehend it absolutely, Mademoiselle,' I said. 'And, indeed, I would very much like to cast my eye upon the five hundred Silhouettes . . .'

'You mean you doubt me?'

'I do not doubt you.'

'Then why pester me to see them? Making them is all that counts.'

Again, I looked over to Louise, but she was silent, working at some piece of complicated embroidery, and did not raise her head. Abandoning the conversation with Mademoiselle Corinne, I thus found myself the only one in the room with nothing to occupy me and this sudden Idleness I found irksome. I remembered what Pearce used to say when I went fishing with him – that I was always and ever 'too restless' – and I therefore tried to remain still in my chair and watch the fire in the grate, and put from my mind all thoughts of what the night might or might not bring.

I looked down at my legs. I had put on a set of taupe *canons* for which I had paid the Tailor of the rue de l'Oiseau a goodly sum. But now the appearance of my legs, which are somewhat thin and puny (in contrast to my stomach, which is still substantial, despite my diet of Oatmeal and Peas at Versailles) encircled with these ridiculous ruffs, such as Vultures have on their horrible, scaly shanks, struck me as sublimely ridiculous and I could not prevent a great wave of melancholy from overcoming me.

'You are a foolish mortal, Merivel,' I said to myself. 'You have been seduced by something which has no future. And the next time you wear these *canons* will be in the *Galerie des Glaces* at Versailles, where your role as Supplicant will have no end, except an end in failure.'

I could not sit still on my chair any longer. I got up and bowed to the ladies and apologised, as cheerfully as I could, that all my 'wonderful geographical wanderings about the city' had wearied me enough to make me wish to retire to bed.

'What did he say?' piped Mademoiselle Corinne.

'He said that he is tired,' said Louise. 'I have exhausted him.'

Determined to behave as though I was expecting nothing further to happen to me that evening, I undressed and washed myself

and got into bed. I hung my wig upon the door handle. I lay in
my linen sheets, scratching my head.

Hoping that I had not contracted lice from my time with Hollers, I nevertheless felt moderately glad, all of a sudden, that my
hair, though wiry and coarse (and likened by me in *The Wedge* to
'hog's bristles') was still quite thick, whereas many men of my
age were persecuted by an uglifying Baldness. Unlike some, I
was not afraid to be seen without my wig and I said to myself
that *were* Louise to come to my room, she would not be unduly
affrighted by the sight of me.

But alas, she would not come. Of this I was now almost certain. She had been tender and very flirtatious towards me, but at
my crude suggestion that she should take me as her lover she
had suddenly drawn back. This I had not expected at all and, I
admit, I was still at some pains to understand why she had acted
in this way, but I knew that she had her reasons.

I lay in the dark and asked myself: 'What would King Charles
do now, finding himself in this ambiguous position?' But then I
reflected that in all probability no such problem ever perplexed
him, for that no woman *ever* refused him or drew back from his
embrace. They fell before him like daffodils before the scythe.
Instead of lying alone, as I was, scratching himself, he would
already have been in Louise de Flamanville's bed.

But then a new wondering assailed me. Was it possible that
Louise, having led me on, even so far as to tell me about her former lovers and the great Incapacity of her husband, wished, as it
were, for *me* to take up the baton and conduct the next movement of our little private piece of music?

She was a person of great Intelligence and Finesse. Was it not
very probable, therefore, that her woman's sensibilities, when
goaded to invite me to a physical union that might have great
consequence for both of us, had found themselves too tried? The
only way forward, in this case, was for *me* to act.

I lay very still, listening to the sounds of the Paris night, which seemed much quieter than the night in London. I was indeed quite weary and part of my mind instructed itself to go to sleep without more fuss and ado. But the other part could not help but imagine how it would be to lie in Louise's arms and how, if I could become her lover, the coming days would unfold before me in a wondrous parade of glories.

I was on the very verge of rising and making my way to Louise's room when it came upon me that if I went there and she sent me away, I would feel far *worse* than if I had not gone there at all. I therefore tried to measure this potential *Worseness* against the risk that, even as I was lying here and not moving, she was, in fact, waiting for me and would feel angry and humiliated if I did not come to her . . .

While these two alternative possibilities turned and returned, turned and returned in my mind, I fell asleep.

I woke in the half-dark of early morning. I could hear a solitary Blackbird singing.

Without any fear or fret, without any hesitation, I drank some water to refresh my mouth, then put on my coat over my night-shirt, opened my door and made my way to Louise's room.

I opened her door. She lay asleep, with her candle still burning, yet almost on the verge of guttering out, by her bedside. Her brown hair was spread in soft waves upon her pillow and on her features was the wisp of a smile. I stood over her and admired her stillness and her beauty, and then she opened her eyes.

'Oh, Merivel,' she said. 'I am so glad you understood.'

The joy I had predicted I would feel if I could become the lover of Louise de Flamanville did not tarry, but came into me and filled my being the moment I held her and felt all my passion reciprocated in her.

Seldom, I reflected, is the ardour of two lovers equal; there is always one who feels more. But with Louise, it seemed to me, we took our pleasure with a kind of exquisitely matched reverence for it, being neither hasty nor slow, but only strong and tender, each for the other, and whispering all the while words of passionate attachment.

Afterwards we lay in a swoon of love. We slept a little, entwined, and woke with the Blackbirds singing loudly and a cold grey light at the window.

'You must go,' whispered Louise. 'The servants will be stirring. And Corinne . . .'

But I could not go before I had loved her again, this time very quietly, for fear of disturbing the Household, and she clung to me silently, with her mouth held to mine and only cried out with a stifled breath when she came to her pleasure.

It was when this second blissful Exertion was over and we were lying in a silky sweat together, letting our hearts return to their normal beating, that we became aware of a commotion below in the driveway. A carriage, drawn as it sounded by four horses, was arriving.

For a moment neither of us moved. Then Louise threw back the bedclothes with a look of terror on her face. 'De Flamanville!' she whispered. 'I recognise the sound of his coach!'

I leapt from the bed, searched the floor for my nightshirt but could not find it. I caught sight of my coat upon a chair and flung this on.

'Quickly, Merivel!' said Louise. 'He must not know! He *must* not know!'

I cast a kiss towards her with my hand and hurried to the door. I listened for a moment, but could hear nothing in the passageway, so I scurried out into it as silently as I could and went along towards my room, trying to mimic the quietness and agility of a rat.

How ridiculous I appeared, in my unfastened coat, with bare legs and my hair all damp and crazed with my recent Endeavours, I only realised when I was back in the safety of my room and caught sight of myself in the large looking-glass. But I did not stop to contemplate my image.

I hurled away my coat and hid, naked and cold, under my covers, and pretended to be asleep. Now I could hear numerous feet upon the stairs: Servants woken in the last minutes of the night and hurrying down to their Master, whose loud tread was soon enough heard on the flags of the hall.

To my great relief, this tread did not embark upon the stairs, but progressed towards the *Salle à Manger*, where Colonel Jacques-Adolphe de Flamanville began calling for his breakfast.

9

Very fortunately for me and for Louise, Colonel de Flamanville had long ago ceased to share a room with his wife. When he had taken his breakfast and come upstairs, he went straight to his sister's room and did not therefore subject himself to the sight of Louise's rumpled bed, scented with my unmistakable presence.

Indeed, he did not come near his wife, so she was able to wash and dress herself, and descend to the *Salle à Manger* at nine o'clock for her own morning repast, looking clean and calm.

I, too, managed to attend to my person sufficiently so that no trace of Louise's perfume clung to it. I even soaped my head and dried it, and shaved my face. Only my left ear-lobe, very red where Louise had bitten it, suggested any Misconduct beneath de Flamanville's roof, but my wig concealed this, so that all in all I appeared the very Picture of an Innocent Guest, who has passed a chaste night and risen moderately early, refreshed with sleep.

I did suffer, however, from a ravening appetite, and in a very short space of time, consumed no less than four lamb cutlets, together with a dish of Coddled Eggs and three bowls of Chocolate.

When I saw Louise smiling at this I said: 'My servant in Norfolk, Will Gates, is always amused by my gourmandising. He considers it may be bad for my heart.'

'Oh,' said Louise, 'I do hope that is not the case.'

It was at this moment, when my snout was once again hidden in the Chocolate bowl, that Colonel de Flamanville strode into the room.

In common, I suppose, with many military men, de Flamanville was a tall person of exceedingly upright bearing. He even held his head fiercely high, as though perpetually undergoing some exercise to stretch his neck. This, coupled with his long Nose, gave his person a kind of haughty Authority, upon which, I surmised, he depended to get his way with people he considered beneath him, such as myself.

Yet there was something in his deportment that could not help but remind me of a Giraffe, so despite all that I had done in secret to cause his extreme displeasure, I found that I was not in the least afraid of him.

He sat down at the table and asked Louise how we had passed the time since leaving Versailles. I set aside my Chocolate bowl and wiped my face.

Louise remained very still and calm and said: 'We have mainly been at work in my Laboratory, *mon chéri*. You remember that Sir Robert Merivel is a Doctor of Medicine? His knowledge of my compounds is impressive.'

'Ah,' said de Flamanville, 'I did not know that. A Doctor? You do not look like a Doctor. Are you in the employ of Monsieur Fagon?'

'Monsieur Fagon?'

'The King's Surgeon. You do not know him?'

'No,' I said. 'I came out from England with a Letter from King Charles, for whom I have worked for very many years, recommending me for some medical appointment within His Majesty's circle. Unfortunately—'

'You know how difficult it always is,' interjected Louise, 'to get the King's attention and Versailles is so crowded at the moment. But I also saw that it was important for Sir Robert to come to Paris, so that his English attire could be . . . ah . . . *adjusted* to the standards of the French Court. His best coats are with Monsieur Durand undergoing Alteration.'

The Giraffe raised his neck still higher and stared down his nose at me, wrinkling it slightly, as though I might have been a morsel of vegetation upon which he was planning to graze. 'And then what is your plan?' he asked. 'When your coats have been altered?'

'Well,' I said (and once again the ghastly image of the room I shared with Hollers came, unbidden, into my mind), 'I shall of course return to Versailles. I have great faith in my Letter.'

De Flamanville looked at me for a moment longer, sniffed and stood up. 'I play Billiards in the morning,' he said. 'Will you join me?'

I looked over at Louise, who nodded her head in the most inconspicuous of assents, so, obediently, I rose from my chair. Yet I must confess that the idea of a Billiard Game with Colonel de Flamanville wearied me most intolerably. My very bones ached at the thought of it. I had never been skilled at this game, which consists in having a hand steady enough (and a mind empty enough) to knock balls of Ivory through wooden hoops on a table covered with carpet, for hours upon end. It had always seemed to me to be the reverse of a 'pastime': indeed, a stupid activity in which Time was stretched out to such an unbearable degree that one despaired of it ever being 'past'.

But here I am now in the room Colonel de Flamanville calls his Library, but which does not appear to contain very many books. I meditate that if you are a Colonel in the Swiss Guards, as well as being a member of the infamous *Fraternité*, there is some possibility that you have little leisure for reading.

Chief in the room is the gigantic Billiard Table, upholstered with a very intricate tapestry carpet, and I am at once invited to choose my 'weapon', from a pile of seemingly identical weapons, for pushing the balls around.

I have forgotten the correct name of these implements. It

amuses King Charles to call them 'spoons', for that they are tilted up at their wider end and I suppose that one might be able to eat a Broth from them, if no other cutlery was at hand. I choose one and examine its fine workmanship. (I am beginning to form the impression that, in France, most Things are better made than in England.)

The Billiard balls can be made of Lead or Ivory, and these, of course, are Ivory, very finely wrought. Colonel de Flamanville likes to hold a spare ball in his hand while he watches me begin my lamentable play. He has also acquired the habit of sniffing and snorting disdainfully when his opponent plays a weak shot. I imagine the mucus in his Giraffe nose in a perpetual state of confused Flux.

The Score starts to mount irreversibly in his favour, and this notwithstanding the fact that, as well as sniffing, he talks all the while to me, asking me questions about my work for King Charles and my station at Whitehall, and the Measurement in hectares of my Estate at Bidnold, together with much else (such as my marital status, most exceedingly ambiguous in a Catholic country and about which I am forced to lie, as I lied to Louise) that I have no particular wish to touch upon and which I do my best to circumnavigate.

After a while, when one of my erratic balls has bounced into the structure of a hoop but distressingly failed to pass through it, he suddenly says: 'I am returning to Versailles tomorrow. I suggest you come back with me. I have the ear of the King from time to time, and I will do my best to get you an Audience.'

My heart fills with dread. 'Colonel de Flamanville,' I say, 'that is more than kind of you. However, I do not think that my Coats will be ready by that time . . .'

'Ah,' he says. 'Your Coats. What adjustments are being made to them?'

'Well, alas, they were quite without Shoulder-Ribbons . . .'

De Flamanville looks down at me with all the Disdain that a Giraffe might demonstrate towards a vexing little wild dog yapping round its feet. 'So this is all?' says he. 'The sewing in of ribbons?'

'Yes.'

'And how might that take more than one afternoon?'

'It is not only the ribbons,' I lie hastily. 'While I was at Monsieur Durand's admirable Premises, I clearly saw that a finer Coat than any I possess might be made for me there and I was so extravagant as to order one. I am to go for my first fitting on Monday morning.'

De Flamanville plays a deft shot, sending his ball through the hoop and simultaneously knocking mine wide of it. He straightens up, measuring his next move, which is to attempt his first hit on the End Post. Then he turns to me and says: 'And while you are going through with fittings and so forth, where do you intend to lodge?'

I have not anticipated this question. I find myself desperately wishing that Louise were in the room and could intervene on my behalf. But I know that I must answer with the greatest possible composure. 'I admit,' I say, 'that I had not given this my attention, Colonel, only because your wife has been kind enough to invite me to reside here. If this arrangement is in any way inimical to you, I will leave straight away and go to one of the excellent-seeming Auberges I glimpsed along the River.'

De Flamanville makes no comment, but only continues to pace about, snorting, on his side of the Billiard Table, still apparently measuring his ball's distance from the End Post. 'Are you absolutely sure,' he says after a moment, 'that you do have a Letter from King Charles?'

'Yes. It is upstairs in my Valise.'

'Very well. Perhaps you would be kind enough to fetch it.'

On the stairs, en route for my room, I meet Mademoiselle Corinne. Louise has told me that she never appears for breakfast, but takes this in her bedroom, under the blind and watchful eyes of her five hundred paper Silhouettes.

'Ah,' she says, while I wait patiently and courteously for her to descend. '*You.*'

'*Bonjour, Mademoiselle Corinne,*' I say. 'I trust you slept well.'

'No, I did not sleep well,' she says. 'I was woken before dawn by the sound of people Moving About. If it had not been so cold, I would have risen up to investigate.'

'I assume it was the Servants you heard, making preparation for the Colonel's early arrival.'

'I doubt it. They are a lazy and dim-witted assemblage, who leave everything to the last minute. No. I do believe it was you. The footsteps had an English Echo to them.'

'An English Echo?'

'Yes. French people walk more elegantly. You flap your feet like Penguins. I distinctly heard a Penguin.'

I cannot help but laugh at this, thus incurring Mademoiselle's greater displeasure.

'And there is another matter, Monsieur *le "Docteur"*. I simply do not understand what you find to laugh at all the while. Is not the suffering in the world great enough for you? Have you not presided over the deaths of Patients? Are many not betrayed by those they love? Was Jesus Christ not murdered on a Cross?'

'He was,' I say quickly. 'But He rose again. 'My laughter comes all from my joy at the Resurrection, which gives hope to us all, Sinners though we may be.'

At this she closes her toothless mouth and says no more. She comes on down the stairs with infinite Slowness, but as she passes me she jabs my chest with a bony finger, and declares: 'I am watching you! You may depend upon it. And so is Jacques-Adolphe. For I have told my brother everything.'

Now my fear of the Giraffe is suddenly woken. I curse my Fortune that I have fallen in love with the wife of a Colonel in the Swiss Guards. I know that there may be no limit to the wounds, both social and physical, such a Soldier might decide to inflict (even one who belongs to the *Fraternité*) in order to defend his supposed 'honour'. Coward that I am, I look helplessly around my room, wondering if I should try to make some immediate escape from the house. But I conclude very quickly that this would be foolish and quite probably fatal.

One night . . . I think with sadness. I had but one night with Louise and now I am to be ignominiously thrown out by a husband who has never ever loved her . . .

I decide to play the Innocent Man insofar as I am able. I reflect that neither Mademoiselle nor the Colonel knows anything with any certainty, unless – a very agitating thought! – my Nightshirt has been found in Louise's room.

Taking a deep breath, I return, outwardly contained and calm, to the Billiard Room and present my letter to the Colonel, who snatches it out of my hand.

'The Seal is broken,' he says at once.

'The Seal was broken by one of the *Surintendents* of the *Grand Commun*. I remonstrated with the man, but he was unmoved.'

'If the Seal is broken, your Letter is worthless.'

'Well,' say I, 'it is compromised, I agree, but it is not worthless. I have no doubt that King Louis will recognise that this is the hand of King Charles, his cousin. Did you know that they used to play together as children, by the way?'

'That changes nothing.'

'My Master, King Charles, told me that they used to play very gravely, sometimes almost in silence, so conscious were the two Princes of the Grand Destiny that awaited them . . .'

'I think you are prattling, Monsieur. Let us return to the matter in hand. Your Letter from Whitehall is made worthless by the broken Seal and is very likely to be seen as a Forgery by King Louis.'

'On my honour, Colonel, it is not a Forgery. The breaking of the Seal does not mean that the Seal was never made. For here it is. You may still plainly see the initials imprinted in the wax, here, C.R.'

De Flamanville peruses the Letter for a brief moment, then hands it back to me. 'It is of no value and will obtain you nothing,' he says. 'You have wasted your money on new fashions in vain. Your return to Versailles is now quite pointless.'

He makes this assertion with such a degree of venomous certainty that for a moment I can find nothing to say.

'What I suggest,' he says, 'is that you pack your Valises and my coach will take to you whichever Auberge you select. In this way you may stay in Paris long enough to collect your new clothes and show them off in England when you return there. I'm sure they will be much admired.'

'If you wish me to leave,' I say as calmly as I can, 'then of course I will. I am never a man to trespass on anybody's Hospitality, as my King would certainly vouch. But I would remind you that I am only here because your wife expressly invited me to stay and would take no refusal.'

With his own spoon, Colonel de Flamanville now beats harshly against the edge of the Table. 'My wife,' he barks, 'does nothing without my Permission! Her invitation to you is withdrawn.'

I look down at the half-completed Billiard game. In the haphazard arrangement of the balls on the tapestry carpet I fancy I can clearly see the wandering dispositions of my hand, and the unerring, arrow-straight trajectory of his.

'Very well,' I say. 'As you will.'

I lay down my spoon. I bow to the Colonel and walk to the door. As I open it, I hear some sweet music being played on a spinette and I know that it is Louise who is playing, and this fills my heart with agony. I hesitate at the door, listening to the melody.

From behind me de Flamanville shouts: 'Let me say to you, further, Monsieur, that I *will not* have my sister tormented by lewd behaviour under this roof! If I hear from her that you have returned to my house, I will have you killed.'

10

That a paltry thing, the alteration of my Coats, kept me in Paris a while longer was, as it transpired, a matter of some consequence.

Though I had little idea how, knowing no one, I should spend my time, except to walk about and admire the great wintry city, it afforded me some space for reflection upon my state.

This reflection chiefly took place, two days after my departure from de Flamanville's house, inside the great Cathedral of Notre Dame de Paris, where I had walked the length of the Nave, passed through the Transept and sat myself upon a stone slab in the Chapel of the Seven Sorrows at the eastern End of the Choir. Here I kept the company of some melancholy-seeming saints, frescoed in pale colours upon the southern wall.

These figures, put there, by my reckonings, some three or four centuries ago, when all their coloration may have been vibrant and bright, were so faded by Time that they appeared to me to embody the Transience of each and every living thing – even when some attempt has been made to make those living things eternal in Art. For let the years pass and we perceive that by some terrible, soundless trick the Art, in its turn, has faded and flaked away.

One of the saintly figures, dressed in a sombre brown robe, reminded me of Pearce. His face was thin and his expression agitated. In his hands he held a large cross, which he clutched to him in precisely the way that Pearce used to clutch his soup ladle, as though fearing, at every moment, that some Thief or highwayman was intent upon its misappropriation.

'Pearce,' I whispered to this Fresco, 'my life has once more pitched me into Confusion and Muddle. And I really do not know where I am to go.'

The immovable face of the painted saint regarded me with sorrow. In the quiet of the great church I fancied I could hear Pearce sigh.

'Shall I go home to Norfolk?' I asked my departed friend. 'Or shall I try, by some means, to come again to Louise, for whom . . . (and I hasten to add this, Pearce, because I know that you regard all my Amours as shallow and driven only by lust) . . . for whom I have the very greatest regard . . . and from whom I have some proof of reciprocated Affection.'

'Reciprocated Affection?' said Pearce. 'I doubt it.'

At this moment a young Priest passed by the Chapel of the Seven Sorrows, and when he saw me there, talking to myself, he paused and asked: 'Is there anything that I can do for you, *mon fils?*'

'Ah,' I said, 'no, I do not believe there is.'

'Do you wish to make a Confession?'

'A Confession?'

'Yes. Only if you wish it.'

I did not say to the Priest that I had been brought up in the Protestant Faith, nor that this Faith had deserted me after the terrible death by fire of my innocent parents. I did not admit it, because, at this particular moment, for some reason the idea of a Confession – of a laying down of my Burden of Sin, Failure and Indecision onto the thin shoulders of this man of the Church – appealed very strongly to me.

I followed the Priest to the Confession Box, which, being a very confining space, has always put me in mind of some kind of prison cell, or Oubliette, but I endured it. From sitting on the stone slab in the Chapel of the Seven Sorrows, my bottom was somewhat cold and aching, and the wooden plank of the Confessional did nothing to alleviate this. And I fell to pondering whether it might not be wise to supply cushions in Confessionals, so that the Sinners are not tempted to hurry through their Transgressions, or leave some out altogether, for the simple reason that their arses are in distress.

Through the grille I could see the Priest's eye, very brown and bright, like the eye of a Mistlethrush, regarding me.

'Go on, my son,' he said. 'Speak.'

I turned away from the Mistlethrush and looked down at my hands. I knew that I should really begin upon an account of my Chief Sin, which had been to fornicate with the wife of another man, but a welling up of loyalty to Louise prevented me from doing this, my Amours with her now seeming to me both private and precious, and having nothing to do with any Priest.

Instead I said: '*Mon père*, I confess that I am lost. Out of ambition and greed, and out of a kind of restless Loneliness, I came to France in the hope of some Preferment. But I have not got it and now I do not know which way to turn.'

'Go on, my son,' said the Priest again.

'That is all,' I said. 'I do not know what more to add. I confess my Greed. But I have no reward for it, only bitter Disappointment. And now I am running short of money. I would that God might tell me what to do next.'

There was a short silence from the Priest's side of the Box. Then he cleared his throat and said: 'God does not give Instructions. To find what you should do, you must look into your own heart.'

I spent some time sitting alone in my room at the Auberge St Denis, where de Flamanville's coachman had deposited me, and which was on the Ile de la Cité, looking outwards to the shining River.

It amused me to watch all the Commerce that passed on the waterway. I saw barges carrying wood and Sea Coal and bales of wool and heaps of sand and shale. I saw one piled up with furs and another with onions and another with live ducks in wooden crates. And the shouting of the Bargemen and the cries from the other Oarsmen, ferrying passengers up or down or across the Seine, sounded, to my ears, much as they did upon the Thames, all intent upon Trade and nothing but. And I thought how England and France were as one in their commercial souls, and how the two countries should, by rights, be squashed into a commodious Confession Box, there to divulge all their avarice.

Around the steps and wooden walkways that descended to the water clustered raggle-taggle packs of beggars, just as they clustered in London, with their hands outstretched and their eyes wide with Hunger. And remembering, from my first night at Versailles, what terrible pain real Hunger can cause, I here and there gave them a few *sous*.

But I had not lied to the Priest when I said that I was running out of money, so I could not part with much. And, indeed, it was this awareness of my own forthcoming Penury that led me, on my second night at the Auberge St Denis, to write the following letter:

To Wm Gates,
Bidnold Manor, in the County of Norfolk
Angleterre

My dear Will,
I write to you from Paris, where I have taken Lodgings, and not from Versailles, where I expected to be, but am Not, for the Reason that His Majesty King Louis has Doctors enough surrounding him and has no need of Me, to add to their Number.

I have thus decided that, before Christmas comes, I shall make my return to Bidnold. I know that Miss Margaret stays in Cornwall until Twelfth Night, but I will nevertheless come back, and hope I may devise some Lively Entertainment to cheer us at Christmastime, so that no Angel of Melancholy will visit us and no more Handkerchiefs will be worn out.

Please make ready the House for my return a week or so hence.

I remain,
Yr Affectionate Master and Friend,
Sir R. Merivel

I sat at my window a long time, with a candle burning low.

I was trying to decide whether I should write a second letter, this one to Louise, before leaving Paris. Even if de Flamanville had returned to Versailles as he had planned, I reflected that I could not be certain that any letter of mine would not fall into Enemy Hands – those of Mademoiselle Corinne – before it could be given to the admirable woman for whom it was intended.

I decided, at last, to write a simple brief Note, which ran as follows:

Chère Madame,
It grieves me that I was forced to leave your House without saying goodbye.
I return to England shortly.
Please favour me with your Presence in the Jardin du Roi, near the place where the Bear is caged, on Tuesday afternoon at two o'clock.
I remain,
Your Humble Servant,
Merivel

I sealed my letters and took them downstairs, requesting that they be put in the Post Bag forthwith. And when I had done this I felt a kind of *soulagement*, a lessening of anxiety and fret, for the simple reason that I made some Plan.

Now it is Tuesday.

Yesterday I collected my Coats from Monsieur Durand and I am pleased with their altered appearance. The feel of the ribbons fluttering and cascading down my arms is oddly enjoyable, as though they might be wings, ready to lift me off into the white winter sky. They seem to lend me a lightness of tread.

When I go through the gates of the *Jardin du Roi*, telling the Guard that I am a 'close Acquaintance' of Madame de Flamanville, I see Respect upon his features as he looks me up and down. Yet I know this Respect is not for me, but for my clothes, and I marvel afresh at the magic that can be worked by fashion and fashion alone.

The day is mournful, with the last of the Plantain leaves flying off and drifting to rest on the gravel pathways, and dark clouds promising rain. But the thought that in a few moments I may see Louise creates in my heart a little nugget of warmth, and I place my gloved hands there, where I know my heart to be, and the cold in my fingers becomes less.

I approach the Bear. It has ceased to howl and is sitting in a puddle of its own excrement, staring out at the world.

I do not know why the plight of animals moves me so greatly. Perhaps it is that I have never overcome my own Animal Nature and if animals could talk to me, and laugh at my jokes, why then my closest friends would be not only dogs, but also cattle and sheep.

I draw near to the cage. There is a stench from it, both of excrement and of Animal Terror. I can do little but stand and contemplate the creature. It does not move, but its rheumy eyes regard me with a kind of passive tenderness, as though it knew my own helplessness in regard to it. Then, suddenly, it lumbers to its four great feet and comes towards me, and sticks its snout through the bars of the cage.

Drool seeps from its mouth. I long to give it water or food, but have neither.

I go a little nearer and hold out my hand, and the Bear utters a noise, which is not precisely a howl, but only the low sound of yearning.

A voice at my back says: 'The Bear has not gone to Versailles, I see. I fear it is not sleek enough for the King.'

I turn and see Louise, wearing a cloak trimmed with white fur, and I walk away from the Bear and go to her and bow, and lift her hand and place on it an ardent kiss.

'Louise,' I say, 'I am so sorry for the hasty nature of my departure. I wanted to come to you before I left. There were a hundred things I wanted to say to you, but your husband's Manservant stood over me, even while I packed my things, and then conducted me straight to the open door and the carriage . . .'

'I know,' says Louise. 'And I could not come to *you*, for fear of what Jacques-Adolphe would do. And so we were parted.'

We stand and gaze at each other, both of us aware that this Reunion will be brief and is only, in truth, the prelude to a new Departure. My longing to take Louise in my arms is so great that I look about me to ascertain whether we are alone in this part of the *Jardin* and, expecting no one to be near us, I am extremely discomforted to see two Guards approaching at a fast pace, bearing muskets.

'Louise,' I say. 'I do believe I am about to be shot.'

She turns and sees the Soldiers. Her hand flies to her mouth and she positions herself bravely in front of me. 'He would not dare!' she whispers.

The men come on. I expect them at the next instant to stop and raise their weapons, as though part of a Firing Party. But instead they click their heels and offer us a little bow, at which sign the heavy beating of my heart is stilled somewhat. Louise reaches out and clutches my arm.

'Madame, Monsieur,' says one of the Guards, 'you may wish to withdraw a little . . .'

I stare at them and now I realise what it is they are about to do: they are going to kill the Bear.

I ask myself whether I should not be glad at this, the creature's existence being such a wretched thing. But something in me is repelled by it. My knowledge of animal anatomy is sufficient to tell me that this Bear, for all its pitiful state, is still young. And the notion that its Whole Life will have consisted in being caged and starved and tormented with thirst offends me deeply.

'I was told,' I say firmly, 'that the Bear was to be transported to Versailles.'

'Yes,' replies one of the Soldiers, 'but His Majesty has changed his mind. He has wearied of large animals.'

'So you are going to shoot the Bear?'

'Yes, Monsieur. If you and Madame would care to walk away . . .'

'No!' I say suddenly. 'Please do not kill it!'

'I'm sorry, Monsieur. Those are our orders.'

In an instant I have done the most surprising thing. I have whipped off my glove and held out my hand, on which I am wearing the Sapphire ring given to me by King Charles – the very one I almost lost to the Highwayman on the Dover Road.

'See this Jewel?' I say to the Guards. 'It was given to me by the King of England. It is worth ten *pistoles* – or more. And it will be yours if you put down your muskets and do as I instruct.'

Louise looks at me in amazement, as well she might. All I can whisper to her is: 'It offends me, Louise. I cannot bear the *offence!*'

The Soldiers confer with each other. They believe, I am sure, that I am quite mad, yet are perhaps saying to themselves that very few madmen can afford the kind of shoulder ribbons with which my Coat is adorned, so fashion comes, yet again, into the Equation.

'Listen to me,' say I. 'I leave for England tomorrow or the next day. I will pay you to commission a cart to take the Bear, in its cage, to Dieppe and see it safely delivered to the Port there. From Dieppe I will ship it to England. King Louis need know nothing of this. But you, you will live well for some time on the value of this ring, which any good Parisian jeweller will be ecstatic to buy from you.'

The Soldiers gape at me. I take off the dazzling Sapphire and hold it before their eyes. They glance at it for a moment, then shake their heads. 'How do we know,' says one, 'that it is a real Jewel and not a Counterfeit?'

'Well, surely, you have only to *look*! This ring came from the Royal Coffers at Whitehall: His Majesty's atonement for beating me at Tennis so very frequently.'

'Tennis? *Tennis?* What is this all about, Monsieur?' What in the world will you do with a Bear?'

'I will care for it!' I burst out. 'I have a very beautiful park surrounding my house in England. I will make a compound where it can live out its days in tranquillity. I will study its nature and learn something from it. It will give me far more knowledge and understanding than a Sapphire ring could ever yield.'

Louise's hands flutter about my arm, as if to restrain me from my wild idea, but I am angry now and not to be restrained. Sensing that I am serious, the Guards withdraw a little to confer. Then they turn to me and announce: 'We will do it for the ten *pistoles*. You must sell the ring and get the money. Then we will do it.'

I sigh. I did not want to spend the rest of my time in Paris haggling with Jewellers, but I see that there is probably no choice. I reason, also, on the instant that if I am lucky enough to get more than ten *pistoles* for the jewel, then all my pecuniary anxiety will fade away.

I take out a small purse from my pocket and give it to the Guards. 'Very well,' I say. 'I will sell the Jewel. You must buy meat. Let the Animal eat and drink this afternoon. Let the cage be cleaned. On Thursday, by midday, I will expect to find everything shipshape on the Quayside at Dieppe, at which place and time the *pistoles* will be given to you.'

The Guards examine the Purse. They confer once more in whispers with each other and I fancy I can hear them plotting to purchase meat for themselves and to give nothing to the Bear.

'If this animal is not fed,' I say, 'It will attempt to eat *you*. Do you wish to risk that?'

'Yes, it certainly will,' affirms Louise bravely. 'You can note from its saliva how famished it is. Its inclination will be to bite off your hands.'

Upon this cue the Bear opens it jaws and lets forth a mighty Roar. The Guards retreat further from it and regard it anxiously. They grip their muskets more tightly.

'Well?' I say. 'What is to be? Ten *pistoles* or nothing at all?'

They confer yet again. Both are looking somewhat pale.

'We will do it,' they say, almost in unison.

'Good,' I say. 'You have made the right decision.'

I go to them, hold out my hand and they shake it each in turn. They are still convinced that this beribboned Englishman has taken leave of his senses, which, looked at in one way, is true, but it would not be for the first time, nor for the last.

On the eastern side of the *Jardin du Roi* there is an Evergreen Maze, whose bosky paths rise to a wooded pinnacle, from which the view over the city is most serene and fine.

Louise and I climb up, hand in hand, to this most excellent place, and when we have admired Paris enough, turn to each other and embrace. That I may never hold this woman in my arms again chokes my heart so much that tears come to my eyes and spill down my cheeks.

Louise licks them tenderly away. We kiss again and I sense in her no diminution of the passion we felt in her bed. So we go deeper into the little wood, where we are hidden from the path, and I take off my new Coat and lay it down on the forest floor, and there, in the cold winter's afternoon, we are lovers once more.

Lying together afterwards, very still and with no inclination to move, despite the chill in the air and the diminution of the day's light, Louise says to me: 'I have decided, Merivel. In the summer I am going to Switzerland. I shall stay for a long time. Perhaps you could come to me there? I know my Father would be glad to see you. He has never approved of my Marriage and he knows how unhappy I am. I will make sure that he welcomes you into his house.'

I stroke Louise's hair. Into my mind comes a wonderful imagining of mountains and wild flowers and skies of cobalt, and some lofty castle sitting among firs and pines. I tell Louise to send word to me as soon as she is there, and I will once again entrust myself to the roads and the sea.

Part Two
The Great Captivity

I saw the Bear, in its cage, safely stowed on the deck of the boat by French sailors, who asked me what manner of animal this was.

'It is a Bear,' I said. 'It has come from the Forests of Germany.'

'Bear meat is a delicacy in England, is it, Monsieur?'

'No. I'm not going to eat it.'

'What are you going to do with it?'

I did not really know what to answer to this. I had been so intent upon saving the animal that my mind had not proceeded very far towards any Destiny for the creature. I saw only a safe and commodious compound, like a Stockade, in the park at Bidnold, and here the Bear would be fed and cared for, and Margaret and I would come there and visit it, as a wondrous new pastime, and when I had guests at Bidnold (including the King) they would also be amused to spend time in contemplation of a creature they had never before beheld.

However, what I heard myself say in reply to the French sailors was: 'I have got the idea of starting a Menagerie, like that to be seen at Versailles. I am hoping, in due time, to hold captive a Giraffe.'

As the boat drew away into the Channel, on a morning of freezing and impenetrable mist, with only the cry of gulls to remind us that our Vessel was not the last and only thing on the surface of the World, I did not go below to my cabin, but positioned myself upon some wicker Chicken Crates and sat very still, regarding my captive.

This stillness was now and again disturbed by the Chickens rudely attempting to peck at my bottom through the gaps in the wicker-weave, but I found some sacking and put this over the Crate, and after that the Chickens showed me a little more courtesy, fancying, perhaps, that night had suddenly descended.

In better spirits than when Louise and I had seen it in the *Jardin du Roi*, the Bear occupied itself for some time with a piece of meat, then turned in a circle and shat copiously, drank water from a tin bucket and after that settled down to regard me, with a settled Quiet, in much the same way as I was regarding it.

Some words of my beloved Montaigne, written, I think, about a dog or a cat, came to my mind. 'Of Animals,' he said, 'silence itself can beg requests', and I asked myself what request the Bear might be begging of me, or I of it.

For I could clearly perceive that both of us were in Transition from one time to another and that very many Confusions tormented us. The Bear had no understanding of the element – the sea – on which it found itself, nor any concept of Future Time. As for me, it was not difficult to imagine myself as the animal in the cage, constrained as to what success I could ever achieve, after the lament-able failure of my effort at Versailles, and constrained as to whom I could love, without finding myself thrust through with a sword.

To the Bear I said: 'The boat beneath us moves over the water towards England, my poor friend, but the mist holds us in a ghostly Shroud of Unknowing.'

Cold began to cramp my limbs, but I stayed sitting on the Chicken Crate and comforted myself with my remembrance of Louise, of her sweet warmth and her lively conversation, and her ample breasts, and I asked myself whether, after fifty-seven years of my life, I had not at last found Love.

'What d'you think?' I asked the Bear. 'Am I deluded?'

And the animal, for answer, lay down softly and closed its eyes.

I stayed a night at Dover, at a poor Inn, where no fires burned.

From here I made preparations for a cart to convey the Bear to Norfolk, and had to pay dearly for it, for it was difficult to find any man of Dover willing to make this journey. I do think that all Dover men are salted by their nearness to the sea and do not like to travel far from the ocean. Had I asked them to conduct a Whale in a great water barrel to Bidnold, perhaps they would have done it, out of a Natural Affinity with this monster of the deep, but the warm-blooded Bear and the distance they would have to travel in its company affrighted them to the tune of seventeen shillings.

Luckily, I was well provided with money, having got twelve *pistoles* for the Sapphire ring, from a Jeweller acquaintance of Monsieur Durand's, of which only ten had been promised to the Guards of the *Jardin du Roi*, and in the time to come I would be grateful for the extra two hundred *livres* the transaction had gained me.

Only at moments did I chide myself for having sold something so precious and which I could never, ever come by again.

The moment my hired carriage turned, at last, into the drive at Bidnold, where the park was dusted with snow, I had the sudden feeling that something attended me at my house that I would not like. I cannot say why I felt this, except that, arriving there as the dusk was falling, everything appeared to me very shadowy and dead-seeming, with no Deer in sight, nor any bird or animal at all, and my habitual gladness to find myself once more at my beloved Bidnold was strangely absent from my heart.

As we drove up to the door, Will Gates came out – as he was

ever wont to do – to greet me. But on his face I could read at once a very Great Anguish, and when I stepped out of the carriage he reached out to me and took both my hands in his and looked up at me with eyes glittering with tears.

'Will,' I said, 'tell me the Matter at once.'

'Oh, Sir Robert,' said Will, 'I can barely say the words. 'Tis Miss Margaret, Sir. Taken very ill. And nobody knows what to do for the best.'

No news could have been more terrible to me than this – save news of Margaret's death. Stiff from my journey, I felt myself falter and almost sink down where I stood outside my front door. Will, all bent over as he is, was able to take hold of me and helped me inside, where my frame collapsed itself onto a wooden settle in the Hall.

'Where *is* Margaret?' I managed to say. 'Is she not far away in Cornwall?'

'No, Sir. Sir James and his family could not leave for Cornwall. Miss Margaret was taken ill on the eve of their departure. She could not travel. They are nursing her at Shottesbrooke, and hoping and praying . . .'

'What is the illness, Will?'

'All I know is she has been a-bed for more than thirty days. And there is no sign that she rallies. I sent Tabitha over to help with her care. We would have gladly nursed her ourselves here at Bidnold, Sir Robert, but Lady Prideaux thought it best that she be not moved. So I did not know what more to do . . .'

I sat huddled on the settle and Will stood over me, and I could hear his congested breathing and see his gnarled old hands wringing themselves in Desolation. And then I became aware that Cattlebury and some of the other servants has come into the Hall and were standing silently round me.

'We are mighty sorry, Sir Robert,' I heard Cattlebury say. 'I am making broths with choicest Marrowbone and taking them myself to Shottesbrooke. And Lady Prideaux, she says to me: "Your broths, Cattlebury, they are keeping her alive, for she will take no other thing . . ."'

'Thank you, my kind man,' I said. 'That is most considerate.'

I looked round me at my Household and saw the silent cluster of faces, all watching me with great tenderness of feeling, and this loyalty, for which I felt most heartily grateful, made me try to rally myself. I stood up, unaided by Will, and announced: 'I will go to Shottesbrooke without delay. Bring me a cup of Alicante, Will. Simmer it a little with cloves and cinnamon, to warm me. I will take it in the Library. Then I will set forth.'

'You had best take some food, too, Sir Robert.'

'I have no appetite.'

'I will bring you some broth,' said Cattlebury. 'It will revive you.'

I thanked Cattlebury and the other Servants for their kindness, and walked with slow steps to the Library, where, to my great comfort, a fire was burning.

Will helped to settle me in a chair. As he removed my cloak and caught sight of the new ribbons sewn into my coat seams, he could not refrain from asking: 'What are these strange Adornments, Sir? I have never met the like of these.'

'Nor I, Will,' I said, 'until I came to Versailles. 'And costly they were, yet they brought me one piece of good fortune. But none of that signifies now. Is my daughter going to die?'

Will made a great Performance of folding my travelling cloak over his arm, smoothing it down and down, until it could be smoothed no more. 'I cannot say, Sir Robert,' he said.

It was dark night when I arrived at Shottesbrooke Hall.

Sir James and his wife came down and greeted me, in their night attire, and gave orders that a bed be made ready for me. Then Arabella Prideaux clung to my neck and wept.

'It is our Fault, Merivel!' she cried. 'We got from Lowestoft some boiled Shrimps, to give Margaret a taste of what she might eat in Cornwall. And she did not like them, but Mary and Penelope urged her to try more . . . And in the night she was very ill, vomiting everything she had eaten, and then came on a high fever and a great Headache and a pain in her stomach . . .'

'Her stomach we have managed to soothe a little, with Asses' milk and the excellent broth your Cook insists upon bringing to us,' said Prideaux. 'But the fever will not abate, nor the great Agony in her head. She has been purged and bled. We have tried Cantharides and all else that Dr Murdoch can think to do, to try to get the fever to subside. Sometimes it breaks for a little and the Pain lessens. But then it always returns. And she is getting very weak.'

I felt a chill sweat break on my skin.

'Are you telling me,' I said, 'that nobody has put a name to the thing she from which she suffers?'

'Dr Murdoch does not know,' said Arabella.

'Dr Murdoch is a Quack,' said I, 'and always was. Who else have you summoned?'

'Another physician from Attleborough, Dr Sims. But he could not diagnose any cause, either,' said Prideaux, 'beyond a poison got from the Shrimps.'

We stayed silent for a moment. Then I asked: 'Is there, on Margaret's face or body, any sign of redness or rash?'

'There is a rash,' said Arabella, 'in the area of her neck and breasts. We have tried washing her with Nettle Soap, to draw out the sting of the rash, but it is stubborn . . .'

Now the sweat on me was like ice and I felt it course down my body. I stared at Prideaux and his wife, all helpless in their nightshirts and with their hair in embarrassing disarray, and holding in their hands each a trembling candle. And though I knew that they were good and honest people, I wanted to howl and scream at their ignorance and at the ignorance of the doctors.

'She has Typhus,' I said.

She lies in a high, spacious room, in soft, clean linen. A fire burns in the grate.

Outside, in the freezing night, Owls cry. And the sound they make, which is one of great Desolation, echoes the sound I hear inside myself, as I sit by her bedside.

I have instructed the household that no visitors must come near Margaret any more, for that Typhus is a deadly Contagion, and I would not see sweet Mary and her sisters follow my daughter to this Place where she is.

To Tabitha, who will not let herself be moved from her Mistress's side, I have given instructions that she must tie rags about her own face – as I myself shall do, just as I did when I visited victims of the Plague in the year 1666 – when we are near her. 'And when we wash her,' I instruct, 'we must afterwards wash ourselves and be always washing, so that we do not get any Contagion from her skin or from her mouth.'

Margaret sleeps in uneasy rest. I see the rash creeping up to her chin and onto her cheek. I long to stroke her cheek, but I do not. Her hair is damp and tangled on the pillow, and this, too, I want to caress and smooth with my hand, but I do not.

I talk softly to her. I tell her that I will fit out a carriage with furs and cushions, and take her home to Bidnold on the morrow.

'This Bidnold of ours,' I say, 'was once described to me by the King as "the place where we shall come to dream". He understood that it is a house of great Consolation. If you cannot get well at Bidnold, even though it be cold winter, you cannot get well anywhere on the Earth. And I swear to you, in the King's name and in the name of my long-lost friend John Pearce, whom I could not save from Death, that I will do everything in my power, as a father and as a Physician, to make you well.'

She stirs awake and sees me by her, and I know from her eyes that she has recognised me, and I take a little comfort from this, for that I know, in its Last Stages, Typhus muddies the brain, and it is by this that you may know that the sufferer is near death.

I tell her once again that I am going to take her home. 'And when you are well,' I say, 'we shall go out into the snow and there, in the Park, will you find a great lumbering beast, a Bear, which I have rescued and brought back from France. And in time we shall get to know its ways, and perhaps it will dance for us.'

'I did not know this,' she says. 'That bears could dance.'

'Oh,' I say, 'that is just another of my follies. I was afraid you would not recognise me unless I said something foolish.'

'I recognise you, Papa,' says Margaret, 'except your clothes are a little different.'

'Ah,' I say. 'Another folly: Shoulder-Ribbons! Even Will, with his poor eyesight, remarked upon them.'

'They are very becoming . . .'

She smiles, and to see this smile of hers gladdens my heart so much that I want to raise her up and hold her against my breast, but I do not.

I ask her about the Pain in her head, and she tells me that this is the worst thing and the most difficult to endure, and I tell her that I will get Opium for her from my Apothecary in Norwich, and when she has taken this the Pain will be less.

She closes her eyes and I imagine that she is drifting back to sleep, but she says quietly: 'Tell me about the King of France.'

I hear myself sigh. I realise at this moment, and not at any moment before, how weary I am and how great is my longing for sleep, but I force myself to begin on some small anecdotes from Versailles, to entertain and soothe her.

'The King of France,' I say, 'calls himself Louis *Dieu-donné,* Louis Anointed-by-God. He is a man of Glory, who also likes to compare himself to the Sun – *Le Roi Soleil.*'

'Does he resemble the sun?'

'Yes, very much, for that he dresses himself in gold and the colour of his wig is a burnished copper, like your own beautiful hair, and the great Heat he creates in a room is a very Palpable Heat, and I have felt it myself and seen others almost swoon at it.'

'Swoon and fall down?'

'Yes. Faint clean away! For he is barely mortal, you see. He was born, I am told, with two teeth already in his head, translucent as Pearls, and this was taken as a sign that he was indeed God's chosen child and would survive his infancy and reign for ever and ever . . .'

'Nothing is for ever and ever, Papa,' says Margaret.

'Are you sure?' I say. 'What about my love and affection for you? I cannot see why these should have an end.'

12

No winter in my life was ever as cold as this one, the winter of 1683–4.

In my park the Great Frost spread its burning rash over every leaf and every twig and stone and every blade of grass. Birds, roosting in the trees, dropped to the ground and died. Red Squirrels clawed and bit at the earth, where their stores had been hidden, but the earth was turned to Granite. The Squirrels grew ragged and thin, and disappeared.

I ordered that the deer be rounded up and brought to the shelter of the Cow Barns, but even there the water in their trough still froze in the night. The animals clustered all together for warmth and their sweet faces, regarding me in a silent, reproachful bunch, reminded me of Pansy-flowers.

'It will end,' I said to them. 'It is a finite Season.'

But it did not show any sign of ending. The Woodsmen, who had been charged with making the Stockade for the Bear, came to tell me that they could not, even with the sharpest iron picks, make any hole in the ground for the setting of the posts. The Bear, therefore, could not be given its liberty, but was forced to remain in the cage, and the children of the Woodsmen, ragged in their woollen clothes all tied together with string, came and trespassed on my land, and threw sticks and icicles at the creature to vex and torment it.

'They must not do it!' I scolded the Woodsmen. 'You must constrain them, or I shall throw you all off my Estate.'

But where should I throw them? To the Workhouse? And I depended upon these people for my supply of chopped wood, for Cattlebury's stoves, for the fires that warmed my rooms, for the blaze that was kept burning, day and night, in Margaret's Sickroom.

And when I considered how these Woodsmen and their families lived, in poor hovels, built of mud and lathes and thatched with Reeds, and how I lived, with all my French furniture and stone Fireplaces and Hangings of tapestry and brocade, I suffered a worm of sorrow for their lot, and was mightily glad that Pearce was not at Bidnold to reproach me with all the Unfairnesses of the World and to blame me for them.

Yet, still, the taunting of the Bear angered me. 'Throw sticks at me, if you must,' I wanted to say to the rude lads and ragged little wenches, 'but spare this animal, for it has done you no harm.'

Christmas was upon us, but I commanded that there be no feast.

Snow fell silently and made walls and mounds all around us where none had ever been, and I began to be afraid that we would want for food, for that no Butchers' nor Fishmongers' carts could pass in the great press of snow on the drive, and many of our Chickens were dying, and all our winter vegetables were smothered three feet deep in the ground.

I sent for Cattlebury and asked him how we stood as to Supplies, and he assured me that he, 'sensing in my bones a cold Season', had been laying down Potatoes, Onions, Neaps and Carrots, as well as sacks of flour, in the dark of the cellar and that we would all live off these 'and not suffer for it'.

'And when these are gone?' said I.

'We will kill the Deer,' he said. 'Venison is a lovely meat, Sir Robert.'

I sent him away. I climbed the stairs to Margaret's room, where

Tabitha, draped in Muslin round her face, kept quiet watch. For all that a fire burned there, and every window was tightly closed, it felt chill. And when I approached the bed I noticed, for the first time, a foul Cancre blistering the skin of Margaret's lip.

Every incremental torment brought to her by the Typhus – from the looseness of her stool to the Convulsions of her stomach and the great Agony in her brain, relieved only by Opium – caused me such helpless anxiety that I had almost lost the art of sleeping at all. And when Tabitha and I undertook to wash Margaret, which we did very often, for that she soiled herself and could not help it, I now began to see that her body was wasting away.

And I was taken again in my mind to that time when John Pearce began to die, and I remembered how his coming death had been visible to me in the scanty flesh that clothed his bones, and how I had known – for all my long studies in Medicine – that I could do nothing to save him.

As I stared at the horrible Cancre on Margaret's lip, I began to have the feeling that her life was lost. I knelt by her side. I clung to her sheet, twisting it in my hands. And my prayer was to Pearce: 'Help me! For the sake of our past Friendship, help me to save her!'

His only answer was that sudden quiet – in which all the World seems to withhold its breath for a long minute – that I have termed 'The Silence of Pearce'. Though, many times in my life, I have got consolation from this strange taking away of sound and movement, its manifest uselessness to me now put me into a sudden anger. I wanted to scream and cry, and break my hand hitting out at the wall.

I ran downstairs, snatched up my warmest Cloak and went out into the snow, hoping that a walk in the icy park would calm me. The Servants had cleared a passage through the great drifts from the house to the Barns and I followed the narrow path they had made, and for a companion I suddenly had a Hen, who appeared from I know not where and, with delicate steps, hastened along beside me.

The Hen and I, with bright and hectic eyes, looked out at the frozen land.

The Beech Trees, which had borne the tracery of the Frost with sumptuous grace, now looked lumpen and shapeless, with the great weight of snow upon them. And I was afraid that their limbs would break under the burden of it, and the thought that my trees would be brought low made my fury increase.

I walked on. My breath billowed before me in a blueish Vapour and I felt the sharp stab of the frozen air in my lung. The green parkland around me had folded itself into sweeping white Dunes, shaped by the wind. To the Hen, who had to make little flapping runs to keep up with me but seemed determined to do so, as though she lacked companionship, I remarked: 'These snow Dunes are like the sands of a Desert.'

That same night, lying on a rug on the floor in Margaret's room and sleeping a little, I had a dream of Pearce.

He walked towards me along a riverbank, and the river was silvered with the sun and all the weeds that grew along the bank were lush and vigorous and bright.

'Pearce,' said I in my dream, 'here you are at last. Tell me what I can do to save my daughter. I *beg* you to tell me.'

Pearce sat down among the weeds, which seemed to hold him securely in a green Chair. He would not deign to look up at me, but after a moment or two had passed, while the water flowed sweetly on, he said: 'Go where you always go. Go where you cannot prevent yourself from going.'

I was silent. It was always one of Pearce's most perturbing tricks to talk to me in Riddles, and very often these Riddles would not come to any solution at all, and I would be left only with a sense of my own obtuseness.

'Where is that?' said my dreaming self. 'You must tell me where, Pearce.'

But, to my dismay, he rose from his soft chaise of greenery and made as though to walk away from me.

'Don't go!' I pleaded. 'Tell me what I must do!'

He stopped and stood still, and I saw that he carried in his hands the blue-and-white soup ladle, and I cried out: 'I am glad that you have got the ladle, Pearce! I am very glad for your sake that it is not lost.'

Ignoring this, yet cradling the implement to his thin body, he said: 'Imagine you are a Slave at the time of Julius Caesar. That Slave suffers from that same deep forgetfulness of his own Absence of Freedom that afflicts you, does he not?'

'Well—'

'Imagine, then, if you were that same Slave and a terrible affliction or sadness came upon you; where would you go to ask for help?'

I hesitated a moment, then I said: 'I suppose that I would go to Caesar.'

'Of course you would. For in your heart you *love* your servitude to him; that is why you are still a Slave. So there is your answer. You must go to Caesar.'

Your Majesty, I wrote,
Your Servant Merivel sends you his Affectionate Greeting from the Snow Deserts of Norfolk, where we are walled up in a Great Whiteness, the like of which I have never before seen.

I do not know how this Letter will reach you, for that no Letter-Bearer, nor cart can make its way to Bidnold. But I write, in part, to try to assuage my Mind, which is in Mortal Anguish.

Sir, Margaret is dying of Typhus.

I am trying every remedy that I know of, but I do see that, as the days pass, these remedies are failing. If any Physician at Whitehall, with better knowledge of this foul Disease than I, has some counsel I might follow, I humbly beg of you that you write it for me. For I do think that to lose Margaret would bring me swiftly to my own death, and then I would no longer be able to entertain Your Majesty with my follies and Jokes.

The Great Captivity

*I pray you are well, Sire, and not suffering in the great Age
of Ice that has come upon our land.*
From your Faithful Subject, and Loyal Fool,
Sir R. Merivel

Each day I prayed that the snow would melt, so that my letter
could be conveyed to London, but no Thaw came. I began to
believe that Margaret's life hung upon this letter and that if I
could keep her alive until the roads were passable once more,
then she would not die, for some counsel would come from
Whitehall to save her.

My medical books told me that there was no certain Remedy
for Typhus. All I could discover was that the disease was wont to
have a duration of eight or ten or twelve weeks, at which time the
Patient would very likely display some sign of recovery, such as
a marked lessening of the Fever and a Calmness in the Bowel.
But if these signs did not come, why then, what would occur
would be a growing Confusion of the Mind, followed by Uncon-
sciousness and Death.

Both I and Margaret were thus in the hands of Fate, or (as my
Parents, no less than John Pearce and the King himself would
have insisted) in the hands of God. All that I, a mortal Doctor,
was able to do was to relieve her symptoms a little. With Cattlebury's broths I fed her Opium. I bled her from time to time, to try
to calm the choler in her veins. I washed the sweat from her
brow and from her body. On the Cancre I laid a smear of Louise's
Beeswax and Plantain salve and in a few days, to my great delight,
the Cancre was reduced.

This small success with the Cancre cheered me for a while and
I blessed Louise for its invention.

I spent much time talking. I reasoned that if I could keep Margaret's mind alert, then I would stave off its gradual sinking into
Unknowing. I told her the stories of her Childhood, beginning
with that of her Birth, in the year of the Great Fire, and how it

was I who, to save her life and her mother's too, had cut her from Katharine's womb.

She had heard this tale many times before: how that I had been convinced I would be able to save them both and failed. The first time I told her, she wept for her Mother and asked: 'Why could you not save her, too, Papa?'

And I explained that no matter what I had tried, and what the Midwife had tried, we could not staunch the bleeding in Katharine's womb, so her life drained away. But I reassured Margaret that her mother did not suffer, but only drifted into a beautiful sleep. And so died very calmly.

All of this was true, but Margaret had also grown up with one terrible lie concerning Katharine. She believed her to have been one of the Quaker Sisters helping Pearce and his Friends to care for the Mad People at the Whittlesea Bedlam. But it was not so. Though she was a beautiful and seductive woman, Katharine had been one of the Hospital's most tortured inmates. Pearce had warned me, again and again, to keep my distance from her. But I had not kept it. Lust, once more, had led me to a fatal place where I should never have trespassed.

I had further told Margaret that her mother and I had married at the church of St Alphage, where Katharine is buried, but no such ceremony ever took place, for the simple reason that I, being still estranged from the King, was unable to procure any agreement to the Annulment of my marriage to Celia. And I was not prepared to commit Bigamy with Katharine.

Now, fearing that Margaret would die, I asked myself whether I did not owe her some Correction of the untruths surrounding her Mother's short and fretful life.

I knew that I shrank from it. I told myself that it was not just to inflict such cruel revelations upon an invalid. But when I stared into the flames of the fire that was kept always burning in her room, I also imagined how, upon hearing of her Mother's insanity and the lamentable advantage I took of this poor, helpless woman, Margaret would suddenly turn from me, her only living Parent, and wish I might be devoured in Hell.

The thought that, living or dying, my daughter would withdraw from me all her love was more than my exhausted mind could bear. So I stayed silent.

Walking, one frozen morning, about the house, to try to judge how the very building itself was withstanding the wrath of the snow and the winds, I went into the room I had always designated the Olive Room. It was no longer decorated in Olive greens (with scarlet tassels above the bed), but in a plaintive watery blue, which was much to the King's liking but a little too insipid for my taste.

A great French Armoire, made of veneered Walnut, had always stood in this room and now I opened its doors, to draw into my lungs the scent of this cupboard, which was the Scent of the Past.

I stood there, breathing hard through my nose. I reminded myself of an animal sniffing the air, to see what sustenance or carnal delight it might find riding on the wind; or a Connoisseur of Wine, snorting into his goblet, pretending to smell Blackberries and Wood of Elm and I know not what else in a beaker of Claret.

What I could smell was my youth. A memory of its Delectation filled my veins and warmed me. In this very room had I lain with Violet Bathurst, and torn at her clothes and been made weak by her shameless demands. In this same place had Will and I nursed Pearce for thirty-seven hours. On this spot had I held baby Margaret in my arms, to show her each room of the house that had been restored to me in 1668 and would one day be hers.

My young self, I recalled, was always in a lather of Heat. So explosive with Plans and Mad Wonders had it been, that I could recall no wintertime – except one – when it had felt cold. And I was just beginning to marvel at this when I noticed a large bundle, wrapped in Linen, at the bottom of the Armoire. And I remembered what it contained.

I lifted it up and set it down, and spread out the Linen wrapping, and there before me lay a great heap of Badger Furs. They had been fashioned into Tabards by my Tailor, old Trench, in the Winter of 1665, which, I now remembered, had been of long and icy duration, and in the course of which I, no less than the next man, had begun to shiver.

I had insisted that all my household servants follow my own example by wearing these Badger skins, 'to prevent chills and Agues'. I had warned them that we would, every one of us, appear a trifle foolish, draped in these singular Garments (with the snout of a dead Badger rearing up on each shoulder), but that upon them might depend our survival of the cold. 'Of what account is mere foolishness,' I asked them, 'compared to Death?'

All had agreed to wear the furs. All except Will.

Will had turned aside from me and would not, under any threat of Punishment whatsoever, put on his Tabard. I had endeavoured to coax and cajole him. I had warned him he might suffer from all manner of ailments if he did not keep his body warm in this way, but he utterly disregarded me.

'I shall not, Sir Robert,' he informed me, 'and that is that.'

Now the Tabards were a little mangy with Moth holes, and spiced with the Dust of Time, and the snouts no longer reared up, but hung down somewhat mournfully, and many of the glass eyes, sewn in by Trench, had fallen out. However, when I shook out the garments I could feel that there was still much warmth in them. And so it came to me that I would brush them down and wash and dry them, as carefully as I tended my wig, and lay some of them upon Margaret's bed. Reserving one for myself, I would distribute the others among the servants. 'Pay no attention to the Moth holes,' I would say, 'but only consider the heat they will bring to the area of your hearts.'

I stand in my Library, distributing the cleaned Tabards.

When Will comes in I expect him to refuse to put his Tabard on, but he does not. He heaves the garment over his head and laces it round his bent old form.

'Very good, Will,' I say. 'I am excellently pleased you have consented.'

He moves slowly across the room, making for the door. The Tabard sways below his knees as he walks and he reminds me of a poor Bison I once saw in an engraving, with its head hanging low and all its fur in tatters.

I do not know whether I am about to laugh or weep at this. I feel something welling up in me, some Great Emotion, but it seems to lodge in my breast and not come out.

As Will reaches the door, he turns and says to me: 'I am doing this for Miss Margaret's sake, Sir Robert, so that I may play my part in her recovery, and that is the only reason.'

13

In the first week of February we were entered upon the ninth week of Margaret's illness. There was no change, for better or worse, in her condition. Typhus, it seems, is a thoughtless visitor who assumes a Right of Habitation in the body and sleeps there, and forbears to leave.

Looking at my Almanac one morning, and calculating the weary succession of days, I began to believe that we would be walled up for all time in our helpless Arctic prison and slowly die there. And this thought put me in mind of that other bereft prisoner, the Bear, whom I had woefully neglected.

I walked out to the place where the cage stood and I saw that the snow was so deep in it that there was hardly any place remaining for the animal's body. Though it kept trying to move, the packed, frozen snow constrained it, whatever it attempted. The weather, in short, was constructing a Coffin round it.

I called to me one of the Grooms and together we began shovelling out snow, mixed with animal faeces, from the between the bars of the cage, which was awkward, arduous work, but after an hour, labouring up a Great Sweat, we had released the Bear from its hapless position and it was able to turn, very slowly, in a circle.

I could see from the way the animal moved that its limbs were stiff and sore from its confinement, and I told the Groom to fetch me some strong chains from the stables.

'Chains to what purpose, Sir Robert?' he asked.

'Only fetch them,' I said, 'then I will show you.'

He came back, hung about and rattling with the chains, like some Ghostly Spirit come out of the grave, which made me smile, for that he was a very fat man to whom Death no doubt appeared a most unfair and inimical Thing, and I took them off him and found one that I could pass through a ring in its end.

'Now,' I said, 'I am going to reach into the cage and loop this chain round the Bear's neck, like a leash round the head of a dog.'

'To do what, Sir?'

'When I have the chain secure, you will open the gate of the cage . . .'

'Not I, Sir Robert!'

'Yes, you, my good man. I cannot do this all alone. But have no fear. I will have the animal on its leash. You have only to stand safely behind the open gate and I will lead the Bear out.'

'Heaven deliver us! What if he pull the chain from your hand?'

'He will not do that. He is weak. You have seen how confined the poor creature has been.'

'He could still eat you alive.'

'Why then you will have no need to bury me in the ground.'

'I was not joking, Sir.'

'Nor I. For digging a grave in this frozen earth would be a pitiless labour.'

The Groom stared at me, as though lamenting that he was employed by a madman, then he looked up at the sky, which, as we laboured in the snow, had darkened over Bidnold, promising us yet another Blizzard.

While he watched me, I pulled my thick leather gloves up almost to my elbows and, holding the Chain, slowly reached into the cage and encircled the Bear's neck. Feeling my hand upon it, the animal threw back its head and almost dislodged the Chain, but I managed to hold tight to it, and with my other hand reached for the Ring and tugged hard on this, till I had his head in a necklace.

The Bear let out a little noise of protest, but it did not resemble the howling I had heard it make in the *Jardin du Roi*, so I was emboldened to talk to it.

I said: 'My poor friend, we are going to go for a walk. We shall go slowly, so that you can find the feeling in your haunches and in your feet. We shall not go very far.'

'Lord, love us!' said the Groom. 'You are taking a wild beast for a *walk*?'

'Yes. If it will come with me. Animals who do not move die soon enough.'

'And what if it escape your Chain? What if it savage my horses, or the cows?'

'It will not. It has been fed every day – or so I commanded. Animals such as this will only attack when they are hungry.'

'How d'you know that, Sir Robert?'

'Only by ordinary Logic. Would you slit the throat of a lamb to eat it if you were not famished?'

'Yes, indeed I would, Sir. I would save it up for later.'

Seeing my 'logic' so easily annihilated by this fat Groom, I found it best to discuss the matter no further. The sky was darkening all the while and I did not relish the idea of walking very long in a Blizzard with the Bear. It was attempting to shake off the collar, but the Chain was strong and my grip was firm, and I now commanded the gate of the cage to be opened.

The gate was secured by two iron bolts, but these the frost had welded almost to their housings, and I was afraid the Groom would run away before he had persuaded them to move. While he struggled with the bolts, the Bear regarded him hungrily.

To move its thoughts from biting off the Groom's hand, I stroked one of its ears, and it turned its face to me with a look of poignant Reproach.

'I know,' I said, 'I promised a fine Stockade. I promised branches to climb and a place to walk or run. But we cannot build them yet. Everything at Bidnold is captive to the winter.'

When, at last, the bolts yielded and the Groom tugged open the gate, the Bear looked out at the white landscape before it, but did not move. The Groom clung to the open gate, shielding himself in terror. I held fast to the Chain and in my left hand carried a stalwart stick, which I knew would avail me almost nothing should the Bear decide to attack me, yet it armed me in some inadequate way and helped my Resolution not to falter.

Then I walked forward, endeavouring to pull the Bear after me, and slowly, with a limping gait, it followed. I shouted back instructions to the Groom to clean and swab the cage, and to put down clean straw and fresh water.

I led my poor Captive down a cleared pathway into the park. Some Crows clustering on the topmost branches of a frozen oak tree at once set up an irritable clamour, but the Bear paid them no heed and we ambled on.

I kept looking behind me at the creature, chiefly to make sure it was not about to claw me to death. I remembered the autumn day with Louise in the *Jardin du Roi* and how the Soldiers had come to shoot the Bear. And then I remembered the price I had paid for its life, which was exceedingly great, for that the King's Sapphire had been very precious to me – and I thought how difficult it may often be to measure the Value of one thing against another, and how men can frequently come to ruin by the complexity of this Arithmetic.

But I did not dwell upon this. After my labours with the shovelling of snow I felt warm and, though the sky was dark, it seemed suddenly to me that the Degree of cold in the air had lessened. And this lessening of the cold cheered me, so that my heart felt more light than it had done in a long while.

We walked a good distance across the park, to where the cleared path ended and mounds of snow reared up at us, blocking our way. When I stopped, the Bear sat down and looked at me. Its look was so sorrowful and tender that any lingering fear I had of it vanished.

I leaned against the wall of snow and reached out and stroked the Bear's head. And the thought came to me that perhaps the animal, brought wild out of the forests of Germany, had been already *tamed by Man* before it had been taken to Paris.

And then my next, ignoble, idea was how I – to make a great show of my courage and skill – might pretend to my future guests at Bidnold that Merivel alone (who had long ago got himself a great preferment by the saving of the life of one of the King's Spaniels) had made it docile and obedient, for that he had a singular and unique understanding of animals and the workings of their souls, and was able to speak directly to them.

This made me smile. And in the next moment something extraordinary happened: a great rushing wind swept suddenly across the place where I rested with the Bear and it began to rain.

All night I listened to the sound of a great river, as the snow and ice became water once more, pouring itself into every ditch and dell, and flowing away down the drive in a surging torrent.

I pictured my letter to the King riding on this torrent, like a paper boat, and arriving after a short space of time in His Majesty's bathtub, where he would exclaim, 'Ah! A message fashioned into a ship! How brilliantly unusual!'

And his long fingers would pluck it out of the water and read my words, and then he, still taking his bath, would call to him all the great physicians at Whitehall and say: 'Write for me every known remedy for the typhus sickness. Write them now, at once, or lose your positions at Court!'

And they would start anxiously scribbling down their recipes, which, though their writing might be blurred a little by the steam from the hot water being poured over the King's back, would in a short time arrive here at Bidnold.

Then I would ride to my apothecary on byways no longer choked with snow. And after that it would not be long before Margaret was well again.

⚐ ⚑

What succeeded the Thaw was a fortnight of mildness so sweet that I fancied I could smell the Spring in the soft air. The building of the Stockade for the Bear was begun. My letter to the King was sent to London.

I thought that everything would find some Amelioration now. But it did not.

I was walking in my Hornbeam Alley one late February morning, looking for signs of new leaf, when Will Gates, still obstinately attired in his Tabard and sweating a little inside it, came hurrying to me in what passes for a run in his ageing frame and summoned me to the house.

'What is it, Will?' I asked. 'Why such Olympian haste?'

'Tabitha sent me,' panted Will. 'It's Miss Margaret gone into a Confusion and not knowing where she is . . .'

I reached out for the grey stem of one of the Hornbeams and chung to it, to stop myself from falling.

Will came to me and held my arm to steady me. 'Sir Robert,' he said, 'it may be but a temporary Confusion . . .'

'No, Will,' I said. 'I have read the medical papers. It is the beginning of the end.'

Will shook his head furiously, side to side. 'It cannot be!' he burst out. 'I am still wearing my Badger skin!'

I sit at Margaret's bedside. I hold her hand. I say her name aloud.

She says to me: 'I am afraid of the cave.'

'What cave?' say I.

'I went in,' she says, 'and there was a Fledgling trapped in there, and I took it in my hands to bring it out . . .'

'And then?'

'I have forgotten. There was nothing in my hand. Only vile phlegm.'

I stroke her forehead, which is no longer burning hot as it has been, but cold as clay. I ask her where this cave might be and she replies: 'Cornwall.' And this gives me a little hope, for that she remembers the name of Cornwall, where she should have been with her friends, and does not say Mesopotamia or Ipswich or Lyme Regis.

Though I detest to do this, I send Tabitha for my Medical Instruments, and I open a vein in Margaret's arm and let blood from it. But I perceive that her poor arm is well-nigh wasted away, and to see my child in this Condition brings such a rage to my heart that I can barely stop myself from screaming.

I bind the arm, all the while cursing my own inadequate medical knowledge. But I know that I am seeing before me a body that lacks nourishment and I send Tabitha to Cattlebury with the instructions to make a Milk Posset.

'Will he remember what that be?' asks Tabitha. 'Mr Cattlebury is got forgetful lately, Sir.'

'Milk!' I shout. 'Milk, white wine, egg yolks, Sugar, cinnamon and Nutmeg. Whipped till it thickens. Go on your way!'

Tabitha glides away like a little shadow and I berate myself for shouting at her, a very gentle girl, who has risked her life and gone without sleep many nights to nurse Margaret.

It is very quiet in Margaret's room and I do not like this Quietness, for in it I find myself thinking about the Quietness of the Grave. To fend this away, I begin to prattle in a disordered kind of fashion, telling her once more about my Parents' Haberdasher's Shop and all the soft little ends and bits of things that it contained. 'There were feathers of all sizes,' I say, 'and cards of Lace, both Breton Lace and Lace interwoven with gold and silver thread. There were strips of finely brushed felt and pieces of fur and satin Ribbons, like those sewn into the shoulder seams of my Coats, and Buttons of every kind, including Buttons of Bone . . . but fire came and all of these things were burned, even the silver and the gold . . .'

Margaret regards me gravely. The pupils of her eyes are very large. I cannot tell whether she hears me or understands what I am saying, or whether she is already sliding away on some lonely sea to Oblivion. And the Pity of this, that my daughter might find herself alone in an approaching dusk, with everyone and everything she had loved lost to her for ever, overwhelms me, so that I begin to cry and, once begun on my weeping, give myself to it entirely, so that I am all washed about in a tide of tears, and a deal of time passes and I do not know how to come out of it. I seem to know that, in this silent room, my World is ending. It is ending.

My chest aches from my sobbing. And I think how this pain is but a slight wound compared to the great slaying of my soul that is going to come when Margaret is gone. And I say aloud: 'I do not know how I shall bear it!'

I repeat this, helplessly, many times, with my head buried in Margaret's pillow and my arms enfolding her frail body. *'I do not know how I shall bear it!'*

And then, in my damp darkness, I hear an answering Voice. The Voice is hushed, almost inaudible. It says: 'You shall not need to bear it, Merivel.'

I try to restrain my sobs and raise my head from the pillow.

The room is dark, with the curtains drawn against the spring day, and only a solitary candle burning. I wipe my eyes on a corner of Margaret's sheet and look towards the door, and I see a tall figure standing there, dressed all in Black and with a white wrapping binding his face. And I think that I am in the presence of Death, who has come, unheard, into the room, and all my flesh turns cold.

Death moves very slowly and walks towards the bed. And I catch the scent of him as he nears me; but, strangely, Death does not smell of any foul Thing, but of the most beautiful and refined Perfume. I breathe in this Perfume and know that it is familiar to me, but I cannot remember from when or where.

I wipe my eyes again to try to see more clearly. Death stands motionless at the bedside of my child. He wears black gloves. Above the white Muslin binding his face, his eyes regard me with a fierce Intensity. 'Merivel,' he says. 'I will touch her, as I touch men for the Pox. If the King touches, God very often saves.'

Weak from my weeping, I stumble to my feet. I try to execute my oft-practised bow, but I have to reach out my hand to stop myself from falling onto the bed.

'Your Majesty . . .' I stammer. 'I mistook you for Death.'

'Did you?' says the King. 'How interesting. Monarchs and Death are both burdened with Dread. I expect that is the reason.'

'No,' I say. 'There is no Dread of you in my heart.'

'Good. I did not think there was.'

'Only a very obstinate love.'

'That I know. It is, of course, why I am here. So let us both be silent a moment. And then I will touch Margaret and we will pray, and you shall see that in a short space of time she will recover. Kings must believe in their own Power or they are lost. In this belief is all their strength and might. And this I know from my long years of Exile. Even sheltering in my Oak Tree at Boscobel, with all my battles lost, I knew it.'

I try to stand very silent and still, but I am aware that my nose is running, and that a dribble of mucus is coursing down over my lips to my chin and beyond onto my collar. I have no rag with which to wipe it away, so I use the sleeve of my coat, and it is only then that I recall that I am wearing an old, frayed brown Garment that I like to put on when I make solitary visits to my garden, it seeming to be the nearest thing I own to a kind of Camouflage, wearing which I feel free to talk to the Hornbeams and the Beeches. I feel ashamed to be in such poor attire before the King, but I cannot give this shame any attention, for I know that it has no importance. What is occurring in the room is so unexpected, so extraordinary, that I know I must give it all my soul. And as if to reinforce this knowledge, I glance over to the door and suddenly catch sight of Will, hung about as always with his Badger Tabard, kneeling on the floor with his hands clenched in prayer.

The King moves close to the bed. Margaret opens her eyes and they flicker with some kind of Recognition, then close again. The gloved hands reach out and, folded one upon the other, alight on Margaret's forehead.

'Kings have no Power of Healing,' says King Charles, 'but God has that Power and He may work through us. In God's name, I touch you, Margaret. May God heal you and make you well.'

'Amen,' murmurs Will.

'Amen,' say I.

14

The King intended to stay no more than one night at Bidnold, and so had arrived with a very small Retinue consisting of two Coachmen, one Officer of the Royal Guard, two Valets and one dog, his favourite Spaniel bitch, Bunting.

He and Bunting were lodged in the room that used to be called the Marigold Room, where once Celia had lain, complaining all the while about my vulgar decorations and my absence of taste. But the King admires this room, upholstered now in a flaming sunset of corals and magentas, only cooled a little by an abundance of cream satin cushions. It has a very beautiful view of the Park and, as he entered there once again, the King said: 'Ah, yes. Here I am at Peace. Now I shall rest awhile.'

Leaving Tabitha with Margaret, I summoned all my servants and gave instructions for a bounteous Feast to be cobbled together before evening, so that the King might dine in as much splendour as my house could afford, given so brief a notice.

To Cattlebury's suggestion of 'a rich game pie with Marmalade' I said: 'If you will, Cattlebury, but then let us *navigate* around the pie with oysters and anchovies, and a saddle of Lamb with a Madeira Sauce, and a Chine of Beef, and follow it all with a Rum Syllabub and baked Apples. His Majesty has travelled a long while to be with us and will be as hungry as a lion.'

'Or as a Bear, you should have said, Sir,' remarked Cattlebury.

'If you ask me, that creature will be devouring deer before the spring is out.'

'Thank you, Cattlebury,' I said. 'I am always interested in opinions.Now. I wish the Dining Room to be thoroughly cleaned and polished as to woodwork, silverware and Pewter, and all the best Linen got from the chests and ironed and laid out. Nobody shall rest or stop for one moment till everything is shining and clean. And I want fifty candles lit before Supper is served. Both His Majesty and I are fond of light.'

I then took Will aside into the Servants' Pantry and said gently: 'Will, the time has come to take off your Tabard. This evening you will put on your best Livery, so that you may serve the King at table.'

Will picked up a corner of his Tabard, and looked at the Moth holes and the Mange with which it was afflicted, and shook his head sadly. 'Sir,' he said, 'I swore I would not take this off until Miss Margaret was well again. Of what use was my promise if I now break it?'

I regarded him, stooped and sad as he was, with almost as much decay on him as was on the Badger skin, and saw that the day had come when I could not let him perform any more duties in the Dining Room, for that he could not hold the plates and dishes up.

And so I perceived, not without some feeling of shame, that his insistence on his wearing of the Tabard had saved me, perhaps, from a Catastrophe of spilled oysters and dropped sauce boats, from a general mortifying supper-time Chaos, and so I said: 'Very well, Will. An oath is an oath and you are an honourable man. Keep on the Tabard. Only—'

'I know, Sir Robert, I cannot appear at table. I would give the world to serve His Majesty again, but I will stay out of sight.'

After a hastily assembled luncheon, the King invited me to take a turn in the Park with him.

In the strong sunshine I could very clearly see the creases that Time had engraved on the King Charles's face and I saw, too, that his skin – always a very sweet Caramel colour – had become pale and spotted with liver stains, and I wanted to protest at these signs of ageing: at the Discord they engendered in my mind, which childishly believed the King to be ageless and immortal.

I led him first to my pleached Hornbeam Alley, which he admired, professing himself enamoured of the 'French style of gardens, where everything is Geometry and Order', and I began to relate to him (for that I knew of his abiding interest in the state of other people's hearts) how, in Paris, I had fallen in love with a woman 'of infinite learning in regard to plants'.

'Ah,' said the King, 'how delicate of you, Merivel. I would not have taken you for a man who could be seduced by Botany.'

'Nor I,' said I, 'but then, all my life I have been surprised by what moved me. It is as though, despite the excellent exhortations by Montaigne for men to "know themselves", I still do not comprehend my own Nature.'

'Very probable. But the reason may well be that you still yearn to entertain and surprise yourself. Am I not right?'

'Well,' I said, 'I yearn to surprise and entertain *you*.'

'Ha! How considerate of you. And you succeed most of the time. But this Paramour in Paris, do you amuse her?'

'I believe I do, Sir. But I am endeavouring to forget her. Her husband is a Colonel in the Swiss Guards and he has threatened to kill me with his sword the moment I show my face at his house . . .'

'Oh, how infantile! Mistresses should be married and husbands should know their place – as once you learned, to your cost. Perhaps the Swiss Guards stand too much on Dignity, do they?'

Into my mind came an image of Colonel Jacques-Adolphe de Flamanville, sniffing and snorting as he massacred me at Billiards, and I said that the maintenance of his Dignity did indeed appear to count strongly with him and that I had nicknamed him 'the Giraffe'. But in fairness to his fellow soldiers, I also conjured for the King (who, of late, did not enjoy going beyond the shores of England and so had not seen Versailles for some time) the Stoicism of the Swiss Guards, standing so still in the frozen moonlight and playing their drums with such infinite softness that the sound seemed, almost, to ascend out of the ground.

'This I like,' he said. 'When the strong restrain their strength and are subtle.'

We walked on and came soon enough to the newly built Stockade, inside which the Bear was pacing round and round.

The King stopped, and held to the wooden posts of the Stockade and regarded the Bear with fierce attention. Bunting began to bark and he picked her up and cradled her in his arms till she was quiet.

'Does the creature have a name?' he asked after a while.

'No,' I said. 'I cannot think of a name substantial enough.'

The King smiled, then in silence watched the Bear, as it lumbered away from us and came to a place of uneasy rest beneath a tree branch. Then he said: 'I believe his name should be Clarendon, like my former bear-leader. The animal is Cast Out and alone. He may soon enough die.'

I was shocked for a moment. I had no wish to entertain the thought that my Bear would 'soon enough die'. But then I looked at the stricken creature and remembered how the affluent, pompous old Earl and Chancellor, who had believed he would be at the King's side to advise him and guide him all his life, in the end *outlasted his own usefulness*.

And so Clarendon, who had risen so high and made so mighty a Fortune, was sent away into France and never returned to inhabit the great house he had built for himself. Lady Castlemaine and others at Court laughed and rejoiced at his disgrace, and his Coat of Arms was defiled, and a charge of Treason (never put) began to circulate about his absent person.

The King, who had been driven into fury by Clarendon's overbearing presence for so long, at first joined in the mockery and derision of a man who had advised him all his life, but some years later, after Clarendon had died at Montpelier, he compared him to Shakespeare's Falstaff and himself to Prince Hal. 'I was cruel,' he said. 'Clarendon died of heartbreak. I should not have punished him so completely.'

Now, the thought that my Bear, whose saviour I had imagined myself to be, was enduring some kind of terrible Exile here at Bidnold caught me in a sudden sorrow. I saw that I had not been able to give the creature one moment's happiness. I had saved it from death; that was all.

'Was I wrong to save its life?' I asked.

The King held the dog close to him, as though for his own comfort as much as for her protection, and asked: 'Why did you *want* to save it, Merivel?'

'I believe I thought it might play a part . . .'

'In what?'

'In my future understanding of my own Nature.'

The King turned and looked at me. It was a look of unconcealed Disdain, that I remembered from long ago and which caused me sudden pain, for in it I always and ever saw reflected my own Inadequacy.

'I see you have not lost the habit of turning all Things towards yourself,' he said with a sniff.

We returned to the house and ascended to Margaret's room. She was sleeping.

We stood and watched. Her sleep appeared calm and Tabitha told us that she had taken some of the Milk Posset before closing her eyes once more. Her thin, bandaged arm lay still, in an attitude of surrender, on her pillow. Each of us touched this languorous arm, then the King, whose mood was now sombre, went to rest once more and I descended to the Kitchen, where I found Cattlebury cleaving the heads from a brace of Mallard Duck.

'I did not order Duck,' I said.

'No, Sir Robert,' replied the impudent cook, 'but they walked of their own accord into my larder and I says to them, "You are done for, my lads!" And they quacks back to me, "Will the King eat us?" And I says, for that I am a Man of Wit – as I hope you have noticed, Sir Robert, over all these years – "The King eats everything in the land, so why should you be spared?"'

'What did you mean by that – "the King eats everything in the land"?'

'Only what I say, Sir. If famine comes, will the King starve? No. He will take from the people the little that they have, to stuff his own gob.'

'Be quiet, Cattlebury!' I cried out. 'I will not have seditious talk under this roof.'

Cattlebury left the Duck and came towards me, brandishing the meat cleaver. As I flinched away from him he said: 'He will be your ruin, too, Sir Robert. Mr Pearce was always right, the King will be your ruin.'

I went out into the garden and gathered some Hellebore leaves. I had imagined these plants so wounded and suffocated by the frost and snow that they would be brown and dead, but they were not.

I made an Infusion of Hellebore and Honey – another recipe of Pearce's, for the benign treatment of mental infirmity, used to some effect at Whittlesea. I took this up to Margaret's room, where Tabitha had resumed her watch. I apologised to the girl for shouting at her before and told her to go and rest.

Margaret had not moved at all in her sleep. It was as if, since the appearance of the King at her bedside, she had been cast into a gentle Oblivion, such as once afflicted her Mother, and I prayed that she would not slide from this into Death.

I tried to hold in my mind to that moment in the Drama of King Lear, where the poor mad Monarch is cured of his confusions *by sleep* and wakes to find his daughter Cordelia at his side and, after a while, recognises her, whom he has not seen in a long and cruel while, and cries out: 'Do not laugh at me, For as I am a man, I think this Lady to be my child, Cordelia' and she replies, 'And so I am, I am.' And upon this last repetition of the words 'I am' – if they be well said by the Actor – I can never hold back my tears, for what moves me most in the World is seeing that which was once lost to us restored.

I roused Margaret gently, and she opened her eyes and looked at me. I helped her to sit up a little.

'Margaret,' I said. 'The King is come to Bidnold. He laid his hands upon your head and prayed to God to make you well. So now you will be well.'

She said nothing, but only looked at me with the compassion invalids often feel for those who nurse them. I stroked her hand.

'I have made an Infusion for you, to calm your mind. Will you try to take a little?'

I held the cup to her lips and she took small sips, like a child. The skin of her face was pale, but yet with some blush of sleep on it, and her hand was warm and dry.

I began to relate to her how the King had sent no word of his arrival, but arrived like Jove Descending in his Chariot at the gate, forcing Will to such a stumbling and tottering rush to the front door that his heart almost ceased before he could appear at the King's side.

'But appear he did, Margaret,' I said, 'and to his great joy, as he tried to make his bow, His Majesty raised him up and said: "Gates! Our very excellent man! How glad we are to see you!" And Will's heart almost stopped a second time from wonder. Imagine the scene . . .'

I watched her face carefully, to see whether she had understood my little account.

For a moment her features did not move at all, but then the ghost of a Smile lifted the corners of her mouth. 'I am glad,' she said.

I helped her to drink half the cup of Hellebore, after which she lay back on her pillow and would take no more. She closed her eyes again. I sat without moving, asking myself whether, in any degree, I believed that a King can cure his subjects of grave maladies, and I knew that, in all truth, I did not believe it.

Yet neither could I assent to the idea that the King's arrival at my house was to be entirely without some beneficial Consequence. I knew that had Pearce been here he would have said: 'Once again, Merivel, you enter a state of Delusion. Doctors may aid healing, but Kings do not. And only God cures.' To which I would have replied: 'I know, my friend. I believe that even the King himself knows that. And yet, perhaps you leave out a vital consideration: the power of the mind to entertain those Delusions that sustain it.'

Considering the unreliability of Cattlebury and Will's inability to supervise him, the Supper that appeared in the Dining Room was far from lamentable.

The candles had been lit. Everything was clean and shimmering. The King sat with Bunting on his lap and fed her morsels of Roasted Duck and the somewhat overcooked Chine. Cattlebury's Game Pie came decorated with a pastry Crown, filled with shining Marmalade and set with Currants, as though with jewels – a courteous little act of repentance, I fervently hoped, for his outbreak of anti-Monarchist feeling.

For a while, disconcertingly, His Majesty talked to the dog and not to me, but I knew better than to interrupt him. It seemed to me that something important was turning in his mind and I was not wrong. At length, as the Pie was broached, he raised his eyes to me and said: 'I have not told you, Merivel, how tired I am. I do not mean from my journey to Norfolk, which – once we were clear of the curtilage of London, which is much contaminated by Poverty – gave me great gladness, but from Matters of State.'

'I can imagine that, Sir,' I said.

'The very sight of any Business – fees unpaid to the Navy men, money owing for a thousand other things, Petitions from this or that Society or Guild – makes me feel ill. There are mornings when, after my little Constitutional in the Park, all I am capable of doing is going to Fubbsy's apartments and lying down by the fire and having her stroke my head, so terribly does it ache.'

'Maladies of the head are hard to bear. I know it well.'

'I could almost wish – and I have never in my life had such a thought before – that somebody else could be King.'

'That would never do, Sir. None that I can think of have the Legs for it.'

The King smiled and took a drink of wine.

'There are so few, so *very few* at Court who entertain me any more, Merivel. All is Gravity and Reproach. I am even supposed to be making war with France! All bound together with the Dutch and their competitive mania for Trade Monopolies. But wherefore would I do such a thing, when the only money I have to call my own comes from loans from King Louis?'

'War is a bitter scourge . . .'

'Quite so. I will not go to war – with France or with anyone else. What I long for is peace.'

Bunting, at this moment feeling herself neglected, began to whine for a morsel of pie. While this was safely procured for her I said: 'You know that you are welcome to stay at Bidnold for as long as you want . . .'

The King stroked the dog and looked at me. 'I was coming to this,' he said. 'I have always found this place very comforting. I was intending to go back to London tomorrow morning, but I feel that I simply cannot do it. I need sleep and fresh air. I shall remain at Bidnold.'

I bowed and said I was honoured, which I was. But in the next moment, taking in the true implications of the King's announcement, I was also mightily discomfited. For Bidnold – what with the Infirmity of Will and the Mortal Illness of Margaret, the absence of provisions after the great snow, not to mention the seditious utterings of Cattlebury – was not really in any state to endure the prolonged Presence of the King.

I myself was weary and worn down. It was going to be difficult for me to be attentive to the Sovereign when all my thoughts were with Margaret. I was also undergoing great tidal fluctuations of guilt about my neglect of my Patients. My excuse, in these recent times, had been that I should stay away from them lest I be a carrier of the Typhus. But the truth was that during my absence in France, and in the long and terrible cold winter, I had given them virtually no thought, blithely assuming that old Dr Murdoch (that Quack!) and Dr Sims were doing their best for them, and that they had explained to them my great predicament in regard to my daughter's sickness.

But I had hoped to make amends very soon by visiting them, every one, and now I saw that, more than ever, I was Captive in my house and that all my endeavours would have to be for Margaret and for the King alone. Habitually, the King arrived here with sufficient of the Court to entertain him and I could play the quiet Host, popping up with jests and fooleries, as required or requested, from time to time. But here he was at Bidnold with only two Valets and a spoilt dog for company. I began anxiously to wonder how we might pass the coming days.

When we left the Dining Room the King stopped and turned and looked back at the table, and at all the fifty candles dripping and burning. 'Where is Gates?' he said. 'Was he not always faithful to the serving of Supper?'

'Yes, he was, Sir,' I said, 'but his hands are become a little unsteady . . .'

The King nodded gravely. 'I see,' he said. 'I believe you told me that in London. But I do so much dislike it when things I have appreciated come to an end.'

15

Spring came in.

Each day, as it spread its sugaring of green on every tree and hedgerow, I saw signs of Amelioration in Margaret's condition. She began to eat the small, tempting meals I persuaded Cattlebury to make for her: milk puddings, coddled eggs, celery hearts baked with cream. The colour crept back into her cheeks.

I made sure that her hair was washed and curled, as she liked it to be.

Sometimes I helped her to rise from her bed, and we would sit at a little table in front of the window of the room where she'd lain for so long and play a few games of Rummy, and I saw from these that her mind was sharp and clear. To the heartless God who had let my innocent parents perish in a fire I expressed my gratitude.

I unearthed my tarnished oboe from its case, shined it up and, to Margaret's amusement – and the King's – led my daughter down to the Music Room and played for the two of them some of the old, badly remembered melodies with which I once entertained the mad of Whittlesea. At one of these sessions the King stood up and took Margaret by the hand, and led her to a short but stately dance, after which we three applauded enthusiastically, as though we had been at some marvellous new Drama at the Duke's Playhouse.

I sent word to Sir James Prideaux of Margaret's recovery and

invited his family to dine with us, and when the women understood that the King was here and would be part of the company
they all – so Sir James wrote to me – requested new dresses and
new ribbons and new shoes, 'and your soirée will quite bankrupt
me, Merivel, but of course I do not care a whit, such is our rejoicing to meet the King and to know that Margaret is with us again
in the world'.

They came in and filled the house with conversation and
laughter. Each in turn embraced Margaret and Mary wept with
such joy to see her friend restored that Arabella had to hide her
face with her fan to conceal her own tears.

To the King, the family gave great and immediate delight.
Though he had made much of telling me how 'staid and comfortable' he was with Fubbsy, I could at once perceive that the arrival
of four beautiful young women in my house lit up his eye with
its old Fire.

Penelope was but fifteen, but to her as well as to Mary, Jane and
Virginia, he showed the kindest attention, impressing upon her the
importance of her lessons in Dancing and Geography. 'Grace *in* the
world, Penelope, and Knowledge *of* the world,' he said to her, 'my
Father taught me to value these things, before his Head was
unkindly cut off. Therefore, in his name, you must pay attention to
them.' And all the company fell silent and we did not know where
to look, and it was as well that Will (at last divested of his badger
Tabard and wearing a suit of red-and-gold Livery too large for his
bones) came in at that moment to tell me that the net that I had
requested for a game of Shuttlecock had been rigged up in the hall.

We took turns to play in different teams and whoever played
in the King's team won, for that his agility had diminished little
since I used to play Tennis with him, and his strokes were very
strong and keen. But nobody seemed to mind who won or who
lost. Our capering about with Racquets, chasing a Feathered Ball,
brought to our hearts an extraordinary gladness, and though we
were short of breath and thirsty, and I had to send to the kitchen
for Ale and Lemonade, we did not want these games to end.

At midnight we were still playing. The only spectators were Arabella and Margaret, who was not yet strong enough to run about and sweat and risk a fever, but they, too, were caught by the laughter in the game and sat by the guttering candles, sipping Lemonade and cheering on the teams. And I thought how there had not been an evening as sweet as this one at Bidnold for many a long time, and how it was as if all my Melancholy had been swept from my heart and sent by the Shuttlecock into some faraway void.

True to what he said he would do, the King spent long hours walking alone in the Park in the early sunshine and as many quietly resting in the Marigold Room. 'I am at peace,' he kept repeating to me, 'I am at peace in this place.'

Letters followed him, more and more as the days passed, but he did not open them. He said that the very word 'Parliament' made him feel faint, 'as though I were a youth again and in Exile', and he made me vow never to utter it.

He spent the evenings dining with me and with whatever amusing Company I could procure for him, including my Lady Bathurst, my former Amour, Violet, now widowed and quite aged, yet still beautiful in a ruined kind of way and with her Wit as sharp as ever it was.

And one evening, after we had drunk a great quantity of wine, the King took her to his bed, and when I myself retired some time later, I (and no doubt Margaret, as well as all the Servants at Bidnold) heard the familiar shouting and screaming of Violet Bathurst, who could not find herself touched by a man without making of it an almost ungovernable Riot.

At breakfast the following morning the King did not appear. Violet, looking pale, and with a fine Bruise on her neck, and drinking weak Cinnamon Tea, turned to me and said: 'I did not tell you, Merivel, that I am dying.'

'Well,' I said, 'we are all dying, Violet . . .'

'But I am dying more utterly than you. There is a Cancer in my breast.'

I was eating Porridge. I looked at its grey lumpishness and felt my gorge rise. Before I could say anything Violet said: 'Now that I have been fucked by the King, I can die happy. Is this not so?'

She was smiling her familiar, challenging smile, which used to cast an agreeable spell over me, but to which I now felt myself to be almost immune.

'How can you be sure that what you have is a Cancer?' I said.

'Well, it is great *Thing* near my armpit, which should not be there. What else might it be? But I did not let the King's hands discover it and he took, I think, much pleasure in me, as once you did, too.'

'I have no doubt he did.'

'But he may not come to me again . . .'

'Why not?'

'I believe I exhausted him!'

Margaret came into the Dining Room at this moment, so Violet and I ceased to talk of these things. Margaret said 'Good Morning' to Violet, but would not look at her, being, I think, embarrassed to have overheard the night's frenzy and not knowing whether all Normality in the house was henceforth to be altered by it. When Violet announced her departure, my daughter looked relieved.

I accompanied Violet to the door. As she left the house I said to her: 'I will come to Bathurst Hall tomorrow and examine your breast. Perhaps what you have is a mere Cyst, which I can drain.'

She brushed my lips with her hand. 'Thank you, Merivel,' she said, 'and for giving me the King. What delights I have always found under this roof!'

Then she drove away in her carriage and I returned to my Porridge, which was cold, and to Margaret, who was very subdued and quiet.

'I have made a decision,' I said. 'Tomorrow I shall resume, in some measure, just for an hour or two, the rounds of my Patients.

Will you entertain the King, if he should request any entertainment, while I am gone?'

'Yes,' said Margaret. 'Shall I teach him to play Rummy?'

My unfortunate Patients . . .

For a long time they had been at the mercy of Dr Murdoch,
whom I have known since my Days of Folly. He is old now, and
from his nose and ears sprout vigorous hairs, like rats' whiskers
and I pity the recumbent Sick, who are forced to contemplate
these whiskers and be repulsed by them, and fear the scratching or pricking of them, as Dr Murdoch bends down towards
the bed.

Though, like Pearce and myself, Murdoch once worked at St
Thomas's Hospital in London, he did not last long there and he
has never, by my measurement, been a bona fide Physician, but
merely stumbled through his life in a stupor of half-knowledge,
dispensing this or that remedy at his ignorant whim.

He is prone to muddling one Patient with another. To a man
who had lost a great quantity of blood from inadvertently tripping
over his own feet and falling onto his scythe while haymaking,
what does Murdoch do but let *more* blood, misremembering him
for a patient with choleric seizures – for the only reason that
both men were large and bald. And so the scythed man dies,
having almost no blood left in his body, and his poor wife says
to me, 'It were the Doctor that killed him and no mistake.' But
she has no money nor status in the world and so can bring no
Suit against him.

Murdoch has got very rich on his paltry skills and by pursuing
his Patients to the grave, and beyond, for his payments. He has
built himself a fine house at Walsham and acts as though he were
a lord, demanding Deference from all and sundry, and disliking
me very intensely, for that I am an Intimate of the King and Murdoch very prone to jealousy.

In recent times, Murdoch has been assisted by a younger man,
Dr Sims, who was called to Margaret when she first fell ill at Sir

James's house. Neither he nor Murdoch understood that she had Typhus, so I conclude that this Sims, too, is a Know-nothing fool, scarce better than the old rat-man. And I remember Pearce often saying to me that half the Physicians in England were imbeciles, and that this was a great tragedy for the people.

'Do you include me in the Imbecile Category?' I asked.

'No,' said Pearce. 'On the contrary. You are a very fine Physician – when you give your mind to it.'

I set out with these thoughts turning in my brain, and guilt in my heart for my abandonment of so many of the sick and needy all through the bitter winter. I hoped that word had spread of Margaret's illness and that I would be forgiven on account of it.

The first Patient I visited was a Wool Merchant named Mr Percival Maybury, whose one great affliction – and that, he said, blighting his whole life – was his abiding Constipation, and because all his thoughts turned, day by day, upon the making of a good stool to relieve the pain in his bowel, his Wool business was neglected and going down towards ruin.

He had grown very thin. He told me that Dr Murdoch had prescribed Clysters of bitter almonds, but that these 'produced stools that are black and burning' and causing him great agony as they passed out of him. And so he now forbade himself to eat, almost, so much did he fear the blocked passage of food in his gut.

'This will not do, Mr Maybury,' I said. 'We must find some other remedy.'

In previous times I had tried Clysters of Turpentine for him, and these would bring him 'great relief' for a while and then, I know not why, cease to have any effect whatsoever. I now told him that I had been told of an excellent device to sluice out foul matter and this was called an Enema Pump, made of a Sheep's bladder, attached to a carefully sewn leather Pipe, and the bladder filled with salted water and squeezed into the anus through the Pipe, with a force that sent the liquid up the large intestine. And when, in time, it forced itself out again, why then, all the stools followed its downrush and came out with no hurt or strain.

Percival Maybury looked marvellously cheered by this and asked me how he could come by such an instrument. I told him that I would ask my Apothecary in Norwich to procure one for him.

Meanwhile I advised him to eat Oatmeal and peas, this diet – to my certain knowledge – having a very loosening effect upon the bowel. And I recounted to the poor Wool Merchant the flavour of my time at Versailles, in my shabby room with Hollers and drinking water from the garden fountains, and this made him laugh exceedingly and I was cheered, because I know that in laughter may reside Forgiveness.

I proceeded on to an asthmatic Patient, Mr Joshua Phipps, once a Moneylender and Pawnbroker, but now forced to stay out of every city for fear of the vitiated air and what it did to his breath. Yet Moneylenders cannot prosper unless they be visible, and people see their Sign and come to beg loans or to trade their pitiful possessions for coins, and so Phipps, like Maybury, grieved both over his bodily state and over his failing enterprise.

'I am doing battle with fear, Dr Merivel,' he told me. 'I cannot conquer my Asthma, but I am endeavouring to conquer my *fear* of it, testing myself to see how long I can last without breath till I inhale my Mint Balsam and get some air into my lungs. Now, by virtue of practice, I can endure *two minutes*.'

'Two is heroic,' said I. 'I am sure that I could not last one minute.'

'Fear constricts,' he said. 'Fear begins in the throat. Perhaps, if I can truly banish my terror, then I will banish the disease.'

I replied that I thought this an admirable aspiration, but meanwhile conjured for him my sea voyage to France, and how the briny air had filled me with gladness and seemed to rinse me clean of some foul Humours.

'When summer comes,' I said, 'why do you not get a boat from Harwich or Felixstowe, and stay on the deck and breathe, trying to fill your lungs with the West Wind?'

He looked at me gravely. 'I have never been inclined to go to sea,' he said. 'I prefer the company of dry things: Bills of Sale and Money Orders and nicely written Receipts.'

I then rode on to Bathurst Hall.

This house is very large and was once the scene of some Mad Revels, with a black Stallion being led into the Dining Room and shitting everywhere, and all the Fops mad with laughter and lust, and old Lord Bathurst himself rolling on the floor, shrieking out his half-witted nonsense, and Violet pirouetting on the table, and then everybody singing and copulating in corners or puking and falling asleep in the mess, and all the poor Servants toiling back and forth to try to clean everything up.

When I think of this time, I feel a blush creeping up my cheeks, especially at the prolonged and immodest couplings I enjoyed with Violet in various Corners of the house and even on the stairs, as we crawled to bed, like dogs. Never, I think, have I known any woman quite as wanton, deep in her soul, as Violet Bathurst, and she led me on to great extremes of licentiousness. Had Pearce witnessed one *half* of what I did with her, his heart would surely have ceased long before it did.

Now I was shown once more to her Bedchamber, a room I knew well, but which seemed, suddenly, to have become very dark, with heavy drapery drawn across the windows and stinking of Oil from the lamps that guttered near to Violet's bed.

She lay there, stroking a grey cat, with her grey hair coiled in a heavy plait and her face pale, yet painted with two spots of Rouge on her cheekbones. And when I saw her like this, what I felt was a terrible Pity for the passing of time, which had taken away her beauty and my lust, and left us as the mere husks of what we had once been.

I tried to make my countenance cheerful. I felt glad that, if she were indeed dying, she had had at least one night with the greatest lover in the land. And when she saw me she was immediately drawn to tell me how fine her night had been and how the King's mouth was still 'of a great voluptuousness and brought me to Pleasures deep as an ocean, Merivel, deeper than any that you gave me, so that I almost lost consciousness' and how His Majesty's prick was 'as large and silky as any woman could dream of'.

'Good,' I said weakly. 'I am very glad, Violet . . .'

'Do you not wish to hear more, Merivel?'

'Is there more to tell?'

'Yes indeed, for he is a lover of wondrously new Positions. Do you not wish to hear about these?'

'No,' I said. 'I am not particularly in the mood for hearing about them. And I must return to Bidnold very shortly. I have left the King in Margaret's care.'

'Oh,' said Violet. 'That is very unwise. For he will surely make love to her.'

'*What* did you say?'

'Well, I merely stated what should be obvious to you. Margaret is now a very pretty young woman. Why should the King not try—'

'Hush, Violet!' I burst out. 'Do not say such a terrible thing. The King is my friend and will not ravage my daughter while I am gone to visit my Patients.'

'How do you know?' retorted Violet. 'It was plain to me within five minutes of arriving at your house that he intended to take me to bed. He cannot help himself, and now, I warrant, he will *help himself* to Margaret!'

'Stop!' I said, putting my hand over Violet's mouth. 'Or I shall leave. D'you wish to show me your infernal Lump or not?'

Obediently she now pretended a great Contrition, kissing my hand and stroking it with her lips. Then she lay back on the pillows, holding the cat to her for comfort, and looked up into my eyes with a most piteous expression.

I waited a moment, trying to calm the agitation in my breast. Gently I raised Violet's arm. Then I reached out for one of the lamps, and brought it near to the arm and saw by its yellow light the 'Thing' she had described to me, where her left breast descended to her armpit. It was purplish and a little shiny, and hard when I touched it, and I saw at once that it did indeed have the appearance of a Cancer and not a Cyst, as I had hoped.

I felt very keenly the quietness of the room, disturbed only by the purring of the grey cat and my laboured breathing. I took up my Instrument case and selected a sharp needle, with which I made a quick stab into the Thing, causing Violet to scream with pain and the cat to fly from the room.

'I am sorry to hurt you,' I said. 'If this is a Cyst, then the liquid will now begin flow out from it. Bear the pain for a moment longer and we shall see . . .'

But no liquid came out when I withdrew the needle. What it had probed was a solid, fleshy thing. I hated the sight of it. I wanted to take up my Scalpel and cut it out there and then, but I knew that the agony of this would be too terrible to bear without a great quantity of Opium, and that I would need a Nurse to hold the patient down and to help stem the bleeding.

Where the needle had entered a little Blood was let and I wished I had some of Louise's Salve to soothe the wound I had made. I laid a square of muslin on it and kept my hand there, to hold it in place awhile.

'Well, Doctor?' said Violet. 'Am I dying, or not?'

'I will cut the Cancer out,' I said. 'It is not large. You will not die of so small a thing.'

'Ah,' said Violet, 'and yet I feel that I am dying. Why should that be?'

'I cannot say.'

'Will the King die, Merivel? He told me last night that he sometimes felt himself to be immortal.'

'The King will die,' said I. 'But I do not wish to see it. I shall endeavour to die first.'

Great agitation was still in my heart as I started for home. The idea Violet had put into my mind, that the King might seduce my daughter, had wounded me as fatally as any Cancer.

As I travelled towards Bidnold, I felt a sickness rise in my stomach, so that I had to rein in my horse and dismount and vomit up my breakfast by the side of the road. I stood there, shivering and afraid. An image of my poor wife, Celia, in her attic room with her needlework and an old Crone for company, visited my mind and distressed it further. I leaned against my horse for a moment, to feel the warmth of it. Then I rode on.

16

Two Letters came to me at this time.

The first was from my Dutch friend, Hollers. He wrote to tell me that when he had quite used up all his provisions – including those few jars of peas I had left behind when I departed so suddenly for Paris – and had almost no money left and saw no way to live but to return to Holland, his clock had at last been returned to him.

A Note, in Madame de Maintenon's cultured hand, had informed him that his clock 'will not serve, Monsieur Hollers, for that it advances by more than one minute per diem on the Time told by the Chapel clock. It is thus *stealing Time* from God, at the rate of eight or nine minutes per week, and God has much Work to do; He does not like Any Moment to be taken from Him.'

So alas, Hollers wrote, *all my endeavours at Versailles have come to nothing. All the Time (that capricious commodity!) which you and I spent imagining my Future was vainly wasted. I am back in my Shoppe in my own city, and when I look around me, I see, on the sudden, that this Shoppe is a poor place and all my Timepieces, made with such loving care, give me no pride nor pleasure at all. I do not even bother to dust them any more. I shall never be Famous, Merivel! My chance of Fame is gone! I shall moulder to nothing, here on the dull Canal-side. Oh, tell me, my friend,*

what I am to do! I am at pains to go on with my Life in any
way at all.

Sadness on Hollers's account made me melancholy. Though I
knew that being back in Amsterdam could not possibly be a
more agonising Test of Endurance than our terrible habitation at
Versailles, I could nevertheless imagine the Clockmaker grinding
his molars in frustration and sorrow.

When I recounted my friend's story to the King he said: 'Oh, I
had often heard that Madame de Maintenon is a Pedant. And she is
not even a beautiful Pedant. How unfortunate for my cousin Louis.'

At this moment Bunting began a clamour to be taken out for a
walk, so the King rose, ever obedient to her commands, and
went out, and nothing more was said on the subject of Hollers.
And I felt this to be a dereliction, too – that the King had seemed
to give no thought to my friend's pain.

Yet I do not know why I should be surprised. The King is the
King and cannot take into himself the burdens and sorrows of all
his English Subjects – never mind the inhabitants of the Low
Countries as well. And, now I come to think of it, he has no fondness for the Dutch. He finds their language unpronounceable
and he has told me more than once that his Dutch Nephew, William of Orange, is a Prig.

While the King was gone on his walk, I wrote a reply to Hollers,
begging him to bear up and to rediscover his joy in his own
endeavours and in his own city, and to dream no longer of Fame.

As I wrote, I reflected how astonishing it is that Man attempts
any Thing of Significance – any Thing that might alter his life –
when part of him knows, that if he fails, all his former contentment will be lost. He cannot go back to a Time Before the game
began. He has, as it were, the chains of the imprisoned debtor
dragging down his spirits and his body. He wishes himself unborn
of his strivings. He accounts himself a fool for having ever
attempted them, but can do nothing about it.

None of this did I write to Hollers. I mentioned only that I *knew* him to be a fine Clockmaker and strenuously wished that I myself were capable of manufacturing with my own hands any comparable wonder. *In my whole life*, I wrote, *I have never made an object of perfect beauty. You have made many.*

I then turned my attention to my second letter, which was from Louise de Flamanville.

Though, in my waking hours, I had had little leisure to think of her, she had very often crept into my dreams and these dreams had had a strange, repetitive beauty to them. In them, Louise and I were to be found sitting side by side in her Laboratory, boiling Herbs and Mineral Compounds, which gave to the air a wondrously sweet Perfume, and which we then alchemised into medicines of startling efficacy. We saw blind men regain their sight and barren women delivered of children. Magic attended all our work. Louise said to me: 'It is because there are *two of us.* Alone, we could do little. Together, we work miracles.'

Now, with the arrival of her letter, a great longing for Louise was woken in me again and my hours with her in Paris returned to me in all their sweetness.

I thought ardently of the summer, when I might visit her in Switzerland, and this distant promise was given greater substance by her News.

She informed me that Jacques-Adolphe had taken a new lover, a young soldier of Russian origin, named Petrov.

This Petrov, she wrote, *who is really a mere Boy and apparently blushes exquisitely when anybody speaks to him, has so captivated my husband that he has become Careless with his behaviour. He takes note of almost nothing but of how, when and where he can come to Petrov and do those Things with him that the* Fraternité *yearn for above all other Experiences on earth. So it is, dear Merivel, that when I mentioned idly to Jacques-Adolphe that I would go to Switzerland to see my Father once the warm weather arrived, he said merely: 'Do what you will. Only do not ask me to come with you, for I must stay close to Petrov. If I am taken away from him, I will die.'*

'I hope therefore, to travel to Switzerland at the beginning of June. And how very pleasant my visit there would be if you could be persuaded to join me at my Father's Château. Does such a journey tempt you? Or have you quite forgotten me? Shall we walk together in the high meadows? The scent of cut hay, you may remember, is very potent and sweet.

I sat with this letter for a long time, imagining the hay. Above the sloping field I conjured a setting sun, burning red, as it tilted towards the Swiss mountain top. Louise lay on the grass and the sun lit up her face, and my hands caressed her smooth neck and the tops of her breasts. Somewhere nearabouts a brown-eyed cow feasted on a bank of buttercups in scented shade.

Then, I put the letter away. I knew what reply I longed to make to Madame de Flamanville, but for the time, I was unable to make any plans or promises whatsoever. I was captive at Bidnold. And now my Captivity was to be made unbearable by the Surveillance that I felt compelled to keep upon Margaret and the King.

I began the wretched habit, when the King, Margaret and I were in company together – which was very frequently – of looking from one to the other, back and forth, as though I were at a Tennis game. It was as if I believed this vigilance would entrap any amorous glance that might pass between them – catch it like a Butterfly in a net and stifle it.

This was, of course, a stupid notion: it stifled nothing. Glances of this nature will always find some clever escape, at the edge of vision. And one evening, as we played Rummy, the King burst out: 'Why do you keep looking at our faces and not at your cards, Merivel? You will not be able to tell from us whether either of us has the Jack or Ace of Spades you would like to put with the King and Queen you have already picked up.'

I apologised. I gave my attention to my Hand, which was by no means promising, and I predicted myself coming last again in the score – for the third time that evening. And I knew that I deserved at least this punishment, or one far worse. For I had begun to feel an intense *dislike* for myself, behaving as a Spy and an Inquisitor. I cursed Violet. I vowed that from the following day I would end my pitiful Vigil.

I did not seem able to end it.

Margaret had grown very fond of Bunting and it was sometimes the case, in the warm May weather, that she accompanied the King and Bunting on their walks about the park. When these had first begun I had only rejoiced to see Margaret out in the air once more, walking with a firm step and throwing sticks for the dog, and sometimes skipping along with the sheer joy of finding herself alive again. I had stood at my Library window and watched them – the two people I cherished most in my heart – and understood myself to be the most Fortunate of men to have them here, living and breathing by my side.

But now, when they announced a walk, I heard myself stammering out futile utterances (what Pearce once dubbed 'the freakish piffle that you sometimes spout, Merivel') such as: 'Ah, a walk! An excellent idea! I am much in need of exercise myself. I shall come with you.'

And so the three of us would set out, I mired in shame at my own ridiculousness and even blushing at it. And then, to compound it, I would either keep up a perpetual prattle about the weather and the wild flowers and the shapes of clouds and I know not what other Subject, to prevent them from talking to each other, or else I would let myself fall a little behind my beloved companions, to try to gauge, from the way they held themselves and the frequency with which they turned their heads towards each other, whether any Understanding was brewing up between them.

One morning, when the walk had taken us towards the Bear's compound and we were standing in a line regarding poor Clarendon, who sat motionless beneath a ragged ash tree in a heap of Sadness, Bunting suddenly took it upon herself to slither under the stockade fence and began to scamper towards him.

Margaret screamed. The King began calling urgently to the dog, but she only turned for a moment at the sound of His Majesty's voice, then went forward again, drawn on by the scent of the animal, wagging her feathery tail and stopping a mere few paces from the place where Clarendon sat.

Clarendon looked at Bunting. As I tried to fathom what might be running in the Bear's mind, he hauled his great weight onto his four feet and let out an angry roar.

I then realised that the King was attempting to climb up the heavy posts of the fence, which was designed precisely so that it cannot be climbed – by bear or man. Calling to him to desist, I began to run to where I knew the gate of the Compound to be. As I ran, I heard another roar come from the Bear and, not for the first time, cursed myself for bringing Clarendon to England, and saw some terrible Ruin falling upon me – all for some sentimental idea about the sorrows of a wild animal. The next noise I expected to hear was the snapping of Bunting's bones.

I reached the gate and put all my strength into drawing back the bolts. I could hear Bunting barking. Slowly I pushed open the heavy door. As I went in, I saw the Bear advance upon Bunting. I picked up a fallen branch of ash and agitated it madly, while shouting the dog's name. Bunting was low on her haunches, growling. Clarendon was three or four feet from her. In the midst of terror I admired the little dog's courage.

Then Bunting raised herself up and sped towards me. I dropped the ash twig and held out my arms. These little Spaniels can run fast and, almost before Clarendon could decide whether to follow her or not, I gathered Bunting to me. As I turned, I saw the Bear come lumbering forward. Holding the dog so close to my breast that I almost suffocated her, I panted back to the gate. I could smell the Bear now and hear its laboured breath. I knew that all could yet be lost, including my life, for the heaviness of the gate made it impossible to close with one hand.

But as I reached it and slipped out of the compound, other hands took hold of the bolts and began wrenching and pulling. I tripped and fell backwards on a tuft of grass, and saw Margaret and the King straining to draw the bolts into their housings. And when the task was complete and they knew that we were all safe, they fell into each other's arms and Margaret laid her head on the King's breast and wept.

He stroked her hair and comforted her. Then he turned to me, perching breathless on my grassy tuffet, with my bottom a little bruised and Bunting still clasped to my heart.

'Well done, Merivel,' he said. 'You saved the life of a Royal Dog once more. I believe I owe you some Reward.'

'You owe me nothing, Sir,' said I. 'You saved Margaret's life.'

I sit alone with the King.

Will has struggled along to my Withdrawing Room with a jug of Mead, causing the King to remark, upon the entrance of my decayed old Servant: 'Good evening, Gates. We see too little of you. May you not be more with us in the Dining Room?'

Will bows as he sets down the Mead, which almost topples and spills. He looks anxiously at me as he replies: 'Begging Your Majesty's pardon, but Sir Robert, and I too, feel I am not fit to serve there.'

'Not fit?' says the King, choosing, it seems, to become blind, all of a sudden, to Will's many infirmities. 'Have you not, for as long as I can remember, been the Master of this Household?'

Will smiles his foxy, sidelong smile. 'I am not the "Master", Your Majesty. I am the Servant.'

'In French you are the "Master": *Maître. Maître d'hôtel*, you see? And we would like to have you by us at mealtimes. It would remind us of the Old Days.'

'Oh, Sir, I know not what to say. I do fear spillage and muddle.'

'Well, never mind a little of that. It might be amusing. But let us suggest a simple role for you, so that we may avoid too much Calamity. You shall stand behind our chair, Gates. When a Plate arrives for us, you will move a little to the side and take it from the Footman's hands and set it before us. When we have finished with the Plate, you will take it up again and pass it to the Footman – and so on through the meal. How does this simple task appear to you?'

Again, Will looks at me, as if for guidance. I nod encouragingly, wondering nevertheless whether Will is capable of remaining Upright in one position for the long duration of a meal, but hold out my hand, gesturing for him to make his own reply.

He bows very low, so that I notice, for the first time, the top of his periwig is almost *bald* and find myself suddenly distressed by this, revealing as it does my stinginess and lack of vigilance towards the well-being of my servants.

'From tomorrow, Your Majesty,' says Will, empressing his arthritic right hand into an approximation of a Military Salute, 'I will take up my post. I shall not move from behind Your Majesty's chair, except to turn little sideways to take Your Majesty's Plate from the Footman, and to return it to him again.'

'*Voilà*,' says the King. 'An admirable Arrangement.'

We both attack the Mead. I know that the night is going to be long. I ask Will to bring from the kitchen some Caraway Cake and a dish of cherries.

The King produces for my perusal a letter from his brother the Duke of York, which berates him, albeit in a tolerant, brotherly way, for his 'too-long absence from urgent matters of State' and urges him to return to London without delay. The document further mentions 'tumultuous Petitions for the Recall of a Parliament, which, I remind you, Your Majesty has not entertained since that which attempted to sit at Oxford in 1681'.

'Parliament!' says the King. 'I am too *old* for parliaments, Merivel. For they must always be up and doing things, and suggesting Remedies for those Matters which go on perfectly well and so need none. And they are too fond of wars. I know that the people like to be left alone. They do not want False Remedies and they do not want any more wars. They want what I want: food in their bellies, comfortable nights, a little profitable Trade, a drop of Mead from time to time, a few inspiring sermons, a good death. Is this not so?'

'Yes,' I reply, 'I believe it is.'

I do not mention that Poverty is still a great scourge across the land, for I know that it is the King's opinion that Parliaments, crammed with Ambitious souls seeking their fortunes, do very little for Poverty and that he himself, by employing so many in his service and by his dispensation of Alms, and by his sheer love for his People, does more. Yet it has seemed to me, from riding about Norfolk to see my Patients, that the Poor have grown in number in recent times, for that they are more visible in the villages or on the roadside, begging or stealing, and I have heard it said that all the Workhouses round about are full to breaking. And in time, men will surely blame the King and look to him for some remedy.

I glance at the King who, by long Royal habit, sits very straight in a chair, but who is now slumped down in an attitude of great Dejection. I am about to suggest that we talk no more about Parliaments, when the King says: 'Guilt, Merivel. Now it claws me. Sometimes, even here at Bidnold, I wake in the night and think of all my transgressions and my betrayals, and then I cannot breathe . . .'

'There is no human life, Sir, free from Transgression.'

'That may be. But did you know, my friend, that I appropriated ninety per cent of the Dues from the Postal Service to pay for Barbara Castlemaine's Pension?'

'Well, no, I did not, Sir, but—'

'I did it for the sake of Quietness – that she would not nag me any more. But men have suffered because of it. They have lost what was rightly theirs. And a hundred other things have I done, which come to haunt me.'

'A mere hundred? I marvel at so few. Pearce once accused me of committing a hundred follies a week!'

A smile spreads across the King's countenance. It is a familiar smile, one that says 'this is why I like you, Merivel, why I *love* you, even, because you lighten what is heavy and make laughter from sorrow'.

But now I want to make some reply to this. I want to say: 'If you take my daughter from me, if you treat her as you treated my unfortunate wife, Celia, then I can no longer be your Fool; I shall become your Enemy.'

These words form endlessly in my mind, but do not force themselves into my mouth, and I tell myself that for all my deep anxiety on this score, I can, in truth, do nothing at present except to be patient and to see what Time brings forth.

An image of the King holding Margaret to him beside the Stockade and stroking her hair comes into my mind, but I force it away, telling myself to read nothing into it, only the King's kindness and readiness with comfort, after the moments of danger to us all and the near loss of a precious dog. I must not see Transgression where there is none.

Will reappears at this juncture with the Caraway Cake, apologising that there are no cherries, 'for that Cattlebury cannot send them up'.

'Why can he not send them up, Will?' I ask.

'Beg pardon, Sir?'

'You heard me perfectly well. Why cannot Cattlebury send up the cherries?'

'Well, Sir Robert, I cannot rightly say . . .'

'Perhaps I can "rightly say" that he cannot send them up, because he has eaten them?'

'Well, he did, Sir. But he ate them only because he had a little difficulty with his Stools, Sir, and a cherry will loosen the Stool, as you informed us, but he did not mean any harm.'

At this the King lets out a great roar of laughter. 'Oh,' he says, 'this has cheered me! *He did not mean any harm!* There is Anarchy in the kitchen, Merivel, but it is apparently quite harmless!'

'It is *not* harmless,' I say with unheralded but emphatic severity. 'Please tell Cattlebury, Will, that my patience is at an end. One more transgression of this kind, and—'

'And what, Sir?'

'It is the End of the Road. He will be cast out.'

Silence falls in the Withdrawing Room. The King and Will both regard me with astonishment. Then out of my mouth come the words that I wish to be heard elsewhere, but address instead, via Will, to my disobedient cook.

'Remind Cattlebury,' I say, 'that I am a man of good humour, a man to whom Loyalty towards those I care for and who depend upon me was ever a solemn pledge in my heart. But remind him also that my Loyalty can be tested too far! Please impress this fact upon him. I can be pushed to anger – as when I saw Farmer Sands whipping his Shire horse till it died. And Sands, in time, had to yoke himself to his plough to till his pitiful fields. And did I feel one jot of sorrow or pity for him? No, I did not. My anger had taken away all my compassion. And so it shall be, Will! So it shall be with Cattlebury, if I am tested too far.'

Under the burden of these unexpected words, Will sinks down onto the floor and his bald wig falls aslant his face. The King rises to help him to his feet.

I, too, rise up, but not to help Will, only to snatch a slice of Caraway Cake from the dish and cram it into my mouth, to stop myself from bursting into tears.

17

I could not for too long delay my promise to Violet Bathurst to cut out her Cancer.

Though I shied from the task, I knew that I had to discover in me some will to do it, before the Thing spread. For the thought of Violet dying alone in her dark chamber was a very sorrowful one. I do hold and believe that the deaths of those who have taken irrepressible pleasure in their moment-to-moment existence – in a world where many people seem sunk in a physical and spiritual twilight, or half-life – are to be especially mourned.

The Nurse I wanted to help with the Cutting was one Mrs McKinley, a bonny and kind Irishwoman, whose Catholic family had fled to England after the Protestant Settlements in Ireland in 1641. Mrs McKinley, now in her fifties and grown a little stout, had the gentlest, surest hands I have ever beheld in all my work with Nurses. More than this, her voice is of a great sweetness of tone and this, I have often observed, brings comfort to the Patient.

It also offers to me an accompaniment of amusement as I work, for that, in her Donegal accent, she addresses me as 'Sir Rabbit', and no matter how many times she says this, it always brings a smile to my lips and thus, though my fingers may be in a tangle of flesh and gore, I am afforded enough Lightness of Heart to be able to carry on.

To buy Opium for Violet, I first had to visit my most favoured

Apothecary, Mr Dunn, in Norwich, a member of the Worshipful Society of the Art and Mystery of Apothecaries.

Of this designation the King had observed that the word 'mystery' appeared to him to be 'an inconvenient noun', which should not belong there.

'One does not wish there to be any *mystery* in the matter,' he pointed out. 'One wishes, on the contrary, that the Apothecary's knowledge be proven, or at least theoretical, as opposed to hypothetical, let alone mired in the Unknown. Is this not so, Merivel?'

I agreed that it was. The King then announced that he would be interested to talk to Mr Dunn and to inspect his premises. We thus travelled to Norwich together in the King's coach, and by the time we got there a great press of people, recognising the King's Livery on his coachmen, had surrounded us.

I descended first and savoured the disappointment on the faces of the Crowd when they saw me (a mere Sir Rabbit) and not their Sovereign. But then I reached up my hand, and the King took it and descended in elegant style, notwithstanding the little limp that the obstinate Sore on his left leg has given him, and a great cry of rejoicing went up from the people assembled, and they reached out to try to touch the King, and a woman passed him her baby to hold in his arms.

I could see Mr Dunn, standing at the door of his Apothecary's Shoppe. I had not been able to give him any warning about the King's arrival, and when Dunn caught sight of his Sovereign, his body began to jerk in spasms of incredulity. He took off his Spectacles and put them on again, fearing his eyes were deceiving him. Then, suddenly bethinking himself of how he appeared that day, he cavorted into his Shoppe to remove his Wig and replace it with a better one.

Some time passed before we could make our way inside the Shoppe. Still holding the baby, the King embarked upon numerous conversations with the Crowd, enquiring after the Wool Trade in Norfolk and the Herring Fleets, and hearing how, in all honesty, the times were not very good 'for that people go short of money, Sir, after the hard winter storms, when the Fleets could not put out' and when 'many sheep had their breath frozen in their gullets by the ice and snow'.

I saw that the King listened attentively to these tales of dead sheep and unfished herrings, but offered no remedy. All he could find to say was: 'You must hold on. You people of Norfolk are stubborn and true. We are in May weather now. Better days are coming. You must hold on.'

When he said this, one man, a poor Fisherman, barged his way through the press of citizens to show the King his naked ribcage, which was so scantily clad with flesh, it could only put me in mind of Pearce's body just before he died. The man beat upon his ribs with his fists and cried out: 'I'm a beggar in Norwich now, Sir! Look at me! I had a Herring Boat at Yarmouth, but it was lost in the January tides and all my livelihood with it. And I have five children. Tell me how I am to "hold on"!'

At this the King passed the baby back to its mother and turned to me, snapped his fingers and said: 'Coins, Merivel! Give this poor Fellow a shilling or a half-crown immediately.'

Then, as I scrabbled in my pockets for my Purse, he said to the Fisherman, 'Sudden loss is part of Life, as I, who lost my Father so cruelly, know well. And all we can do is to bear it. But here . . . here is kind Sir Robert Merivel, who will furnish you with a shilling or two, and tonight you and your family will eat your fill.'

Hands reached out to me – not only the filthy hand of the Fisherman-Beggar – and in less than one minute I was obliged to part with every bit of money that I had, for in a Crowd you can-not give to one and ignore the rest. The reaching out to me for coins only ended when I turned my purse inside out, to show that I had not one penny more to give. Nobody thanked me. And when at last we were able to turn and walk into Mr Dunn's prem-ises, the King did not seem to have absorbed the fact that now I had no Means with which to buy the Opium I needed for Violet's

Cutting. All he said was: 'I do not like it when I am face to face with Poverty and Want.'

Suspended from the ceiling in Mr Dunn's Shoppe is a strange variety of Stuffed Creatures: an Alligator, a Turtle, an Eel and a brace of Toads.

When you enter here, the slight stench from these Exhibits, which have hung there for a goodly time, might incline you to turn and walk out again, and I saw the King's nostrils dilate, and he produced from his sleeve a handkerchief scented with Lavender water and held it to his nose awhile.

Then the scientific curiosity, which impelled him to start his own Laboratory at Whitehall and to give a Royal Charter to the Society for the Improvement of Natural Knowledge by Experiment, led him to forget any bodily inconvenience. He began to pick his careful way around Dunn's dark emporium, noting what the jars and galley pots and gourds contained, and setting aside his handkerchief to sniff at them. Then he suddenly turned to the Apothecary and asked: 'Where did you acquire your knowledge, Dunn? Was it properly come by?'

Adjusting his wig, Dunn stammered out that he had been apprenticed to an Apothecary as a boy of sixteen, and being 'both curious and reckless', had tried very many types of Physick on himself, 'to see what they would do to me . . .'

'How interesting,' said the King. 'Curiosity and recklessness may both be fine attributes in a man. I have often thought it.'

'Well, and in this way, Your Majesty,' said Dunn, stammering no more, 'when the Physicians prescribe, I can sometimes make a Correction, for that I have kept a Notebook of everything I tried, with all the quantities and manifestations of symptoms, and special notice of all the False Cures.'

'False Cures?'

'Sir Robert knows,' said Dunn, 'the quantity of Mountebanks in this country! They will sell anything, Sir, call it "a Beautiful and Efficacious Vomit", say, and sell no matter what for a shilling and sixpence. It might be Rat Poison. It might nearly kill you. But some Physicians, they scarcely know what preparation does what to what, so then the Apothecary's knowledge, if it can, must be the Corrective to a False Cure.'

The King nodded approvingly. *'Nullius in Verba,'* he said quietly. 'The Motto I gave to the Royal Society. *Take no man's word for it.* All should be done by proper experimentation. And you, Mr Dunn, seem to have followed this dictum admirably, by testing Compounds on yourself, though I warrant you may have got near to dying for it!'

'Well, I did, Sir. More than once. But here I am, alive. And what I like about my Trade is that there is no end to Medical Knowledge. Sir Robert, here, has taught me many things I did not know before.'

The King looked at me in mild astonishment. 'Has he? Has he really?'

'Many things.'

'Really? We know him chiefly as a Jester. A Jester and a Friend. But would you say he is a Good Physician?'

'Very good, Your Majesty.'

'Ah. How interesting. He once achieved a miraculous cure upon a favourite dog of mine, did you not, Merivel? But I think this was a Cure by Neglect, was it not?'

'Well, I would prefer to call it a Cure by Nature, Your Majesty. As the Great Fabricius said: *"Non dimenticare la Natura."* I merely gave Nature time to work.'

'While you drank some fine Alicante and ate some figs and slept . . .'

'Only in order to *pass* the time.'

'Ha! You see, Dunn, why we love this man. He keeps laughter alive. But now to our main Business. We need a plentiful supply of Opium and neither of us has any money, for we have given it all away to poor Fisherfolk and the like. Will you accept the King's Credit?'

I wished to work upon my Cutting of Violet's Cancer in bright daylight, so that I could properly see what I was doing.

I rode to Bathurst Hall and told her that I would come early on the morrow, and commanded her to have her bed removed nearer to the window.

'Mrs McKinley will accompany me,' I said, 'and I have stocked my bag with a great Quantity of Opium, so you will not feel any pain.'

Violet was sitting quietly in her *Salon* that day, doing Needlework, and finding her thus occupied cast me into gloom, for that I had never seen Violet Bathurst taken up by so static and conventional a Pastime.

'Violet,' I said, 'it hurts my soul to see you doing that. Pray let us have no more Embroidery once your Cancer is taken out!'

She raised her head and gazed at me sadly, holding out the work, which – unlike Celia's Needlework – was very inelegantly done, with bits and ends of thread hanging down in loops. 'Merivel,' she said, 'do not be so dense. Look what a novice I am. But I must learn to stitch in case, after the operation, it is *all* that I can do. Do you imagine that a woman with half a breast can play at Skittles?'

'Yes,' I said firmly. 'After a little Time of Recovery has passed. Indeed, I shall organise a party of Skittles at Bidnold and you can partner the King.'

Violet shook her head. 'You are dreaming,' she said. 'It will not come about.'

I rose early and collected Mrs McKinley from her house in Bidnold Village, and I noted how everything about her was clean and scrubbed, from her pink fingernails down to her polished boots.

I showed her the Opium I had got from Dunn and she said: 'Lord, Sir Rabbit, you could put an Army to sleep with this Quantity!' And an Image came to me of the Swiss Guards in the Place des Armes at Versailles, lined up in their ranks, and then falling over in an Opium-induced trance, one by one. And I smiled.

'I am only anxious that Lady Bathurst does not suffer too much,' I said. 'But I warn you, she is much given to screaming, it is in her nature and you must try not to be too distracted by this.'

'No, no, Sir. I shall not be distracted. All my children were Screamers. I just shut my ears and said my prayers, and all went into a lovely Quietness.'

We arrived at Bathurst Hall and straight away were shown up to where Violet lay on her bed in its new position near the window. She looked very pale and the fierce easterly light etched lines on her skin that I had not noticed before. When I bent over her she reached up and pulled me towards her. 'Merivel,' she said, 'I am afraid . . .'

'It will be quick, Violet,' I said. 'In less than five minutes it will be over. We shall then stay by you while you sleep.'

I had commanded that a fire be lit in the room and a cauldron of water set on it to heat, and this had been done as I had asked. While I positioned a chair near the bed and prepared my Scalpel, Mrs McKinley mixed a good quantity of the Opium powder with Brandy to make Laudanum and Violet swallowed this down. I watched her eyes flicker as it began to enter her blood.

Mrs McKinley then gently removed the top part of Violet's nightgown and took out clean muslin rags and washed the area of the Cutting in hot water and then with Tincture of Witch Hazel. After this she lifted Violet's arm and cleaned that also, saying, ''Twill be Nothing, My Lady. You shall see. In a trice it will be gone.' With the cleaning done, she laid a square of linen under the arm, strapped Violet's wrists to the bedposts and begged her to stay as still as she was able.

At the door stood Violet's maid, Agatha, a pretty dimpled girl, torn, I could see, between wanting to stay with her Mistress and desiring to flee. I turned to her and said: 'Agatha, go downstairs and heat a Warming Pan. The shock of a Cutting can make a person very cold. I shall call to you when I want it brought here. Find woollen blankets and bring them too.'

The girl curtseyed and fled away. I looked over at Mrs McKinley.

'We shall give the Laudanum a little more time,' I said, 'then we shall begin.'

Mrs McKinley pressed a white linen cap onto her head and rolled up her sleeves. She took Violet's hand in hers, gently stroking the palm. This stroking seemed to calm Violet, and we saw her eyes close and heard her breathing become deeper.

I raised the Scalpel. I told Mrs McKinley to press upon the breast, to draw the skin tight for the Cutting. As she did so, the Thing seemed to enlarge itself and I saw now that some small outcrop of it extended down into Violet's armpit, and this dismayed me, for I thought it would be a clean round Nub I was taking out, as if removing an eyeball from its socket, and now I understood that my Scalpel would have to make a second cut and then a third.

Mrs McKinley saw this too. 'I think 'tis more than it at first seemed, Sir Rabbit,' she whispered to me. 'Look there. And you will have to get it all.'

I took a breath. I cannot ever cut into another person's body without remembering how I had to hack deep into Katharine's body to deliver Margaret, and in consequence I remain calm, for I know that nothing could terrify me as profoundly as that operation did.

I made two swift cuts, like a cross, in the centre of the Cancer. Not much blood flowed. I lifted back the skin and investigated how deep I would have to go to bring out the lump of Cancerous matter, which was mottled purple and white in its colour and looked to me like some Sea Creature clinging to a rock pool.

Violet had begun to moan. Mrs McKinley spoke to her softly, telling her that the worst would soon be over.

I began the cutting. My blade went deep, circling the Cancer. Mrs McKinley dabbed at the flowing blood with her muslin rags. Violet began crying out in agony and her body arched and moved, so that my hand was jolted and the blade stabbed deeper than I had intended. Violet screamed. The scream was so loud and distressing to my head, it was as if Sound suddenly got in the way of Vision and blurred it. I blinked. With one hand Mrs McKinley was trying to hold Violet still and with the other swabbing blood from the wound.

'Try a prayer?' I hissed to Mrs McKinley.

'Oh, yes, a prayer. I will, Sir.'

She began a very low mumbling to God, asking him to give us Quietness.

I blinked again and turned the scalpel so that now I was cutting – or hoped I was – *underneath* the Cancer.

'I am almost there, Violet,' I said. 'I almost have it out . . .'

'No!' Violet cried. 'Let it alone! Close it up, Merivel. I can bear no more!'

'My Lady,' said Mrs McKinley. 'Sir Rabbit must take it all out, or it might grow again.'

'Let it grow!' cried Violet. 'I'm old and ugly now! Let it smother me and take me away with it!'

Mrs McKinley acted to swiftly to pour more Laudanum into Violet's mouth and this – more than the prayer, I shall admit – quietened her. I took up the muslin and swabbed and swabbed, to get the blood away. Then, probing with my finger, I felt the Cancer loosen from the flesh on one side. I cut again underneath and it loosened more. Blood ran over my hand.

Two more cuts and the Thing was loose. With my Spathomele I prised it out and set it in a glass dish. Pressing a wad of Muslin hard on the wound, I stared at the Cancer and I thought how strange and terrible it was that the body, in its darkness and secrecy, produces Additions that can bring it to the grave.

Violet was quiet now, her breathing shallow. Dearly I wished that I could sew up the wound and there would be an end to the Cutting, but I knew that my labours were not done. In the armpit lay two Satellites of the main Cancer and these could not be left in Violet's body.

I took up the Scalpel again. I had promised that the whole Cutting would take no more than five minutes, but my struggles with the elusive Satellites took more than thirty-five, for they, it seemed, were welling over with blood and I could not cut without pausing while Mrs McKinley swabbed and swabbed.

By the time I came to sew up the skin, Violet was pale with deep Shock and was hiccuping violently, and both Mrs McKinley and I began to fear she would be seized by Convulsions, or that her heart would cease.

Together we bandaged the wounds, then we cleaned our hands and arms with black Soap in hot water, and I called for Agatha to bring the warming pan and the blankets. We untied Violet's wrists and laid her right arm by her side, but placed the left arm on the pillow, away from the wounds.

Mrs McKinley, touching Violet's forehead with her strong hands, whispered to me, 'Lord, Sir, but she is terrible cold . . .'

Agatha came in, and when she saw the bloody rags all around and her Mistress pale as a Ghost, and the Cancerous tumours in the dish, almost fainted clean away. I took the warming pan from her and wrapped a blanket round it, and told Agatha to bring more hot water and bowls of Chocolate for me and Mrs McKinley.

Both the square of linen and the sheet underneath Violet were crimson and damp with blood, and Mrs McKinley and I knew that we had to get them away. But here was a difficult task, for the pain of movement would be very great for Violet. I put my arm under her right shoulder and neck, and lifted her forward, and Mrs McKinley peeled back the linen and the bloody sheet, then I laid her down again and raised her back and her buttocks, so that the sheet could come out. Then we spread out clean linen and pressed soft Pillows round the wound, and began to try to get her warm, setting the warming pan near her feet and covering her with the Woollen blankets.

Into her mouth Mrs McKinley dribbled yet more Laudanum. The hiccups continued for another ten minutes. Then they stopped and Violet lay still and quiet before us. I lifted her wrist and felt for a pulse, and got it, faint, but ticking there, as the morning began slowly to pass.

Mrs McKinley took off her white cap and wiped her brow with it. 'Lord, Sir Rabbit,' she said, 'the Chocolate will be a lovely thing.'

We sat out all the daylight hours in Violet's room. The sun glanced on us, then hid itself behind cloud and the room darkened, as if promising rain.

My mind kept wandering to Bidnold and what the King and Margaret might be doing there, but I tried to put these ugly thoughts away. I knew that I had to remain with Violet until the morrow.

I watched her face, once almost beloved to me. She snored in her Laudanum sleep. I said in a low voice to Mrs McKinley, 'It was not done as cleanly as I had hoped.'

'Well,' she said, 'it was as difficult as any I've seen, including my own.'

'You had a Cancer in your breast?'

'I did. But it was cut out of me long ago, before I met you. And look at me, Sir Rabbit. Strong as a horse. I shall die ancient in my bed. You can lay a fat Wager on it.'

18

We passed a most wretched night, with Violet starting to vomit up the Laudanum she had swallowed and then, because the quantity of Physick in her body had diminished, being afflicted with unbearable pain.

We cleaned her and tried to soothe her and get her comfortable, but her body was still icy cold and her lips dry and cracked. We gave her water and Mrs McKinley fumigated the Bedchamber with Frankincense, and then went down to the kitchen to make what she called 'a Potato Broth', such as her family used to consume in Donegal, and always efficacious for 'cure of poison'.

I sat alone with Violet. I kept the fire brightly burning and tried to put more coverings on the bed, but Violet said they were too heavy on her wound and she could endure nothing touching it.

To try to take her mind off present sufferings, I invited her to tell me more about her night with the King and I did see a frail smile appear on her wounded features.

'Well, he is very talkative during the Act,' she said. 'And I do adore sexual discourse – as I remember that you do too, Merivel.'

'Sometimes . . .' I said.

'But afterwards, when we had quite exhausted several Positions, he began to talk about the Queen, and how he has betrayed her with a hundred women, and how he has pacified her, through all the years, with Religious Gifts.'

Violet then pointed over at her bureau near the fire. 'See the little wooden box on it, Merivel. Bring it here and I will show you something.'

I fetched the box, which was finely made in the shape of a Sea Chest and studded with small Brass nails. Violet told me to open it, which I did, and found inside, on a lining of blue velvet, a curl of white hair.

'It belonged to Bathurst,' said Violet. 'He bought it in Rome for a large sum. As you recall, he was a mad and credulous man. He had been told that the hair in the box had been cut from the head of St Peter and he chose to believe it.'

'Ah, it is hair, then, that has survived almost seventeen hundred years?'

'Precisely so. How could anything Human not perish and turn to dust after all that time? I pointed this out to Bathurst, but he was unmoved. He used to mumble his prayers over it. He used to ask it to bring him luck at the Horse Races.'

'And did it so?'

'I cannot remember, Merivel. He was the worst of Gamblers, until he went mad and forgot about it. But I bethought myself, after the King left, that his Queen, in her Catholic piety, might believe it too. So I want you to give it to him to give to her – to atone for all that he did with me of a wild and filthy nature!'

'I will,' I said stroking Violet's forehead. Then I said, in a hushed and choked voice: 'Violet, tell me something else. Do you really believe that the King will try to seduce my daughter?'

'He does not *try* to seduce anyone. He succeeds.'

'Will he not think Margaret is too young?'

'I have no idea, my friend. But what can it really matter? To lose your Virginity to the King of England . . .'

'It matters greatly to me! When I remember the misery that it brought to Celia.'

'Celia was a stupid girl, Merivel. I always marvelled that you had any feeling for that mousy and dull creature – especially when you had me to attend so ardently and efficaciously to the needs of your prick. But Margaret is not credulous and weak, as Celia was. She will not let herself suffer.'

Mrs McKinley returned at this moment with the Potato Broth, so this conversation had to cease.

We raised Violet up a little in the bed. I could see that Dawn was creeping towards us beyond the windows. I spooned the broth into Violet's mouth, and prayed she might keep it in her and not vomit it up again. Then we laid her down again, and I touched her cheek and felt that the good Broth had warmed her a little. The scent of Frankincense in the room was heady and strong, and I felt myself yearning for sleep.

At eight o'clock, before leaving Bathurst Hall, I went down into the vast Kitchen, where, in times past, meals for thirty or forty people were prepared and the ovens seemed to be roaring day and night, and the savour of roasted meat was so strong, it used to seem to me as though you might live only on this – on the fragrance alone.

Now all was very silent, with every surface scrubbed and cold. Violet's cook – 'Chef Chinery' as he likes to style himself – stood looking out of the window, wondering, it seemed, what to make of the breaking day and how to pass it.

'Good day to you, Chinery,' said I. 'Are you well?'

'As well as Time permits, Sir.'

'Good enough. Now, *permit me* to give you some orders. Lady Bathurst's Nurse, Mrs McKinley, will be staying until Her Ladyship recovers sufficiently to be nursed by Agatha. Nurse McKinley made a very efficacious Potato Broth for Lady Bathurst last night, which calmed her digestion, so please ensure there is a plentiful supply of potatoes.'

'There are always potatoes. The earth of Norfolk heaves with them.'

'Good. I would also request that you make sustaining meals for Mrs McKinley . . .'

'Irish, be she?'

'Yes, she is originally from County Donegal.'

'Then all she will need is potatoes. That be what they live on there.'

I stared at Chinery, a large, ageing, vexed-looking Norfolk man, who had had an unaccountable fondness for the old mad Earl and has not been happy in his work since Lord Bathurst's death.

'Pray do not assume,' I said, 'that Mrs McKinley will be happy to live on potatoes. Her nursing work will be arduous. She will need Meat and Bread and Fish and fruit and Ale. She must be kept strong.'

Chinery returned to his gazing out upon the stable yard, quite as though he had not heard me.

'Chinery!' I said sharply. 'Please pay attention. I am very tired. I would like to take some Coddled eggs and bread and Coffee before I leave the Hall. Please make sufficient for Mrs McKinley, too, and send them up forthwith.'

I stayed just long enough to see Chinery turn and nod his assent. Then I strode out of the kitchen, attempting to hold my head high, and pleased I was not wearing a Sword, over which I might have tripped and fallen.

On my arrival home, longing to sleep, I was immediately taken aside by the King, who told me he had a Matter of great Importance to discuss with me.

At once my exhaustion fled and was replaced with a terrible agitation.

We repaired to the Library, where the King began pacing about, till I was giddy with his coming and going.

At last he halted and said: 'I have decided, Merivel. I cannot stay at Bidnold any longer.'

My lips were dry and my voice weak as I asked: 'Has anything *happened* while I have been away, Sir?'

'No. Nothing has happened, except my Conscience has been pricked.'

'May I ask by what, Your Majesty?'

'By all that I am neglecting. I cannot go on in this vein. The Duke of York is right: things will come to ruin if I do. I am the King. I must return and govern.'

'This is very sudden, Sir . . .'

'Not really. Ever since my brother's letter I have not felt at my ease. There is so much in the Land that seems to be falling apart for want of money. I must set about trying to raise it, by some means.'

'How will you raise it, Sir?'

'By further Loans from King Louis, I suppose. Unless some alternative can be conjured from the Air, or you yourself have an inexhaustible supply of half-crowns. Oh, but listen, Merivel, let us talk no more of it. Shall we not have one more happy evening at dinner and Shuttlecock games with the excellent Prideaux family before I depart? Will you invite them on Thursday?'

'Yes . . .'

'And perhaps, this time, Margaret will be strong enough to join in the play?'

'I am not sure, Sir.'

'I think she will be. She can play on my team. Now, tell me, Merivel, how is Lady Bathurst?'

We both sat down. I was yearning to see Margaret, but I was forced to remain with the King in the Library, to give an account of Violet's operation.

He listened gravely. He said that he considered Violet Bathurst 'an exceptional woman, of wondrously furious desire'. He asked me if she would survive the Cutting of the Cancer.

'She may survive this, Sir,' I said. 'But the Cancer may return. I have, for the moment, done everything I can.'

It was then that I remembered the Box with the curl from St Peter's head, and I fetched this and gave it to the King, and told him it was a gift from Violet for the Queen.

He lifted out the curl and sniffed it. Then he wound it round his long index finger and examined it.

'I am most interested in the role of Superstition and Delusion in a human life,' he said. 'These things are very easy to deride, but I do not set them aside lightly. I have seen how the Queen is comforted by the Relics she has amassed. She kisses them with such passion! In her mind they are the Loving God made Manifest. It matters not that they may be some old knuckle bones from a Poorhouse graveyard in Kent, or a scrap of linen from a Bazaar in Egypt. What matters is what they are *to her.*'

'I agree with you, Sir. Montaigne says that the end of Delusion may be the end of Joy.'

I was then moved to recount to the King how, long ago, the present of an Indian Nightingale in a gilded cage had been given to me, and how I was most moved and fascinated by this bird, and kept trying to get it to sing to me by playing my oboe to it.

'But at length,' I said, 'comes my Friend John Pearce, the Quaker, and says to me, "Merivel you are a Dupe. That is not an Indian Nightingale. That is a common Blackbird with a few painted feathers!" And I saw that Pearce was right and that my beloved Indian Nightingale was no such thing – and nor, perhaps, does an Indian Nightingale exist at all on this Earth? But yet I had savoured my State of Delusion and the ending of it caused me much grief.'

'Ah,' said the King. 'Of course. You had held Wonder in your hands and then you lost it.'

We both, then, were sunk in a silent, contagious Gloom. After a while the King replaced the curl from St Peter's head on its blue velvet bed and closed the box and said, 'The Queen will like this. I shall tell her that a Priest in Norwich – to which city, long ago, St Peter travelled and made friends with a Barber-Surgeon – put it into my hands.'

We laughed at this and then the King said: 'All is in the *story*, Merivel. No artefact can come to its full significance without the telling of the tale.'

On Thursday evening the 23rd of May, came the Prideaux family and we all dressed ourselves in our finest Finery, and one of my

French-adjusted satin coats, with its cascade of Shoulder-Ribbons, was both mocked and admired.

I had had a long talk with Cattlebury. He seemed somewhat chastened after his eating of the Cherries and ready to put his heart into a fine Banquet for the King's last evening. A quantity of Trout was ordered, and Capons and Hazel Nuts, and a Shoulder of Mutton and other delicacies to which I knew the King to be partial, and some fine wines were brought up from the cellar.

The dinner was very successful and splendid. At my command a hundred candles had been lit, so that a veritable fire danced and flickered all around the room, and when I looked at all the faces lit by this fire, what I saw on them was happiness. Even on Will's face, as he stood at his post behind the King's chair, wearing Livery now far too big for his shrunken body, I noticed a foolish smile, which he was unable to suppress, except when he took up a plate from the Footman to set it before the King, and this he did with most morose Concentration.

Margaret was wearing a turquoise gown, with turquoise ribbons in her auburn hair. She seemed to blush a great deal, as though at her own beauty, and I marvelled that I, with my flat nose and my Hog's Bristles and my fat, speckled stomach, could be father to such a lovely girl.

After Dinner, too weighed down by food and drink to play at Shuttlecock, we began on a game of Blind Man's Buff in the Withdrawing Room and got great mirth from watching him or her who was the Blindfold Catcher staggering about on my carpet from Chengchow, while we ran and hid behind chairs and curtains, and called out taunts and provocations.

When it was the King's turn to be the Catcher, he declared that he could recognise each one of us by our Smell and, because we could not hide from our own Perfume, it did indeed come about that he caught and identified us more quickly than any other Catcher, and I thought how it seems to be his gift to know people by their scent, or their gait or by their breathing, and sometimes to ascertain, with strange precision, what is in their minds.

When we were tired of the Buff, we made up two tables for Rummy, and a Mead was served with delicate Vanilla biscuits, crafted by Cattlebury, and it came about that Sir James Prideaux was revealed as a true Master of the game and outdid us all, and collected to himself a great pile of the ha'pennies for which we were playing.

'Ah,' said Sir James, laughing as he gathered up his money, 'this is excellent! Now I shall afford to take us all into Cornwall once again, and this time, Margaret, you shall come with us.'

'And see Puffins,' said Penelope.

'And collect Cowrie shells!' said Mary.

'But eat no shrimps!' said Arabella.

Margaret blushed and smiled, but, to my surprise, said nothing. At this moment the King stood up and walked over to where Margaret sat, and raised her up by the hand, then bowed to me and said: 'I did not tell you beforehand, Merivel, for fear that you would try to dissuade me, but I have suggested to Margaret that a place at Court be found for her and she has consented to come – if your blessing be given.'

I sat very still and suddenly cold in my chair, while all the Prideaux family gaped with wonder at this announcement.

'Why . . .' said Sir James, accidentally letting fall a cascade of his ha'pennies, 'that is wonderful, Sir. Wonderful for Margaret . . . and for Sir Robert . . .'

'The Duchess of Portsmouth has written to me,' the King continued, 'asking that a new young Lady-in-Waiting be found for her, so this seems to fit very nicely. I shall go to Whitehall tomorrow and set all in hand, as to lodgings and Allowances and so forth, and then, if her Father is willing, Margaret will come to London at the beginning of June. May I assume your consent, Merivel?'

Everybody looked over towards me. Only little Penelope, I think, understood what I was feeling, for she came to me and solemnly took my hand in hers.

Still holding Penelope's hand, I stood up and bowed to the

King. 'I am honoured. This is . . . a great Honour,' I said. But my voice came out very thinly, as though I might have been choking on a Parsnip. 'But you will not be offended, I trust, if I feel obliged to ask Margaret to say – before Your Majesty and before all the Company here assembled – whether it is an honour she truly wishes to accept.'

The room fell silent. The hour was late and what candles were still alight dripped, with a steady ooze, into their sconces.

'I do,' said Margaret.

I stand in thin moonlight by Clarendon's compound and look for him in the near darkness. I can hear him breathing, but I cannot see him.

Then I feel a Shadow at my side and I know that it is Pearce.

'Well,' he says in his ghostly voice, 'what are you going to do, Merivel?'

'There is nothing I can do,' I reply.

I hear Pearce sigh – or perhaps it is the sighing of Clarendon, or the sighing of the Ash trees in the Bear's Stockade . . .

'This bitter night had to come,' whispers Pearce. 'The King will betray you now.'

Part Three
The Great Consolation

19

Margaret has gone.

I accompanied her to London and saw her installed in the Duchess of Portsmouth's apartments in Whitehall Palace.

Margaret's room is not a dark attic space, like Celia's, but a spacious chamber, with a high bed hung with blue Brocade, and a carved mahogany fireplace, and a table laid out with silver Brushes and Combs. I stood at the window of this room and looked down upon what she was going to see each day, and I saw in a little courtyard a stone fountain in the shape of a Nymph, pouring the water from an Amphora, and the sight of this innocent figure gladdened my heart. In the basin of the fountain there were some bright golden fish, swimming around the feet of the Nymph.

The Duchess of Portsmouth, the King's beloved 'Fubbs', came to us and was very gracious and kind to us, and took Margaret in her arms and kissed her, and told her that her life would henceforth be a beautiful life. And I could see that Margaret believed her, and was full of joy and excitement, and I did not want to disturb this happiness by showing the Fears and Suspicions that still crawled in my mind.

Fubbs may lead a 'beautiful life', but she is not a beautiful woman, and this lack of beauty in her only augmented my agitation that the King could look to my daughter for Satisfaction – or had already done so. Fubbs is short and plump, with big eyes in a round face and a little beaky nose. She reminded me of a Wood Pigeon.

I said to the Wood Pigeon: 'Margaret is all I have.'

She came and took my hand and said: 'The women in my care are my little ducklings and I am their tender Mother Duck.'

And I laughed to hear her choose a bird metaphor, when I had just labelled her a Pigeon, and at this moment the King appeared and we all fell into our bows and curtseys, and I felt my heavy Sword jangling about me, like a loose bridle bit on a horse, and the King said to his Fubbsy: 'Margaret taught me to play Rummy. Now I am very good at it. She will teach you, if you are nice to her.'

The King was wearing a sober brown coat and looked tired, and his limp seemed to have grown more pronounced since he left Bidnold. To me he said:

'I miss Norfolk, Merivel. How is Clarendon?'

'As ever he is, Sir,' I said. 'He is lonely.'

He looked at me with tenderness. 'You will be lonely, now that I have stolen Margaret from you,' he said, 'so what are you going to do?'

I did not know how to reply. The echo of Pearce's ghostly words I heard in this question troubled me for a moment. But more than this, I had not been able to think what I *would* do, beyond grieving for Margaret. I had had an image of myself, standing at the Bear's compound for hour upon hour, watching the animal's sad perambu-lations round the Stockade fence, but not knowing how to improve his lot, or mine. But then I heard myself say: 'I have an invitation to travel to Switzerland, Your Majesty.'

'Ah,' said the King. 'Very good. But can you be certain that no Giraffes will come there?'

'Giraffes!' said Fubbs. '*Que voulez-vous dire?*'

'Merivel knows what I mean. He would not want any long-necked thing spoiling his revels.'

'What "revels", Papa?' said Margaret.

'Why none,' said I, 'but it is merely that, as His Majesty knows, on the subject of Giraffes one cannot be too careful!'

At this, both I and the King fell to laughing, while the women looked at us with that profound irritation one feels at being excluded from a secret joke.

Then the moment came for me to say Goodbye to Margaret.

This I had dreaded exceedingly, both for the sadness of it and the fear that I would make myself ridiculous by weeping. So I readjusted my Sword and stepped boldly up to Margaret, as though presenting myself with punctuality at a meeting of the Overseers of the Poor of Bidnold Parish, and took her hand in mine and bade her take good care of herself, and to write me letters as often as she could.

But she drew me to her and put her arms round my neck and said: 'I love you, my dear Papa.' And this threatened to weaken my resolve not to cry, so I held her for a moment and kissed her cheek, and then I turned away from her and, after making a clattering kind of Obeisance to the King and Fubbs, left the room.

And so I returned once more (after so many Departures, so many Returns) to Bidnold and sat in my Library, sipping wine, trying to advance my mind in the direction of *doing something*, but failing utterly. All I did was sit there drinking. I was in such a Trance of Inactivity that it felt to me as though I might never move again and be turned to stone in my chair.

After a long while of this petrified Stillness, I thought how difficult it had become for me to believe that *I had ever done anything*. When Will came in to light the fire, as a cool summer evening fell, I said to him, 'Tell me, Will, have I ever moved from my position here in this chair?'

'What are you talking about, Sir Robert?' asked Will.

'It feels to me as though I had sat here always . . . and all of Existence had gone on without me.'

Will shook his head in perplexity. Fussing with his tinder box he said: 'Well, you once rode to London with a brace of Roasted Quail in your coat pocket, and we could never quite remove the stain of them. But if you do not believe you have ever done anything, why do you not read a little from the Book you wrote about your life? There must be some *Doings* set down there.'

I looked towards the escritoire, where I had hidden *The Wedge*. I had in recent times given it very little thought, but now I was suddenly anxious to peruse it, if only to reassure myself that I had had the capacity to live through momentous happenings and still breathe.

While Will's fire broke into hesitant life, I walked stiffly to the desk and opened the drawer where *The Wedge* lay. I picked it up, all dusty and corrupted by mouse droppings and fly shit as it was, and returned to my chair. Will regarded me anxiously.

'Is there, in your Book, Sir, any mention of me?' he asked.

'Yes, Will, there certainly is,' said I. 'Many a mention. And look here, near the end, here is a letter, copied out, that you wrote to me when I proposed a visit to Bidnold, never imagining that it would be mine again, yet yearning to see it once more.'

'I remember that visit, Sir.'

'Do you want to hear what you wrote?'

'Yes . . .'

'Here it is, then: "*Oh, Sir Robert! You cannot know how much we are all here every one of us who remember you filled with joy at this great Coming Event, which is your arrival at Bidnold. Please, Sir, be assured we will make all very fit and Nice for this fortunate Returning . . .*"'

'My sentences were not very good,' commented Will.

'Your sentences were excellent.'

'"Fortunate Returning" is not correct, is it, Sir?'

'I think it is marvellously correct and apt. For, if you remember, Will, this was a Fortunate Return. I had thought the house lost to me, and then the King arrived, with a great many dogs, and it was on that day that he restored to me the West Tower and told me it was mine for ever.'

'I shall never forget the rejoicing in my heart, Sir Robert . . .'

'Many times I took Margaret up there, to that white space and showed her the Fantails on the window ledge and the great view of the Park . . .'

'And I *knew* it would all be yours again one day. I knew His Majesty would give it back to you.'

'Well, I did not know it. I did not dare to hope. But now it is mine again. Only Margaret is gone.'

'At least, thank the Lord, she is not gone to Heaven.'

'No. But I am afraid of what will happen to her, Will. The Court has brought a thousand young women to ruin. I am so afraid that my limbs seem to have adhered to this chair.'

I managed to consume a little food at supper, but I kept thinking to myself, 'I need more than food and wine to console me: I need some kind of Oblivion . . .'

Then, I remembered that I still had in my possession a fair quantity of the Opium I had bought from Apothecary Dunn for Violet Bathurst's operation, and without further consideration went to my room and got it, and made up a jar of strong Laudanum.

I undressed myself, put on my nightshirt and got into bed. Outside, the bright June night was still lively with birdsong. I opened *The Wedge* and began to turn the pages, looking for every mention of Margaret. Here and there I saw that my Handwriting was very poor and slapdash, as though I had been in a terrible haste to set things down.

Sipping the Laudanum, I forced myself to read the passage where I cut into Katharine's womb to deliver Margaret. And though it was very terrible in its detail, it created in me a kind of rapture, knowing that I and I alone had brought Margaret alive and breathing into this world, and, but for my medical skills, the baby would have died. And so I thought, this I did, at least. In the paltry sum of my life, there is this one marvellous thing: I saved Margaret from death.

I sipped more Laudanum. I imagined myself young again (or

almost young, at forty years of age) and lifting my daughter into my arms, and I saw great beauty in the scene, as though it had been captured there and then by an Artist in a painting, and the light in the painting was golden and soft.

When I opened my eyes from this Reverie, I saw that the veritable night had come. I listened for the sound of Clarendon wailing in the darkness, but could hear nothing. I knew that sleep was about to enfold me and I laid my head down. The last thing I remembered was the sound of *The Wedge* falling onto the floor.

When I woke, I did not know where I was or what was happening.

I heard a voice saying: 'Wake up, Sir Robert. Wake up!'

I saw dawn light at the window and fancied myself in some room at Whitehall, with a fountain outside and golden fish swimming in circles.

'Men are here,' said the voice, 'and very angry. You must get dressed and come down.'

'What men?' I managed to say.

'Village folk. Farmers. And they have Weapons about them in the shape of pitchforks and shovels, and some kind of Gun.'

'*What?*'

'Come along, Sir. I smell that you have been quaffing Brandy, but you must get up, or I fear they will march in here.'

'Where am I? Am I in London?'

'No. You are at Bidnold. Now, I have your coat and Breeks, Sir. Kindly step out of the bed so that you can put them on.'

I now realised that the voice belonged to Will. I looked up at his crumpled face and a shiver of remembrance came into into my afflicted mind of all the Laudanum I had sipped as the night fell, and what dreams and wonders I had beheld.

But now those wonders were well and truly fled. I took Will's outstretched hand and pulled myself into a sitting position, and I saw the room turning about me in wild circles.

'Will,' I said, 'I am not well. I cannot get up.'

'You must get up. Or do you want to be pitchforked in your bed?'

'Pitchforked in my bed? You are talking Nonsense, Will. You belong in a Bedlam. Now, kindly let me sleep . . .'

'No. For once you must do as I say, Sir Robert. Something grave has occurred.'

'Something grave?'

'Alas, it has.'

'What time is it?'

'Just before six. Please hold yourself up, Sir Robert, while I put your Breeches on.'

I sat there swaying, wondering whether I was going to vomit upon Will's ancient head, while he stuffed my nightshirt into my Breeks.

'What grave thing can occur so early in the morning? I am not usually awake at this hour . . .'

'I know you are not, Sir.'

'I have always imagined that nothing could veritably happen until I was . . . Now hand me the pisspot, Will. I am going to be sick.'

Will scrabbled to find the pot and held it before me just in time to receive a stream of brown vomit, stinking of Brandy and Physick. This was as horrible a vomiting as any I had ever made, and I felt sorry for Will who had to see it and smell it, but its effect was salubrious, for after it my mind felt a little more clear.

Wiping my mouth and blowing my nose, I said: 'What "grave thing" has visited us, Will? Is Lady Bathurst dead?'

'Not Lady Bathurst. But a sheep.'

'A sheep?'

'Yes, Sir.'

'And why am I being woken for this? Do not sheep die all the time? I seem to remember that in the Bible they are always tangling themselves in Thorn Bushes or else being Sacrificed . . .'

'It is your Bear, Sir Robert. Escaped from the Pound and killing livestock. Now, stand up, please, and put on your wig. Your hair is very distressed.'

I stood, while Will brushed my wig and put it on me.

'There must be a mistake,' I said. 'The Stockade Fence is mighty strong and I have never seen the Bear attempt to climb it.'

'Well, it is out somehow. Now you must face the farmers' anger.'

I went shakily down the stairs. My legs felt as though they would buckle under my weight. In the hall I saw a group of five men, carrying forks and shovels, and with one among them hoisting a Blunderbuss upon his shoulder.

When they saw me they all – without any courtesy or politeness – began to talk at once, telling me that a Wild Beast was roaming their fields and that they were holding me accountable and would be presenting Bills for each and every loss. As they carried on shouting at me, they threw down onto the stone flags of the hall the bloodied carcass of a sheep.

'I cannot tell what you are saying if you all speak at once,' I said. 'Am I to understand that my pet animal, Clarendon – so named by His Majesty the King – has done harm?'

'He may be your pet animal, Sir Robert,' said the Blunderbuss man, 'but he is a Beast! Look at this ewe. Mauled and half eaten! 'Twill be our children next.'

I looked down at the angry faces. I had met these folk before, several times over the years, but never in my house, and it was only here, in my grand Hallway, that I understood how poor they were, with their clothes bundled together out of rags, and their boots heavy and worn. They stank of the earth and of unwashed flesh. A new wave of sickness rose in me and I sat down quickly on the stairs.

'What would you have me do?' I said weakly. 'As you see, I am not well today . . .'

'We cannot help that, Sir. Will you let us be ruined, with all our livestock taken? Will you let our children be killed?'

'No. Of course that should not be. The Bear must be recaptured.'

'Recaptured? *Recaptured?* Pray, do not insult us, Sir Robert. If you put him back, what will he do but come out again?'

'I will build the fence higher.'

'And meanwhile? Sheep, goats, chickens . . . All gone into his great maw. And us sinking into poverty.'

I looked helplessly at the men and they looked helplessly at me. 'What would you have me do?' I said again.

'He must die,' said Mr Blunderbuss, whose name I now remembered was Patchett, and who lived on a poor farm just outside Bidnold Village, where the fields were choked with Ragwort, and all his toil was in trying to get this Ragwort out, so that it would not afflict his cattle with Gripe, but every year it returned. 'We are sorry about it,' Patchett continued, 'if he was your Pet. But a Bear is a mighty strange Pet, and he must be put away.'

I rubbed my eyes. My sickness was passing a little. Poor Clarendon, thought I, your 'protector' has failed you. I sold a Sapphire ring that you could live a better life, but I did not contrive it well. All I gave you was a little piece of ground and some trees for shade, but you were an Outcast and knew no joy.

I stood up. 'I shall come with you,' I said, 'to help you find him. But he must be despatched cleanly. He must not suffer. Do you have powder for your Blunderbuss?'

'Yes, Sir.'

'Use that, then. I know the power of your weapon. I saw a man's head blown off with that on the Dover Road.'

The men mumbled among themselves at this, as though they thought that I, being wealthy and pampered, had seen nothing disagreeable in my whole existence. I heard myself sigh.

Will was still at my side and I sent him to fetch me a warm cloak, for that the morning felt cold to me and my body was all a-shiver.

'Take a sip of Chocolate to restore you, before you go out, Sir?' said Will.

'No,' said I. 'I will take it on my return, to console me then. I shall surely need it.'

We roamed over the park. We stared at the empty Compound and the marks of the Bear's claws and the splintered wood, where he had climbed the fence.

From here, we tried to follow a trail on the dewy grass, but it only led us on and on until we came to the field where the sheep had been slain.

We stopped and I sniffed the air, for the smell of Clarendon was, by this time, very familiar to me, but I got no scent of him. I had the fanciful notion that he had already travelled miles and miles away, far from Bidnold and far from Norfolk, knowing he could never return to me. And the image of him wandering on and on, along desolate roads, with no purpose and no destination caught at my sentimental heart. 'Clarendon trusted me,' wailed I to myself, 'and now I have no other course to follow but to betray that trust.'

Rain began falling. My emptied gut cried out in pain. But still we trudged on, down green lanes, and over wide meadows and fields of corn and apple orchards and pig pens and scrubland covered with Gorse.

By a circuitous route, and without the least sighting or sniffing of Clarendon, we arrived at Bidnold Village, where a tavern I knew very well, the Jovial Rushcutters, was just opening its doors, and I said to the men, 'Let us go in and I will buy us a good drench of Ale to fortify us. Then we shall go on.'

They did not refuse. We sat on benches among the Sawdust, quaffing beer, and never has any Ale tasted as fine to me, and my poor stomach was much calmed by it. After drinking two jugs of it I would willingly have lain down on one of the Rushcutters' hard settles and slept, but I knew that I had to keep to my word. I paid for the beer and we went out again into the bleak morning.

The rain kept up its steady fall. It was one of those summer rains, invisible almost, yet soon enough dampening your clothes and your spirits. And I was so tired, after several hours of walking, that I was ready to drop down in a field of clover and let Clarendon find me and bite out my heart.

In this field was a barn, where the first of the summer hay was piled up in great mounds. And as soon as we came near to this barn I knew that this was where we would find the Bear. I could see his paw prints in the clover, leading there, and then I caught his scent on the breeze, in spite of the rain.

I halted the posse of men. I told Patchett to make ready his Blunderbuss.

I said: 'He is in there. Go slowly and he will not come at you. Aim at his head or at his heart.'

The farmers all hoisted their pitchforks and their shovels, and Patchett got his great gun primed for its firing. Then they walked forward in a Column, the pitchfork men keeping safely behind Patchett.

I stood in the clover. I waited to hear the explosion of the Blunderbuss and, when it came, I felt a kind of deliverance come upon me, as though all my duties to the World – at which I failed so ruinously often – had been taken away and nothing more would ever be asked of me.

20

I told Patchett and the other men that I wished to bury Clarendon and asked them to help me to dig a pit. They regarded me as though I were a lunatic.

'Forgive me, Sir Robert,' said Patchett, 'but look at the Meat on him! Enough for ten families. In my house we have not eaten Meat since springtime.'

The Blunderbuss had shot Clarendon near the heart, laying open the bloody sinews of his chest and dislocating his left arm, but his head had not been touched and it lay on the mound of sweet grass as though on a pillow. One eye was open and one closed. The open eye oozed blackness and I did not know what this was, whether black tears or some discharge of his brain, dribbling through the skull.

All is perplexity, thought I.

'Bear Meat will be strong . . .' I said feebly to the farmers. 'The taste of it will not be to savour.'

'We can bear strong Meat,' said Patchett. 'Never you trouble yourself about that. You go home, Sir Robert, and we will skin him and portion him up between us and have a fine Roasting tonight. We can bring you the Pelt, if you wish it, but the Meat is ours: a fair exchange for the slaughtered Ewe.'

I could not argue with this logic, though the thought of Clarendon being eaten made me sad for the world: for its pitiless Arrangements. I said I would accept the Pelt, wanting, I suppose, to possess something of my Bear, even though the animal was dead. I thought that a Norfolk Tanner might make of it some great Rug, which, when the dark winter came again, I could lay upon my bed and feel it, warm and heavy on me, in my loneliness.

I made my way back to Bidnold, going slowly through the orchards and the fields of clover, as the rain ceased and a bright morning sun began to beat upon my skull.

As I walked it came upon me that, tired though I was, I had an urgent task to perform and this was to send a letter to Louise de Flamanville, asking to be taken in by her, into her Father's house in Switzerland.

This escape – to her and her only – I now saw as the thing for which I suddenly longed beyond all longing. I yearned to be transported there on the wings of some mythical Bird, without the glittering fatigue of a sea journey and the slow travail of coaches and the discomfort of wayside Inns. For, with Margaret gone into the King's clutches and my poor Clarendon dead, my weariness with Bidnold and with all of England was suddenly so great that I could not conceive how I was going to endure the next twenty-four hours in it, unless with a return to the taking of Laudanum.

As I approached the house I saw a strange Conveyance, like a small canvas-covered wagon, drawn up at my front door. I at once assumed that some gypsy pedlar had come a-calling and prepared my strongest and least compassionate voice with which to send him packing on his life of scavenge and barter. But Will, seeing me come staggering home at last, tottered out into the drive to tell me that a gentleman, 'a Quaker by the garb of him, but with a name I could not catch, is here to see you, Sir Robert'.

'Oh, Will,' I said, 'I have walked round half of Norfolk and got wet through, and now I have been sweating in the sun and my poor Bear is dead. I swear I cannot do anything more today but lie down . . .'

'I understand that, Sir,' said Will, helping to remove from my aching shoulders my saturated cloak, 'and I am sorry about your Bear, but the Quaker Person is very intent upon seeing you and I think you should converse with him, for that he says he was a friend of Mr Pearce.'

This last statement caught my attention, as Will knew it would. I was immediately intent on talking to the man. Telling Will to send to Cattlebury for Lardy cake and boiled Chocolate, I dragged myself to my close-stool, where I pissed away the ale drunk at the Jovial Rushcutters, then changed my clothes, put on my wig and descended to the Withdrawing Room, where I expected to find my visitor.

There was, however, no sign of him. I called for Will, who explained to me in a whisper that 'this man, being a Quaker, Sir, I thought the splendour of the Withdrawing Room too great for him to bear – as it always was for Mr Pearce – so I put him in the Library. By the way, Sir Robert, your wig is all awry.'

'No matter!' I snapped at Will. 'Let me just come to the Quaker and see what he wants, and then I shall go to my room. I must write to Switzerland. Please make sure I have ink and quills and paper. I will take my Luncheon on a tray.'

'Yes, Sir,' said Will. 'And would you like me to interrupt you with an urgent Message?'

'What are you talking about, Will? What Message?'

'Would you like me to come into the Library, Sir, with some supposed Important Communication, so that you may make your escape from the Quaker and he be forced to leave, so that you may write your urgent letter?'

I looked down at Will's creased and trusting face. He is like some little animal, I thought, whose sinews I must preserve, at all costs, from the destruction of the Blunderbuss.

'Yes, Will,' I said kindly. 'Now I understand you. That is a capital idea. Come in in ten minutes. Say that a Messenger from the King has arrived unexpectedly.'

'I will, Sir Robert. Unexpectedly.'

I entered the Library and there found a tall, gaunt figure, dressed in the black Quaker Garb so familiar to me. The man had taken off his hat (a thing which Quakers do not normally like to do, for fear of conceding any mark of Respect to any individual including the King himself) and the hair on his head was white. He had a small beard, also white, yet of a russet colour at its end, as though it had been singed.

He came towards me and held out his hand. His eye, still lively in his worn face, lit up with obvious emotion. 'Robert,' he said.

And in this saying of my first name he revealed himself to me. Only a few people in my life have ever addressed me as 'Robert': my dear dead parents, John Pearce, and his Quaker Friends at the Whittlesea Bedlam, where I worked before Margaret was born. And this man was Ambrose, one of those same Quakers, a person of very kindly disposition who, after Pearce's death and my seduction of Katharine, had to perform the terrible task of sending me away. This sending away he had managed to do with great tenderness and sorrow, so that I did not, in any guise at any moment in my life, blame him for it. I was at fault; he performed his duty and that was that. Katharine and I were driven away in a Dray Cart.

'Ambrose,' I said, seizing his hand. 'Oh, what a goodly day that we meet again!'

He nodded. It appeared that the sight of me, older by some seventeen years than when he had at last seen me and with the sorrows of the morning still visible, perhaps, on my features, had choked him, so that he could not speak.

'I have ordered Cake and Chocolate,' I said. 'Come, Ambrose, and sit by the window, where you will have a nice view of my park, and we shall talk of former times.'

Ambrose produced a ragged handkerchief from one of his black pockets and wiped his eyes. 'I am sorry,' he said.

'Think nothing of it. I am forever weeping. But tell me at once, dear Ambrose, what became of your Bedlam? Ten years ago I drove there with my daughter, for I wanted you all to meet her, and she you. But the place was abandoned and in ruins.'

'It is sad that you saw it so.'

'I went to John Pearce's grave and got some briars and bram-
bles away, for that they offended me. I saw the remnants of the
barns, where our Inmates had had their existence, but the wind
sighed through all. I believe you were long gone.'

Ambrose was now seated in a chair. He placed his hands under
his chin in a familiar, characteristic steeple position and looked
away from me, out towards the summer morning.

'I can hardly bear to tell you, Robert,' he said. 'We depended,
for all our needs, upon Quaker Charity. And as the years went on,
it seems the Spirit of Charity diminished in England, with everyone getting and grabbing for himself. We became very poor and
could take no more Distressed People into our care.

'We could barely feed those we had, nor feed ourselves. We
had to resort to getting wild food. Daniel went out each morning
to net larks, as they rise up with their song. We ate ground acorns
and grass soaked in milk . . .'

At this moment one of my immaculately liveried Footmen
came into the Library and laid down a jug of steaming Chocolate
and some large slices of Lardy Cake.

Ambrose ceased talking and stared at the beverage and the
Cake as though they might have been a box of jewels, and
seemed to lose the thread of his discourse, so great was his
wonderment.

I instructed the Footman to serve the Cake and Chocolate to
my guest, and only when Ambrose had consumed a large morsel
of cake and taken a deep draught of the Chocolate did he go on
with his story.

He told me how, for a year or more, the Quaker Keepers and the
Inmates had subsisted 'on wild birds and the little root vegetables
we could grow', but the truth was that they were starving.

Eventually they had to summon the Inmates – those who had
survived the hunger – to a meeting and tell them that the Whittlesea Bedlam would close its doors before the next winter. 'This
was harsh news,' said Ambrose, 'and every one of them stood

helplessly gaping at us, for we had been their protectors and they thought our Protection would go on for ever, but it could not.'

The Quakers helped the Distressed People to write letters to their families, asking to be taken home once more. 'But there were three men and two women,' said Ambrose, 'who had no families, or could not remember having any, or whose families refused to take them, so what were we to do with these?'

'I know not, Ambrose . . .'

'We asked the Workhouse at Marsh to accommodate them, but they would not.'

'For that they could *work*?'

'They could not. And we were almost resolved, as our last and desperate Resort, to send them out into the lanes to beg. But it was Daniel who saved us from this and found them shelter.'

'Sweet Daniel. He was but a boy when I was at Whittlesea. Tell me where he found it?'

'In Cambridge. He knew a man who presented a Spectacle of Performing Animals: elephants, dogs and one Tiger from India. And he went to this Showman and stood before him and said: "We can help you add to your Spectacle, and so charge a higher fee for entry. We can give you five Lunatics. And they will screech and tear their clothes and perform any Lunatic action you ask of them to entertain the crowd. And they will demand no recompense, only food and lodging . . ."'

'Ah. I see Daniel's resourcefulness, and yet . . .'

'I know what you are thinking – that they would be degraded and seem no better than bears in the minds of the spectators.'

'Well . . .'

'You are right, of course. And so it proved, for they were put in a Cage to make the Crowd more affrighted by them, and when I heard about this Cage, I felt mightily sad. But if the Showman had not taken them, Robert, they would have died. Which would you have us procure for them, death or Degradation?'

I was silent, unable to answer this on the instant. I took some Chocolate into me and was glad of its warmth and sweetness.

Ambrose, pausing in his tale, looked at me pleadingly. 'I beg you, Robert, do not blame us. We could not help them to live another *day*. We ourselves were so weak and thin and suffering from every Ailment that we could hardly perform our tasks or conduct our prayers, and I do not exaggerate when I say this. The Showman saved five lives.'

'Caged lives,' I said.

'Alas . . .'

'Yet I do not blame you, Ambrose,' I added quickly. 'I understand that you had tried every other avenue. When famine visits, desperate measures may be required.'

I was about to embark upon a vain little disquisition on the subject of knowing something of Hunger myself, at the Court of Versailles but, recognising – just in time to stop myself from uttering it – that what I had suffered was as naught to what the Quakers and their charges had endured, I merely asked: 'And when the Inmates had all departed, where did you go, Ambrose? Where did Daniel go, and Hannah and Eleanor?'

'Ah,' said Ambrose. 'Well, we had no other way but to beg our Relatives to take us in. We parted ways, with much sorrow to leave each other and for the failure of our endeavour, and went back into the world. I went to my Brother's house in Ely. And by and by, I was able to get a little Trade begun. I will show you the fruits of it in my wagon, if you have the time to give me . . .'

It was now that the Library door opened and Will entered. He bowed to Ambrose. He shuffled towards my chair and announced, almost inaudibly: 'A Messenger has arrived, Sir. From the King.'

'Not now, Will,' I hissed.

Will cleared his throat and said again, more loudly, 'Begging your pardon, Sir Robert, but there is a Messenger from His Majesty who craves your presence.'

'Ask him to wait, Will,' I said.

Will looked at me in cross-eyed perplexity. Then, not knowing what to say to me, he reached out and held on to the back of a Settle, to steady himself to turn and walk out again.

To my consternation, Ambrose made as if to rise and said: 'Do not let me detain you, if you have an important message . . .'

'No, no,' said I, 'it is nothing important. It will be some little matter . . . erm . . . to do with Giraffes for St James's Park . . .'

'Giraffes?'

'Yes, that is what it will be. Giraffes from King Louis of France. I was lately at Versailles and promised His Majesty I would procure at least one for his Menagerie at St James's. Please sit down, Ambrose, and continue with your story. And Will, kindly inform the King's Messenger, that the Giraffe matter is in hand and serve him some of this excellent Chocolate.'

Will, now almost at the door, swayed with drunken Confusion. But, pausing only to scratch his old head, he went obediently out.

Offering Ambrose more Lardy Cake, I settled myself to hear the rest of his tale. He had barely begun upon this when the Library door opened again and my Footman came in, bearing a letter, which he laid beside me, and when I saw the Post Mark 'Helvetica' upon it, my heart lurched: the letter was from Louise! Realising this, I could not prevent myself from staring at the letter on the table beside me, so urgent was my longing to read its contents.

Ambrose had fallen silent. Now, he rose and said: 'I see I have come at a bad time, Robert. Messengers and Letters need all your attention. Let me trouble you no longer.'

'No, no!' I said. 'Business can wait. These are trifling matters, but your visit is not trifling. You said you had some things to show me in your wagon. Why do we not go and look at these now?'

Placing Louise's letter in the pocket of my coat, already feeling a kind of warmth radiating from it into my hand, I followed Ambrose out into the drive.

Here, he folded back the canvas flaps of his wagon and what I saw, standing shoulder to shoulder like little trees in the cart, was great quantity of dovecotes, painted all in different colours and with different designs to their roofs and nesting holes.

'My word, Ambrose!' I said. 'How did you come by so many dovecotes?'

Ambrose reached in, took down one of them and set it on the gravel. It was painted white and it was, I had to admit, an object of some beauty, and reminded me all at once of the white doves, which still came to settle on the roof of my precious West Tower at Bidnold.

Ambrose's hand caressed its roof, which was made of Reed thatch. 'I make them,' he said. 'With my last farthing, when I had my shelter at Ely with my brother, I bought cheap wood and began to fashion small things from it: bowls and ladles and simple boxes, and these I sold in the Market.

'And people told me my work was fair. So I began upon designs for other things, but what I longed to make was these; I cannot tell you why.'

'You longed to make them because they are beautiful.'

'Yes, they are. And they have saved me. I live upon these. I no longer try to bring Souls to God. I bring birds to a place of refuge. I suppose it is a very small thing.'

21

I bought three dovecotes from Ambrose. The white one I kept for myself. The other two were painted a sweet grey-green and I intended to make gifts of them, in due time, to Violet Bathurst and to the King.

Before he left, I asked Ambrose to tell me a little of what had become of Eleanor, Hannah and Daniel.

'Oh,' said Ambrose. 'Well, their hearts were locked into our work at Whittlesea. You remember how dedicated they were to our Cause. When that Cause failed, they could not find any other thing to do, and before ten years had gone by, both Daniel and Hannah passed away.'

'They died? Even as young as they were?'

'They did, alas.'

'Died of what, Ambrose?'

'Of nothing in particular. Nothing that I know of. Merely that they – even as devout Quakers – could not find in themselves the means to continue, for all their True Endeavour had been taken away.'

'Ah. The terror of finding that life no longer has any Meaning! How much I fear that state. And Eleanor?'

'She found a good man to marry – a Quaker farmer. And they live from the earth and have raised a beautiful child. That is all I know.'

'I am happy for her. She would have made a good mother. She was a kindly "mother" to me often enough!'

Ambrose made no comment upon this, but turned and began searching again in his wagon. He then put into my hands a leather bag, which I immediately recognised.

It had belonged to Pearce. Indeed, it had been a *gift* from me to him, long ago when we were both medical students at Cambridge and he a poor Sizar (forced to wait upon the Master and Fellows at table, to pay his way) with no money to his name and nothing in which to carry around his Work. I remembered that he used to wear the bag hanging round his neck, as though it might have been a horse's Nosebag and all the Learning in it so much Hay, and the sight of him thus draped about used to give me much mirth.

'When we left Whittlesea,' said Ambrose, 'I found this at the bottom of an old cupboard in what was once Pearce's room. His clothes, such as they were, we had given to our Charges, but this remained where it lay. There is a book in the pouch, by Hieronymus Fabricius—'

'Ah, the Great Fabricius!'

'Yes. But a strange work: *De brutorum loquela*, published in Padua. Perhaps you know it?'

'I know *of* it. The subject is interesting. Aristotle says in the *Politics* that Man is the only animal with the gift of Speech, but this is at least open to Question, and I imagine Fabricius is questioning it here.'

'My Latin is not good enough to read it. I said to Eleanor and Hannah, "It should be given to Robert. It is what John would have wanted."'

'I am not certain about that, Ambrose,' I said. 'I expect you will remember that all John gave me, when he knew he was about to depart this world, was his soup ladle.'

'Which you put into his grave . . .'

'I did.'

'So now you have a treatise on the Language of Beasts. And the leather bag, though it is old, has the Stamp of Austell's of Cambridge, so it is surely well made.'

'I know it is. I bought it for John.'

'Ah. Well, now it returns to you. Generosity sometimes moves in a circular direction.'

Ambrose departed in his wagon. He left me with regret in my heart that I had not been more hospitable nor made something more of the visit. And though I had paid him well for the dovecotes, I knew that he was disappointed too, and as he drove away he turned on me a look of Severity. His horse had been neither fed nor watered.

Louise's letter, which I had been so impatient to read that I had rudely cut short my time with Ambrose, lies on the floor. My lunch of Boiled Tongue and Carrots, for which I have no appetite, lies on its tray, congealing.

I close my eyes. I yearn for Oblivion. But certain sentences in the letter keep returning to my mind: '*I can only conclude, from your Silence, that what passed between us was of no real consequence to you.*' '*I therefore think it best to consign our fleeting Amours to History.*' '*Though I suggested you might come to me here in Switzerland, I see now that this Invitation was too hastily made, and so I must withdraw it.*'

Now I lie in bed, sipping Laudanum, my only Consolation.

Bitterly I reproach myself that I had not replied to Louise's letter but, Captive as I was, first to Margaret's illness and then to the King's presence in my house, I had truly been unable to travel to Louise – even in my mind. I had foolishly assumed that she would somehow comprehend this from afar and wait out the months until I could come to her again. But I had been wrong. She had not comprehended it. How could she? She had known nothing of what was occurring. And so, being hurt by my neglect, she had decided to let me slip away.

On being told that I have eaten no lunch, Will comes to my room and stares reproachfully at the Laudanum jar.

'You will be sick again, Sir Robert,' he says.

'I do not care,' I say. 'Indeed, I care about nothing on this Earth. It is certainly time that I left it.'

Will fusses with my coverlet, trying to straighten it. 'I remember that you uttered some Foolery about dying long ago,' he says, 'but you were in the Dining Room and I said to you, "Do not die here, Sir. It is not seemly. If you are determined to die, pray go somewhere else."'

'I am not in the Dining Room now, Will. I am in my Bed. This is as good a place as any.'

'Well, if you must, Sir,' says the impudent Will and goes out at once, leaving me to my fate, without any attempt to cajole me from it. I am stung by his sudden and unexpected Indifference. Stung to my core. Awash with self-pity, I fall asleep at last.

I slept for twenty hours and woke feeling much restored, despite some clumsy dreams of Giraffes rampaging about my park.

After a hearty breakfast of Porridge, followed by Bacon and Muffins, washed down with a little Ale, I gathered up the pages of Louise's letter, took them to the Library and began to write as follows:

My dear Louise,

Oh what a wretch I am! But how much more wretched is this wretch made by your harsh words!

May you not forgive me?

I pray you, listen to what I shall relate. My life, through Winter and Spring, was thrown into bitter confusion by the Severe Illness of my daughter Margaret, whom I helped to nurse through many weeks of agony, before, at last, she returned to Health and Life. It was all I could do to live out each day without Despair, to come only to short nights, full of Agony and Terror and I had neither Time nor Space . . .

I had got thus far, buoyant upon the notion that this letter might turn everything round in Louise's heart, when my Footman announced the arrival of a servant from Bathurst Hall, who urgently requested to see me.

I asked that he be shown into the Library. By his sombre face I could tell that he had bad news for me and he blurted out that Lady Bathurst had been 'struck down with Pain in her side and terrible Vomiting, and all she can say is that you must go to her at once'.

Reluctantly I set aside my letter. As I did so, I began to wonder whether the world was not, in some guise, conspiring against me, interrupting me at every turn to prevent me from seeing Louise ever again. But now I had no choice but to go to Violet.

I gathered together my Medical Instruments and such as remained of the Opium grains after my quaffings of Laudanum, and followed Violet's servant to his coach, telling the Coachman to stop in Bidnold Village at the house of Mrs McKinley to collect her on our way.

Thankful for my long sleep, which had left my mind clear, I now attempted to deduce, from the scant information that I had, what might be happening to Violet. I knew from my studies that a Cancer, though cut out from one part of the body, may sometimes mysteriously recur in another part, and that this second coming of Cancer may be more fatal than the first. When Mrs McKinley climbed into the coach I said to her: 'We must pray this is but some slight infection and not a return of any Tumour.'

To my dismay, Mrs McKinley said: 'If you ask me, Sir Rabbit, 'tis a likely Return, or rather a Spreading, for to tell the truth, Lady Bathurst has never truly rallied since we took the Breast tumours out of her.'

And then I thought, it is not only Louise I have neglected; I have been so occupied with Margaret's going away to Court, and then with the loss of my Bear, that I have neglected everything and everyone else. I should have visited Violet many times, but I did not. And I thought how, whatever is neglected by man soon enough sickens or departs, and I said to Mrs McKinley: 'I see what these times are: they are a Time of Leaving.'

'Pray 'tis not so,' said the kindly Irishwoman. 'Pray to Our Lady, Sir Rabbit.'

The moment I saw Violet I knew that she was dying.

Her eyes, once so very beautiful, seemed to have retreated into her skull, as though trying to escape from seeing what was before them. Her cheeks were sunken, blueish in colour from the shadow of the cheekbone upon their poor cavity. Her thin hands clawed at the sheet.

'Lord-a-Mercy,' whispered Mrs McKinley, when we came into the room. 'You were right, Sir. See how she claws . . .'

I went to the bedside and sat down. The grey cat was in the room, but had retreated to one of the window seats, as though it knew that some Catastrophe had befallen its Mistress. Mrs McKinley stood a little apart, at the bed's end. Violet looked up at me ardently, like one who is praying, and said in a faint, beleaguered voice: 'Merivel, now all is sorrow.'

I took her hand in mine and caressed it. For the moment I could find no words of consolation. After a little while I said: 'Where is the pain?'

'Entire,' said Violet.

'You mean that it is everywhere?'

'Yes.'

Mrs McKinley now began to unpack my instrument bag. She took out the small glass Beakers I use for Cupping – burning the skin with their heated edges, so as to raise blisters on it, through which much poison may sometimes come out. I do not like performing this Cupping, for that it causes yet more suffering to the Patient, but I have also noted its beneficial qualities of Distraction, as well as of Evacuation. While the pain of the burning lasts, other symptoms may be masked by this.

'We shall do a Cupping,' I said to Violet and nodded to Mrs McKinley to make a flame to heat the glasses.

While she did this, I persuaded Violet to let me examine the breast wound. When I unwound the Bandages I saw that this was healing well, with no sign of any new Tumour. But then I noted that Violet's stomach was strangely swollen and lumped up, and when I put my hand there Violet screamed with pain.

I stroked her hair. The thinness of her features troubled me so much, I wanted to put some veil or piece of Gauze over them, so that her skull would not be so visible to me. I found myself wishing that Violet Bathurst might have died on the night when the King made love to her. This, I thought, would have been a fitting end for her: a surfeit of delirium stopping her heart – not this wasting and falling in of the flesh.

When the cups were readied, I gently turned Violet and unlaced her nightgown. Her back now lay before me, pale and thin, with each nub of Vertebra pressing up, as though yearning to break free of the skin.

I laid my hand softly on her neck, to hold her still, while Mrs McKinley set down the Cups. When they began their terrible blistering, Violet reached out for me and clutched my knee.

She began babbling to me of her old passion for me. I grew hot in the face with embarrassment when she reminded me of our Fornications on the staircase and how, at that time, nobody but I could give her the satisfaction she craved.

I did not dare glance at Mrs McKinley, but only saw, at the corner of my eye, her deft hands continuing their work. And she uttered not a word.

''Tis the role of a Nurse,' she had once said to me, 'that she sometimes be deaf.'

After reminding me of yet more violent Amours we had contrived together Violet said: 'There was affection, too, Merivel. Very deep. I shall not call it love, yet love it almost was. And how many people can one veritably love in the world? Those we hate or despise far outnumber those we adore. Our souls are similar, yours and mine: always hungry, always frail. 'Tis quite miraculous we have both endured so long. I am content with that.'

'This is not the end, Violet,' I said to her. 'We shall play more games of Shuttlecock . . . in the autumn . . .'

'No,' she said. 'We shall not, Merivel. A Shuttlecock is light and I am heavy. I am falling to earth.'

After the cupping we gave her the Opium, very strong and raw, made her as comfortable as we could and kept watch by her side. She soon enough slept.

Mrs McKinley took out her Knitting and, as the day became evening, the clicking of her needles was the only sound.

'What are you making?' I asked her.

'Merely a square, Sir Rabbit,' she said softly. 'See? Made of fine string, not wool. A square may become any Thing in the world you wish it to be.'

Towards five o'clock, food was brought up to us from Chef Chinery: a plate of Cutlets in Gravy, a dish of Cabbage and Potatoes, and a flask of Cider.

Both of us were hungry, so we set upon this meat and drink with great Attack, seated at a little table near the window. But I blush to relate that we ate so greedily, filling the air of the room with our slurpings and munchings, that we did not hear the constricted sounds of dying that Violet Bathurst began to make. The cat heard them and fled from the room. But I paid this no heed. I thought it was we who had chased the animal away.

Only when I had scraped my plate clean and wiped my mouth with the fine Damask napkin did I look over at the bed, and see Violet's eyes wide and staring and her jaw gaping. 'She is gone,' I said. 'She is gone.'

We went to her, and I closed her eyes and kissed her forehead, then Mrs McKinley bound her jaw with Buckram. After this binding, her work done, she got stiffly to her knees and took into her hands the wooden cross she wears ever about her neck.

'Our Lady of Heaven,' she said, 'I pray you receive the soul of Lady Bathurst in your gentle heart. Forgive her all her trespasses. Let her rest in peace. And, if it please you, in your infinite mercy, look kindly on good Sir Rabbit who is but a mortal man.'

The evening was coming upon us, very soft and luminous, with all the white roses of the garden shining in the descending light.

I walked to the lake and tried to picture the row boat, painted red, in which I had once ravished Violet, before falling into the water. I now remembered that when I fell, my Breeks were all a-tangle round my calves, preventing me from kicking out in a proper swimming stroke, and for a moment, in the icy lake, I thought that I would sink and drown.

Then I saw an Oar come down to me, and I grabbed at this and felt the boat tilting above me, and expected Violet to come plunging in, with her skirts billowing out above the waterweed, but she did not. She held manfully to the Oar and I held to it too, and my head bobbed up and it was at this moment that I felt my Breeks slide off my legs and fall away.

'Violet,' I shouted, half choking and spouting water like a Whale, 'I am naked below!'

'So are we all!' she cried, and her laughter sounded loud in the warm air.

22

The summer is slowly passing.

I languish in my bed, slave to fevers and dreams. To Will, who urges me to get up, I say: 'I cannot. I have seen too much of Death. I must preserve my life by remaining here, to think my thoughts. Please make sure that I am left alone.'

The August weather is fine and warm, and the trees I can see from my window have not yet turned to any autumn colour, nevertheless I note, from the way the leaves move and clatter, that all the Freshness is gone from them. They have had their season and will soon fall. And I reflect upon the way my mind and body have always longed for summer and warmth, and how, in this year 1684, I am letting these go by without taking any pleasure or comfort from them. And part of me recognises how stupid a thing this is; I should be walking in my garden to catch the last scent of the roses, or riding at an easy canter along the Chestnut *allées*, or hosting Picnic parties. But for none of these can I summon the necessary joy.

I say to Will: 'I am a leaf, Will, doomed to fall.'

And Will replies: 'Pray do not offend me with Poet's Piffle, Sir Robert. It is not worthy of you.'

'Worthy of me?'

This, I ponder: my Worth in the vain world.

I let Clarendon die. I let Violet die. The hospitality I showed to Ambrose was miserly and unworthy. I may even have lost Louise.

And the King, who has always and ever lodged in my heart as God lodges in the heart of true Believers, has, by taking Margaret away to a destiny that may prove to be her ruin, almost vanished from it, leaving behind only the merest hint of his presence there: a whiff of perfume, a cascade of laughter. Yet I feel this Absence not as a relief, but only as a terrible wound in my breast.

My dreams, however – though this be strange – are of a sweet, consoling nature. Often, in them, I am a five-year-old boy again, with my Mother in the Woods of Vauxhall, looking for badgers. She places a rug on the earth and sits down there in the first drift of evening, and I sit beside her, snug within the circle of her arm, feeling against my leg the warmth of her body, and she says: 'If you are very quiet, a Badger will come from its sett and you will see its black-and-white face.'

And then, after a short while one of the animals appears, and it turns in circles and pirouettes on its hind legs, as though dancing for us, and I am held by the spell of this, and I feel my Mother's gladness as she holds me close to her.

Yet, in reality, though we went again and again to Vauxhall Woods, no Badger ever came to visit us. I suppose I was never quiet enough, but too restless and prating. So then I understand that my dreams are showing me *what might have been*, had my own conduct been different. And I begin to wonder: can a dream ever instruct us how to be *in the time to come*?

I know not what that time holds for me. At present it appears to contain Nothing at all. I lie above a Precipice. The depths below me are black and silent. I listen for the sound of the wind, or for the calling of a human voice, but nothing is heard.

I send one of my Footmen, by the name of Sharpe, to Dunn in Norwich, with a note from me ordering more Opium. Though I have been trying to resist thinking about this excellent Consolation, my mind cannot quite turn away from it, so tempting is the absence of suffering that it procures.

But, alas, Sharpe does not return. The price of Opium is high and I sent him with a substantial Purse. And Will comes to me and says: 'Sir Robert, that damnèd Sharpe, it appears, is a Naked Villain and a Thief. For off he goes with all his clothes in a sack, and his every possession bar his Livery of the Household, knowing he would not come back to Bidnold, but live off the Opium Purse for a goodly while. What do you think to that?'

'What do I think?' say I. 'I think it lamentable. But what am I to do?'

'You should pursue him and catch him and let him be hanged for Knavery and Theft!'

I stare at Will. Though I am shocked that any Servant should steal from me and like me so little that he betray my Trust in him, I hear myself say: 'Alas, our England does not prosper, Will.'

'What is that to do with Sharpe, Sir?'

'Well, only this, that more and more do people drift from their trade or occupation, or are thrown from these, to fall into a general Criminality of Mind – even Footmen, who are schooled in humility and obedience to command from on high. And I do not know what is to be done.'

'His Majesty must pass laws . . .'

'His Majesty has convened no Parliament through which to pass them.'

'So all is coming to ruin, is it, Sir Robert?'

'Ruin compared to what was hoped for. At the Restoration there was a time of Opportunity, which you and I saw with our own eyes, but it is squandered and gone.'

'So what is to become of us?'

'I cannot tell, Will. Now, I am going to give you a purse. Tomorrow you must take the coach to Dunn's of Norwich and get me the Elixir that I need.'

'I beg your pardon, Sir?'

'You heard me.'

'I heard the word Elixir and that is all.'

'And you shall ride to Norwich to procure it.'

'I am not permitted to procure any "Elixir".'

'On the contrary, I am giving you permission.'

'I mean that I cannot do it. I mean that I *will* not do it. And there's an end of the subject.'

Will, who has been standing near the bed, where I lie in a state of unwashed catastrophe, turns from me and walks, surprisingly fast, to the door, which he opens and closes with a bang in the manner of a child undergoing a tantrum.

This amuses me fleetingly. Will's stubbornness has often occasioned me some mirth. And now that he is so old, I see it as proof of his obstinate desire to Continue, which consoles me, for were Will to die, why then I see that my Solitude would be complete. As long as he argues with me, he means, perhaps, to outlive me.

But then I begin to see that unless I haul myself into a coach I will not come by my Opium by any Means, for now I can trust no other Servant but Will. And no sooner have I realised this than a terrible Craving for it overcomes me and all that occupies my mind is how I can send for it.

I fidget and turn in my rumpled bed. My limbs ache. My mouth is dry. I feel like the most wretched specimen of the Human Race. I hear myself call out to Louise de Flamanville to save me.

Days and nights pass.

My one refuge, in the absence of Opium, is in my dreams, where sometimes I am with Rosie Pierpoint, long ago when she was young, and the two of us lying together in delirium on her piles of Laundry, and I wake in an Ecstasy, imagining myself inside her. And the sweetness of her lingers long in my mind and body, and soothes them to something like peace.

The only letter that comes is from Margaret.

'*The King,*' she writes, '*spends much time with those of us who attend the Duchess of Portsmouth, and this is most flattering and agreeable. He tells me that he prefers to be here in our apartments than with his Queen or with his Privy Council or anywhere in Whitehall or in the Kingdom, save Bidnold.*'

She then goes on to relate how she has become the favourite 'maid' of the Duchess, who spoils her with new dresses and pieces of Jewellery *'and if the King come not to her at night, she sometimes wakes me and takes me into her bed and puts her arms round me and we fall asleep together, like children.'*

Though this image troubles me, I force myself to see in it only the Duchess's affection and I reason, furthermore, that the King might draw back from betraying his Mistress with her favourite Maid-in-Waiting.

But then follows a new thought. I imagine how, waking in the night full of lust, the King might go to the Duchess and, finding Margaret there in her bed, be suddenly enamoured of the idea that the *three* of them might make Revels all together. And I feel very hot and sweating when I think that my daughter might be so corrupted, and immediately take up my pen and write: *'Stay on your Guard against any Sophisticated Practices of the Bedroom, for that they may degrade and punish you with Shame, in the end. Keep yourself pure and unsullied, Margaret, and only seduce the world by showing your Talents at Music and Dancing and your Comprehension of Latin.'*

When I read what I have written, however, I do see that the tone of it is one of vile Priggishness and Pomposity, and I tear it in pieces. Instead, I force myself to write:

How happy I am, dear Margaret, to hear you are so favoured by your Employer. She is right, of course, to single out one of so sweet a nature, and all that you are getting for yourself is got by that – by your own Goodness and Kindness. And how much I look forward to seeing your new dresses and Jewels, surpassing any that I could afford! I shall come to London before September. Meanwhile, I send you my deepest affection,

From your loving Papa,
R. Merivel

I arrange for despatch of my letter, and soon afterwards Will informs me that Sir James and Lady Prideaux have called upon me and attend me in the Library.

'Ah,' say I, 'how kind of them. No doubt they heard that I was ill.'

Will draws back the curtains in my bedroom, that I have kept half closed to keep out the August sun, and opens the window. 'You are not ill, Sir,' says he, 'you are horridly malingering. And you stink like a dead rat.'

'Now, now, Will,' I say. 'Have a care how you speak to me.'

'I only speak true. I will get hot water brought up to you, that you may wash yourself and put on some clothes before you come downstairs. Meanwhile I shall serve a Cordial to Sir James and his wife.'

Had my Visitors been any other than the Prideaux, perhaps I would not have stirred from my Inertia. But to these I feel bonds of affection (for Margaret's sake as well as for my own), so I scrub my body, put on the clean garb Will has laid out for me, clamp my wig to my head and, on legs very weak and trembling, make my way downstairs.

When I see the Prideaux I am cheered. What consoles me in them is their sanity or normality. Their lives go on, as lives should but seldom do, arranged around a quiet prosperity and domestic comfort. They are never heard to complain about anything, for, in truth, they have very little to complain about. Yet they do not seem smug.

They commiserate with me about the Bear. (This story is out around the County, and no one except James and Arabella Prideaux appears to sympathise with my loss, but all take the side of the Farmers who killed and ate the creature.)

'What did you intend for your Bear?' asks Arabella.

'Oh,' say I, 'I intended that he should have an untroubled life. Once I talked about starting a Menagerie here at Bidnold, but I did not, in the end, want a Menagerie, I merely wanted Clarendon to be happy.'

'Happy?' enquires Sir James.

'Yes. Many do not consider animals capable of what we would call "happiness", but I believe they are wrong. We have only to observe a pet Spaniel made aware that he is to be taken for a walk . . .'

'Dogs are perhaps a particular case, Merivel, having chosen Man to be their protector. But your Bear was named Clarendon, you say?'

'Yes. The King named him, after the late Earl.'

'Thus, perhaps, unfortunately consigning him to an *unhappy* end?'

'Indeed. Though His Majesty did not intend this. Watching Clarendon absorbed him. He observed that something in the demeanour of Bears reminds us of ourselves. They have the faces of Outcasts.'

'Outcasts? The King is not an Outcast.'

'For eleven years he was. He never forgets it – not for one day. The place he visits most frequently in his dreams is Boscobel.'

The Prideaux nod gravely. After a while Arabella asks: 'Have you any Souvenir of the poor Bear?'

'The Pelt was brought to me. To look at this empty skin, with the head still attached, was a fearful thing. But I have had the Pelt taken to be cured, so that I may use it as a rug.'

'Ah,' says Arabella. 'I saw such a thing once, made from a Tiger skin. But a little Stench adhered to it, unfortunately. I could not bear to be near it.'

I change the subject swiftly. We talk about all our girls and they give me news of Mary's new beau, who is the eldest son of Sir Reginald Brocks-Parton and worth ten thousand *livres* per year. And we exclaim over this sum, and find ourselves embarrassingly short of breath, as visions of True Riches make us pant.

Then James Prideaux says: 'We fear you are much alone, Merivel. Why do you not come and stay at Shottesbrooke with us until the end of summer? We can make up some parties of Whist and I shall invite musicians to entertain us, and there is a hanging on Mouse Hill next week . . .'

'We would be so glad if you would come,' says Arabella. 'This was all the purpose of our visit. And it is such a while since we have had a hanging in Norwich. We could take a picnic and enjoy the Spectacle together.'

I look at my friends, so nicely seated in their chairs, holding their glasses of Cordial so correctly, and find that, for the first time since I have known them, I do not, after all, absolutely *like* them. Though I am disconcerted by this and hope that it may be a temporary feeling, it infects me with a sudden stubborn Optimism on my own account and courage enough to reply: 'That is the kindest offer. But I have made my plans. Before the month's end I am to set sail for France and Switzerland.'

Thus, it came to me.

Why wait for a letter that might never arrive? Why not profit from the last of summer to make a long and absorbing journey across France into a land I have never seen? Immediately I began imagining all the wonders I might encounter: castles upon crags, forests of deep darkness, shining lakes, glaciers, mountains rising to the waning moon, fields of Gentian flowers, a Carillon of bells at sunset, and wayside inns serving Rhenish wine and wild boar.

And if, when I arrived at the Château de Saint Maurice, Louise's father's abode, I were refused all entry to it and to Louise's life, why then at least I would have travelled somewhere. I would have breathed the pure air of the hills, stood higher in the world than I have ever stood, to see what view was there. I would have Tales to tell.

After James and Arabella Prideaux had departed, I called Will to me and told him: 'You were right, Will. I have been malingering. But you shall suffer no more of it. I shall make plans to depart for Switzerland forthwith.'

'Switzerland?' said Will. 'I would not go there, Sir Robert. I heard tell it be even colder than Scotland. How shall you keep your blood warm?'

I was about to reply that I would drink a great deal of the excellent liquor they call Schnapps, known for its body-heating properties, but instead I said: 'It is still summer, by the calendar. Summer will gently merge into Autumn as I go, but then I shall see golden Beeches and stately firs and snow on the mountain tops. And on my arrival I shall be the guest of the Baron de Saint Maurice, in whose house great fires burn . . .'

'Forgive me, Sir, but has he veritably *invited* you?' said Will.

'Yes,' I replied. 'The invitation is of long standing. Merely, I have not been at liberty to take it up.'

'And how long do you plan to be absent from Bidnold?'

'I do not know. A few months, perhaps. All shall depend on how long I am welcome in the Baron's château.'

'And us, Sir? Cattlebury and Myself and the other servants. What are we to do in your absence?'

'What you always do. Keep the house. A portion of the King's *loyer* will be left in your personal care to cover all expenses. I ask only that you conceal the money in some place where none but you can come to it – for after Sharpe's absconding with my purse, we are able to trust nobody. Make sure that you have everything always in readiness for my Return.'

Will stared at me. Then I saw that his face had creased itself into an expression of troubling sadness and he began shaking his old head, as if in exasperation at my recent changes of Tune and Whim.

'What is it, Will?' I asked.

'Nothing, Sir,' he said. 'Except I know that I may feel somewhat lonely and abandoned . . .'

'You are not "abandoned", Will. It is only for a short space of time. And please bear in mind also that, although I shall not be here, His Majesty has the right, by the generous stipend that he pays me, to take up Residence at Bidnold at any time. Thus the

Candelabra in the Dining Room and all the Silver and Pewter Ware must be in a perpetual state of shining readiness.'

'I will bear it in mind . . .'

'And do not believe that I shall not be thinking about *you*. Every morning, when I wake in some Medieval tower and look north-westwards towards England, I shall imagine you rising in your room at Bidnold and drinking your bowl of Chocolate, then giving your Orders for the day as to what is to be scrubbed or rearranged or polished or brought in or taken out.'

'Will you really, Sir?'

'Yes. It is most certain.'

Will nodded. His features unclamped themselves a little from their creased state, but something of sorrow remained stubbornly in them as he turned and left the room. For his sake, I knew I might yet be dissuaded from my audacious plan to travel to Switzerland, so I went immediately to my escritoire and took up my pen.

My dear Louise, I wrote,
I have made up my mind: I am setting forth to find you.

23

I embarked on my journey.

Always in my mind was a many-turreted castle. To these turrets led stairways of stone, winding in upon themselves, chill to the touch.

Before taking ship I set down in London and found my daughter in great Rapture with her life.

Fubbs whispered to me, 'Margaret is much noted by the young Beaux of the Court. The youngest son of Lord Delavigne, the Honourable Julius Royston, is vaporous with longing, but I have forbidden Margaret to lose her virginity to him. She must hold out and that way she may get a proposal. *Un Match très, très aus- picieux, mon cher Merivel! La noble et riche famille Delavigne!* And he is such a charming young man, you cannot imagine . . .'

Fubbsy's delight in Margaret was, I observed, a tender and affecting thing. When Margaret was talking, Louise de Kéroüalle's bright bird eyes fixed their gaze on her, as a Mother's gaze fixes itself encouragingly upon an infant in its efforts to walk or speak. When they moved out of a room, Louise linked arms with Marga- ret and they leaned close together like conspirators.

Only one thing troubled the two women, and this was the vexed condition of the King's health. Fubbs told me that he had suffered a Convulsion very suddenly that morning, while having his moustache trimmed, and fallen into a Faint. When I asked if I might see him she said: 'He is sleeping. But when the Queen heard of it, she insisted that he be moved to her Apartments and I cannot take you there.'

I walked with Margaret round the gardens and noted subtle changes in her bearing. Where, before at Bidnold, she had tended to skip about and be careless, like a girl, now she moved with a slow grace, holding her head still and high, and when she took my arm I saw that she was careful to arrange her hand upon it so that her fingers were prettily spread, as though at some stately dance. And those people who passed us – mostly gatherings of fops draped about with heavy Swords – smiled at her and inclined themselves in small, unnecessary bows.

'My word, Margaret,' said I, 'I see that you are quite noted here. How has this come about?'

'I do not know,' she said sweetly, 'only that the Duchess is much noted and I am frequently by her side.'

'And are you also at the King's side?'

'What do you mean, Papa?'

'Do you sometimes walk out alone with him?'

Margaret lifted her face to look sideways at me, but then walked on without answering my question. Only when we reached the shade of a young oak tree did she stop and say: 'When you are in Switzerland, my dear Papa, I shall hope that you will not worry your head on my account. Fate has smiled very kindly on me. I did not die of the Typhus. And now – see where we are walking! I believe you should have trust in me, in my good Sense.'

I placed a kiss upon her brow. There was very much that I wanted to say, but I discerned in Margaret a great Unwillingness to hear it said. So we walked on, and I tried to get my mind away from all the things that still troubled it, and press it forward to where Gentian flowers might spring up at my feet.

My way through France was plagued by burning weather.

In the succession of coaches, every passenger, both man and

woman, fell to complaining about the heat, fanning themselves and blowing and puffing like Pug dogs, and loosening their Attire, or taking it off, so that bits of their bodies, damp with sweat, might be exposed to the air.

The stench in these Conveyances was worse than any I had ever endured and I shall not soon forget it.

Then, in one of them, there occurred something most Singular and shameful, which I am embarrassed to set down, yet I have determined upon doing so. (There is surely no purpose to the writing of one's Life unless it include the base and vile things, as well as the dutiful and the benevolent?)

On our way to Besançon my companions were all men, except for one woman sitting opposite me. This woman was a Matron, aged about fifty, of great girth and with skin whiter than lard, and she had furnished herself with a jar of meat pâté, from which she ate continuously, sucking noisily on a spoon.

Some twenty miles from Besançon, plagued as we all were by the sun burning upon the carriage roof, this creature did decide, unceremoniously and without any by-your-leave, to remove her drawers. She pulled them clean off and bundled them away, and hitched up her skirt and did not care that the passengers saw her Cunt. On the contrary, fanning out her great thighs so that all her private Anatomy was visible to us entirely, she observed nonchalantly that women must take precautions against a Sweating Cunt, 'for in the sweat can the Pox come in'.

'Ah,' said I, averting my eyes a little from a sight she appeared so keen to display to me, 'I have never heard that said before, Madame, and I am a Physician.'

'A Physician? Well, Monsieur, let me add to your score of knowledge, for it is well know how scant that may be in your Profession. My own Mother died this way, from a Pox got in a Tropical Heat, and by this heat alone and not from the prick of any man.'

After saying this, she continued to eat her potted meat and I could not refrain from staring at her – at her mouth gulping the pâté, and at her Cunt, very dark and glistening with sweat, and pushed forward on the seat opposite me. And I knew that for all that she disgusted me, I would, had we been alone in the lurching carriage and she willing, have fucked her well and truly. And I thought, with pity for myself, how Solitary a thing my life had become, devoid of any animal love.

I closed my eyes and slept a little, and woke with my mind and body in a boil of lust, but could do nothing to relieve it, and I cursed the fat woman for torturing me so, and wished myself to be a Bear, with no scruples or modesty, that I might take out my member, grown very large and aching, and thrust it in her without ceremony, and get my pleasure and release forthwith.

Then I saw that the woman had set aside her jar of pâté and had moved herself further forward on the seat, so that her bottom hung almost over the edge of it. And her glance was now fixed upon me.

I looked round at the other passengers, three men of differing ages and kinds, and they, too, had fallen to breathless silence, and were regarding me with expressions of Excitation and amusement on their faces. And after a few moments the man next to me, a red-faced Squire with large wens upon his nose, nudged my thigh and whispered to me, '*Allez-y, Monsieur. Pourquoi pas, si elle l'invite?*'

So then it came to me that all along – with her ostentatious sucking and swallowing of her rich pâté, and her tales of the Heat and the Pox – this ageing Drab had been manufacturing an invitation to Copulation and had only waited to see which one of us would accept it.

My breathing was now very laboured and hot. The carriage jolted on along the burning road. The woman raised three fingers of a fat hand and pointed to my pocket: *three livres* would be the price of it. I hesitated only a moment more, then I scrabbled for my purse, found the money and gave it to her, and in a trice I was kneeling and unfastening myself, and putting myself in her and tearing at her bodice to take one of her fat breasts in my mouth.

I rammed her very hard, and she lifted her legs and they clenched themselves round me. I closed my eyes. The excitation I felt was as fierce as anything I have ever known. I could feel the lascivious gaze of the other three men upon me, regarding the cheeks of my bare Arse moving just like a Chimpanzee in rut, and feeling the coach tremble and rock. And I thought that never in my life had I imagined myself doing such a thing, in front of strangers, on a burning foreign road, and I knew I should feel great Shame, yet I did not. I was Pure Beast and could only continue on in my crazed need to Spend, until it came and all my longing drained away.

When it was done, I fell back into my seat. I wanted to hide myself away.

I thought that never would I be able to tell anyone, man or woman, what I had done in a swaying coach on the road to Besançon.

I closed my eyes. But when I opened them again, what did I see but the Drab with her legs stretched out, chafing her Parts with the fingers of one hand and with the other, pulling at the nipple I had taken out from her bodice. And this, it seemed, filled every man in the carriage with such excitation (for that their wives or mistresses might never be so wanton as to pleasure themselves in front of them) and when she had brought herself to a palpably ecstatic *Jouissance* with a long shivering sigh, each now produced money, and one by one reached out to her. And so it was that they all took her, either rutting upon their knees as I had done, or pulling her onto their laps to bounce her great weight upon their erections. In not more than half an hour all four of us had had her, and she had got herself twelve *livres*.

When it was over the woman (whose name none of us knew, or cared to ask), being tired and sore, I supposed, laid herself down at our feet. She did not seem to notice or care that the coach floor was clotted here and there with Semen. She merely laid her head upon her arm and covered herself, and covered the money secreted between her breasts, and she fell asleep silently, while the men around me snored and farted, and the stench in the coach became worse than the stench of a Brothel. And I was overcome with a great sadness.

I longed to reach Switzerland. I imagined that there the world might not be so susceptible to a sudden raging Disorder of the senses as the one I had just been part of.

I put up at an Auberge in Besançon and washed the sour smell of the coach and the Drab from me, and slept a full twelve hours; and on the next day I crossed the border into Switzerland and followed the road to the great lake of Neuchâtel.

When my coach came within distant view of the water, I asked to be set down in a small village named Bellegarde. Here, in soft sunlight, I walked about, noting with tenderness very many vegetable gardens growing beside poor houses of wood, and orchards full of apple trees, heavy with fruit, and gaggles of Goats, hung with bells about their throats, grazing on sloping fields.

I paid a young boy two *sous* for a mug of Goats' Milk and drank this as thirstily as I had once drunk milk at the gates of Versailles. Then I sat down upon a tuffet of grass, with my single Valise at my feet, and pondered what I should do, now that I was so near my destination.

I had the fancy to go riding in to the gates of the Château de Saint Maurice on a fine horse, thus making me seem, in the Baron's eyes and in the eyes of Louise, a greater and taller man than I was. I thought longingly of Danseuse. No horse had ever seemed to me as beautiful as Danseuse, or had possessed so serene a nature. But she was long gone.

I called the goat boy to me and asked him where, in Bellegarde, I might hire a horse. But he told me that none there owned horses, only donkeys and mules, and though this dismayed me for a moment, I was then, all of a sudden, amused by the vision of myself on a biting mule. I remembered that what Louise de Flamanville had seemed to like in me was my ridiculousness and helpless absence of Vanity, and that all around our brief amours had trembled the sound of laughter.

The goat boy told me that the Château de Saint Maurice was but three or four miles from Bellegarde, 'but higher than we, and they say you may have a very fine view of the Lake there', and calling the goats into their pen, he took me to his father, a stooped man, sitting in the darkness of a low house, intent upon carving a pipe out of Meerschaum.

The mule he owned was small and thin. It had a hectic look in its eye.

'Will its back be strong enough to carry me and my Valise to the Château?'

I enquired.

'Yes,' said the man, 'but she will not walk.'

'The mule will not walk? Have I misunderstood you, Monsieur?'

'No. She will not walk.'

'Then how am I to arrive anywhere at all?'

'You mount. And then you will be whisked into a trot. Walking she will not do. Trot-and-stop. Trot-and-stop. This is her nature. Take it or leave it.'

So it was that I *bounced* my way up the forested path to the Baron's house.

The sun was just beginning its decline, and the great oaks and firs that stood sentinel along the way took on a deeper and deeper blackness as I and the mule approached. Once again I had the disconcerting sense that it was my eyesight and not the sky that was fading. And I strained with all my might to bring light to the path, so that when the house appeared at last I would see it and recognise the circular turrets I had for so long imagined.

Then I saw it. It was built of stone, with a high slate roof, and high Mansard windows and tall chimneys – but no towers. I reined in the mule and, as if in astonishment at finding itself confronted by a turretless building, the creature deigned to walk slowly towards it.

Step by slow step, then, we neared it. I had been somewhat preoccupied by my bottom – its great soreness from coach and mule travel – until this moment, but now I was preoccupied by my heart, which set up a great and suffocating clamour. Sweat broke on my lip. My legs, in the too-short stirrups, felt weak.

And then, lo! Once again the wretched mule decided upon a trot and, as it strained forward, I was pitched back in the saddle, lost the reins and lost my balance altogether and – just as we began to circle the knot garden laid out before the great front door – found myself tipped out onto the gravel.

Relieved of my weight, the mule now began a mad canter round the knot garden, past the door, and returned at great speed the way we had come, with all my Possessions still strapped to its bony rump. The dust from its flying hooves was flung into my eyes.

I pulled myself to a sitting position. My left shin gave me some stinging pain. I sat there, breathing hard, wiping dust from my face – a round-shouldered lump in the fast descending dusk.

Nobody came out of the house. I could hear, far off, the sound of lake water breaking on a stony shore.

'Merivel,' said I to myself, 'this is a fine Kettle of Sprats.'

24

A copious amount of blood began to leak from my leg and soak my stocking. Now, all at once, I could see and hear Buzzards circling above me in the twilight, so I attempted to scramble to my feet to avoid being pecked to death. As I brushed the grit and dust from my coat, a Servant in a periwig arrived at my side and gave me his arm to lean on, and lighted my way to the house.

I discovered myself in a wide hall, paved with stone flags, where a fire of pine cones was burning. Louise descended a wide staircase. She said my name softly. Behind her came her Father, the Baron, a tall man with a bald crown to his head, but with long white hair flowing out beneath, like the petals of a ragged daisy.

I bowed to them. They regarded me with plain astonishment, as though I might have been the Man in the Moon, suddenly fallen out of it. Near them two wigged Footmen stood at brisk attention, casting only sidelong glances at the blood from my leg dripping onto the stone.

'Forgive me my sudden appearance,' I managed to stammer. 'I had hoped to make a more . . . appropriate arrival, mounted on a horse, but all I could get at Bellegarde was a mule, and veritably it liked me no more than I liked it and so threw me into the dust, and . . .'

'Hush,' said Louise. 'You are horribly pale. You may faint if you talk any more. We shall see to your wound. Papa, this is Sir Robert Merivel, come out from England, and we must care for him.'

The Baron glided gently to me and shook my hand. I saw at once that in his lined face there still resided very lively hazel eyes.

'You are welcome, Sir Robert,' he said. 'My daughter has talked much of you. Now, do you have a trunk to be taken upstairs?'

'Alas,' I said. 'Though the mule did not take to me, she was much enamoured of my Valise and has cantered back to Bellegarde with it on her back.'

At this the Baron de Saint Maurice let out a whoop of laughter. 'Ah, animals!' he said. 'How they surprise us.' Then he snapped his fingers to the Footmen and I found myself lifted from the ground in a kind of Chaise, made only of the linked hands of these strong Servants, and carried upstairs.

Louise herself washed and dressed the wound on my leg, and applied to it some of the Salve that had been so efficacious for the rash on Margaret's face.

While she dabbed and cleaned, I remained silent. I stared down at her sweet head. As she tied a bandage round my calf she said quietly: 'My Letter was too hasty, Merivel. I am sorry. I could not know that your daughter had been ill. I was hurt by your Silence, but I was wrong to write as I did, in so petulant a way. I should have trusted you.'

She then raised her face and looked up at me. I might have kissed her, but I did not. After my shameful behaviour in the coach on the the road to Besançon, I found that all my carnal inclinations were stilled and that what I longed for was merely to be by Louise's side, to savour her companionship, and only later – possibly many days and nights later – take her to my bed.

It was the hour when dinner was to be served and the thought of sitting at a fine table, with firelight dancing near, and the conversation of Louise and her father playing like a complicated melody in my ear, filled me with gladness. I imagined that – after long months of travail – my heart would at last be at peace.

There remained only the problem of my torn stockings and my general absence of clothes, but Louise at once found for me a fine crimson coat, frogged with gold, belonging to the Giraffe, with black Breeks and white silk stockings, this ensemble enhanced by an enormous white shirt, with lace fluffing out at throat and wrists.

Regarding myself, swamped by these garments made for a very tall man, I reminded myself of nothing more nor less than a Regimental Flag, a billowing ornamental thing, raised on a standard in some far-flung Field of Battle. As a Regimental Flag, quivering in the wind, I would have had some dignity, but as a man I looked utterly farcical. I descended to Dinner thus, with the crimson coat flapping round my calves and the lace at my wrists flouncing down over my hands.

The meal was delicate and served with wine produced on the Baron's Estates. Louise had dressed herself in a low-cut blue velvet gown and laced ribbons in her hair. She wore at her throat a very fine pearl necklace and, seeing her thus, at her Father's table, wearing exquisite yet unostentatious jewels, I understood how far she exceeded me in her Birth and Position: she was the daughter of Baron Guy de Saint Maurice of Neuchâtel in the Pays de Vaud, and I was the son of a humble Glovemaker from Vauxhall, and I had prospered in life only because I had a talent to amuse the King of England.

The Baron, however, being a man of courtesy, treated me quite as though I had been the most important Guest to have sat at his table in a long while – this notwithstanding the vexatious tendency of my lace cuffs to flop into the food, thus becoming horridly stained.

Having let me narrate the sad tale of Clarendon and his sordid end, he drew me into a conversation about animals and insects, in which we both agreed with those philosophers who refuted (at least as proven truth) the Cartesian notion of these creatures as automata and who were content to speculate on the existence of Souls among certain species.

'Consider the ants,' said the Baron. 'With what selflessness they strive! I have even observed them forming a Bridge, claw-to-claw, across a little streamlet in the woods here, that the Queen might be carried over upon their backs to a new site for a nest, and some of them were pressed by the weight of her so low in the water that they drowned, and all without a sound. Does this not argue for a consciousness of the Greater Good, even of the need for self-sacrifice and thus for a soul – be it ever so small?'

'Or else, as has been said many times,' said Louise, 'it is mere *instinct*, as that which drives them to forage and to copulate. But we shall never know.'

'Why might we not know?' said I. And I then went on to mention that same work, *De brutorum loquela*, by Fabricius, which had been given to me in Pearce's Nosebag. In all truth, I had not opened the book, but yet felt emboldened to state: 'Fabricius has much to say on the *speech* of beasts.'

'Ah, yes, Fabricius . . .' nodded the Baron.

'*De brutorum loquela* takes outwards into new realms the very notion of Language among the animals,' I continued, with a feigned air of Authority. 'Thus we might deduce that new Enquiries will take forward the notion of *souls* in animals.'

'But who will write these "new Enquiries"?' said Louise. 'For do we not all secretly agree with Descartes, even if we do not like to use the word automata, so that we can trample scorpions to death, and slaughter sheep, and feel no blame?'

At this mention of Sheep and Blame, Clarendon came swiftly into my mind – Clarendon as dead meat. I thought of Patchett and his friends carving him up and boiling his bones and gobbling him down.

'I give you scorpions and sheep,' I said, 'but I do not give you Bears. You were with me when we first saw him in his cage, Louise. Will you tell me that the piteous looks he gave us were not *speaking* to us for his salvation?'

'Yet he could not speak, Merivel.'

'He spoke to me.'

'In a language I could not hear?'

'In no language. He spoke to me soul-to-soul.'

The Baron nodded his pink-and-white head vigorously at this and began writing in the little Book he kept at his elbow through the meal.

'Soul-to-soul,' he said. 'This is well put, Sir Robert. I sometimes think this is how Constanza speaks to me.'

Constanza was Guy de Saint Maurice's dog, a grey Lurcher puppy, with long, soft limbs that reminded me of willow branches furred with lichen. This dog had lain quietly at our feet during the supper, but now, hearing her name, her trembling nose appeared from beneath the tablecloth. The Baron stroked her head.

'Yes, Constanza,' he said, 'and what do I ever refuse you? You plead so eloquently for walks and attention that I almost always consent, even when I do not really want to go for a walk. You *speak* to me.'

'Montaigne said something very similar about one of his dogs, Baron. He said he was not afraid to admit that his Nature was so "childish" that he could not refuse the play this dog offered him, even though it might interrupt his work.'

'Ah! Well, I am one with him. And always, as no doubt he found, I am gladdened by the walk with Constanza. My head clears. My whole *conception* of the world alters in its favour.'

Louise smiled tenderly at her father. She said: 'Papa's *conception* of the world is already admirably favourable, *n'est-ce pas*, Papa? Tell Sir Robert why you keep a Notebook always at your side.'

The Baron laughed. He picked up his book and waved it about. 'I am afraid to miss wonders, that is all! At my age memory is weak, but all around me the world grows more and more interesting. So I note everything down.'

'Papa keeps a pen and an Inkhorn in the head of his cane, so that he has the means to write at all times.'

'A lot of what I put in is futile, Sir Robert. Absolutely futile. But there are wonders, too. That is the point. Among all the dross are always the shining bits of gold.'

I expressed my admiration for this habit of Notation. And then, because my heart felt at peace (and because I had drunk several glasses of the Baron's excellent wine) I admitted to Louise and her Father what I had never admitted to anybody except Will Gates – that, long ago, I had attempted to write the story of my life.

'Oh, tell us more, Sir Robert!' said the Baron. 'Was it not arduous to set down?'

'No,' said I, 'for it amused me to try – as Montaigne says we must – to explore my own Nature. Louise knows that I am a man of impulsive appetites and haunted by the terrifying prospect that life will pay me no attention. But I am also very melancholy and prone to self-indulgent weeping – particularly at my own mistakes. And so it amused me to see how these differing sides of myself formed themselves into a Story.'

'I like this excellently,' said the Baron. 'And where is that Story now? I mean, where is the Book?'

I told them that the Book had lain under my mattress for sixteen years, gathering the excreta of bedbugs as it lay, 'and who am I to say whether even these minute creatures did not have souls?'

'Indeed! But might you not ask that it be dug out from the mattress and then you could send for it, and Louise and I could sweep away the dust of the bedbugs and read it?'

'Well,' said I, 'I think it is locked in the drawer of an Escritoire now, and indeed my servant, Will, could send it. But what it charts are all the follies of those times, all my venal habits and my neglect. The picture you would take of me from it would not endear me to you.'

'You might be mistaken about that,' said the Baron. 'What I have always prized in men is Honesty, above all else and certainly above small human failings. I assume your Book is honest, or else there would be no point to its existence.'

Silence fell in the grand room. Louise and the Baron stared at me, waiting for my reply. At last I said: 'When I wrote it, I believed it to be honest. But now I see that it is full of lies and self-delusions.'

⊣⊨

The room I was given in the Château looked out over the forested gardens to the Lake.

A high wind got up and I lay in a high bed listening to the sighing of the Firs. And it seemed to me that I was standing on some kind of Pinnacle of my life, from which place I could see both before and behind.

I slept in perfect peace and had a dream of Pearce. He stood before me, while I, with admirable flourish and *attaque*, dissected a corpse laid out on a table in the old Anatomy Theatre at Caius College, Cambridge. The body resembled me, but was not me – only somebody I might conceivably have been, or had endeavoured to be.

As my Demonstration progressed, Pearce took many Notes. He did not once – as was his usual way – question my findings or interrupt me, and when I ceased my Performance, he came to me, put his arm round my shoulder and said: 'You told me much, Merivel. And you strayed very little into Error. It was altogether admirable. Let us drink to your new competence.'

Whereon Pearce produced a flask of Sack, and we passed it from hand to hand and slaked a thirst, which was not of the body but of our minds, yearning for Knowledge and for our old friendship. And this was as sweet a dream of Pearce as I had had in many years.

When I woke in the night, it was to remember that all my Possessions were gone.

Even now I was encased – as in a linen cocoon – in an enormous Nightshirt that belonged to the Giraffe and on the morrow it would be his stockings that I would have to put on.

And this wearing of his clothes vexed me not a little, for it reminded me that he, Colonel Jacques-Adolphe de Flamanville of His Majesty's Swiss Guards, was still and always the husband of the woman I had come here to know and love, and that I was a poor Sir Nobody. I remembered that de Flamanville might arrive any moment to send me packing on a mule.

But then I began to consider what weapons I had with which to protect myself, and I knew that, already, I had one. And this was the great courtesy shown to me by the Baron de Saint Maurice. This elderly man, with his Notebook and his Inkhorn and his great good humour and wisdom, would, I decided, find some means to keep me from harm.

On the morrow he had promised to show me his Library, wherein, he said, he had books on every subject – from Botany to Demonology, from Gymnastics to Pharmacology, from the Tides of the Oceans to the Tanning of Leather, from the Art of Cathay to the Study of Superstition in the world, from Marriage to Mythology, from Zephyrs to Zoology . . .

And so I imagined all this knowledge, which was now freely available to me, as a shield around me, even as an invisible Curtilage of Enlightenment, keeping me at a little distance from all those who would make an enemy of me and seek to end my life.

25

What blessed my first days at the Château was a sweet quietness in the weather.

After breakfast on my first morning, while Louise went to her Laboratory, the Baron led me on a tour of his Estates and I saw his acres of vines, brimming with near ripeness in the soft sun. He had wide plantations of Poplars, for the marketing of their timber and, in the bright, steep grass meadows, cows led a slow, well-nourished life.

His orchards were magnificent with ripe plums, apples and pears. There did not seem to be any land that had not been put to bounteous use. Of fallow or wild spaces there were none. And the Formal Gardens had been planted with a great quantity of herbs and medicinal plants, which had led Louise to her experiments on salves and potions. The controlling mind that I saw at work here was orderly and averse to waste.

To this same mind I said: 'This makes me see that, at Bidnold, I have not been as ingenious in my use of land as I should have been. Much of it is mere Parkland, supporting nothing except my little herd of Red Deer.'

'Well,' said the Baron, 'Switzerland is a small country, half of it pushing up towards the sky in peaks and crags. We must be resourceful here or die.'

After which remark he was silent for a space, then he turned to me and said: 'Sir Robert, we must now enter upon a delicate conversation.'

'Ah,' said I. 'Well in matters of delicacy I prefer to be addressed as Merivel and not "Sir Robert".'

'Merivel? Well, yes, certainly, if you wish it. Names are important. So now I must tell you, Merivel, that my daughter endures that most fearful thing, an unhappy marriage . . .'

'I know something of this . . .'

'I blame myself for having agreed to it, yet de Flamanville courted her with great courtesy and discretion, and we did not know then that he has never loved women. But it has been a true Torture, because he is a cruel man, and there seems to be no end to it – or, at least, no end with any Honour in it. So I have hoped for some time that Louise might discover love elsewhere. Your visit will make her happy, I am certain of it.'

We were passing through an apple orchard and the Baron plucked a fine red *Délice* and gave it to me. I stared at it in my hand. Its perfection, shining in the sun's even light, was so striking, it was as if Saint Maurice had given me a jewel.

'I have been much alone in recent years,' I said. 'But when I met Louise, I felt life returning to me. She is exceptional among women. Let me assure you I have the greatest respect for her, Baron, most particularly for her gifts as a Botanist . . .'

'Her gifts, yes. They are considerable. You shall shortly hear her compositions upon the Harpsichord, which are very fine.'

'I shall be honoured to be among her audience.'

'But – please forgive me if this does not regard me – I thought you were lovers? She told me you had become lovers.'

'Yes . . .'

'She is forty-five, Sir Robert. And like mine, her nature is very passionate.'

'Yes . . .'

'She should not grow old unloved.'

'No, I do not intend—'

'She told me you did not go to her last night.'

'No, I did not.'

'So I do not quite understand . . .'

'Well, I was not sure how I should conduct myself in your house . . .'

'I see. Let me ask you how you think your King Charles would have conducted himself?'

I turned the *Délice* in my hand, feeling the cool of it, imagining its firm flesh. 'He would not have hesitated,' I said. 'He would have made love to your daughter.'

The Baron and I had walked a long way in the warm sunshine and were returning rather slowly along the drive, when we heard behind us the clip-clop of a horse.

Into my mind immediately came a vision of Colonel de Flamanville, astride a formidable stallion, with his sword held in readiness to slay me with one stroke as a prelude to dragging Louise back to Paris or Versailles.

Glancing round, however, I discovered the horse to be a mule – indeed, the very same mule that had thrown me off its back into the gravel, and on her back the goat boy who had loaned her to me.

The mule was reined in and skittered to an inelegant stop. Then I saw that slung onto the creature's rump was my lost Valise.

'My word!' said I, 'but this is an Honest place, Baron.'

'Well,' said the Baron. 'The air is clear here. Everything can be seen and nothing hid. And so we tend towards honesty. Is that very dull?'

After the walk I went to my room, opened my Valise and took out the things I had brought with me, which were not many, but did include Pearce's Nosebag with *De brutorum loquela* inside it, and now I was glad, given the supposed vastness of the Baron's Library, that I would be seen to possess at least one book. I took *De brutorum* out of the Nosebag and laid it upon my Night Table.

'Pearce,' I said. 'Do you see me? I think you would be proud of me now. I have come to a fine place of learning.'

I had packed, too, the coat I had had made in Paris, complete with its cascade of Shoulder-Ribbons. And I decided, as I hung this up, that for Louise's sake I must also attempt some learning in regard to my Appearance, striving always for elegance and decorum, so that I did not embarrass her in front of her father and his aristocratic Acquaintance.

I was sitting on my bed, surrounded by pairs of underdrawers and a quantity of crumpled shirts, when Louise entered my room.

I endeavoured to rise but she said: 'No, no, Merivel, do not move.'

She carried a glass on a pewter salver and set this down by me, saying: 'I brought you a Cordial. Father says you are quite fatigued from the great tour he has taken you on. Why do you not make yourself more comfortable, then take a sip of this, which is made of Elderberry and Rose Hips, and will strengthen you in a very short time.'

I did as she proposed and lay back on my pillows, with my lingerie heaped around me. And she came and sat near me and held the glass to my lips, very tenderly, as though I might have been a child.

I drank the Cordial. Louise watched me with fascinated attention. I asked myself whether she had come to my room in the expectation that I would make love to her now, in the Interlude between my walk with the Baron and the midday dinner.

I found her presence near me very sweet and comforting, but I realised once more that, since my contemptible behaviour in the Besançon coach, all sexual desire seemed to have left my body. I had often heard whispers at Court about certain fops who, having prodigiously used themselves in a thousand bedrooms, were now quite unable to perform coitus, unless it might be with the stimulation of obscene and unmentionable Orgies at work all around them. And I prayed that this would not be my case – that the Besançon whore had so slain me with illicit excitation that ordinary tender love was no longer possible for me.

I looked at Louise, remembering our amours in the *Jardin du Roi*, hoping this might make me a little hard. But all that would come to mind was the extreme winter cold that had enveloped us and how this cold, on the bits of our flesh that were naked to the air, had nipped and stung, and I felt this cold again and shivered.

'Louise . . .' I began.

But, as if anticipating the apology I was about to utter for being at the moment so unlike the lover she had known, she placed her fingers gently on my mouth and said: 'Hush, Merivel. I think you should close your eyes. Try to sleep a little. I will arrange for food to be brought to you later on, for I know that when one has taken exercise one needs fortification.'

I slept the day away and only awoke in late afternoon.

On a table in my room a plate of breaded chicken and pickled cabbage had been placed, and I devoured these with unseemly haste. At least, thought I, hunger has returned to me. I am not dying, therefore! And after eating I went to my close-stool, and shat very copiously and felt much relieved by this, telling myself that I was now cleansed of my all my Foulness.

I put on a clean shirt and went downstairs, but I could find neither the Baron nor Louise. Assuming them to be out on some further inspection of the vines and the orchards, both now coming to perfect, yet fleeting ripeness and asking to be gathered, I entered the Baron's Library.

Gazing at the great quantity of books (far outnumbering the volumes in my Library at Bidnold), smelling them, taking deep draughts of all that they contained, I felt a sudden Great Quiet come upon me. I sat down at the long oak table that ran the length of the room. I did not take any book to read, but only sat and breathed invisible words.

And what came to my mind was Margaret's exhortation to begin upon what she called 'some enterprise of Writing', and I knew now that this was what I longed to do. Indeed, thought I to myself, this is perhaps why I have come here, not merely to be Louise's lover, but to press my mind to some Proper Work, and in this will lie all my Consolation and some proper template for my Future.

Louise found me, sitting very still, like some Actor in a Tableau, at the Library table. The light at the window was golden, coming towards sunset.

She led me outside, to a charming terrace, where the Baron was taking his ease with a glass of wine, with Constanza at his feet.

A Footman poured wine for us. Just beyond the terrace was a coppice of Hazelnut, where a pair of sparrows were fussing and chirruping, and the sound of these birds in the soft evening sunshine was extraordinarily sweet, as though, for as long as this song lasted, nothing could be amiss in our world.

'So, what did you choose to read in the Library?' asked the Baron. 'Perhaps your tour took you no further than the A Cataloguing: Aesop's *Fables*? Aristotle's *Dialectica*? Aubrey's *Lives*?'

'No,' said I, 'no further than A. Or not even as far. Yet I *felt* the power of the books very forcibly. That seemed to be enough . . .'

'Yes? But you know you may treat the Library as though it were your own. Please borrow anything you wish from it.'

'Thank you, Baron.'

'Winter is not very far away. There will be great snows here at the Château. If we all have our Work, we shall endure them with fortitude, *n'est-ce pas*, Louise?'

'Yes. And I meant to tell you, Father, that I am working on a Preparation to keep the flies from pestering you.'

The Baron put his hand on his bald dome, above the ragged daisy petals of his white hair. 'Scourge of my existence, flies. For I sweat in my head and down they come to sup on this moisture.'

'I could lend you a wig, Sir . . .' said I.

'Ah, wigs. Now there is a vanity I am not fond of, begging your pardon, Merivel, for indeed yours is very nice and clean. But the thought of this ton of mouldering Curls on me . . . there is something in me which rebels at it.'

At this moment one of the sparrows flew down from the Hazelnut bush onto the grass, where it began to peck about. I watched it for a moment, envying the birds their absence of sartorial choice, and in the next second the bird was gone. A great grey Sparrowhawk had cascaded out of the air and carried it away in its claws.

We three stared at the patch of grass where the little bird had been. Its mate left the Hazelnut and landed among the fallen leaves and looked about, hopping this way and that. We watched in sorrow. It flew back to the topmost twig of the bush and balanced there, trying to see where its lost companion had gone. Then, it began a desperate calling: 'Sip-sip, sip-sip . . .'

This call was unlike the merry chirruping we had heard earlier. It was the sound of grief. And we were silent, listening to it, and Constanza began a plaintive whining.

Stroking the dog's ears to calm her, the Baron said: 'Who shall any longer say, when they witness this and hear the bird's lament, that Creatures have no souls? Does not Aristotle say in his *De anima*, that "voice is the sound characteristic of what the soul has in it"? Will you tell me there is no soul to inform that cry?'

'I shall not tell you so,' said I.

'And I shall tell you that we do not know,' said Louise.

We dined and went to bed, and I undressed and washed myself and put on a clean nightshirt. I lay in my linen sheets, listening to the owls in the firs and to the sound of the lake far off.

My head boiled with thoughts. Although I have, over the past year and a half, continued to set down my own Story, and this writing has often calmed and assuaged my melancholy, and sometimes brought me mirth, I do also see that my own life, for all its Singularity, has not sufficient significance to imbue this task with any real merit.

What I would fain discover is some Subject – such as Sir James

Prideaux's *Treatise upon the Poor of England* – which might absorb all my attention and lead to a Work of Proper Distinction, sufficient to get me some marvellous hearing at the Royal Society, whose Fellows incite in me both admiration and envy in equal measure.

These were no banal speculations, but considerations of the most audacious kind, leading to a momentous question. 'Why,' said I to myself, 'should it not be I, Robert Merivel, who brings the full power of his mind to this subject of the Souls of Animals and tries to explore it further?'

Why not, indeed? Why not?

I knew that many men had speculated upon the question, and that I could not proceed in ignorance, without first perusing these speculations. But I also assumed that many of them might be found in Baron de Saint Maurice's admirable Library, and thus be accessible to me in the coming days and weeks.

My lack of any formulated opinion on the question troubled me a little. I had, as yet, no coherent Hypothesis, let alone a Theory. But I remembered how Pearce had often said to me, on the subject of Anatomy (at which I excelled and he did not), that understanding is, of necessity, a slow journey and that, at the outset of this journey, one should proceed with humility. 'One cannot,' he said, with a flourish of complicated Pearcean logic, 'know in advance the infinite number of things which one does not know.'

What I knew I had – which many other men did not – was a great Affinity with God's Creatures, from a Starling I had first dissected as a child, to the Badgers I longed to find in the Vauxhall woods, from the great deception attending the gift of my Indian Nightingale and my attempts to save its life, to the sweet dog, Minette, who had been my companion through months of adversity. And so onwards unto Clarendon, my poor Bear, who cost me the price of a priceless ring, and whose soul I seemed to hear talking unto mine and asking to be set free.

Might it not be the case, I reasoned, that this Affinity – though I knew myself to be no scholar – would enable me to arrive at perceptions hidden from drier and colder men? And from what did this Affinity arise? Surely, from my own animal nature, to which my entire existence had been such a fearful slave? And thus, would not my attempt at this Treatise teach me not a little more only about birds or bears and their place in the world, but also about my own place and my own soul, thus enabling me to conduct the last years of my life with greater dignity than heretofore?

All of this thinking put me into a state of great optimism and excitation. The sweet sound of the lake, the calling of the owls, the sighing of the wind in the firs, seemed to set up the perfect orchestration to this agitation of my mind. I knew myself to be furiously happy. Almost, I desired to go down to the Library now and begin my search for books. I longed to tell Margaret that at last I had found a subject perfectly suited to me and that I would throw myself into my great Work with all the enthusiasm of which she knew me to be capable.

Though sleep seemed to be far off, as the night advanced and the Moon went down, I felt a beautiful calm steal upon me. I had my Plan and I saw that it was good. I felt like God surveying Creation and congratulating Himself on His excellent work.

And so I fell into a deep and soundless repose, and it was only when I woke with the sunrise that I remembered what I was meant to be doing in the night and had not done. I was meant to be making to love to Louise.

The time was six o'clock. I went quietly along the stone corridor to her room, concealing with my night robe a beautifully erect member. It was as though all my exquisite mental Excitation – compounded by my vision of myself holding forth to the Learned Fellows in the sacred chambers of the Royal Society – had primed me for its physical counterpart.

I went into the room and stole into Louise's bed. She woke and turned to me and I kissed her. When she felt the hardness that I pressed against her, she laughed with joy.

26

Now, for some long while, as the Autumn colours, shining through the lake mists, slowly browned and faded and the first chill of Winter came to our surprised attention, I can truly say that I was happy and at peace.

My days followed a sweet uniformity. After breakfast I would go with Louise to her Laboratory, so that she could share with me the progress of her experiments. I sat beside her, observing the measuring, mixing, heating, and sifting of herbs and compounds. Six different preparations were being tried as a Repellent for flies, but she could not come to any success here, for those that appeared efficacious burned the skin and those that did not burn it seemed rather to attract insects to land upon the Baron's pate.

Yet Louise did not give up. One of the many things I came to admire in her was her Quiet in relation to Failure. And when I commented upon this she said: 'I am merely trying to emulate, in a small way, your sublime Newton. He has demonstrated that on the route to scientific truth, Catastrophe and Error must be continually overcome. What is the purpose of becoming cross?'

After an hour or so, I would leave her to her labours and go to the Baron's Library. Here, in the scented quiet of this room, I had embarked upon Aristotle's *De anima* and begun to ponder long upon his conclusions about the soul, which he divides into three Elements. These he describes as follows: the Nutritive Soul, possessed by Man and Vegetables; the Sensitive Soul, possessed by Man and Animals; and the Rational Soul, which is unique to man.

Though it may prove very difficult to question his reasoning that only man possesses an intellective Soul, capable of Memory and will, I tried not to let myself and my would-be Treatise stumble upon this early obstacle. I reminded myself that Aristotle might be *in Error* when he assigned souls to potatoes and vegetable marrows. And if this was the case, why then he might also be mistaken in believing that animals could not reason or exert their will when called upon to do so.

Instances of animal behaviour, in which the will appears to be exerted, I already knew to be many. In the work of the naturalist, Henry More, I had read to my amazement of a 'Parliament of rooks', which sat upon the high roosts and acted as one to hound from their number those birds that had exhibited 'delinquent conduct'.

Pliny, I recalled, speaks of a troupe of Elephants who, being taught to dance by a cruel Master, were seen to be 'practising in secret', so that they would not be chastised at the next dancing lesson.

And was it not plain to see, thought I, that horses, such as my beloved Danseuse, and dogs, such as Bunting, came very clearly to comprehend the elaborate system of rewards and punishments meted out by their owners, thus arguing for a process of reasoning going on in their heads?

More than this, I had observed in these animals, no less than in Clarendon, a detestation of oppression and a spark of recognition of Justice. For had it not been true that, on the day when I led Clarendon out of his cage, so that his poor limbs, clamped in by the snow and ice, might be freed and exercised, he had followed me very meekly, as though understanding very perfectly my benign intentions towards him?

He could have massacred me for leaving him so long pent up in the cage, but he did not. It was as though he perceived my sorrow at what had happened in that time of the great snows, and understood that I was doing my best to make some amends to him.

While understanding that the road leading to my Treatise (which I tentatively entitled *Meditations Upon the Animal Soul by Sir R. Merivel*) would be very long, I permitted myself to scribble down some first Notes upon it, and this feeling of a true Beginning gladdened my heart so intensely that I could not refrain from taking up my pen again and writing to Margaret, to tell her how precious to me her advice had proved and that I was now embarked on a new field of study, 'which does indeed quiet my mind and has shaken me from all Melancholy'.

I did not tell my daughter that my other 'field of study' was teaching myself how to be a very marvellous Lover to Louise. But these *études* did indeed occupy much of each and every night, and she, being a woman of independent spirit, did not hesitate to instruct me and place parts of my body exactly where she wished them to be, and liked to keep up an erotic commentary upon our every Exertion.

These nights, while bringing me repeated sexual satisfaction, exhausted me somewhat, but Louise appeared to thrive. What I detected in her, as the autumn passed, was a blazing out of good health, despite so much loss of sleep, so that she appeared to look younger than when I had first met her at Versailles.

We did not speak of love. I did not feel able to pronounce the word. Yet I knew that this was what Louise longed to hear from me – that I loved her. And it is true that, in some measure, I *did* love her. But what I loved more was that new Sense of Myself, as a man of seriousness embarking upon a Great Work. For I saw that, for the first time in my life, I was attempting something that would find favour with the two men I had striven so long to please: Pearce and the King.

I pictured Pearce reading my *Meditations*, holding the Treatise close to his face, hour after hour, then laying it down at last and saying: 'Admirably far-reaching, Merivel. You have given me much to reflect upon. For once you have concentrated upon a subject *worthy of your time.*'

And as for King Charles, I saw him bursting out into affectionate laughter and slapping his thigh and saying: 'Animal souls! What a marvellous idea. Upon my word, my dear Fool, I see from this masterful Work that you have joined the ranks of the Wise and must be elected Fellow of the Royal Society forthwith! Let us have a jug of Mead.'

These imaginary scenes brought me unimaginable joy.

If the afternoons were fine, Louise and I would walk down through the winding paths of the estate to the Lake, and watch the sailboats skimming over it, and the waterbirds wading at its edge or bobbing in the water. And this panorama of the Lake, with the soft hills behind it sloping to a rim of firs, and neat houses of wood dotted here and there, with blue plumes of smoke issuing from their chimneys, soon became as pleasing to me as any landscape I had beheld, so graceful was it in its quietness and calm.

Only once, when Louise and I were alone there, on an afternoon that had started fine but had now shadowed to grey, was this calm disturbed.

We were standing, hand in hand, near the water's edge, and a large boat came towards us and tied up at the nearby jetty. From the boat emerged a group of Soldiers – more than eight or ten of them, all in their uniforms and buckling on their swords as they disembarked. I had no idea which Regiment they belonged to, but the dark blue of their coats put me in mind of the Swiss Guards.

At any moment, thought I, Colonel Jacques-Adolphe will appear among them, and he will come storming to me and attempt to gouge out my eyes with a Billiard spoon, and all will be at an end.

The soldiers went past us and no tall Giraffe came into view. But I had begun to shiver in the sudden afternoon chill and I said to Louise: 'We are living as though your husband is dead and will not come to take you back to Paris. But he will come one day.'

Louise was quiet. She touched my cheek, which no doubt had gone pale. 'For as long as his infatuation with Petrov endures, he will not come.'

'And when that is over?'

'He believes that it will never be over.'

'Will he not come at Christmastide?'

'No. That season is inimical to him. He cannot abide to imagine any nativity.'

In the evenings, after an always excellent dinner cooked by one of the Baron's two chefs (both neat-mannered men, unlike my poor Cattlebury), we would often repair to the *grand salon* and listen to Louise performing for us on the Harpsichord.

She played very finely and could sing well. And, listening to her voice, I could not but be put in mind of those evenings at Bidnold, long ago, when Celia sang for me and the delusion that I was in love with her stole so catastrophically upon me.

And I asked myself, between the sound of one woman's voice and another's, sixteen years later, what had I truly achieved in the world? And all that I could answer was that *I had persevered*. This perseverance had brought me here, to a fine château in Switzerland and to the bed of a clever woman. And this seemed to me to be fortune enough.

Louise not only played the Harpsichord, she also composed music. Her arrowy spirit flew straight to the mathematical heart of composition, without appearing to encounter difficulty. Her musical notations were deft and flowing. What melodies she heard in her mind, she could quickly underscore with moving harmonies. Certain bass Chords of hers – in their brilliance and surprise – brought even the most inattentive listeners back into the fold of Wonder.

Some of these listeners were men and women with far more musical knowledge than I possessed. The Baron liked to entertain at a Friday evening soirée, and so it was that I came to meet some of the Society of Neuchâtel, which included in their number Artists and Singers.

To this last category of people I found myself irresistibly drawn. Their great Largeness, whether of chest or bosom, together with the echoey timbre of their voices I experienced as a strange, sexual provocation. That the men, no less than the women, were in the habit of embracing each other created in me a longing to be so embraced. And a Swiss Baritone, by the name of Marc-André Broussel, as though reading my mind, did, at our second encounter, hold me against his massive girth for a full ten seconds, then pressed a sensual kiss on my lips.

This singer spoke five languages and knew London, and had sung for the Duke of York. Upon learning that I was a Confidant of the King, he wished to hear every detail of my life. And, liking his attention and the musky scent of him, I recounted to him the story of how the King had rewarded me with lands and titles in return for becoming a Professional Cuckold, and how I had broken my pact with him. 'Alas,' I told Broussel, 'I did the one thing forbidden to me. I attempted to make love to my wife. And so I was cast into the wilderness.'

'What wilderness? Where?' said Broussel, clutching at my sleeve.

'Well,' I said, 'only the Quakers, in England, believe themselves to live beyond the Great Shadow cast by Whitehall. So I went to them, to work in a Quaker Bedlam with my only friend in the world, John Pearce. But John Pearce was a dying man . . .'

'*Mon dieu, mon dieu, mon cher homme,*' said Broussel, encircling me in his arms, 'how I love this story! Ah, I would like to compose an opera around it. Will you not write it down for me? I am always searching for stories and finding none as good as this.'

So susceptible am I to the kind of flattery that puts me at the *centre* of a thing, and so seduced was I by this Marc-André Broussel, with his Largeness and his wild black hair and his scent of cloves and rose oil, that I heard myself agree, with alacrity, to do this.

He then cried out, for all to hear: 'Listen every one of you! Sir Robert Merivel is going to write down a story for me – his own story! – and I am going to write an opera about him. I shall *play him*! I shall embody him in music!'

The company's attention was greatly attracted by this and, soon enough, all pressed me to tell 'my story'. But I quickly saw that it was one thing to tell it in confidence to the great Singer and quite another to relate it to the Baron's assembled guests. There is, I know, some pathos in the tale, yet it also risks to make me appear lecherous and foolish, and although I have never been averse to ridicule, I did not want to court it here – not least because I did not want to embarrass Louise.

Seeing me hesitate, Broussel stood up and with a dramatic flourish of his arm said: 'I shall tell it, if Sir Robert will not. It is the story of a man who is given Paradise. Paradise, you see – like Adam. But again, like Adam, he breaks the one rule that he must not break. And so loses again all that had been so recently granted to him. But as to detail, you will have to wait until I have written my opera!'

There was a great Outcry at this and somebody called out: 'How does the story end?'

At which Louise said quickly: 'We do not know. None of us knows how our stories are to end.'

Work upon my *Meditations* proceeded slowly. I had at last opened Fabricius's *De brutorum loquela* and found there a very tender passage about mother hens and the hatching of their chicks, which, if my Latin translation was accurate, indicated to me the Master's acknowledgement that *love* might be present in the hearts of birds, as indeed I had presumed from watching the Sparrow on the lawn, mourning the loss of its mate. I copied out Fabricius, thus:

The chick in the egg, needing air, by its chirping notifies the Mother that it is time to break the shell, its own beak being too soft for the purpose.

'There is, however, sufficient Space and Air to permit the chick to chirp loud enough to be heard, as both Pliny and Aristotle bear witness. The chirping may have a pleading sound and to her (the Mother Hen), hearing it and understanding the need, or if you will, eager to behold her chick and most dear child, pecks open the shell.

If a chicken can feel Maternal Love, as imputed to it by Fabricius, then surely he is admitting the possibility that the bird has a soul. People who appear incapable of love we call 'heartless' or 'soulless'. We say that we feel love in our hearts, but it is not the organ we are talking about (which, as Pearce and I discovered, is absolutely without feeling), it is the soul.

We know not where in us this soul resides. Perusing a work entitled *Observations sur l'esprit humain* by a French writer, Jean Duquesne, I read that, in Denmark, earlier in this long century, it was believed that the Devil might steal the soul from the nostrils of unbaptised children.

Superstitious people imagined Satan flying through the air and coming through the open window of a Nursery, and approaching the precious cradle, then reaching in with a curving finger, as narrow and flexible as the stalk of a spring onion, and taking the fledgling Soul, and supping upon it, as a Gourmet supping upon some rare strain of Asparagus. And later it would pass through Satan's body and return to earth as foul faeces, to be trampled into the mire.

Then, alas, the soul-less child would grow up with no Human Qualities within him, and be pitiless and enslaved to appetite all his life. And so, to prevent this catastrophe, the windows of Nurseries were kept closed and locked, and it came to pass that sometimes infants died for want of any fresh air.

All this, though I saw that Duquesne's book was full of fancy, disturbed me much. I sat long at the Library table, pondering it. And it came upon me that the reason why I had chosen this subject of the Souls of Animals was certainly to ascertain whether I, a man from whom Belief in God had long ago fled, and who could not bring himself to imagine any Resurrection, possessed a soul *at all*, or whether I was not merely an Amalgam of vain Longings and Appetites, no better than a morning cockerel strutting about his yard, waking all the world with his inharmonious voice.

Each day the weather was becoming colder, and knowing that Christmas would be soon upon us, I began to buy gifts for Margaret – an ivory brooch in the form of an Edelweiss flower, a small leather Jewel Case and a card of fine Swiss lace. These I despatched to London with the message that I would come home to Bidnold for the winter if she was not happy at Whitehall and wished to return to Norfolk.

I then wrote to Will Gates as follows:

My dear Will,

Your Employer, Sir R. Merivel, sends you good Cheer from Switzerland, where we, like you, are sliding towards Winter, with now and then some light falls of Snow.

Though I cannot yet find it in my heart to quit this very beautiful Place at present, I am always and ever thinking about Bidnold and praying you shall not be walled up in Ice, as we were last season.

Pray send me word of how you are, Will. I do not suppose the King has come to Bidnold lately? I feel very far from you all. But I can relate to you that I have not been idle, but have begun upon some Work, which I do think will please Miss Margaret.

Awaiting your reply, I send you this Christmas Gift of a

Merivel

decorated Almanac, showing the outspread of days for the
year 1685, that will shortly be upon us.
From
Your Affectionate Master and Friend,
R. Merivel

When I showed Louise the Almanac, which had been very nicely
decorated with Astronomical signs and symbols, she said: 'It is
too beautiful to give to a Servant.'

I took it from her hands and began to wrap it. 'No,' I said. 'It is
not.'

27

Christmas came and went, and I received a fine letter from Margaret, saying how contented she still was with Fubbs and mentioning in very affectionate terms her Admirer, the Honourable Julius Royston.

> *I have,* she wrote, *been instructing Julius in the Rules of Gin Rummy and now we two are quite addicted to the game. We like to play alone, without other slower or weaker players to annoy us, so we sneak away from the Duchess, and even sometimes from the King (who manifests a sweet fondness for Julius) to lay out our cards. I fear there may be no cure for our addiction . . .*

At this tender mention of Royston, I felt my fear on Margaret's behalf abate a little. But I instructed myself to remain vigilant in my mind. Margaret is a clever young woman, who has long ago learned how easy it is to turn me round and round, like the Blind Catcher in a game of Buff.

I had no reply from Will.

I tried to imagine the slow Progress of my letter and my gift across France and across the sea, and then going no faster than a horse could trot along the roads of Suffolk and Norfolk. I knew that I should be patient.

But in my dreams I saw my house catch fire and each and

every person and each and every Thing within it burned, as my dear Parents had burned in 1662, and as London itself had burned four years later. And the voice of Pearce said to me: 'There was always going to be a Third Fire, Merivel. Only you were too blind to see it coming.'

Always, when these nightmares woke me, Louise tried to soothe me with caresses and kisses, and these, she ever hoped, would lead to some new immodest act between us at four or five in the morning. Yet sometimes they did not lead there, for what I felt come upon me a was great weariness with the Repetitions of the Human World, and I would get up and retire to my own bed, seeming not to care that Louise might feel abandoned, but only needing to be alone.

Louise had told me, in a whispered conversation one night and quite unabashed, that she was at a point in her life, at the age of forty-six, where, having been denied any sexual pleasure by her husband and her lovers being few and what she termed 'inadequate', she had discovered in herself, through my ministrations, a great and perpetual Yearning for *Jouissance*.

She admitted provocatively (hoping thus to excite me) that it troubled her so much, she frequently became distracted in her work and sometimes guiltily resorted to pleasuring herself – a thing she had seldom been wont to do before she met me. And a set of Songs she was composing upon the Harpsichord, each with a most beautiful Melody, she had chosen to entitle *In Praise of Bliss*. The words she was writing for these songs made me blush for her.

'How will you sing these verses in front of your Father?' I asked.

'He will like them,' she said airily. 'He will be pleased that I have been brought to such a Heat before I grow old. He wants to me to be loved.'

One cold January day, Louise came into the Library in midmorning.

I was scribbling some Notes upon the observable intelligence of Orang-utans, remarked upon by King Louis of France and of some potential Significance in my Argument. I was feeling that rare and pleasant thing, the sense of some *onward progress* in my Endeavour, and did not wish to be interrupted.

But, without any apology, Louise pushed my books away, sat herself upon my knee and whispered her needs of the moment into my ear, then guided my hand under her skirt to bring her to a quick and violent Spasm, after which she almost fainted in my arms.

Thus turned aside from my work, I felt suddenly oppressed by this obsession of hers and the demands it made upon me, and said to her unkindly: 'Louise, shall you not try to calm your appetites a little, before they wear you out?'

'I cannot,' she said. 'Why do you ask me such a thing? It is you who have *awoken* them in me, Merivel. I was chaste before I met you. It is your fault.'

I kissed her gently, to atone for my unkindness, and I thought she would go from me then and let me return to my Orang-utans, but, roused by even my quiet and tender kisses, she began to embrace me with a terrible fervour.

We tumbled off the Library chair onto the floor and I felt my breeks being unbuttoned. I began to protest, but Louise's embraces were such that they stifled my words, making them inaudible. She tugged down my breeks and knelt over me and sat astride me with her skirts pulled up (a position Violet Bathurst had often favoured and chose, sometimes, to spice with exquisite vulgarity and debauch by pissing upon my stomach) but I had no will nor hardness for the Act, and all I could feel was a sudden stab of mourning for Violet. I thus pushed Louise roughly from me and she toppled over onto the carpet.

At this moment the Library door opened. Aghast that the Baron should find me thus, unbuttoned and throwing his daughter aside as though she were some mere Object, I staggered to my feet, tugging frenziedly at my Breeches. My wig had fallen off. My face burned with shame. I turned to begin to make my apologies and discovered myself face to face with Colonel Jacques-Adolphe de Flamanville.

From his great and austere height, dressed still in his uniform of the Swiss Guards, complete with his sword, he regarded me. Behind him stood a Fellow Officer, also uniformed, and also staring in fear and disgust at me, as though I might have been some foul reptile in a cage.

As I reached down clumsily for Louise and helped her to her feet, de Flamanville said: 'I shall be obliged to kill you. You have no Honour, Sir, but to save mine we shall go through the ritual of a duel. We shall meet on Friday morning at first light.'

No words would come to me. All that I could feel was the great *stupidity* of what had happened. Ten minutes ago, I had been quietly at work on my Treatise; now I had sealed my Death Warrant. Or rather, Louise had sealed it.

To my great shame I could not feel any fear for what punishments might be meted out to her by de Flamanville, but only mourn the imminent end of my life with sudden and terrible intensity.

I felt almost faint and held to the back of the chair on which I had lately been sitting. Perhaps it was seeing me so unmanned by the Colonel's declaration that gave Louise the strength to say calmly to her husband: 'With your ridiculous threat of duels, Jacques, you have forgotten to introduce me and Sir Robert to your companion. Is this your lover, Petrov?'

'Louise,' said de Flamanville, 'I suggest you go to your room and arrange yourself. You stink like a Vixen.'

'And you, my dear, stink of cruelty, as always,' said Louise. 'I shall certainly go to my room – *my* room in *my* Father's house, where I shall behave as I please with whom I please. But before I go, I wish only to know whether you have brought your boy-lover under this sacred roof, or not.'

De Flamanville opened his mouth to speak, but now his companion stepped forward, performed a little military clicking of his heels and said: 'My name is Capitaine Beck, Madame. I am under your husband's Command at Versailles. I am not Petrov.'

'Ah,' said Louise. 'Well, Capitaine Beck, may I suggest you take my husband out of this house before my Father returns from his walk and throws you both out. He is Baron Guy de Saint Maurice de Neuchâtel. He will not countenance any duel fought on his land and I warrant he will protect Sir Robert Merivel with his life.'

Beck appeared disconcerted by this, but the Giraffe drew himself up to his full six foot and four inches and said: 'Louise, you have quite failed to understand the situation. No matter what your father does or says, your ridiculous Lover is going to die. My honour dictates it. Capitaine Beck will call upon Sir Robert to set out the formal arrangements. Let it be swords or pistols. It is all one to me, for he does not stand a chance with either.'

He was right. I was no swordsman nor marksman. I could not have been certain of killing de Flamanville with a Blunderbuss at twenty paces. When the two men had left, I sank down upon the chair upon which I had yearned to sit quietly all morning and said: 'Well, that is that, Louise. I have no choice but to play the coward and run away.'

'No!' said Louise. 'For that is exactly what he will expect you to do. He will make the necessary preparations immediately. You will be waylaid and stabbed in the back.'

'These are my only choices then – to die one way or the other?'

'No,' said Louise. 'There is another way we may come at de Flamanville. By money. For he has very little – not enough for his needs in the *Fraternité* – for his father gambled away the de Flamanville family Fortune. All that we own – the house on the Faubourg Saint-Victor, everything – came to me from my father. The Baron will raise a large sum. Jacques-Adolphe will accept it and leave. And you and I shall go on just as we were.'

'And what of your husband's Honour?'

'Ah, Merivel, did you not once admit to me that in your contract with King Charles you had traded Honour for Material Possessions? And does not everyone on earth understand how easy a trade that is? I know Jacques-Adolphe. He will find it *very* easy.'

'Louise,' said I, 'I cannot ask your Father to buy my life.'

'No,' she said. 'I will ask him.'

I sit with the Baron by a dying fire, drinking Claret.

It is late and cold, but we linger there. The Baron is too discreet to talk, yet, of de Flamanville, or of my imminent death, or of what the Baron might do to delay or forestall it. Instead, we discuss the things which hold us to the world.

We turn to the subject of my *Meditations Upon the Animal Soul*, which work he much approves, and I confide to him my vain Vision of myself presenting it at the Royal Society, with all the Natural Philosophers listening attentively to me in that hushed chamber, and feeling at last that I had become a Person of Substance.

'Ah,' says the Baron. 'How interesting it is that we find it so difficult to believe in our own Worth. To me, you are already a Person of Substance, as you call it. With your medical skills and your great compassion, I judge you a worthy man. As perhaps you judge me to be, too. But in recent years it has stolen upon me that, for all my great age, I have done nothing to change the world. I inherited much. I made more. And that is the sum of my life. And so I have set my heart upon a mad enterprise.'

'A mad enterprise? What might it be, Baron?'

The Baron takes up the small Notebook that he carries everywhere with him and shows me pages and pages of sketches of flying machines. 'You see?' he says, 'I am quite deranged. I am nowhere near to solving the problem of Propulsion, or Forward Motion, but if only I could! Then I would feel that I had made some great contribution to the happiness of Mankind. For how wonderful this would be – to fly above the world, like angels. Is it not one of the things we crave in our dreams?'

'And in our dreams we give ourselves that power. Then we thud down to earth upon waking.'

'Precisely. But suppose we could fly above the lake, and then south, even, towards the mountains, or *above* the mountains . . .'

'Not mere angels, but gods!'

'Yes, gods! Ah, Merivel, I fear I shall never solve it. I have not enough time left. Sometimes I feel I have lived too long anyway. I have outlived five dogs. And you know, age does not confer wisdom, Merivel. Age confers Vanity, Foolish Prattle and a terrible concern with Riches. The idea that I could lose my fortune obsesses me not less than the flying machines.'

'It is human to fear poverty. Human, too, to wish to pass what we have to our children.'

'Yes, and this, I suppose, must bring bring us to the question of Louise. You know that she is in love with you? You are now what holds her to the world.'

'I admit I find this surprising, Baron. Nobody has ever been in love with me before.'

'I see in her eyes a desire to devour you! You are the first man to whom she has given herself in this way.'

'Yes . . .'

'So. You must understand that I have never been able to refuse my daughter the things she asks of me. Why should I, when I am so proud of who she is and what she accomplishes?'

'I understand completely, Sir.'

'So here is what I have resolved. I will pay de Flamanville, but not merely to spare your life. I will pay him a fine fortune to have the marriage Annulled, provided you will agree to marry Louise.'

I get up and, on unsteady feet, walk towards the Claret decanter and pour all that remains of it into our two glasses. I am shivering as I say: 'I am infinitely touched by your generosity, Baron, but I cannot accept. I cannot have my life bought for me, nor my future.'

'I do not really see why not.'

I want to say that this *already happened to me* long ago and that, ever since, I have sworn that no debt of this kind would ever be mine again. Indeed, to see such a terrible choice rise up before me again makes me feel faint. It is as though all the life I have lived and all that I have achieved *by my own strivings*, between the first contract with the King and this last one with the Baron, is about to be annihilated.

I gulp the Claret and say: 'The thing belittles me too much.'

'I understand. But you do not need to see it in this way.'

'In my position, Sir, would you accept it?'

'That is a fair question. I think it would depend upon whether I was in love with Louise or not – but pray, do not answer that. Let me merely remind you that, as Louise's husband, you would become Heir to the Château and its Estates. You would live in comfort for the rest of time. And do not underestimate that. When you reach my age you will understand the importance of great riches.'

We fall silent. The ticking of a Long-case clock is the only sound to be heard in the room. Then Constanza whimpers in her dreams.

I have hardly slept at all, or so it feels, when I am woken by a Servant, who informs me that there is a Capitaine Beck here to see me.

'No!' I cry. 'The duel is on Friday!'

'Duel, Monsieur? What duel? Do you wish to dress, Monsieur? Or shall I show him up here?'

'I must dress. I cannot go to my death in my Nightshirt!'

The servant goes out. I haul my body out of the bed, where it longs to stay. It is still dark outside. I feel sick and my mouth is dry from the excess of Claret drunk with the Baron.

I rinse my face and comb my wig, and fumble for a clean shirt. As I am stepping into my Breeks, all aghast in my mind at the morning that awaits me, there is a knock upon my door.

It is Beck. He closes the door silently behind him. Gone is his look of man-afraid-of-a-reptile and he says, with anxious politeness: 'I am sorry to wake you so early, Sir Robert. But I have been instructed to speak to you, and you alone, on a matter of gravity.'

'Gravity?' I sigh, buttoning my breeks as hastily as I can. 'Well, indeed, this is a Grave matter, Beck. I do not mind telling you that I really do not wish to die.'

'I understand. This why I am sent here. To tell you that you do not need to die.'

I sit down on the bed. I note that it is still dark outside my window. Beck approaches and stands with one hand on the bedpost.

'Are you telling me that the duel is cancelled?'

'No. It is not cancelled. But it is not you who will be killed; it is the Colonel.'

'Capitaine Beck,' I say, 'why do you not sit down? Then you can explain to me calmly what it is you mean.'

Beck selects a tapestry-covered fauteuil, but does not relax into it but sits leaning forward with his elbows on his knees. 'Can we be overheard in this room?' he asks.

'No, I do not think so. The walls are stone.'

'Very well. I will tell you. The Colonel came here to the Château, knowing that you were in residence with his wife, to *invite* a duel. The duel is what he wants. In a duel lies Death with Honour. And that is what he seeks.'

I stare at Beck. He appears hot in his uniform, even on this chill dawn, and he begins wringing his hands. He looks as though he might be about to cry.

'I am not quite following you, Capitaine,' I say.

'Let me be plain,' he says. 'The Colonel had a lover. He was a very young officer, almost a boy . . .'

'Petrov.'

'Yes. The Colonel's love for Petrov was very great. He told me it was a sublime love – the love he had always believed might be possible between fellow soldiers, a love *ordained* by God. It put him into a religious and physical fervour. Petrov was as beautiful as a girl and full of grace. The Colonel was a man in Paradise. He

believed his life would henceforth be with Petrov, and be a marvellous and noble and faithful life. But something happened.'

'Yes?'

'Petrov betrayed him. I mean that he left him – for another
Officer. I suppose that this is what those with beauty always do:
they try to ensnare the whole world.'

Beck swallows. I see that he is in great discomfort, but I remain
silent and after a moment he resumes his story: 'The Colonel has
struggled to go on with his life, to fulfil his duties in His Majesty's
Guards. He has been very brave in these struggles, but he does
not wish to endure them any more. If he cannot live with Petrov,
he would prefer to die.'

'Might he not persuade Petrov to come back to him?'

'He has tried. He has prostrated himself before him. But Petrov
is tired of him and enamoured of another, and that is that. Love
is a terrible thing.'

Beck wipes his brow, which is sweating profusely. I rise and
pour water for him and he thanks me. I return to the bed and say:
'Forgive me, Capitaine, but if the Colonel is so hungry for Death,
why does he not kill himself?'

'He is a Soldier, Sir Robert. He has lived by the Code of the
Swiss Guards, which demands "Death with Honour". There is no
honour in suicide, unless as an act of atonement for cowardice in
battle.'

'So he sought *me* out? He pretended all his anger on behalf of
his wife, so that I would be his Executioner?'

'That is correct. On Friday morning you will take your positions for the duel. The Colonel will point his pistol at you, but he
will not shoot. You will shoot. You will aim for the heart.'

We sit in silence, staring at each other. After a few moments I
say: 'How am I to be sure that this is not a trap? Colonel de Flamanville has always felt a great Detestation for me and I can
readily imagine that it would give him satisfaction to kill me.'

'I understand your suspicions, but I swear to you, Sir, this is no
trap. I have lived with Colonel de Flamanville, as his Adjutant, for

many months. He is a man bound upon a rack. The mental anguish he endures makes him cut his own flesh. He does not eat nor sleep. Did you not remark how thin he has become? When he catches sight of Petrov he trembles and faints. He is in Hell. He thinks only of death.'

I look over to the window and see the first streaks of a pale dawn laid across the earth's edge. 'There is . . . a difficulty,' I say.

'Yes. What is that?'

'I will not be able to kill him.'

'No,' says Beck. 'We had foreseen this. You are unpractised. We have devised a remedy.'

28

When I woke again I looked out of my window and saw Louise walking alone in the Knot Garden with its covering of snow. She wore a cloak and her pace was measured and forlorn.

I stared at her for a long while, feeling great tenderness towards her. But this tenderness was mixed with the sorrow that my love for her was not as overwhelming as hers was for me.

In deciding this, I cursed my own Obstinacy and Refusal. Louise was as graceful, cultured and marvellous a woman as I could ever hope to have by my side. I should have rejoiced to be the recipient of her passion. And in part – and especially when my carnal desire for her was equal to hers for me – I did. Yet the thought that I would spend the rest of my life with her wearied me. It wearied me because I knew that she would expect too much of me – from my body and from my mind. *I knew that I would fail her.*

I dressed and went down into the Dining Room, where I found the Baron eating plum pie and drinking coffee. When these restoratives had also been served to me, and revived me a little, I recounted to him the Content of my meeting with Capitaine Beck.

At once he said: 'I fear some trap, Merivel. The story strikes me as too extreme and fantastical for a Military man. This is done, I think, only to ensure that you keep the pledge of the duel.'

'It may be, Baron. But Capitaine Beck seemed very distressed on behalf of the Colonel, as though he *felt* his suffering in his own body. It is difficult to doubt what he said.'

The Baron sipped his coffee. Then he said: 'Let me go to de Flamanville this morning with the proposition I described to you last night. Perhaps he will accept. If he accepts, then we shall know that all mention of despair and suicide was but a ploy to bring you to your certain Execution. And he will live the rest of his life very happily, free from the constraints of marriage and with sufficient money to indulge his heart elsewhere. He will get from me the house in Paris, of course, but I do not think that Louise is very fond of it.'

Into my mind, when I thought about this house, came the terrible image of the Colonel's Sister, Mademoiselle Corinne, with a morsel of boiled Parsnip hanging off her chin and shrieking at me through her toothless mouth, and spending her mournful evenings cutting silhouettes out of black paper.

'No,' I said. 'I do not think that she is fond of it.'

'And you and Louise may live on your Estates in England. There is room in your grounds for a Laboratory, I assume?'

I looked distractedly down at the remnants of my fruit pie. I knew what this question signified. The Baron saw my discomfort and leaned towards me and said gently: 'Though I admire you, Sir Robert, and would very much dislike to see you killed, I am doing this for Louise. We should both understand what is at issue here. If you cannot promise to marry her you must tell me now. Then you will have to take your chance with the duel.'

A silence followed. The Baron, with his clear hazel eyes, observed my struggle to utter words we both knew would change my life. I knew that I was perched upon some dreadful promontory, where the Void gaped on two sides, and my feelings of Vertigo were fearful. I wished only to retreat to where I had once been safe, but knew I could not. To my own dismay I heard myself stammer: 'There is plenty of room for a Laboratory at Bidnold.'

I watched Louise for a long while, pacing back and forth in the garden, sunk in her thoughts. Then I went to the Library, as though I imagined I was about to begin upon some Work on my

Meditations, and went so far as to lay out my papers and my quills. But I knew that this was no time for work. I merely sat at the table, feeling wan and chill, staring at the wall.

I longed to be young again: sculling on the river, sporting with Rosie Pierpoint, fishing with Pearce, playing the fool for the newly restored King – before my destiny was changed by him. I longed, in sum, to be a free man.

But I was not free. I was either going to die on the morrow, or pledge myself to marry Louise de Flamanville.

I told myself that as her husband I would be the envy of many men. They would observe her passion for me and want to bed her, but she would refuse them. And, if she did, they would look at me anew, wondering what Trick I possessed to keep such a woman enslaved to me. I would be revered.

Further, and most important, I would be wealthy. Louise would bring with her a bounteous Dowry. I would have no mean Old Age. I would have no Death through Poverty. I would be able to provide for Will. I would, when my daughter married, give her a sumptuous wedding . . .

So now all my thoughts toiled upon money and upon status. I would not only be rich; I would have a permanent and honourable place in the Baron's Society. Broussel would write an opera about me. I would hear myself immortalised in sound . . .

I found, to my shame, that in a short space of time I was much consoled by these things. Indeed, I was made cheerful enough by these material and artistic considerations to risk going to Louise, knowing that I could now be tender towards her, my future wife.

I found her in her Bedroom, brushing her hair. I took the brush from her and told her that I loved her.

She was shivering after her long walk in the snow and I held her close to me to warm her, and she kissed me and told me we would be happy together 'as neither of us has ever been'.

But all that I was veritably thinking about was how, next to her skin and next to mine, from now on, there would always be silk or satin or fine linen. And I put my head between her breasts and laid my face on the silk Camisole that she wore, then took the edge of the garment into my mouth and caressed it.

At lunchtime the Baron returned. 'I have seen it for myself,' he said. 'I would not have believed it of this hard-hearted Soldier, but it is true: Colonel de Flamanville is lost to grief.'

'Is it your belief that he genuinely wants to die, Sir?'

The Baron sighed and called a Servant to bring him a glass of Hock. 'Yes,' he said. 'De Flamanville's mind is on Death. How a man may lay all his hopes upon the whims and desires of another being I have never understood. But this is what he did. He was unsparingly honest about it, to my distress. I could have wished him to be more circumspect and modest, but he seemed to yearn to tell me all. He said that when he found Petrov he found himself, and when he lost him he lost his own Soul.

'So there we have it. He wishes to die. My offer of money moved him no more than the touch of my hand on his shoulder. He has no interest in worldly things. He does not even wish to return to the house in Paris, for that he once took Petrov with him there, and he says he cannot bear to look on it again if Petrov is not by his side and in his bed.'

'Is he not concerned, even, for his beloved Corinne?' enquired Louise.

'He did not mention her. I think he is concerned for nothing and no one. He told me that he has but one aim in view: an honourable Death. So there we are. The duel must take place.'

Terrible visions came to my mind.

First I pointed my pistol at the Colonel and fired, and my shot pinged against the trunk of a tree and ricocheted back towards me and took out my eye. Then my second attempt to kill him missed by an inch and only shot off his hat and a little tuft of his hair, thus making him appear quite ridiculous. Third, so blinded by the moment was I that I swivelled the gun round and killed Beck. And to end it all, I forgot the etiquette of the duel so absolutely that I pointed the gun at myself and shot away my heart.

'Baron,' I said, 'let me remind you that I am no marksman. I am not in the habit of shooting anything at all, let alone a man. I can by no means be confident of killing the Colonel.'

'He knows that,' said the Baron. 'Beck will take care of it.'

Now Friday morning has arrived.

As I dress myself in my best black-and-gold Coat, to walk out to the duel, knowing that a chance still remains that I will be dead in half an hour's time, I force myself to ask, what care I for Death? Those I love will merely go on without me. Margaret will marry. Will must go to his grave soon enough, whether I am there or not, and Pearce has already gone before me. As for the King, he may not even notice that I am gone . . .

Yet I find myself wishing, as I tramp through the snow, that I had some belief in God or His Heaven. Then, I reason, I would cross over in the hope of seeing Pearce, dressed in his Quaker garb, waiting for me, and, seeing me, break into his stumbling run and call out my name: 'Merivel! Welcome! I had not thought to find you *here*!'

But I know that what awaits me, if I am killed, is not my friend, but only Darkness. So vivid am I to myself, in all my moods, in my goodness and foulness, that I find it impossible to imagine my own absence. I cannot see my rooms at Bidnold without putting myself in them. I cannot imagine Cattlebury concocting meals that I am not going to eat. I am able to visualise my grave, in Bidnold Churchyard, with a nice Headstone and flowers and branches of fir laid round it, but not my dead body beneath it. The concept of Not Being fills me with outrage.

The morning is full of sunshine. I walk through the Forest and I see the snow-laden trees glittering with beauty. I notice the traces of animals – foxes and Deer – and envy them their free-

dom and their joy, as they scamper through the great wood in all
its Winter glory.

There is no wind. The silent trees seem to watch and pity as
we pass, walking in line, I leading, followed by the Baron, who
has volunteered to act as my Second, wearing a vast coat of fur
that cannot help but remind me of Clarendon.

The date is the 15th of January in the year 1685 and I am fifty-
eight years old.

We come at last to the clearing where the duel is to take place.
Nobody is there.

I stop walking and turn to the Baron. A robin flutters down
from an ash branch and regards us. I consider how terrible it will
be to see blood on snow.

The Baron looks all about him and we start to listen for footsteps, but none are heard. I lift my face to the blue sky and think,
perhaps after all there will be no duel. The Colonel will return to
Versailles and succeed in seducing Petrov back to his side. There
will be no Annulment. There will be no marriage with Louise . . .

The Baron has brought with him a flask of Brandy, and he
opens this and we drink. And then we see the two Soldiers coming silently towards us down a narrow path.

They have put on their Dress Uniforms. As they turn towards
us, they seem to understand that their long legs carry to this terrible fray an image of Male Perfection, which will never be sur-
passed. By comparison, I know that I, in my black Coat with my
breeks a little too wide, appear like some lowly supplicant *waiting for their favour.*

We move forward to the middle of the clearing, and bow and
then clasp hands as is the custom. The Colonel's face is white and
thin. It betrays nothing.

Beck carries the weapons. The two pistols are housed in a
wooden box, which he offers to us each in turn, as though he
might be offering cigars or sweetmeats. As I take up my pistol I
think of the Highwayman on the Dover Road and the death he

got, which he had not expected. And I understand that I still do not know how this day is to end.

Beck produces from his pocket two bullets. He holds them in the palm of his hand and the lead shines in the sun. We take them up and put them into the pistols.

Then I look, suddenly, in anguish at Beck, for he appears to carry no weapon. He asks me if I am ready and I reply that I am, and I feel the Baron's hand touch my arm before the two Seconds withdraw.

I now stand back-to-back with Colonel de Flamanville. On the First Command, we are to start walking away from each other, making 'good strides'. When the Seconds have counted ten paces, they will make the Second Command, calling for us to stop. Then we are to turn and fire.

The First Command comes and I begin walking. The gun is heavy in my hand. Far above me I can hear rooks turning in a circle and crying out.

Part Four
The Great Transition

29

Once more I find myself travelling across France, this time in a North-Westerly direction. Far out, and still separated from me by many weary roads and a churning sea, lies England.

Dusk creeps round our Coach as we make progress towards Dijon, with a fine snow beginning to fall.

There are but two travellers in the Chaise, myself and an elderly English Priest. He is scribbling sermons till the daylight fails. Having nothing to read, I have begged to borrow his Bible, which precious Book, I note, is stained and squashed, with a pungent scent to it, as though the Priest cradled it to his body every night (or else kept it under his mattress, with the bedbugs and the mice, like my *Wedge*).

To try to cheer myself, I read of the Miracle at Cana and how the niggardly hosts have not provided enough wine, so that poor overworked Jesus is compelled to fashion it out of mere water. But I am again struck not only by the parsimoniousness of the hosts, but by something else that has always troubled me about this story.

It is set down, in a self-congratulatory kind of way, how the best wine – that made out of the water by Jesus – was 'saved till last'. But this strikes me as very stupid. For, in regard to wine, I am only too familiar with the Progress of any party. When, in my Former Life, I gave great dinners at Bidnold (and there were many), I always instructed Will to serve my best wines *first*, he and I both understanding very well that when men are as intoxicated as my guests invariably became, and those at Cana probably were, they cannot tell one wine from another, or even one kind of *drink* from another, and will just stupidly keep quaffing whatever is put into their hands until they fall over. And in this state, the 'best wine' would be horribly wasted upon them. The Saviour might as well have made cheap or ordinary wine, and I find myself wishing that I had been there to tell Him this, in case the Miracle of the good wine was a greater Effort for Him.

I thumb another Miracle, which is the Raising of Lazarus, but I do not enjoy this one very much either, worrying about the Stench that may have lain upon the cadaver in the heat of a Judaea afternoon, and turn from it at random to the Book of Ecclesiastes, where I read: '*That which befalleth the sons of men befalleth beasts; even one thing befalleth them: as the one dieth so dieth the other; yea, they all have one breath, so that a man has no Pre-eminence above a beast.*'

Death is much on my mind. It aimed at me, but it did not strike me.

I departed from the snow-covered clearing in the woods, but Colonel de Flamanville did not. He lay upon the ground, shot in the heart by Beck. His blood pooled upon him, above and below, crimson and bright. Beck knelt down beside him and wept and kissed his face, and all Beck's fine uniform was stained red. And I thought how courageous was this Capitaine to hide his weapon so that he might fulfil such a fearful pledge. I knew, on the instant, that he had done it for love of the Colonel.

I returned to him the pistol, which I had fired far wide of my adversary, inadvertently despatching a Pigeon, which plopped down from a frosted bough. I shook his hand very warmly, then the Baron and I walked back towards the Château, leaving the grieving Adjutant to make arrangements for the corpse. At first we were silent as we walked, then the Baron said: 'You were courageous, Merivel. There was, I now perceive, a chance that you might have died.'

I wished to say that, in my understanding of a complicated and Uncertain Situation, there was a deal more than 'a chance', but I did not. I did not want to taint, by cynical words, my feelings of gladness to be alive.

We walked on. The sun was full up and shining on the snow. Far above us the great mountains peered down upon us, immovable, indifferent. I found in me a great Thirst for Sack.

At length the Baron said: 'We shall let a suitable interval go by. Then we shall arrange your wedding to Louise. I shall invite all of Neuchâtel. Marc-André Broussel will sing for you. I shall spare no expense. It shall be the finest celebration I have hosted in my life! Perhaps, your daughter will travel from England and bring the Duchess of Portsmouth with her? We would be greatly honoured . . .'

From what I knew of her, I could not imagine Fubbs wishing to rise from her Chaise Longue and transport herself and her Wardrobe, and her mountain of jewels, halfway across a Continent to bear witness at the wedding of a Glovemaker's son, so I said to the Baron: 'My daughter tells me the Duchess is not very fond of fresh air, so perhaps Switzerland, with its abundance of air of impeccable freshness, may daunt her? But of course she shall be invited.'

And then I fell to thinking whom, indeed, I might invite, and it came to me that the person whose presence at my Marriage would move me most would be Will. I longed to see his features afflicted with a sudden gladness of heart.

But of Will I had no word. Every day I looked for some chaise or mule that would convey to me a Letter from Bidnold, but none arrived. I would have risked writing to Cattlebury to enquire after Will, but Cattlebury is almost incapable of reading, 'Unless, Sir Robert, it be a Recipe and all laid out on Individual

Lines, with numbers writ as Numbers, and then I can comprehend it.' So this did not seem a very useful thing to do.

I had now resolved to write to Sir James Prideaux, and beg him to ride to my house and give me some report of how things stood there, but so taken along by the anxieties of the Duel had I been that this I had not yet done.

'What say you to a May wedding?' said the Baron suddenly.

Towards evening, as Louise and I lay in her bed, exhausted by the afternoon's Exertions, celebrating our forthcoming marriage, she said: 'Oh, I forgot to tell you, Merivel. A letter arrived for you this morning.'

At once my heart flew to Will. But it was not his laboured hand upon the letter, it was Margaret's, and she wrote thus:

My Dearest Papa,
I pray this letter reaches you and is not Stopped by snow.

You must forgive me for disturbing your sojourn in Switzerland, but I have no choice but to do this. The King is lately taken ill with terrible Convulsions. He has rallied a little, but we are all able to tell, by his Countenance, that he is weak. He has much pain in his Bladder and in his Kidneys. His leg is very Sore.

Dear Papa, I would not trouble you with this, but today he comes into our Chambers and lies down upon the Duchess's bed and sends for me. He takes my hand and says to me, 'Margaret, I pray you, write to your Father and ask him to be good enough to come to me. I know not what is coming upon me, whether I am bound for Death, or no, but I know that my Spirit would be greatly cheered by having your Father near me, to attend on me and to make me smile.'

So, Papa, please come at once. I beg you to come. The Duchess is full of fear that His Majesty is going to die. I know that you would do anything to forestall this. You can

be housed in the Duchess's apartments, so that you may be
near the King, day and night.
We shall await your arrival every day.
From your loving daughter,
Margaret

I sat very still and petrified on Louise's bed. Seeing me thus
turned to stone by the letter, she took it from my hands and
read it, and, being a woman of admirable Judgement, she said,
without hint of disappointment or self-pity: 'You must go at
once. Father's Coach will take you to Neuchâtel in the morning, and from there you may get a Chaise to Dijon and on to
Paris.'

I brought Louise to me and kissed her cheek. 'You are right,'
I said. 'I can do no other.'

'I shall wait for you, Merivel. I shall not let Life take you away
from me for ever.'

'No, indeed. And I shall visit the King's Jeweller in London
and buy you a ring.'

'Shall it be Sapphire, like the ring which saved Clarendon?'

'It shall be of whatever stone pleases you.'

'Bring me a Ruby, then. As hot and fiery as my blood.'

Louise clung to me and wept when I departed. It was as though
we were making some terrible adieu.

As I got into the coach, the Baron thrust into my hands a
sheaf of Papers, torn from his Notebook. I hoped that these
might be his own Observations on my Treatise, in which he
seemed to take a passionate interest, but the Baron's Papers
contained no thoughts upon my Great Subject. They were mere
lists of all the People he would invite to my wedding, and plans
for what Entertainments we might have and the Songs Broussel
would sing for us, and the Banquets we would devour.

I barely glanced at them, but only thrust them into my Valise,
remembering as I did so my wedding to Celia long ago and

how I had first wept at it, and then later found myself imprisoned in a Closet, watching through a crack in the door as the King made love to my new bride.

And I thought how all the Arrangements of my life had flowed out from this Wedding, which had not been real, but only Counterfeit to suit the King's lusts, and how, in my fifty-ninth year, I was now headed towards a second Marriage Ceremony, which did not, in truth, seem quite real to me either, and which was being arranged to gratify the late-flowering lusts of Louise de Flamanville.

Looking over at my Coach companion, the Priest, garbed all in black, sleeping now as the coach jolted through the darkness, I imagined that it was not he but Pearce who sat opposite me. But Pearce did not sleep. He cast upon my features a stare that was without Pity.

'What are you doing, Merivel?' he said. 'What is the *meaning* of this Second Wedding?'

I imagined leaning towards Pearce, and taking one of his cold hands in mine and putting it against my heart to try to warm it.

'I am going to be honest with you, Pearce,' I said. 'I shall not lie. I have great admiration for Louise de Flamanville. Among women, she is remarkable. And there are more than a few moments when I feel love for her. But truly, this marriage is about riches. It is about the getting of a great Estate and a life of ease.'

'Just as it was the first time.'

'If you will.'

'And you are not ashamed?'

'Only a little. Not as ashamed as you would wish me to be.'

''Tis a great pity, my friend.'

'If it is such a "pity", what else would you have me do?'

Here I could not guess what Pearce might say. His voice came no more. All that now haunted the coach was that Silence of his, which is like no other silence on earth, and this I had to endure without flinching. I let go of his hand. I closed my eyes and turned my thoughts towards the King.

On the 29th of January 1685 a Barque named *The Kentish Maid* took me across the Channel, and although the seas were lumpy and flecked with foam, and spray was hurled again and again onto the decks, I remained well and was once again made strangely happy, finding myself in this new Element, where Man can alter nothing, but only Accept what the wind decrees and try to steer his fragile tub to safety.

And I thought how, in my restlessness and longing for Wonders, I might have made a good Mariner and come at last, perhaps, to be the Captain of some trading vessel, bound for far-off continents and never settling anywhere, but always moving across the Globe under crimson skies and uncountable stars.

And it seemed to me, too, that there is a kind of peace to be found on the ocean, a beautiful quiet that is almost always absent from life upon the land, where both men and objects have the habit of *calling out* to us and importuning us with this or that demand, and there is no stillness anywhere.

And I wondered whether, had I spent my life at sea, I would now be a person of Stoical calm, accepting without complaint all that Time and weather could cast at me, and inhabiting at last that mantle of serenity with which Pearce always longed to clothe me, and always and ever failed.

I fell into conversation with the Captain of *The Kentish Maid* and told him how the beautiful intricacies of his ship made me glad, and I could tell that this cheered him very much. He caressed the wooden rail upon which we leaned and said: 'She is a darling vessel, Sir. She will sail to the very blade's edge of the wind without complaint. She has been through some mighty storms and ridden them down – she and I together. But she is old, alas, and leaky now. She may not see out another season.'

'Ah,' I said. 'Poor *Kentish Maid*. And now this same Anxiety must we feel with regard to the King.'

'What, Sir?'

'I am travelling home to be at the King's bedside. He is a sick man.'

The Captain gaped at me. He shook his white head, disbelieving. 'He cannot *die*,' he said. 'You are not telling me that Charles Stuart is going to die?'

'I know not, Captain. All I know is that I have been summoned. I am a physician and the King's old friend.'

The Captain shook his head again, staring down at the shifting, shimmering water. 'He made us Comfortable,' he said sadly. 'As though we were Hove-To. When he came in, we all sat down where we were and breathed a sweet Sigh.'

30

On the evening of Saturday the 31st of January I arrived at the Duchess of Portsmouth's apartments and found there no scene of lamentation, but only Fubbs, a little fatter and dressed in a crimson velvet gown, taking a quiet supper with Margaret. With them was a young man, who was introduced to me as the Honourable Julius Royston, youngest son of Lord Delavigne.

Both women greeted me with delight. Margaret, looking wondrously pretty in a dark-blue dress trimmed with the Swiss Lace that I had sent her, seemed most anxious that I should make the immediate acquaintance of Julius Royston and, knowing that this was the young man who had been paying court to my daughter, I turned on him my sternest gaze.

Little daunted by my look of severity (which I do think is never as severe as I might sometimes imagine it to be) this Royston folded himself into an immaculate bow and babbled that he had been 'most impatient' to meet me and was only sorry that the occasion of my return was the illness of the King.

'How goes His Majesty?' said I to Fubbs.

'He is sleeping now,' she said. 'He likes to retire early. But in these last days he seems to be more himself, does he not, Margaret?'

'Yes. And he even took a short Constitutional yesterday, just as far as the Crocodile. He will be so glad to see you, Papa. Every day he has asked me if you were yet come.'

I sat down at the supper table, and one of Fubbsy's Servants laid a place for me and brought me almost immediately a very refreshing cold soup of potatoes and leeks. Between ardent spoonfuls, I regarded my daughter and Royston, and saw pass between them those looks that only enamoured Lovers send to each other, and I began to pray that this son of an Earl was an Honest man.

He was handsome in a sallow kind of way, reminding me somewhat of the King when he was young, with large brown eyes and dark curls, and a smile of some sweetness. I could not but be inclined to like him. I put his age at about twenty-two or twenty-three and, studying his features, I could not discern on them any signs of Debauch or Wickedness. His voice was mellifluous.

'So tell me, Royston,' said I, taking up the glass of white wine set before me, 'what brought you to Court?'

'My father is Secretary to the Earl of Buckingham, Sir,' said Royston, 'and found for me a Position in the Office of the Superintendent of the Royal Palaces. I have studied Horticulture in Paris and all my fervour is in the Design of landscapes and gardens. I hope to make my mark in this field.'

'Gardens?' said I. 'I myself am very consoled by gardens, as perhaps Margaret has told you?'

'Yes, Sir. She has described to me your recently planted Hornbeam Alley at Bidnold Manor.'

'*C'est quoi*, "hornbeam"?' asked Fubbs. 'Do you mean "sunbeam"?'

'No, Your Grace,' said I. '*Hêtre blanc* in French, I think.'

'Ah, *Hêtre blanc. Oui, je vois. Très joli.* Anyway, you see, Merivel, that our dear Julius is a man of ambition. A man who understands the direction of his life.'

'Yes, I surmise this . . .'

'You will not remember, Sir Robert,' said Royston, 'but I was brought once to Bidnold Manor when I was a child.'

'You were?'

'By Lady Bathurst. She was my Godmother.'

'Violet Bathurst was your Godmother?'

'Yes.'

'Is that not a coincidence, Papa?' said Margaret.

'Yes,' I stammered. 'Yes it is . . .'

'I remember that I was kept with your Manservant a while, for that my Godmother had some private business in your house that I could not attend, and that your Man was very kind to me.'

'Ah. Dear Will. I'm sure he was. Indeed, he would have been.'

But into my mind there passed a flagrant memory of Violet, arriving in haste at the house, in the company of a rather captivating small boy, whom she was returning to his parents or to his School or to someone-or-other (but to whom I paid scant attention), and rushing to me, so that she and I could hurry to some indecent Sexual Feast in my bedroom before she resumed her journey.

I could not prevent a smile from crossing my features. I gulped wine and said: 'Dear Violet. She and I were good friends. I swear to you, Royston, that I did all I could to save her when her Cancer came. But I could not.'

'I know that, Sir Robert. And she always spoke very tenderly of you.'

We fell silent for a moment. My soup plate was taken away and a morsel of chicken was set before me.

Turning to Fubbs I said: 'Your Grace, do you have any word from Bidnold? I sent a letter to Will Gates from Switzerland, but have no Answer.'

'No,' said Fubbs. 'We have heard nothing. Have we, Margaret?'

'No. But no doubt all is well, Papa. Letters from Switzerland may frequently go astray.'

After supper, seemingly at some sign from Fubbs, she and Margaret bid us an abrupt Goodnight and disappeared to their chambers, leaving me alone with Julius Royston.

I, too, was tired and looked ardently towards laying my head down. But no sooner had the women left than Royston, his face all suddenly Beet-coloured, leaned impulsively towards me and said: 'I must say this to you before my courage goes. I shall not procrastinate, for the matter is very simple. Sir, I love Margaret. I love Margaret with all my heart and all my might. I have loved her from the moment I saw her. In that very instant, was I lost . . .'

'Ah . . .'

'Sir Robert, I have asked Margaret to be my Wife and she has consented. And I know we shall be the happiest pair in all of England, if you will but give your permission for our Marriage.'

He was an affecting spectacle, his face so red and his curls suddenly damp, and his hands now clenched together as if in an ardent Prayer. Something in my heart was touched by him.

'Let us sit down,' I said. 'And we shall discuss this calmly. As I trust you may have discussed it with your own father. What does Lord Delavigne say to the match?'

'Oh, he is most heartily glad! He thinks Margaret quite adorable, as she is, as she is. No more adorable young woman ever came into the world . . .'

'Might he not have hoped that you would choose a bride from a more Noble family than mine?'

'Well, as to "nobility", His Majesty speaks far more fondly of you than of many Noble Lords at Court. But it matters not for me. I'm the Youngest of four sons. All he wishes for me is that I get a good Place in the world and that I am happy. But, Sir Robert, I shall never be happy, I shall never have one ounce of contentment in my life if I cannot make Margaret my wife. Please say you will consent! Oh, I pray you, do not torture me, but say you will bless us and give your permission!'

I poured a little wine for Royston and gave it to him, and he gulped it thirstily.

Then I took some wine myself and said: 'A happy marriage is something ardently to be sought in the world. My own was brief and full of sorrow. It thus follows that I have always prayed that

Margaret would be luckier than I. But she is very young, Royston. She is but eighteen. And knows little of the world, or of men . . .'

'I will teach her all that she should ever want to know. I will care for her and pledge all my Endeavour to her. I will never forbid her Dancing Lessons or Music Lessons or Geography Lessons, or whatever her heart yearns for. I will make no prison round her, as some men make round their wives, and this I swear. She shall be my wife, but she shall be Margaret, always.'

So intense were Royston's feelings that tears came to his eyes. He wiped them away and continued: 'You do not know me, Sir Robert. If Lady Bathurst were alive, she might vouch for me, but she is gone. You may judge that I should have waited, before pressing my suit, but I could not wait. I could not wait because everyone is afraid that the King is dying, and how could I come to you with this, if His Majesty were to pass away? You would have no time for it. So it is now that I must ask you. Now, tonight. And I beg you to answer me!'

I looked tenderly at the young man. Something in me *envied him* his grand passion, his optimism, his Beet face. I knew that I had never felt as he felt, and I decided on the instant that I would be doing right to put him out of his misery at once. First Loves are often the greatest loves and should not be denied.

Nevertheless, I could not give him his answer until I had spoken privately with Margaret. I told him to wait here, by the Duchess's fire, and that I would go to Margaret and get from her what her feelings were, and then return to him and give my answer.

He could not argue with this suggestion and did not. As I went to the door, he called out to me: 'Margaret loves me! She has sworn it!'

She was sitting up in bed, reading a letter from her friend, Mary Prideaux.

'From Cornwall, perhaps?' said I.

'Yes. Even so. She has collected forty-nine Cowrie shells.'

'A fine feat. Has she seen any Puffins?'

'She does not mention them. Did you talk to Julius, Father? Did he ask you—'

'Yes. He asked me.'

Margaret laid aside her letter and threw her arms round my neck. 'I know,' she said, 'you will say that this is hasty. But it does not seem so to us. We knew this Had to Be from the moment we met. Julius is the dearest, loveliest and cleverest of men, Papa. In time, you will see. And if we cannot be together, then I think I shall be one of the most miserable, wretched women on earth, and all that I could do would be to hide away in some Convent and live on bread and water.'

'Bread and water?' said I. 'We cannot have that.'

At this moment Fubbsy, attired in a billowing peach-coloured Nightgown and with a lace Bonnet upon her curls, swirled, unbidden, into the room. '*Et alors?*' she said. 'I heard your voice, Merivel. Did Royston ask you? Is all settled? Don't tell me you refused?'

Fubbsy sat herself down beside us on the bed. Without waiting for an answer to her question, she began upon a Paean of Praise for the Honourable Julius Royston, reminding me what a good family he came from and how all the young women at Court were 'mad with Jealousy' of Margaret, who had stolen his heart.

'And they love each other so!' continued Fubbs. 'I have never seen two doves more sweetly enraptured. The King himself agrees with me, you must swiftly give your permission for the Marriage and we shall help you plan a sumptuous wedding in the spring. At your lovely Bidmould.'

'Bid*nold*, Your Grace.'

'Well, Bidnold then. Very strange word. But the King is happy there. This will rally His Majesty, to plan a May wedding in Norfolk.'

A May wedding.

I was so far from being able to tell Margaret about my engagement to Louise that I did not even let the thought of trying to do so trouble me. I looked at the two ardent faces before me, eyes

wide with hope and longing for happiness, and let myself yield
to them and to the young man I had left by the fire.

'It shall be,' I said. 'It shall be.'

I returned to Julius and gave him the good News, and he bowed
low to me and thanked me and kissed my hand, and promised,
on his life, that I would not live to regret my decision.

'There is only one thing, Royston,' said I. 'If you are living in
the expectation that Margaret will bring a large Dowry, you are
deceived.'

'No, no . . .' he began.

'I live mainly from the *loyer* the King pays me annually. This is
generous, but I have no fortune amassed. I have just enough to
support my Estates and no more. Margaret will inherit Bidnold
Manor when I am gone, but I have little to give her now.'

''Tis of no concern to me, Sir Robert. As you know, my father is
very rich and will get a house for us in London. But I aim to make
my way in the world with my Landscape designs. Gardens quicken
the heartbeat of the English. I have seen this everywhere.'

'Yes. I think you are right in that. I have noted it too.'

'Even in poor villages will Cottage gardens be kept, and not
just for food and poultry, but for Michaelmas Daisies and Forget-
Me-Nots and rambling roses. And men on the way to a fortune,
once they have a Portrait of themselves and their wives and their
dogs, why then their thoughts turn, by natural progression, to
Gazebos and lakes and fountains and Follies. So I shall not lack
for Commissions, I am certain of it.'

'Good,' said I. 'I think it admirable that you should make your
own way in the profession of your choice.'

'And when I am Established, I hope that Margaret and I will
have children. I know that her own childhood was somewhat
solitary . . .'

'It was.'

'Not that this was your fault, Sir Robert . . . with your wife
dead. Merely, it is our hope—'

'To get a large family.'

'Yes. And my mind runs on, imagining Margaret with our Babes.'

It was at this moment, when Julius Royston made mention of the sweet Future he planned with my daughter and their sons and daughters, and not at any moment before, that I felt come upon me a sudden, miraculous Ending of my Anxiety in relation to Margaret.

It seemed to me that this Anxiety had been massing in my breast, like a spreading Cancer, for an untold number of days and months, and that now a great (yet painless) Cutting had been performed on me to take the growth away, leaving my heart free from Agony. Indeed, all my agitation that the King would seduce Margaret and ruin her life – put into my head by Violet Bathurst – now appeared to me as a pitiful and deluded thing. I felt as certain as I could be that no such seduction had ever taken place.

I sat back in my chair and looked at Julius Royston. He was no Paper Groom. He was a young man ardently in love. I exhaled a long, contented breath.

'I hope,' I said, 'that both His Majesty and I shall live to see them, these Babes of yours.'

It was late when I eventually retired to the room the Duchess had assigned to me, but I knew that one more task awaited me: I had to write again to Will.

Dear Will, I wrote,
I am lately arrived at Whitehall, for that the King, finding Himself a little Unwell, requested my return from Switzerland. I shall see His Majesty tomorrow and pray his Discomfort is but a passing thing, and will quickly vanish.

As soon as he is well again I shall return to Bidnold. I am somewhat worried that I have no word from you, Will. Pray write to me here, to reassure me that all continues calmly and without accident or Catastrophe in Norfolk.

I find Miss Margaret well and liking her Position with the

Duchess of Portsmouth very much. There is some News attending Her Future, which I shall be happy to relate to you when next we meet at Bidnold.

Meanwhile, I remain,

Your Affectionate Employer and Friend,

Sir R. Merivel

31

The next morning dawned cold, yet lit with a bright sun.

At Fubbsy's urging, I made my way to the King's apartments as soon as I had breakfasted and found him standing by a window, looking down upon the glittering day. When he turned and saw me he cried out: 'Merivel! Oh, I dreamed that you were buried in some Swiss Glacier. Your most dear face was all squashed and packed with ice. I tried to talk to you through the ice, but you could not hear me.'

'Well, happily, Your Majesty, I am not Frozen at all, but standing here before you and I can hear you most plainly.'

The King, who looked very pale, limped towards me, put his arms round me and smacked a kiss on my cheek. In the Chamber with us was Thomas, Lord Bruce, one of the King's Lords-in-Waiting, who had always been courteous towards me and he said: 'Now that you are here, to amuse His Majesty, Sir Robert, I'm sure that he will return to Good Health.'

'Bruce and I were about to go for a drive,' said the King, 'to see the new Flamingos in the Park, but Bruce will not mind, will you, Thomas, if Merivel comes with me instead?'

'No, Sir,' said Bruce. 'Not at all. But I advise that you do not stay out too long and keep a fur over your knees.'

To ride alone with the King in one of his many coaches was a thing I have seldom done and I could not but suddenly marvel at finding myself there, wrapped in furs, with four grey horses pulling us along through the cold, bright morning.

Knowing what extreme anxiety the King's earlier Convulsion had stirred in Fubbsy's heart, and seeing him looking so pale and tired, I could not refrain from asking him about his condition. I expected him to dismiss my questions airily, but he did not. He looked out at the People taking the air in the Park and said: 'I do not want to leave them, Merivel, all these who walk up and down and go their ways, and who make up this precious Gathering that is England. But I have begun to believe that the time is coming. And there is so much that I have left undone.'

I could not think what to say to this sad utterance. The King has never in his life been one to court idle Sympathy, so I knew that what he said he truly believed. And if he believed that he was dying, why then, I knew that I had to believe it too. And this left me momentarily speechless.

'When my Mother was alive,' the King went on, 'she said to me that I should, before I left this world, pledge myself to her Religion, to the Roman Catholic Church. My Brother has converted, but I have not done it, Merivel. I have not done it because it has never been Politic to do it. Yet suddenly my soul thirsts after it. What am I to do?'

'If your soul thirsts after it, Sir, why then I think you should summon a Priest and make your Vows.'

'Indeed. But it is not as easy as that. There would be an Outcry from every one of the Privy Council and beyond in the Realm. The King of England cannot go over to Rome without causing a terrible Ecclesiastical and Political Stink. The only way is that it be done in private, so that the Matter rests between me and God and the spirit of my Mother, and no one else except the Priest. But I know not how, since I am now surrounded by Doctors day and night, I am to smuggle any Catholic Priest into my rooms. Will you turn your thoughts to finding me a way?'

'I will, Sir.'

'Would *you* were a Priest, Merivel, and we could do it here and now, in this coach, with no Witnesses by.'

'Ah,' said I, 'what a Priest I would have made! I would have had no time for my Flock, being so taken up with the Confession of my sins and doing Penance for them.'

The King laughed and tweaked my nose; then seeing how we were come close to where the Flamingos clustered, ordered the coach to be stopped.

'Look at them,' he said. 'Was there ever a more startling bird?'

We gazed out at the pink legs, the curvaceous necks, at the fragile membrane of Coral colour their reflections laid upon the water. I noted the delicacy and grace with which they moved.

'There is,' I said, 'a great quantity of Wonder in the world, which I have never seen and now I never will see it.'

'Indeed. I am King of England, but I will not see it either. That is why I have brought Crocodiles and Cassowaries here to St James's. Is your Madame de Flamanville also fascinated by birds and animals?'

'Oh . . .' said I, discomforted by the unheralded Injection of Louise into the conversation, 'I do believe she is. She was most upset by the fate of Clarendon.'

I kept looking out at the Flamingos, but felt the King's gaze very intent upon me. At length he said: 'And what of her, Merivel? Have you returned her to her Swiss Guard?'

'No. Colonel de Flamanville is dead. He was killed in a duel.'

'A duel? We thought they had quite gone out of fashion. Yet how convenient. So now you are free to marry her, if that is your wish. Is it your wish?'

At this moment something startled the Flamingos, and they took off as one and flew, like a fluttering cloud of rosy Magnolia petals, round the lake, to land again on the opposite side of it. I turned to the King and said: 'Another betrothal preoccupies me since my return and that is the betrothal of my daughter to Julius Royston.'

'Ah, yes indeed,' said the King. 'What say you to that? Fubbs is all a-craze for it. She dotes upon your daughter and upon Julius. Will you give your consent ?'

'What know you of Royston, Sir?'

'Well . . .' and here the King leaned over and began whispering in my ear.

'Say this to no one, Merivel, not even to Margaret, for I have the greatest respect for Lord Delavigne and would not wish to cause him or his family any Embarrassment or Grief. But I have always believed that Julius Royston is my son.'

'Your son?'

'Hortensia Delavigne and I . . . well, it was a matter of one night, as it was with Lady Bathurst . . . but nine months later comes the birth of Julius, and he does not resemble Delavigne, who is all russety and freckled; he resembles me.'

I stared at the King. The idea that my daughter would be married to a child of the King's – even if neither of them ever knew it – I found to be a most Colossal thing.

'Naturally,' said the King, 'I feel a fatherly affection for Julius. And Margaret completes him, or so it seems to me. Their natures are similarly kind and tender, and she will encourage him in his endeavours in Landscape. I will give him a little Commission for a new lake and Shrubbery at Newmarket, if I live until the summer.'

I knew that I had to write to Louise and not put this off, as I had done once before, thus causing her deep pain.

Thinking about her and her unembarrassed cravings for *Jouissance* gave me a feeling of slight Sexual Excitation and I bethought me how, in the afternoon, I might make my way to London Bridge and visit my dear Drab, Rosie Pierpoint, and how I would be most consoled by this and behave like a Spoiled Child in her arms, with no Conscience and no Responsibility.

Meanwhile, I wrote thus to Louise:

My dear Louise,

I am safely arrived at Whitehall, where I have just returned from a Short Drive Out with His Majesty to see the Flamingos in St James's Park. From this, you will see that his Health does not appear to be in any immediate danger, and yet some Anxieties persist. The Sore on his leg gives him much pain, and he is very pale. I shall see him again after Suppertime, when he will come to the Duchess's apartments.

I think of you very much and pray that you are well, and the Baron also, and Constanza, and that the Winter treats you kindly. It is cold here, but with a bright sun.

Now, Louise, I must arrive at my Main Tidings, and these are they: Margaret, with my Consent, is engaged to be married to the Honourable Julius Royston, the youngest son of Lord Delavigne. We all here, including the King, rejoice at this union, for the boy is very fine and the Pair most excellently contented. But they, being young and ardent, do not wish to delay their marriage beyond the Spring and the month now set for it is May.

I shall host the Marriage at Bidnold Manor, and there being much to arrange, and oversee, will not be able to return to Switzerland before June. Thus, our own Celebrations, must, alas, be postponed.

I know that you will be vexed by this, as I am. But rest assured that I will return as soon as Margaret is made a Bride, and we shall then turn our minds to our own Futures.

I send with this letter some Purple Sage leaves, survivors of all the Winter winds and driving Snow, as a token of my respect for all your Scientific Endeavours and of my enduring affection.

Your humble Chevalier,

R. Merivel

Reading this letter through several times I could not but be struck by its coldness and formality. I had not intended that it should be

cold and formal, yet I could perceive that it was, and I felt somewhat ashamed of it, as though it might have been Schoolwork,
badly done. But I had not the Patience to rewrite it.

Then another thing began to torture me. As Margaret's future
Stepmother, Louise de Flamanville should, by rights, be invited to
Bidnold for the May wedding. She would perhaps be well aware
of this and look, in the letter, for such an invitation and, finding
none, be made sorrowful by the lack of it.

Yet for all that I had tried many times, I could not imagine Louise de Flamanville playing the role of Mistress of Bidnold. Deep
in my heart lay the memory of her saying that my gift of a decorated Almanac to Will Gates was 'too beautiful' to be given to a
Servant. And I took from this the feeling that she would not
understand my house and how it was arranged, and how my
loyalties were dispersed within it – even unto Cattlebury, all
awash with his sweating Insanity – and how none of my long-
serving Servants could be cast away.

I sealed my letter and gave it up to be posted, so that I would
not compel myself to add some Postscript, inviting Louise to
England.

Finding myself in the street, I began to walk in the direction of
London Bridge, my yearning to visit Rosie being now very strong.
But no sooner had I stepped out than Fubbsy's Chaise drew up
alongside me, and she hauled me inside and began to question
me about the King's condition, and so I was borne back to her
apartments on a tide of Interrogation, and all my wilful desires
fled from me.

Supper that evening, with Fubbs, Margaret and Julius, was most
lively and happy. We were joined afterwards by Lord and Lady
Delavigne, who were courteous and kind to me, and showed me
with great pride a sumptuous Diamond Ring, which was then
placed by Julius upon Margaret's finger.

At this the russety Lord Delavigne began to blub with joy (thus

endearing himself to me as a Weeper who, like me, may have
worn out many expensive handkerchiefs over the passing years).
Wiping his eyes, he put his arm round Margaret's shoulders and
round the shoulders of his youngest son, and made a short
impromptu speech about the elusive nature of Human Happiness
and how it should be caught with what he termed 'a bold
advance', as a Butterfly may be caught in a net.

'Oh, and *pinned down*, Delavigne, I suppose you will say
next?' teased Lady Delavigne.

'No, Hortensia, not at all. If by "pinned down" you infer that I
am talking about some kind of Containment or Slavery, which
indeed I hope you do not mean, you are utterly mistaken. For
when, in thirty years, have you ever been "pinned down" by me
– except at your own desiring in the marriage bed?'

'*Really*, Delavigne! What shocking Discourse is that, in front of
Sir Robert?'

'I do not say anything to shock. I am merely saying that the
commodity of happiness is rare and should be taken when it
offers itself.'

'It is indeed,' said Hortensia. 'We pray for it most ardently.'

The moment had brought the Delavigne family very close, but
I could not refrain from looking at Hortensia Delavigne, who still
had some Beauty attendant on her, and wondered under what
circumstances the Opportunity of making love with the King had
'offered itself' and how quickly or hesitantly she had taken it, and
what she had felt about it since.

I knew that she, too, must know – or at least surmise – that
Julius was the King's son, but had never, in twenty-three years,
breathed a word about it, not even to get some Advantage from
His Majesty, and I thought how this spoke well of her character
and of her love for Delavigne.

Then the King came in and we sat down to a furious game of
Basset, which is a *divertissement* dependent scarcely at all upon
skill, but only upon a high degree of Chance. Here, it was played
recklessly, for high stakes and amid great laughter. This laughter

brought some colour back into the King's face. And I was much
delighted to find myself on such a Winning Streak that I ended
the rounds with more than twenty *livres* won. But, alas, this drove
my mind back towards money and how the wedding at Bidnold
would be very costly, for all would have to be done in a magnificent way and I did not know how I was to afford it.

One of Fubbsy's French Musicians then came and sang sweet
Airs for us, and we all fell silent, thinking of the Time to come
and what it might bring to us of fortune and misfortune. And I
saw, all the while, Fubbs looking sadly at the King, and I thought
how, of all his mistresses, she had perhaps been the most loving
and afforded the King the greatest comfort. And it pained me to
think that, were the King to die, she would be cast out by the
Duke of York and her apartments given elsewhere, and all her
Status gone.

But such are our days. Such are the days and times of Every
Man and, no matter how hard we work and strive, we can never
know when something shall be given to us and when it will be
taken away.

32

A strange sight greeted me early the following morning: Fubbs, topped out with a veritable Rose Garden of Curl Papers, and her cheeks scarlet-petalled with weeping, bending over me, beseeching me to help her.

'What is it, Your Grace?' said I.

'Another seizure!' she babbled. 'More violent this time. And I cannot go to him, so says Lord Bruce, for the Queen is there. You must go, Merivel. He is unconscious! He may never wake. Please, I beg you, go to him for me.'

I dressed as quickly as I could. One of Fubbsy's Maids brought me a dish of Chocolate and I drank it gratefully. Then I took a moment to clean my Surgical Instruments and made my way to the King's Apartments, leaving Margaret to console Fubbs, who was faint with grief and dread.

The Guards on the outer door had multiplied to six. Their faces were horridly grim, as the faces of those brought to witness an Execution, but one of them recognised me and let me pass into the King's Rooms, which were already choked with people.

Pushing my way through this throng of Privy Councillors, Bishops, assorted Lords-in-Waiting, Servants and Doctors, I spied at last the figure of Queen Catherine, kneeling at the His Majesty's bedside, yet seeming to float upon her wide black skirts, as though the King were already embarked upon the fast-flowing

Styx, bearing him to a Protestant Perdition, and she trying to rescue him in her fragile Catholic barque.

He lay on his side, turned towards the Queen. I could not see his face, but I was dismayed to note that there were no coverings over his body, only his nightshirt, crumpled and stained. And from around the other three sides of the bed the Doctors worked their 'cures' upon him. Blood was being let from his arm. His head was being shorn. And, watched intently by a brace of Bishops, mumbling prayers, the Royal arse was being subjected to the tubes and bladders of the Enema Pump.

Pity for the King choked me. I stood very still, watching. And I thought how my profession, with all its agonising interferences, is so often inept and fumbling, and I wanted the Doctors to go away and leave His Majesty in peace. But I could do nothing.

I searched for Lord Bruce, but could not see him in the throng. Then I caught sight of William Chiffinch, the Keeper of the King's Closet and one very close to the King for all of his Reign. Chiffinch had been in the Royal apartments with me on that long-ago night in September 1666 when the Fire began. Two years later, when I returned to Whitehall, he had recognised me and gripped my hand and said, with some emotion, that he was glad I had not perished in the flames.

Chiffinch was now attempting to control seven of the King's yelping Spaniels on their leashes. I took from him three of the dogs, one of which was Bunting, and she, recognising me, began jumping up and tearing at my stockings. I picked her up and tried to hold the others steady, but now, like children, they all wanted to be carried, so I put Bunting down again and voiced a stern Command to her, and the dogs did sit for a blessed moment or two, while Chiffinch related to me what had happened.

'He went to his Closet towards eight o'clock, Sir Robert, and I waited outside. But he was a long time there, so I went in and I said: "How do you, Sir?" He was as pale as ashes, and he could not seem to reply to me, but just puffed out his cheeks a little.

'I brought him to his Bedchamber, where his Barber, Follier, was waiting to shave him. Follier bid him good morning, but His Majesty said nothing, and I and Lord Bruce helped him to the chair and Follier began his shaving, but no sooner had he begun the shaving than there came a terrible sound from His Majesty's mouth, like the shriek or screaming of some wild animal, and he fell back in the chair.

'We got a weak Pulse from him and he was breathing in shallow gasps. We carried him to the bed and began sending for the Doctors and for the Queen, and we have sent for the Duke of York, but he is not come yet, and someone said he was seen sculling on the river, but he has not been found. But the Privy Council Men are all come, and some Bishops, and I wish they had not, for they do nothing but choke up the room and take up all the Air that the King should breathe.'

I was silent for a moment. Then I said: 'I am superfluous here also. Tell me what I might do.'

'Well,' said Chiffinch, 'you could take the dogs for a walk, Sir Robert. Or I fear they will shit over the floor and we shall all be treading in it. His Majesty usually takes them for their Constitutional at this time of the day.'

I thus set out with the seven dogs. I noted that at the gates of the Palace a crowd of people had begun to gather.

The day was cold but fair and I took the dogs along towards the Park, each one trying to go at a scamper, so you could say that *they took me*, and I was forced to make little running steps to keep up with them, with all the while the seven leashes threatening to become tangled in each other and trip me up.

No sooner did they sniff the air of the Park than the dogs decided each to do his or her business all over the place, and I confess I felt a mite ridiculous, standing and waiting while they shat and pissed, and the people who passed me looked at me with disgust, for that I had let some of them do this on the Gravel pathway and had not tugged them into the grass.

But then one man, recognising the Decorations on the seven

leashes as belonging to the King, stopped me with an earnest look
and said: 'I heard a Rumour, Sir, that the King is dying. These are
his dogs, I know. Can you tell me if the Rumour be true?'

I tugged very hard on the leashes to rein the dogs in, and a
pain ran up my arm as I said: 'We do not know, Sir. The Doctors
are with him. He suffered this morning some kind of Convulsion,
since when he appears to be sleeping. This is all I can tell you.'

The man gaped at me. He was a person of about my own age.
He looked back in the direction of Whitehall and said: 'I was
there at his Coming In. I saw his barge sail up the River. I heard
the bells ring out all over London. We called him our Black Boy,
for his dark curls and golden skin. We thought him immortal.'

I nodded gravely.

'Are you one of his Servants?' asked the man.

'Yes,' I said. 'I think that is what you might call me. Very much
of my life has been taken up with trying to serve him.'

'Forgive me if I have you wrong. Perhaps you are some Noble
Lord?'

'No, you do not have me wrong.'

I was aware then that, our conversation being overheard by
others who strolled there, a small group had clustered round us
and all of these, when they heard that the King was gravely ill,
looked stricken. At the centre of the group the dogs leapt about
and whined, and the people reached down to pet them, as though
to touch one of the King's dogs might have been to touch His
Majesty himself.

One woman, very finely attired, picked up Bunting, laid the
dog's head on her bosom and said: 'If the Age is ended, what will
become of England?'

'Papist James will come in,' snarled another onlooker, a man of
fierce, choleric appearance, 'and all will be corrupt and distorted
by the Dictates of Rome, and England will go down in another
Dutch war. And it will be bloody and have no end . . . '

And the saying of this (which Prediction was most likely and
most true) raised an outcry among the little assemblage, which,

by now, others had joined. Some shouted: 'Down with Papists!' and 'Death to Rome, not to King Charles!' and 'God rot the Duke of York'.

I realised after some moments that many were looking at *me* accusingly, as though I might have been the veritable Duke, or perhaps the Pope Himself. I thought this most unfair and unreasonable, but all I could do was try to calm them by saying: 'His Majesty's Life is not yet over! He may yet recover. He may yet grow as old as Father Time. Please set down the dogs that I may continue their walk, Ladies. Please oblige me . . .'

But they did not want to let go of the dogs and the crowd around me grew larger yet, and truly I did not know what to do to escape. And I could not, in the midst of this Captivity, but think about my conversation with the King the day before, almost upon this very spot, in which he confided to me his desire to be converted to the Church of Rome. I was even afraid that some vestige of this secret confession was somehow visible upon my features.

I snatched Bunting from the lady's opulent breast and, clutching the dog to me, tried to reason with the people, saying: 'Gentlemen, Ladies, please hear me. Hush, I beg you. What am I to do if His Majesty wakes and asks for his Spaniels and none is there? He holds much store by them and likes to have them near him at all times. Please, I ask you, let go of the animals that I may take them back.'

As Colonel de Flamanville and many others were aware, I have no 'Natural Authority', but this frail argument did at last prevail and I managed to push my way through the Mob, holding tight, still, to the seven leashes, and steer the dogs home, their feathery tails wagging merrily in the sunshine.

After returning the Spaniels to poor Chiffinch, and noting that there was no change to the King's condition, except that his head was quite bald and his feet were now being Blistered, and that the Duke of York had taken the Queen's place at the bedside, I returned to Fubbsy's apartments.

Margaret and Fubbs were seated before a large fire, trying distractedly to play a game of Rummy. Fubbsy's hair had been deforested of its Curl Papers and she wore a pretty cap over her cascading brown locks.

On seeing me she flew to the bottle of Cognac she kept always upon a little Marquetry table and poured glasses for us all.

'Tell us,' she said. '*Tell us* . . .'

I took a grateful sip of the Brandy (the scent of which does always remind me, wistfully, of Laudanum and make me crave it) and said: 'There is no change. But the Queen has retired. Perhaps you may be permitted to go in, Duchess?'

Having kicked off her shoes for the Rummy game, Fubbsy at once began searching for them under the card table, with her wide French rump all in the air, like the rump of any scullery maid washing a floor, and sorrow for her filled me utterly.

Once she had found her shoes, she called for her blue satin cloak (a favourite garment of the King's) and, winding herself in this, fled from the apartment, leaving me alone with Margaret.

I sank down in an Armchair and gulped my brandy. After my scramble with the dogs in the Park I was sweating. Margaret came to me, and knelt down and put her head on my knee. She was silent for a long moment, letting me recover my breath, then she said: 'Will he die, Papa?'

'Well,' I replied, 'the Physicians are doing their best to kill him.'

Fubbs was a long time gone and I felt glad for her that she had been received into the King's chamber.

Margaret and I sat and talked about her wedding, which, she said, she wanted to be at Bidnold and nowhere else, with all the Prideaux girls as her Maids of Honour, 'and all the house banked up with flowers, and a great Procession down the drive, with the Village folk joining in and banging drums and tambourines, and casting ribbons and posies in the air.

She became very pink and excited, imagining this Day (the images of which could not but remind me of my 'paper' wedding to Celia Clemence in 1664) and while reassuring her that all would be arranged exactly as she and Julius would desire it to be, the likely cost of it still filled me with terror.

If the King died, his *loyer* to me would cease abruptly. The Duke of York would make certain of that. My only way to cover the expense of Margaret's wedding would be to borrow a large sum from a Moneylender in Norwich, promising to repay him the Principal by Christmas – once I had come to some financial agreement with the Baron de Saint Maurice upon Louise's Dowry. But from this – tainted as it was with dishonour – I found myself shrinking.

I then began thinking how my silence towards my daughter on the subject of Louise was also tainted, this time with Deceit, and I took a breath to begin upon my tale of the false duel and my promise to return to Switzerland and marry Madame de Flamanville, but even as I did so the door was flung open and Fubbs returned.

'He has woken!' she cried. 'I held his hand, and at first I thought he did not know me, but when I leaned to kiss his face he whispered "Fubbs bosom" and tried to reach out a hand to touch me there.'

'What do the Doctors say?' I asked. 'Is the crisis over?'

'They are all smiling. They think all their purges have cured him. But I could not stay to talk to them, for the Duke of York commanded that the Queen be sent for. Dearly would I sit by his side all day and all night, but in that gathering round him I am Nothing. I am Nothing!'

Margaret went to Fubbs and kissed her cheek, and took her blue cloak from her, and then the two women clung together and wept.

I strode out once again into the cold, bright day.

Stopping at a Poulterer's Shoppe, I bought a fat Capon and saw it plucked and dressed, then walked to a Dairy and purchased a jar of cream.

I arrived at Rosie Pierpoint's Laundry on the Bridge just as the midday bells were striking, and found her hard at work on her Ironing, with her girls, Mabel and Marie, scraping and sudsing on their Washboards. The stench of Lye was very strong and the room was billowing in steam.

I went to Rosie and kissed her mouth, and the girls stopped their work and applauded. I put the Capon and the Cream into Rosie's hands and said: 'Here is your dinner, Mrs Pierpoint, to share with the girls, and the bird is a fat one and good. So build up the fire of your oven for the roasting, then light a fire in your heart and take me to bed.'

She did not protest. She laid aside a half-ironed lace shirt and gave commands for the roasting of the Capon to Marie, then led me to her Bedroom above. I heard the girls tittering as we mounted the stairs.

Rosie let me undress her slowly, revelling as I did so in the familiar roundness of her body, her breasts very full and her belly a little fat, but then she whispered to me: 'Sir Rob, I heard a rumour that the King is dying. Tell me it is not so.'

'It is not so,' said I. 'He has been ill, but he is recovering.'

'Are you sure he is recovering?'

'No. I am sure about nothing in the world except that my Cock is so hard it pains me. Feel here. Your poor Sir Rob is all tangled in Momentous Times and grown uncomfortably momentous. Take pity on me, won't you, and go to it fast, for I cannot wait.'

Later, spent and comfortable again, I began to kiss Rosie very tenderly, as I might have kissed a wife who was dear to me. The knowledge that the rest of my life would be spent in Neuchâtel and that beyond the summer I might never come here to her again made me feel afraid.

33

The following morning I went again to His Majesty's apartments, hoping to find calm there and to hear that he had passed a restful night, but all was panic and anxiety, with the Doctors trying ever more numerous remedies and the Duke of York flailing about him, giving orders for a Cordon of Guards to be placed around Whitehall and – fearing, perhaps, that some Revolution might be planned by the Duke of Monmouth or by the Prince of Orange – signing Papers setting in hand the closure of the nation's Ports to all who desired to come in or go out.

From this I understood that the News on the King's condition was very bad.

Lord Bruce confirmed to me that His Majesty had undergone another Fit at seven o'clock, and had since recovered Consciousness but could not speak.

It was difficult to approach the Royal bed for the press of Doctors round it, but most of them knew me and knew my profession, and doubted not my loyalty, so at length I was able to come near the King.

A most terrible scene then unfolded. James Pearse, the King's Surgeon in Ordinary, had decided that blood should be let from His Majesty's Jugular Vein. Now, holding up his sharpened Scalpel in readiness, he was attempting, with his left hand, to *find* the Jugular by pressing and pushing and squeezing the King's neck this way and that, and seeming not to note that his patient was being slowly strangled, with his eyes beginning to burst out of his skull.

'I cannot find it!' Pearse cried out irritably, pressing and prodding yet harder. 'There is no vein!'

The other Doctors, working with Cantharides and Plasters, and laying Leeches into the Sore on the King's leg and administering, yet again, the Enema tubes, stared helplessly at the Surgeon.

'God's fish!' he shouted. 'Do not stand there like cattle! One of you help me find the Jugular!'

Nobody moved, so I, who was standing next to Pearse, said quietly: 'You are choking the King, Sir. Will you not let be?'

He then saw, as if for the first time, that the pressure of his left hand was indeed causing great distress and took it away, while swearing under his breath. The King began to retch and vomited up a little greenish slime onto the pillow. I took a handkerchief out of my pocket and wiped the King's mouth, which was much inflamed, with his tongue swollen and coated yellow.

I called for a servant to bring a clean pillow. The stench coming from the bed was noxious and I thought how, all his life, the King had had a very lovely and recognisable scent to his body, which was like honey mixed with summer fruit, and now he stank like a Polecat, and this made me very melancholy.

But I had no leisure to dwell on it, for I found James Pearse's Scalpel thrust into my hand and the terrible command given to me to 'Find the Jugular, Merivel, or no longer consider yourself a Physician worthy to remain in this room!'

Endeavouring to remain calm, I said to Pearse (the resemblance of whose name to my beloved friend John Pearce offended me much): 'Could you not let blood from the arm? If the Jugular be pierced, then a great quantity of blood will come out – more than you intend, perhaps – and His Majesty will be made very weak.'

'We have *let* from the arm,' said Ordinary Pearse, 'but it is not enough. The Distemper will not yield unless the Convulsive Blood be purged. So please go to it and make no more Fuss.'

In all my years as Physician I had never heard the term 'Convulsive Blood', but with all the other Doctors now staring at me, I had no choice but to take up the Scalpel and obey the command.

I leaned down towards the King, laying my hand gently upon his poor neck and talking to him very close. 'Sir,' I whispered, 'it is Merivel. And I have not forgot the Matter we discussed in your coach. I am giving all my thought, now, as to how we may arrange it.'

The King's eyes blinked up at me and he opened his mouth to try to speak. No word came out, but I assumed from this that he had certainly heard me.

I had, I shall admit, no idea how to clear the room of all the people in it and spirit a Catholic Priest to His Majesty's side – no idea at all – but this I did not say.

Meanwhile a more immediate and terrible task lay before me. To my relief, the Surgeon in Ordinary had left the bedside, giving me a little more space and air. Gently my hand felt round the King's ear and down his neck. And I remembered how, at the Whittlesea Asylum, John Pearce had let blood from the Jugular Vein of a very choleric man named Piebald and how, as he felt for the vessel, he had said: 'The Jugular is easy to find, Merivel. It *speaks* to you. It ticks like a clock. Feel here. There it is. There it is not. There is no need to pinch or press to find it. Only listen with your hand to get its voice.'

Not for the first time, I asked the ghost of my departed friend to help me and in this way I was able to remain calm, with my hand steady and my fingers alert for the 'tick' of the vein.

And then I got it. I pressed a little harder, just enough to give me sight of it, but endeavouring to cause the Patient no distress or choking. I called for a dish to be placed near my hand and with the Scalpel pierced the vessel. Bright blood immediately cascaded from the minute incision I had made, spilling over my hand and onto my sleeve. As this happened, so the King cried out and began to retch again. Now two other Doctors hurried to my side.

'A few ounces,' said one. 'Do not let too much. See how fast it flows. Contain it now! It must be contained now!'

A wad of Muslin was given to me and this I now had to press very firmly upon the vein to staunch the flow. The dish was taken away. I began talking to the King again, saying, 'It is done now. It is over. The Convulsive Blood is out.'

I stayed by his side. I wiped his mouth again and dribbled a little water onto his swollen tongue and saw him swallow it. At the other end of the bed the Enema tubes, having done their work of sluicing and voiding, were finally removed and it was not difficult to imagine that His Majesty's poor body had now been deprived of all its vital moisture. I thus continued to give him water and he kept sucking it in, like a helpless babe straining after the mother's breast. After some time I watched his eyes close and sleep come mercifully upon him.

I did not recount this scene to Margaret and Fubbs. I myself was almost faint from the Agony of it. And to my great dismay, when I returned to Fubbsy's apartments, I saw that all was disorder and hysteria there.

The Duchess had decided, it appeared, that the King was not going to survive. In terror of finding herself thus abandoned, she was now gathering up all her clothes and jewels, and all the small objects of value that she owned, and packing them away in four Trunks. Margaret was helping her, flying about, concealing Necklaces and Bracelets inside little gold vases and boxes, wrapping furs in Linen, sorting stockings into pairs.

'Where shall you send the Trunks, Your Grace?' I asked.

'Where?' she yelped. 'For Goodness sake, Sir Robert, where do you imagine? To the French Embassy, of course, where none of the King's family can wrench them from me! For I see how it is going to be: His Majesty will barely be laid in the ground before the vultures come and tell me I am a Common French Whore and put me out into the street.'

'I'm sure they will not do that,' said I. 'Everybody knows what a Consolation and comfort you have been to the King . . .'

'Oh, indeed? And does the Queen know this?'

'The Queen has always forgiven the King his Mistresses.'

'While he breathes, yes. She has had no alternative. But when he has no more breath? Then she will take her revenge on us all and upon our children. She will enjoy seeing us ruined.'

'It may be true, Papa,' said Margaret. 'The Duchess is wise to send her things into safety. Will you help us, for there is much to pack?'

I looked around at the floor, strewn with every manner of thing, from combs to Coffee pots, from Candlesticks to Chinese lacquer vases, from Gold Cutlery to sets of decorated Playing Cards. How much of all this truly *belonged* to Fubbsy or had merely been *on loan* to her as part of the furniture of her fine apartments I had no means of telling.

'What would you have me do?' I asked weakly. 'What task do you wish to give me?'

'Shoes!' said the Duchess. 'I have been trying to assemble them in pairs, but many are missing and must be hiding around the rooms, under beds or chairs or I know not where.'

'Shoes?'

'Yes. You can see from this how slovenly are the Servants charged with dusting and sweeping, but that is another matter. Please, if you will, search for the missing shoes, Sir Robert. Many have diamond buckles, or jewels sewn into the satin, and are of value, so I cannot leave without them.'

Though I would willingly have sat down and been quiet and taken some Brandy, I had little choice but to do as she requested. I was thus to be observed crawling around the carpets on hands and knees, lifting the heavy hems of curtains, craning my neck to peer beneath chests of drawers and armoires and chaise longues, in a vain search for the Duchess of Portsmouth's shoes.

And I thought how Pearce would have mocked me for this and

called me 'the Lackey of a Slut', but I did not really care, for I knew in my heart that my whole world was about to change and how I filled the time between now and the coming in of that terrible Transition was of little concern to me.

I found one shoe. It was an object of beautiful Perfection, made of blue satin, with a high heel, waisted and elegant. The satin was cross-stitched with silver thread and set high on the bridge of the shoe was a flower, made of silver ribbon and having at its centre a little cluster of Seed Pearls.

I held it in my hands and brushed some dirt from it. I noted its smallness and wondered at how petite the Duchess's feet must be to fit into it. Then I thought about the Shoemaker who had toiled over it and striven to make a faultless thing and my mind returned to my Dutch friend, Jan Hollers, who had attempted perfection with his clocks, but yet had failed by so narrow a margin.

Sorrow filled my heart. Sorrow for Hollers, sorrow for the Shoemaker and some kind of sentimental sorrow for the shoe itself, cast so carelessly off.

Very loud in my mind was the clamour of the Promise I had made to the King in his coach, and I knew that I should not *do nothing* about it. Yet I was at some loss as to what I might do.

I knew that it was to the Queen that I should relate my Pledge. But it was impossible, given my known association, through Margaret, with the King's Mistress, for me to go to the Queen's apartments and expect to gain entry there. There was only one other person who might help the King to the secret conversion that he wished for and that was the Duke of York.

The Duke had little liking for me. He once told me that I brought out the King's 'idle and slothful disposition' and so put in jeopardy the running of the nation. But I feared that Time was short now, and did not know what else I could do except to try to talk to the Duke and place the matter in his hands.

After taking a little midday dinner with Fubbs and Margaret, and other of her Women brought in to help with the Duchess's packing, I thus excused myself from the duty of searching for shoes and began to make my way back to the King's apartments, where I hoped to find York and somehow get his private attention.

The corridors at Whitehall, always thronging with People, were even more choked than usual. But it seemed to me that anxiety and sorrow at the King's dying had somehow affected these poor souls' ability to *hold themselves up*. Everybody I passed was either leaning against the wall or slumped down upon the stone benches, or else moving with infinite slowness, and I concluded that all their normal Purpose, which was to see the King and get from him some Favour or Preferment (and towards which they usually proceeded with sprightly alacrity), had been taken from them, so that now they knew not what they did nor where they were going, for they had no true aim, but were yet reluctant to leave.

Trying not to be contaminated by this festering Slowness, I hastened on my way and only paused when I heard somebody call out my name and saw, coming towards me, Father John Huddleston, an old and trusted friend of the King's, who had helped to conceal him during his great flight from Worcester in 1651 and who had been rewarded by being given a position in the Catholic Household of the Queen.

I had known John Huddleston for many years, once saving his life with a powerful Emetic of Rock Salt and Syrup of Buckthorn, after he had imbibed a Porridge laced with poison. The Poisoner (suspected of being a Quaker) was never brought to Justice. But from that moment onwards Huddleston had kept by him a bottle of 'Merivel's Efficacious' Emetic, in case the thing should ever be tried upon him again. He was thus disposed to see me as his rescuer and so to overlook my known debauches and my formerly disreputable Influence upon the King's morals.

We greeted each other plainly and warmly. Huddleston had

always struck me as a man of great humanity, to whom I had once admitted that, after the deaths of my Parents in a cruel and terrible fire in 1662, I had lost my Faith in God altogether.

Instead of berating me, or attempting to Convert me anew (which pious people are so fond of doing), he had asked me whether my Mother and Father had also ceased to believe in a Loving God, and when I told him that they had not, but remained steadfast in the Faith, he had sweetly conjured for me an image of the Paradise in which my Parents now resided.

It was, as befitting my Father's trade, a Haberdasher's Paradise, with clouds made of wool and Feather Trees waving in the wind, and paths strewn with pearl buttons and fields of linen-weave and houses made of Buckram. And sometimes, when melancholy struck me down, I had tried to imagine this fanciful kingdom, with my Mother and Father in it, and my Mother exclaiming, 'Oh, do look, dearest: a Ribbon Grove. Do you see how pretty it is!'

'The news is bad, Merivel,' said Huddleston. 'Very bad. I am going to the Queen and we shall pray together.'

'How is Her Majesty?' I asked.

'She is prostrated. She cannot eat nor sleep. She chides herself that she has not been "a good enough wife".'

'Ah. Yet, perhaps it might be the husband who has not been "good enough."'

'Quite so. But she scourges herself and she is tormented by another thing – that the King, for all his promises to her, has never been received into the Roman Catholic Church.'

'This matter is on the Queen's mind?'

'Yes. She is most upset that it has not been done.'

Here I took Father Huddleston's arm and drew him aside into what I thought was an Ante-room, telling him that there was an urgent matter upon which I had to speak to him in private.

We found ourselves not in an Ante-room, but in a broom cupboard.

'Oh,' said I, looking around at a quantity of Besoms and feather Dusters stacked into this small space, 'this will not do . . .'

I made to go out again but Huddleston said: 'No, on the contrary, it is a fitting place for any Secret and you must know that
Catholic Priests of my age were accustomed to *making ourselves
small* to fit the Holes made for us. When Cromwell's men came
to search Moseley Hall, His Majesty and I slept the night in a
space no larger than this. Of course, we did not have Brooms for
company; we had Fear. Should I be fearful of what you are about
to tell me?'

'No,' I said. 'Not at all. I only ask your help with it.'

The Father sat himself down on an upturned wooden bucket
and I squashed my body in and clutched at the Besom handles
to steady myself as I related to Huddleston all that the King had
confided to me in the coach.

When I had done, he gazed down at his hands, which were
stiff and pale from many decades of Prayer, and said nothing for
a moment. Then he looked up at me and said: 'Thank you, Sir
Robert. You could not have told me words that I would rather
hear. But we must pray it is not too late . . .'

'I still do not know how it is to be done.'

'It shall be done through me. I shall consult with the Queen
and the Duke of York, and we will find a time that is fitting,
before His Majesty slips away from us. I know you do not believe
in the Rewards of Heaven, but if you get there, perhaps you will.'

34

On Wednesday the 4th of February, following a long sleep, the King seemed to rally. I urged that a Marrowbone broth, such as had kept Margaret alive during the Typhus, be made for him, and this was done, and after he had sat up to be shaved and washed, he was helped by me to drink some of this.

The spooning of broth into His Majesty's mouth enabled me to sit very close to him and to talk to him unheard by others in the room. I thus was able to tell him that, once the Duke of York had found the means to clear the Bedchamber of all the Bishops and assembled Privy Councillors, Father Huddleston would come to him, bearing the Host.

'When will it be?' he whispered.

'I know not, Sir,' I said. 'But it *will be*. Trust me.'

At this last injunction, something crossed His Majesty's face that I had not seen in many a long hour, and that was a smile.

'I know,' I said, reading at once what lay behind the smile, 'I once broke your trust, but that was long ago. And tell me, Sir, have I ever betrayed you since?'

The King's jaw worked painfully slowly upon the broth, as though it might have been a gobful of tough meat. Then he said softly and sadly: '. . . betrayed Clarendon.'

'Ah,' said I. 'Clarendon. Yes. But I am atoning. I am endeavouring to compose a Treatise upon the subject of the Souls of Animals, and Clarendon is ever in the forefront of my mind.'

I expected the King to laugh at this, or at least to smile, but he did not.

'Souls of Animals . . . 'tis certain,' he said, nodding as vigorously as his poor afflicted head would let him. 'Animals have souls . . .' Then, he suddenly began clawing at his sheet and asked: 'Where is Bunting?'

I sent a Servant to find where the dogs were being housed and to bring Bunting to His Majesty. I hoped that he would continue drinking the broth, but he pushed the spoon away and said again: 'Where is Bunting? I must have her by me.' Then he looked about him distractedly, at the faces in the crowded chamber and said: 'Why is *nobody* by me? Where are my children? Where is Fubbs?'

I was like a Jack-in-the-Box, during these Last Days, called to His Majesty's bedside, sent away, called to him again, dismissed once more.

This – and I could not but smile at it – resembled an accelerated version of my life, with regard to the King. And I thought that, by rights, this uncertain Condition should have made me nimble and canny, but that it had not. I had always been – as Pearce once commented – Caesar's Slave. And now, a slave still, I was growing old and flat-footed.

Yet I harboured the certainty that, when the hour came and King Charles bid his Kingdom adieu, I would be by his side. Though he might die in the middle of the night, I felt sure that before the moment came, somebody would wake me. Though he might die in the Queen's arms, or in Fubbsy's, yet nevertheless did I picture myself standing near.

On Wednesday evening rumour spread into the city beyond Whitehall that the King was rallying and would soon be well, so we heard the sound of Bells being rung all over London and, looking from a high window, as the dusk fell, I saw the intermittent glow of bonfires. But I knew that the King would not be well. I longed to go about the city and warm myself at the fires, and tell the people to get out their mourning clothes and take all to be cleaned at *Mrs Pierpoint's Superior Laundry* on London Bridge.

Returning to Fubbsy's apartments, I saw that they had undergone a terrible Stripping. Each and every object that could fit inside a trunk and others besides, such as Card Tables and embroidered Footstools, which could not, had been piled into the Entrance Hall, waiting for a cart to trundle them away to safety.

Margaret and I looked about us in some dismay.

'Well,' said I, 'I am glad that she did not confiscate the beds.'

From Margaret's room, however, many precious objects had been removed, so that nothing remained with which she might brush her hair and only one Candle Sconce had been left to her. She sat down on the bed and said to me: 'If the King dies, the Duchess will leave for France. She has asked me to go with her. She has been so good to me, Papa, but I would prefer to stay in England, where I can be close to Julius. What am I to do?'

'You must do as your heart desires,' said I. 'And you should remember that the Duchess, separated from the King, will be nothing and no one in France, so your life may become dull and sad there.'

'Yet she expects me to go with her . . .'

'She cannot hold you to her for ever, and this she surely knows. I shall return to Bidnold, and you may come with me there, if that pleases you, and Julius may visit us and we can show him the Hornbeam Alley . . .'

At this very moment came in Julius Royston and, finding us sitting wearily in an almost empty room, said: 'Oh, misery! What Hovel is this you now inhabit?'

And this gladdened us with laughter, and Julius put forward at once a Plan for Margaret to move into Lord Delavigne's house 'where you may be comfortable again, sweet love, and possessed of a Hairbrush!'

And I could see that Margaret was very taken with this Plan

and would mightily prefer to inhabit Delavigne House on the Strand than to travel to Norfolk in February and be parted from her fiancé.

And so it was arranged that, after the King had made his final adieu, Margaret would live under the protection of Lord and Lady Delavigne, in a mansion where there was no shortage of Footstools or Candelabra, and I would travel alone to Bidnold, where I prayed to find everything made clean and safe for my Returning.

On Thursday the King sent for me again. Wondering whether he might require of me some Medical Intervention, I went to get my Surgical Instruments, but I could not find them.

Since my return from Switzerland, I had kept them by my bed, in the lowest drawer of my Night Table, but when I opened this drawer there was nothing in it – only a little fawn-coloured dust, where a Beetle had been gnawing at the wood.

I searched everywhere in my room, yet knew that my Instruments would not be found. And I could not but conclude that Fubbs had instructed her Servants to snatch up everything of value – regardless of its ownership – and hurl it into the waiting trunks.

This both saddened me and made me angry. The Instruments I had kept safely with me since 1665. They had been a Gift to me from the King, who, wanting to rouse me out of the lethargy into which I had fallen at Bidnold, had had inscribed upon the handle of the Scalpel, the Motto *Merivel, do not Sleep.*

I had cared for them with scrupulous attention, keeping them polished and sharp. It was with them that I had attempted to cut away Violet Bathurst's Cancer. It was with them that I had let blood from Margaret's arm during the time of her Typhus. It was with them that I had attempted to take out the Stones and Tumours of my patients down the span of twenty years. Without them I felt enfeebled.

I nevertheless made my way, empty-handed, to the King's door and was ushered into the room, where I witnessed His Majesty saying goodbye to Fubbsy's son, the Duke of Richmond, the youngest of his illegitimate children, and saw how everybody round the bed had turned their backs on Fubbs and her child, trying to snub them. With her great overload of grief, and now finding herself openly insulted by One and All, Fubbsy's eyes had turned red and Squinty.

When Fubbs and her son had gone out, I was taken to the Bedside and saw at once, from the King's colour and from the shrunken aspect of his face, that he was surely sinking.

'Merivel,' he whispered. 'The time is come. Pray fetch Huddleston and ask that the room be cleared of everyone except my brother and Lord Feversham, who is a Catholic and will bear witness to my Conversion.'

'I will fetch Huddleston, Sire,' I said, 'but I have no authority to clear the room.'

'Then ask the Duke of York to do it. But do not delay.'

The Duke of York was one among the many who had turned his back upon Fubbs. But I now saw that he, too, was weeping, and to interrupt his tears seemed heartless and rude. I nevertheless approached him. He looked at me with Disdain Absolute, but permitted me to come near, and when he heard my whispered Message, he blew his nose very loudly and assented to clearing the room.

I sped off to find Huddleston, who had promised to wait in the Queen's apartments until he should be summoned and, when he saw me, he knew that the moment had arrived and scuttled round him to procure the Host, sanctified by one of the Queen's Priests, and slammed a wig upon his head, so that none would recognise him.

'Father,' said I, 'I do not think the wig will suffice, for all will see your Priestly garments below. Why do you not take my cloak and put it round you?'

I laid my warm cloak round Father Huddleston's shoulders and together we returned to the King's Rooms, to see departing the phalanx of Bishops, who had appeared so fascinated with the

Enema procedures, and I felt glad that these proud churchmen
were Out of Favour and the humble Huddleston brought to sudden significance by the strange configuration of the times and
His Majesty's conscience.

We lurked together outside the Bedchamber, feigning a sudden interest in a tapestry depicting a Wild Boar stuck with the
arrows of the approaching Hunters, until the last of the Lords and
Councillors had departed. Then the Duke of York came to the
door and ushered Huddleston inside the Chamber, and I made as
though to follow him, but found the door closed in my face.

The day was very cold, with a violet sky promising snow.
Deprived of my cloak, and with the door so cruelly shut a mere
inch from the nose the King used to love to tweak, I discovered
myself to be shivering with misery, and I could not but think of
the icy grave that attended my poor Sovereign, as cold as that in
which we had buried Pearce.

I sat down on a stone settle and put my head in my hands. I
knew that these two men – John Pearce and Charles II of England
– had been the guardians of my Soul, passing it from one to the
other, yet keeping it always safe in their hands. And what would
become of it now I could not tell, but could only imagine that it
was destined for a long fall into Darkness.

By and by came Huddleston out of the Chamber, and tenderly
put my cloak back upon my shoulders and whispered to me: 'It
is done. He is received into the True Church.'

I mumbled that I was glad, although, to me, one Church or
None can make no difference to what awaits the King, and that
is the Nothingness from which we came and to which we again
return.

Huddleston sat by me on the settle and I found his presence
comforting, and I said to him: 'Father, when the King is gone I
shall be lost. I shall have no Direction.'

He put his hand on my shoulder, but said nothing, for knowing me even a little, he understood that this was entirely *true*, so

what could he say in the way of any Comfort? And I honoured him for this. One of the things I do detest in the world is people making Light of my Sorrows and saying 'now, now, be of good cheer' and altogether telling me to feel what I cannot feel and consoling me where Consolation there is none.

We sat silently there for a long time. Father Huddleston took off his borrowed wig and examined it for fleas and lice. He found a flea, but did not kill it, but only brushed it away. Then at length he said: 'Sorrow makes one weary. Why do you not go and sleep a little?'

I replied that I had pledged in my heart to Keep Watch until the King was gone, but Huddleston said: 'He wishes to be alone for a Space, to ponder what he has done today. So I advise you to sleep now, in the case that you may be needed in the night, or on the morrow.'

I did as he suggested, returned to my half-empty room and lay down. As the afternoon came on I saw snow falling. Sleep came and went, and came again and went again.

I rose towards four o'clock and found Fubbs supervising the taking away of her Trunks, and said to her: 'Your Grace, I am upset that my Surgical Instruments have been mistaken for Possessions of yours and put into the luggage. May we call the Trunks back?'

'What Instruments?' she shrieks at me. 'What would I want with Surgical Instruments?'

'They were stowed in my Night Table. They are the Tools of my Trade and a gift from the King, and most precious to me . . .'

'I have not seen them. The Trunks are gone. All that they contain belongs *to me* and to no one else. You must have dropped your instruments carelessly in the street.'

Carelessly in the street!

'Duchess,' say I, 'no such thing is possible. The instruments have been by my side, and barely out of my sight, for *twenty years*. They were stowed beside my bed. I have not moved them from there. But now they are gone.'

'And you are accusing me of stealing them for my own use?'

'I am accusing you of nothing. All I know is that something that is very precious to me has been inadvertently taken away. Please may we ask the Servants to bring in the Trunks again . . .'

'No, we may not! *Mon dieu, quelle histoire pour un petit rien!* The Trunks contain my Goods and nothing else, and they must be sent to the Embassy now, without delay, or everything I own will be taken from me. So please do not trouble me with this petty concern of yours.'

'Your Grace,' say I, 'in all humility, this is not a "petty concern" . . .'

'Yes, it is! I marvel that, at such a time, you can think only of yourself! Surgical instruments may be purchased afresh, but if my possessions are taken from me I will not have the means to replace them. The Trunks are leaving now, so please let me hear no more of this matter.'

In her fury to pack and in her Great Sadness, Fubbsy had, here and there across the afternoon, fortified herself with tipples of wine and these tipples had become so numerous that she was now quite categorically inebriated, and could not walk without stumbling, nor focus her eyes upon any Thing, and her breath was very pungent.

I went to her side and took her arm to steady her and said gently: 'I will go after the Trunks and search them as they travel . . .'

Tearing away her arm, Fubbs exhaled a malodorous puff of wine vapour and shrieked: 'What! And steal much else besides and strip me of things I love, as you are stripping me of Margaret?'

'I am not "stripping" you of Margaret, Duchess,' I said. 'Margaret does not want to be parted from Julius Royston, and that is the sum of it.'

'All I asked was that she come with me to France and see me settled. But no, she will not. I thought she had a kind heart, but I see now that, like you, she thinks only of herself!'

Though I was now very cross with the Duchess, I saw that it was of no avail to argue further with her. As she took yet another gulp of wine, I left the room and went down into the courtyard, where the Trunks were being loaded onto a wooden cart. Here I endeavoured to explain my loss of my precious instruments to the Servants charged with seeing the luggage safely brought to the French Embassy, but they did not seem willing to listen to me.

At length I produced a Purse containing three shillings and, given that the number of attendant Servants was two, I showed them that this made a neat Mathematic of a shilling and sixpence each, if they would let me ride in the cart and look for my instruments as we travelled along.

Hastily they took the money and bundled me in, and the horse set off at a foolish, lumbering gallop along the icy roads.

35

I do not know where we were when the cart was brought to its calamity.

One moment I was kneeling on the floor of the conveyance, searching in the topmost trunk, among bundles of silver forks and a fine array of Cream Jugs, Pepper Pots, Salt Cellars and Wine Coasters for my lost Instruments, and in the next second did I realise that the cart was tilting, like a barque in a violent storm.

I clutched at the sides of it, as though attempting to steady both it and myself within it, but neither was to be steadied. The heavy trunks slid towards me and all toppled sideways into the gutter – cart and horse, Servants, Merivel and luggage – and lay there unable to move, as though a mighty wave had crashed upon us.

I was aware of my head hitting the hard road and then of some heavy Thing falling upon my ankle. And that is all that I remember.

I woke in a cold, dim room.

There was a stench in it, sufficient, almost, to make me retch, yet strangely familiar to me. Noises, as of Animals in pain, reverberated around me. I fancied I was in a Zoo.

I tried to remain conscious by wondering what specimens this Zoo contained.

I imagined Ostriches and Camels, Hyenas and Crocodiles. I

longed to hear the cheeping of baby birds, fancying that this sound, which was the sound of Spring and of life returning, would console me.

'Sip-sip, sip-sip . . . come to me, sweet chicks . . .' I murmured.

Then I was swallowed once more, like Jonah by the Whale, into the belly of darkness and nothingness.

When next I came to my senses an old woman in a blue-cloth gown was standing over me and pulling my eyelids about to see into my eyes. Then her hands moved upwards to my head and began to fuss with something there, and I became aware of a most dreadful Ache in my skull and a dryness in my throat that was almost insupportable.

The Zoo still cried out all around me. I fancied I could hear Lions and Monkeys, and the terrible repetitive shrieking of a Peacock.

'What Zoo is this?' I managed to ask the blue-cloth crone.

'Zoo!' she said. 'Lord love us! Stay still, good man, and do not speak.'

I reached up and clutched her arm. 'What place am I in?' I said.

She looked at me more kindly then. She was elderly and poor, with her hair drawn into an unfashionable strangulated Bun on the top of her head, but with something of tenderness in her eyes. 'You are in St Thomas's Hospital,' she said, 'and you are lucky to be alive. You were found spilled onto the road.'

St Thomas's Hospital.

I had not been inside this wretched institution since Pearce and I worked long hours here, when we were learning the Physician's trade, after finishing our Anatomical Studies in Cambridge. I had not thought – because that this is a hospital for the Poor – ever to be a Patient in St Thomas's, trusting to Fortune that I would never be *poor enough* to get shelter here. But here I was.

I turned my aching head, looked about me and saw, indeed, that I was lying on a thin mattress on a wooden bed, with numberless other mortals of a Poor kind of disposition laid out beside me in a reeking Ward.

The air in the room was damp, as though the sun never reached it. On the stone floor had been strewn a quantity of straw, now much mixed with excrement, as in a cattle byre. The Animal noises came from the mouths and Arses of the Sick, all closeted together here, covered only with thin blankets, or else creeping about, like starving dogs and crying, and many passing the time by farting and defecating into tin bowls. Round these bowls, among the saturated straw, scuttled a lively quantity of mice.

I had had it in mind to ask the woman for a cup of water, but she was no longer by me. In the next bed to mine lay a sleeping man, very thin, with his head shaved for the application of Cantharidic Plasters and the deep Scurf of some ancient Pox still visible upon his face. Spittle bubbled up from his mouth, and oiled his chin and his straw-stuffed pillow. And I remembered how Pearce had always been very severe towards all victims of the Pox, looking me in the eye and saying: 'Men who court their own misery by lechery get the fate they deserve.'

Yet for all this remembered severity, I wished Pearce might be by my side now. I wished he might lift me up and get me away from here, and lay me down in my soft bed at Bidnold and watch over me, as I once watched over him for thirty-seven hours. I wished he might sit quietly by me, his white hands playing softly upon his china soup ladle, as though it might have been a lute. I wished he might bring me water and food.

Reaching up and touching my head, I discovered a Bandage there, and the touching of this Bandage brought back into my mind how I had been in the cumbersome cart with Fubbsy's Trunks, and how we had met with catastrophe on our way to the Embassy.

I could not know, from the ache in my head, how broken or cracked it might be, but I knew that I was not gone into Madness, for that my thoughts now began to turn upon whether I might find it in me to rise up and walk out of this place. I was horribly aware that my poor Margaret would be worried on my account. Fubbs had had no idea that I had boarded the cart with the Trunks and, all befuddled by wine as she was and angry with me, and distraught with sorrow, might have told Margaret any Thing of her choosing, viz. that I had taken flight for Norfolk or gone to drown myself in the river.

Pressing upon my arms, I lifted myself a little in the bed. Now I saw that laid next to my poor Pallet was a pair of shoes, which, though caked in malodorous gutter slime, I recognised as my own, and I looked about me for the rest of my clothes and my wig. All that I was wearing were my undergarments. My right ankle, I could now feel, was swathed in a bandage, but my feet were bare.

I could see no clothes anywhere in the vicinity of my bed. The cold in the Ward was very fierce. (Pearce and I had sometimes complained to the Nursing Sister about this, saying 'how are your Patients to recover, if all their bodily energy must be put into shivering?') But there seemed to be no means to ameliorate their lot. Winter was ever difficult to endure in this place.

Far down the room there was, in fact, a large fireplace, in which burned a few Coals, but scarce enough to make the colour of any flame and only sending out wisps of black smoke, which set everybody to coughing and retching. I pulled the thin blanket round me and, moving very slowly like an aged man, hoisted my feet onto the floor.

I stared at these feet and the legs to which they were attached. They did not look like my feet and legs, but indeed like those of a Pauper, as though, to contrive my entry into St Thomas's, my own limbs had been cut off and undergone some fearful exchange with the lower extremities of a Vagrant. I could see, too, that my right leg (or the right leg of the Vagrant) was horribly swollen and the foot a fierce purple colour, and when I tried to stand up, a very malicious pain came up this leg and into my thigh.

From this I deduced that my ankle was either turned or broken and had not been set properly, and that getting about upon it was going to bring me the gift of weeks of pain. And that this pain should have been caused by Fubbsy's Trunks, with their great weight of pewter, silver and gold falling onto my leg, made me more than ever understand how the Rich are detested by the poorest of the Poor, and how they might like to see our heads chopped off and put upon spikes on London Bridge.

Watched by the Scurfy man, now awake again and scratching himself all over, and breathing the vitiated air through his mouth, I managed the few steps that took me to the end of my bed. I then bent and peered underneath it, hoping to see there my shirt and coat and breeches, but all that I found was a little nest of straw and, lying in it and gone quite into Rigor Mortis, a dead cat.

This sight was so vivid and horrible that it reminded me on the instant of all the dead things Pearce and I had found in St Thomas's during the time that we worked here, and upon which we sometimes practised Anatomical dissections.

These included numerous mice and rats, but also dogs, squirrels, foxes and sparrows. In the Operating Room, where the Cuttings for the Stone were performed, we came upon a dead seagull, and in the Privies a dead Monkey, dressed in a little Mountebank's velvet coat. Of the human dead, taken out upon carts to Common graves, we lost count. Many of these lives we had attempted to save, but we had possessed neither the knowledge nor the means, and very often cursed our own profession for all its failures and shortcomings. Pearce, who had tried and failed to save his own mother, was always made angry by Death.

The pains in my leg and head being very severe, I now sat down again upon my bed and pondered what I might do, being thus hurt and almost naked as I was, and it was at this moment that I heard a new sound and that was the tolling of a bell.

I lifted my head to try to see out of the dirty window, but it was too high and all I could glimpse was the sky, which, after the snow that we had seen, was filled with an eerie brightness, sun and dappled cloud being in perfect Opposition, like lamplight trying to shine through a square of flannel, and this sight, for reasons that I know not, brought forth in me a feeling of profound melancholy.

I lay down again, deciding that I was not fit to move or go Anywhere, and could only hope to sleep until I felt a little stronger and able, then, to send some word to Margaret. The fact that my nostrils were now but two feet from the dead body of the cat troubled me somewhat, but there was no other bed to go to; all were occupied.

So I closed my eyes and hoped to dream of something sweet and reviving, and was drifting surely to some temporary Oblivion when I heard the sound of the tolling bell change and become a sonorous clamour. And then I understood that not one, but many, many bells had begun to toll, then more and more, and still more, till the air of London seemed rent apart with a terrible, never-ending thunder.

I lay very still, with my eyes open. Then I whispered it aloud: 'The King is dead.'

All I had to hold to was my blanket and my straw pillow.

I pressed my face into the pillow and cradled my head with my arms to try to muffle the sound of the bells. The straw became so damp with my weeping that from being a dry inert substance, it returned again to Vegetable Matter and began to stink.

In the Ward, silence slowly fell, as the poor Sick of St Thomas's crept about in confusion, knowing what the bells announced, but yet unwilling to believe it, for that it was too mighty a thing to be believed. I did not look at the suffering people, but I was aware of many shuffling footsteps in the room, as those who could move began to move towards the windows, as though to *see* the bells tolling would be to understand what now awaited us all in England under the new Monarch, James, Duke of York.

I cradled my head more tightly. I called out to the King. I told him I was sorry. I said that I had ardently wished to be by his side in his last moments, but that the terrible loss of my medical instruments had prevented this. I imagined him calling out to me, just as he had once called, in jest, in our games of Blind Man's Buff: 'Merivel! Where are you? Where are you?'

And I replied that I had always been close to him in my mind, that for more than twenty years I had loved him, and that though I had sometimes attempted to lay this love aside, I had not been able to do it. I had been, in Pearce's harsh words, His Majesty's Slave. 'But this Slavery I did not mind!' I cried out. 'For what is a human life worth, if it does not discover something greater than itself to serve? If I had not served you, if you had not roused me from my slothful Sleep, I would have been Nothing.'

All through the day the bells tolled.

I lay as though paralysed, wanting to make my way, along with the great crowds of the city, back to Whitehall to pay my Homage. But such was the pain in my skull, and so prostrated was I by my weeping, that I could barely raise my head from the stinking pillow.

Food was brought to me – mutton and bread and a little cup of Ale. A Nurse helped me to sit up and I reached for the Ale and drank it down like a drowning man gulping Air. Then I asked the Nurse, 'Where are my clothes, I beg you? I must find them and go to where my Duty lies, beside the body of the King.'

She consulted with the Sister and this woman came to me and said: 'You were brought to us just as you are, in your undergarments and your shoes. You were surely taken for Dead and robbed of everything else.'

Cursing Fubbsy's Servants, who must have run away and left me to die, despite the one-and-sixpence I had given them, I thought, I shall never get out of here. Days will pass and the body of the cat will rot and I shall rot too, naked and forgotten by all. In this place occurred one of the Beginnings of my life and in this place will it arrive at an Ending I did not anticipate: an Ending through Grief.

Night came and the fire was banked up to warm us a little in our Mourning, but all through the dark hours did the sound of crying and wailing go on and on among the Patients, only enlivened now and then by the noise of a fart or a sudden puking. I lay exhausted on my saturated pillow and listened to all this, and did not close my eyes. I told myself that I was Keeping Watch upon the King's soul.

On the blessed morrow, towards mid-morning, came a face that I recognised, moving slowly through the Ward, examining each patient, and arriving at length beside me and crying out that, at last, he had found me.

It was Julius Royston.

'Julius,' I said, 'I declare that I am Lazarus and you are the Saviour of Mankind. If I could raise myself up, I would fall at your feet and kiss them.'

36

The day that followed the night of His Majesty's burial was like a prolongation of the darkness of Night, with great Crowds, in black Mourning Crêpe visible everywhere from our windows, and a lowering sky above them. And I stood with Margaret at Fubbsy's windows and we watched this Mass of people under the perpetual rolling twilight of the cloud. And I thought about their love for the late King and how it must have been an Obstinate, rolling and reshaping love, like mine, so that nothing could persuade them to leave this place, which was the place where it had come to rest.

Margaret and I, however, were soon enough forced to leave.

Fubbs had sequestered herself straight away at the French Ambassador's house, leaving us with almost no Furniture at all and no clean linen for our beds.

Then, on February the 16th came an order from King James that the apartments were to be 'vacated absolutely' and nothing taken from them except ourselves, who had 'outrun our time'. And so, though scarce able to walk and with the pain in my head very bad, I packed my clothes and such possessions as remained to me, and escorted Margaret to Lord Delavigne's house.

Lady Delavigne, seeing the bandage round my head and my need of a Cane for dragging one foot in front of the other, very courteously invited me to stay awhile at Delavigne House 'till you be a little more mended'. But I was now impatient to get to Bidnold, so after thanking her elaborately I said: 'There is but one thing will make me well, M'Lady, and that is the tender Ministration of my Servant Will Gates. I shall put myself into his hands.'

And so I said Goodbye to Margaret, where she stood on the steps of Delavigne House, and I could not help but notice that, framed as she was by the Grand Portal with it enormous Coat of Arms above, she looked very small. I wanted to run back to her and hold her to me again, but then came Julius to her and he put his arm round her shoulders. The two of them smiled and raised their hands to me in farewell. And, trusting all to Julius Royston, I was gone.

Almost always my heart had lifted at each and every occasion of my arrival at my beloved Bidnold. But now, as I my hired Coach made the turn into the drive and I looked out at my Park, what I saw was not my Park as I remembered it, but some unfamiliar Landscape.

The grass was long and rank with weeds, the trees all girt about with dead leaves and all the ironwork benches gone. In these neglected pastures I saw, where once the pretty Deer had roamed, pigs truffling in mud and a troupe of ragged sheep limping about on the tussocks. Of the Deer there was no sign. And the drive itself, always kept very neat with gravel, was pitted with the ruts of farm carts and host to some terrible Plague of Moss of a brownish-yellow colour.

As the house itself came into view I was aware of yet greater Dereliction.

One third of the west wall was clamped all over by a raging Ivy. I saw panes broken and missing from the windows, and slates gone from the roof. Where once my Curtilage had been neatly squared with plantings of Box and Holly, there now grew among these a tangle of some nameless dead weeds and a poor broken regiment of Hemlock.

I descended from the Coach, with much distress to my ankle, and stared about me. When last I had glimpsed my house and grounds they had been as they ever were, with everything clipped and clean and shipshape. Now, so altered and defiled were they that I was at pains to recognise them. The air itself, habitually very sweet, resembled that of a Farmyard, vitiated by pig stench, and indeed, what I felt myself to be was some poor Yeoman returning to his little acre of grass and livestock, all alone and with no hope of any betterment to his life.

The day was bitter cold. My Coachman stood about, holding the horses, waiting for his money. The front door of the house remained closed. As I fumbled to find a Purse, I babbled to the Coachman, 'It seems I am come in the wrong Season . . .'

I counted out coins for the fare and watched with great anxiety as the Coach departed – much as I had done at Versailles – as though to be abandoned by the Coach put me in some sudden danger.

Then I turned and limped with my Cane towards the door. I began to call out to Will, telling him I was come home at last and as I called, I could not but remember that other Returning after much absence in 1667, and how, though I no longer believed the house to be mine, I was so moved by the sight of it that I let out a great shout of joy, and, when I saw Will and Cattlebury standing here to greet me began blubbing like a baby.

I went in and found the hall in darkness, with no candle burning and no fire lit. Here again the scent of the air was altered. Habitually it smelled of Beeswax and wood smoke, and this homely perfume had always cheered my soul. Now the air felt damp and tainted with something sickly, as though mice or rats had come to die there. I looked down. At my feet was spread out the pelt of Clarendon. His glass eyes stared blindly out into the crepuscular gloom. And I knew that it was from him (my poor Clarendon, inexpertly treated and cured) that the stench arose.

Then I heard – from the direction of the kitchens beneath – the unmistakable sound of laughter. I moved forward a little and listened. More waves of mirth rose up and broke upon the cold and silent strand of the hall. Again I called Will's name loudly and desperately. My head throbbed. My ankle sent shafts of pain into my thigh.

Nobody appeared. Whoever inhabited the house was deaf to my voice, existing only within the bubble of the laughter. Being thus unheard and excluded, I had no choice but to hobble downstairs.

I opened the kitchen door and looked in upon a mortifying scene.

More than twenty people, men and women both, dressed in ragged and dirty clothes, were gathered there, lying and sitting about on the floor and on the chairs and table, all far gone into drunkenness.

On the table was a congregation of bottles of wine – not less than thirty or forty at a glance – taken from my Cellar. And now that these had all been drunk, the company had started upon a shameless and ugly debauch, not caring what they did in front of each other, with two of the men crouched in a corner intent on Buggery, and some of the women with their breasts pushed up clear of their bodices, and the men sucking on their nipples and fumbling to take down their own breeks, as a prelude to Fornication. A boy, no older than twelve, was laughing like a Magpie and pissing in a terrible stream beside the range, upon which a cauldron of rabbit stew sat bubbling and spilling over.

My eyes wandered, in a trance of disbelief, around the room. At first no one paid me any attention. Then I banged upon the stone floor with my Cane, like some foolish Schoolmaster or aged Beadle, and a few heads turned in my direction. Slowly, and with agitated dismay, I began to recognise some of these ragged people as the maids and footmen who had served me and served the King for long years, once so neat in their uniforms and hardworking and as good as any Servants could be, and now descended into a shameless Anarchy of their own devising.

I said nothing, but only stared, and they stared back and the room slowly quietened, and some of the women sat upright and returned their naked breasts to their gowns and pushed the men away. Then, from the end of the table rose up Cattlebury, scarlet with wine and more colossal than ever in his shape and holding in his mighty hands the drawers of the wench beside him, who, further gone than most into her inebriation, still pawed at his great girth. I waited while Cattlebury's eyes aligned themselves sufficiently to rest on me.

'Sir Robert,' he said at last. 'We never thought to see you more.'

'Ah,' said I. 'You never thought to see me more? Why was that?'

'We pictured you gone. Dead was how we saw you.'

'Well, I am sorry to disappoint you, Cattlebury, but here I am. Now please tell me what is the meaning of this ugly Scene?'

He swayed back and forth. Sweat poured down his cheeks. The woman cackled and nudged his arm. 'His Mighty Lordship asks what is the *meaning*, Mr Cattlebury. What is the poxy MEAN-ING of this fine assembly!'

Cattlebury wiped his face with the drawers, and attempted to steady himself and draw himself up in height, so that he could face me down.

'The meaning, Sir Robert,' he stammered at last, 'is the Same Meaning that it was when you and . . . you and Lady Bathurst and all the merry Fops and Lechers from London did likewise, time after countless time, and we . . . we toiled after you to clean up your stinking mess! What other Meaning can there be?'

More crazed laughter broke out at this. The men in the corner, taking this rude statement and the mirth that followed it as permission to resume their Hard unfinished Labours, went to them with sudden haste, quite uncaring that I should see them in this doglike rut.

I looked upon them and upon the whole discomforting spectacle, and thought how, if men could *see themselves close up* when they abandon all sobriety and become animals, why then, perhaps they might not fall, as I had fallen, into so much repetition of sheer wantonness, realising at last how near it came to stealing their souls.

At this moment a young woman came to my side, whom I recognised as Tabitha, Margaret's maid – she who had watched with such unselfish care over my daughter's terrible illness. Tabitha, too, had been drinking, and her hair was dishevelled and falling into her eyes, but her gown was neat and unruffled. Saying nothing, she took my hand and led me out of the kitchen. She went up the stairs and entered the corridor that led to the Library and, not knowing what else to do, I let myself hobble after her, leaving the Debauchery beneath us to burn itself out. She opened the Library door and we went in.

I looked about me. It seemed to me that far fewer pieces of furniture stood here than the room had once contained. What remained was all covered in white dustsheets, and the air was musty and cold. I pulled aside one of the sheets and sank down on chair, and my cane fell to the ground.

'Where is Will?' said I with a long and painful sigh. 'Please go and find Will Gates.'

Tabitha came and knelt down beside my chair. 'Sir Robert,' she said, 'you shall not punish us. We have taken Advantage of your absence and we are sorry for what has been done, but all has come to this Bad Pass, for that we had no money to run the house . . .'

'No money?' said I. 'What do you mean? I left money a-plenty.'

'No, Sir. Beyond November we had none, Sir. Nothing for food or oil or candles or any Commodity at all. We killed and ate the Deer. We had no choice. When the Deer were all gone we let the farmers' pigs and sheep roam in your Park, in return for meat. We could not buy beer, so we drank your cellar. For you did not send us anything, nor any word. We could not but assume that you were dead, or had decided to forget us, and so you are veritably to blame for abandoning us so cruelly. We were not willing to starve.'

'Tabitha,' said I. 'I did not "abandon" you. You know what manner of man I am. I could never have done such a thing. Before I left for Switzerland, half of the King's *loyer* for a Six-month was deposited with Will Gates. This was more than enough to keep the household in every kind of Commodity for a year and that year is not yet gone.'

Tabitha looked down at the carpet. Her fingers played nervously over its intricate patterns. 'We searched,' she said, 'but we could not find it. We could not find any money anywhere.'

'You searched . . . ?'

'Yes. When Mr Gates passed away—'

'What?'

'When Mr Gates left us, Sir . . .'

Tabitha now put her head into her hands, brushing aside the hair that had fallen over her face. She would not look at me as she said: 'He did not suffer, Sir Robert. He died in his sleep on the first of December. When he did not come down that morning, I and Mr Cattlebury went to his room, and he was very peaceful and still upon his bed, and covered with his old Badger skin.'

I stared out at the shrouded Library, clutching the arms of my chair. I did not move any muscle of my face or body, nor say a word.

Tabitha went on: 'We did all correctly, Sir Robert, as far as we could. We sent for the Searchers to determine the cause of death, but they *saw* no cause, except that his heart had stopped beating. They said only that Mr Gates was ready to "become one with the earth".

'We had no money for a woollen winding sheet, but Mr Cattlebury, he said that this did not matter. He ordered that Mr Gates be sewn into some more of the Badger skins, such as we wore last winter, enough to shroud him quite, and then the Undertakers were sent for and they took him away.'

Silence fell in the room. I looked at the empty Fireplace, and longed more than anything in the world to find Will kneeling beside it and laying kindling in a neat stack to start a beautiful fire.

At length I asked: 'Where is he buried, that I may go and visit him?'

When Tabitha did not reply, I asked the question again. Again, she fussed with her hair, trying to thrust it away from her eyes.

Then she said: 'We had no money, Sir Robert, and no friend nor relative came forth to claim the body. We had no choice. He lies in the Paupers' Grave behind Bidnold Churchyard.'

I remained in the Library, unmoving, until the dusk came down. In this twilight I saw figures swaying drunkenly down the drive and heard once more the boy's Magpie laugh. So I rose and went out and stood by the door, and saw my former Servants, together with the nameless others they had invited to their voluptuous revels, staggering away from Bidnold, taking with them all they could carry of my remaining Possessions.

I did not try to stop them. That I should be bereft of much that I had owned did not greatly trouble me. I had once seen a man hanged in Norwich for the stealing of a single bale of cloth and yet these people, under my very nose, were making off with a great hoard of china and silverware, and dispersing out into the wider world, where I would never find them.

Among the stolen goods were very many clocks, and this stealing of Time brought back into my mind a tender souvenir of Hollers and the clock he had attempted to give to Madame de Maintenon, and which she had rejected for that it 'stole Time from God'. And then I thought how Life itself is the greatest Theft of Time, and how all we can do is to watch as the days and months and years slip away from us and make off into the Darkness.

This was a melancholy observation, but what troubled me more and made me so sick at heart that I could barely breathe was the image I had of Will's body, bound and tied in the Badger tabards, carelessly thrown into a Communal pit with Quicklime heaped upon it.

'It shall not be so, Will!' I announced to the descending night. 'It shall not end thus.'

In the empty house, which had never, in all the time that I had known it, been so bereft of people, I could not decide what to do or where to put myself.

I returned to the Library and lit a single candle and sat on among the half-remembered ghosts of footstools and card tables, and a fine Globe that I would never see again.

'Your world, Merivel,' said Pearce's voice suddenly out of shadows, 'is horridly *Shrunk*.'

This made me smile. 'You are right, my friend.' I said. 'It is.'

'What shall you do now?' asked Pearce.

'I know not,' I said. 'I know not.'

I thought about my Work, my *Meditations upon the Animal Soul*, that I had begun with such touching Optimism, and wondered whether I would return to it, or whether, in embarking upon a subject that might never be truly proven or *knowable*, I had not set out merely upon another of my pointless journeys, like that to Versailles, at the end of which the services that I offered would never be taken up and the Conclusions that I sought would never be found.

'What d'you think, Pearce?' I asked. 'Shall I keep the idea of this work alive?'

But there was no answer. Pearce had gone.

I slept a little, then woke feeling racked by hunger. Remembering the rabbit stew, I took up my cane and made my way down again to the kitchen.

Here two oil lamps had been lit and by the light of these Tabitha was slowly and patiently cleaning the room of spilt wine and urine and semen and discarded rabbit bones.

Laid across three hard chairs was Cattlebury, insensible to everything, snoring like a bloodhound. I stared at him and saw that his neck was being almost broken in two by the heaviness of his head upon the seat of the hard chair, and pity for this neck and for the man Cattlebury stung me on the instant so hard that I said to Tabitha: 'Help me to lift him and we will put him in his bed.'

We carried him, by slow and wearisome degrees, to his small room and laid him down and covered him against the cold night. I stared at his fat, ruined face and remembered all the fine fare, all the Carbonadoes and Lardy Cakes and Pigeon Pies and Milk Possets and Mince Tartlets that he had made, and which had sustained my life for so long. And I reached out and touched his forehead and laid my hand tenderly upon it for a moment, before I came away.

37

The following day I gave a few coins to Tabitha and bade her walk to Bidnold Village and hire me a horse and cart, for I could barely limp ten paces on my swollen ankle.

The horse she managed to obtain was a feeble, slow mare, who would not be whipped into a trot, so we travelled wearily, but I did not greatly care. I had but one task in mind.

I arrived towards ten o'clock at the Sexton's house. His name was Sexton Blunt and this had always made me smile, for that he was indeed a blunt man, with no courtesy and no grace. Taking my cue from him, my dealings with him were now curt and unadorned.

I held before his small hard eyes a purse of five *livres* and said: 'You know me, Sexton Blunt, and that I am a man of my word. I here claim kinship with one William Gates, mistakenly cast into the Communal Pit after his death in December, when I was far from England.'

'Kinship?' said Blunt. 'What manner of "kinsman" can a Pauper be to you?'

'He was no Pauper,' said I. 'He was an honest and God-fearing and hard-working Servant to me for twenty years, and I loved him well. And I wish that he may lie in a well-made grave. I shall pay for its digging and for a Headstone. All I ask of you is that you find men today to take him out of the Pit and make a grave for him in the Churchyard. I shall oversee their work.'

When Blunt began mumbling that I should first need to consult the Parish Clerk, I took back the Purse and said: 'Ah, it is thus to him that I should give the five *livres?*'

'No, no,' said Blunt, looking fearfully at the money, 'but it is the *Procedure.* No body may be taken out of the Pit without signature of the Parish Clerk beneath the signature of the Sexton . . .'

Ten *livres,* then: five to Blunt and five to the Parish Clerk for some scribbled Permission. With this piece of naked Robbery agreed upon, Blunt said: 'And you must find your own men to dig in the Pit, Sir. *I* cannot ask any that I know to do this work.'

'I see, Sexton. Are you thus suggesting that, though this matter concerns the Church and is in your Parish, men will do *my* bidding more willingly than yours?'

'No.'

'Well, then?'

'I am suggesting that none will do it at all.'

While the Permission was laboriously written out and signed, I went to the Joiner and Coffin Maker, Mr Shanks, and purchased a Coffin 'Ready-Made for a Small Man or Woman, no higher than five feet and four inches' and put it in the back of the cart. The 'Ready-Made Small' were the only coffins available, 'for that most who die, save children, Sir,' said Shanks, 'are fatter than once they were, and seem to die of this fatness, and I can barely fashion the boxes fast enough'. With the coffin I was furnished also with a Woollen Shroud, for which I was forced to pay a foolish price, but again I did not care.

I then made my way to the lowly dwelling where Patchett resided among his fields of Ragwort – he who had killed poor Clarendon with his Blunderbuss.

I found him wresting Turnips from the hard earth of his vegetable patch and said to him: 'Patchett, I have need of you now . . .'

When told of the terrible task I was asking of him, instead of protesting he smiled. Scratching his Giant's head he said: 'I knew that matters between you and me would not end with the death of your Bear, Sir Robert. I knew that more would be asked of me one day. But I did not foresee this.'

'Will you do it?' said I.

He kept on scratching. He sighed and his weary breath vaporised in the cold air. He was a man who had known Will and been witness to his kindness of heart, so I kept talking, telling him that it was 'for Will's sake and not for mine' that he had to be lifted from the Pit.

At length Patchett said: 'I will do it for money, Sir Robert. Or for Meat.'

I ransacked my person to see what Coin remained to me after my payments to the Sexton, the Parish Clerk and the Coffin Maker, and all that I found was one golden Sovereign. I held this in my palm and Patchett stared at it in awe.

'Here,' I said, 'this is yours, if you can get Will Gates snug into his Coffin before nightfall.'

With the Sovereign safe in his pocket and with his face tied round with rags against the stench and contagion of the Paupers' Pit, Patchett began digging at one o'clock. I stood by to urge him on. I knew that we had only a few hours of light remaining.

I said to him: 'We shall find Will very quickly in this shallow pit, for that his body was wrapped in Badger furs.'

'Badger furs?' said Patchett. 'Could nobody find better nor more fitting to wrap him in?'

'No,' I said. 'They could not. His winding sheet is but this – the skins of animals.'

As Patchett's spade rummaged through the soil and lime, the stink of Death did indeed begin to rise up towards us, and I remembered how, in this one matter of the smell of the dead, I had always been more courageous than Pearce and stayed quite well through the Anatomy lessons, when other students vomited or fainted away. And, to keep Patchett at the work, I began to tell him about the dissections I had once performed at Cambridge, making them sound very bloody and strenuous and exciting, so that it would be these past things and not the present churning of earth and bones that would occupy his mind.

As I had predicted, it did not take very long to come upon the muddy bundle of fur that was Will. Patchett lifted him out and laid him on the grass, and I saw how, among the cords that bound him to his tattered shroud, were visible two or three Badger snouts, and these marled but homely faces lessened my horror by some degree, as though I imagined the animals were keeping company with Will, as a stuffed toy keeps company with a child, making more bearable his long Night.

I would have washed and combed the furs and the snouts, except that I saw the Maggots were already at them and I baulked at combing out Maggots. But I came to where Will lay, not minding the stench of him, and knelt down and put my hand where I knew his face to be.

'Will,' said I, 'I am taking you out of the Paupers' Grave, for never were you any Pauper, but rich as the richest man, with kindness.'

Patchett and I then wrapped him in the expensive Woollen Shroud, and laid him in the Coffin that was sturdy and made of oak, and I closed the lid and nailed Will down, while Patchett started on a grave for him.

The grave – even in February – lay in sunlight, with the thin shadow of an apple tree just glancing across its corner, and I thought it a good place.

As the sunlight departed and the air became very cold, I began to fear that the grave might not be ready before the darkness fell. I went and found a spade and tried, despite my swollen ankle, to join with Patchett in his labours. But in truth, so difficult was it for me to put any pressure on my foot, or to move about in the churned earth, that all I did was hamper him.

At length, and almost in darkness, with one icy star visible behind the apple tree, the grave was ready and we put the coffin in. And I felt a great Relief flood over me at a thing properly done. Then I took up the spade once more and we pressed the rich earth of Bidnold Churchyard over and round the Box, and I told Patchett what words I would get engraved on a Headstone, and these were they:

William Gates, Esquire,

1609–1685

An inestimable man

The nag and I found our way by moonlight back to the house. She was spent and sweating from lugging the cart and I told her that, once there, the Grooms would bed her down in a warm stable and give her hay and water. But then I remembered that there *were no grooms* – only men cavorting in some distant hostelry, exclaiming over the Booty they had stolen from me and no doubt laughing at all my losses.

The stables, however, still stood, and there was straw in them, and I unhitched the poor mare from the cart and led her in, and found among the straw a few carrots to give her, and filled a bucket with water from the well and set it before her. I watched her drink a little and then she lay down.

As weary as the horse, and with the pain in my foot now very biting, I limped into the house and found, to my great joy, a goodly fire burning in the hall. I sank down on a settle beside it and at length came Tabitha, dressed in a clean dress and pinafore, and with her hair washed and tidy, bringing me wine.

'Ah,' said I, 'I am surprised there is any wine left, Tabitha, if every day was like yesterday in this house.'

She lowered her head as she poured the wine for me. 'It was not every day, Sir, but only when Mr Cattlebury had the Heat upon him and invited all and sundry.'

'I am glad to hear it.'

'It was but a few times, Sir . . .'

'Well, God be praised for small Mercies. Now please fetch Cattlebury, Tabitha, for he and I have before us a grave conversation. He must surely know that he could be hanged for all that he has done.'

''Twas only want of money made him do it, Sir Robert. He said to me one day: "Men without money to put food in their bellies turn swiftly to beasts." And I think they do. For we were very wretched here. If Mr Gates had only told us where he kept the King's *loyer* . . .'

'I know,' said I. 'But still, Tabitha, the Ruin I see about me is very bad. What am I to do with Cattlebury? I do not think that he can any longer stay in my employ.'

Tabitha stooped and laid another log upon the fire. Then she looked up at me. 'He left while you were gone today,' she said, 'and will never more come here.'

I stared at Tabitha. Into my mind came a very vivid picture of my former cook, whom I had known for almost twenty years, standing like an Ogre over his fires, always and ever on the precipice of some Mutiny or other, but yet never falling over it until lately, because he had no other home but Bidnold Manor. And now he was gone out into the dark and I could not predict what would become of him.

'Did he leave any word for me?' I asked.

'Yes,' said Tabitha. 'He bade me write it for him, for that he could not form his Alphabet very well.'

'Let me see it, then.'

Tabitha produced a scrap of paper from her Apron pocket and gave it to me.

Sir Robert, I read,
I cling to my Life and shall not swing on Mouse Hill for only taking what was needed to keep my soul within my body.
I bid you adieu. I shall ever carry Bidnold with me in my heart.

M. *Cattlebury*

I read the message several times, then I put it away in my pocket and took Tabitha's hand in mine and said: 'Bidnold goes with us all in our hearts, but it is over.'

'It is over?'

'Yes. I shall put in hand small repairs to windows and suchlike, to make it safe. Then all that remains here will be taken to a Store House and Bidnold Manor will be closed. I shall be gone to London and thence, in summertime, to Switzerland.'

'What will become of the house, Sir?'

'It will be sold.'

'Sold to whom?'

'I know not. I care not. I once set it all to rights, Tabitha, creating my own wild wonders in every room, with scarlet brocade and golden Canopies and crimson Tassels, which almost stopped the heart of my friend John Pearce. I was on fire with my Endeavours. I could scarce sleep for my excitement when I found the Carpet from Chengchow! Bidnold Manor is the only house I have ever owned. I lost it once and then it was restored to me, and I have loved it very dearly. Margaret hoped to be married here. But I shall I have to disappoint her, for I have not the stomach to set it to rights again. It must go on without Merivel.'

'I am very sorry, Sir Robert,' said Tabitha.

'Yes,' said I. 'I am sorry. But all things come to some kind of ending.'

A long silence fell in the hall. Then Tabitha said, in a little shy voice:

'What is to happen to me? Are you sending me out into the dark?'

'No,' I said. 'For I have never forgotten and never will forget what you did for Margaret. Tomorrow I will ride in the cart to see Lady Prideaux and ask that you be taken into her Service. Would you like that?'

'Yes, Sir. If she will take me . . .'

'She will take you. And you will go into Cornwall with the family in summer?'

'Yes . . .'

'Very well. There are Puffins in Cornwall and these are birds that I have never seen, but I promise that you shall see them.'

᪥ ᪥

I slept long and woke just before dawn and knew, instantly upon waking, where Will had kept the King's *loyer*, where none but he would ever go to find it.

So I rose and pulled on my robe, and took a candle and my Cane and made my silent, hobbling way up into the White Room in the West Tower – the room that had once contained my whole existence.

It was empty of all furniture, save a small Turkey Carpet and one Chair, where I liked to sit, sometimes, and watch the Alterations of the sky, and listen to the wind, and feel that I was above the world and yet floating in its beauty, like a cloud. Only Will, of all my household, knew that I still came here.

I laid down the candle. At the four great windows to the north, south, east and west of the tower the light was strengthening and I saw that the day would be fair.

I knelt down and pushed away the chair from its habitual position, and rolled back the carpet. And, exactly as I had anticipated, under a board that had been cut for this purpose lay the leather bag in which Will had ever kept our Yearly Household Accounts. And stuffed in among the papers was a great quantity of the King's gold.

I barely touched the Sovereigns, but only stayed on my knees, looking at their obstinate shine. Then I noticed that something else had been buried by Will under the floorboard.

I reached in and took it out, and saw that it was my Book (the story of my life that I had called *The Wedge*) that had lain under my mattress for sixteen years and was now more than ever creased and torn and soiled with dust and mouse droppings by being squashed into this new hiding place. But I thanked Will for keeping it safe. When so much else had been taken from me, I was glad to find that this little Record of my Existence, all tattered as it was, was still there in the world.

I sat in the chair and began to read. I read how, in the first sentence, I described myself as 'a very untidy man', with a fat stomach and a misshapen nose, and this made me smile.

I then progressed to what I called the 'Five beginnings' of my life, and these, in showing as they did so much haste and foolery and madness in my younger self, amazed me very much. Indeed, the Book so absorbed my attention that I only raised my eyes from it when the light all around me suddenly underwent its great Transition to the deep red of the sunrise. I looked out at the sky. For a moment I seemed to be held within a cauldron of fire.

Epilogue

*Deposition by Mrs R. Pierpoint,
made at her Laundry on the
Eighteenth Day of March
in the year 1685*

These things I here set down, which I swear by all the fishes in the river to be the Truth, as it visited me here on the morning of the 18th of March in the year of the King's death, 1685.

The day was chill. I had lit my fires and put a Quantity of Sheets and Petticoats onto a boil, and I was warming myself, holding out my arms to the Coppers, when my street door was opened and there came in my old and dear friend, Sir Robert Merivel. And when I saw him I ran to him and cried out: 'Oh, Sir Rob, take Rosie in your arms, for she is all a-cold!'

And so we clung together, and sighed together and I lamented thus: 'The King is dead! And it is a Shame, a crying Shame for England and for us who loved him, and for all the bountiful white Cavalier Lace that has sustained the Laundry trade.'

And Sir Robert, he strokes my hair and kisses my cheek, but he cannot speak for that he is all choked with weeping.

And so I led him near my burning cauldrons to warm him, and gave him a Handkerchief, newly ironed, and he says to me, 'Whose is the kerchief?'

And I say, ''Tis no matter whose. For it is yours now and what can anyone care about a Handkerchief when the King has so lately passed away?'

He sits himself down upon a pile of Garments, waiting for the wash: some fine shirts among them, but much of them very worn and used, and hanging by Threads, for that their Wearers are come to impecunious times and cannot afford new, but send me over and over the same old rags.

And Sir Robert, when he has blown his nose and wiped his eyes, notices this and says to me: 'What are these Tatters you are laundering now, Rosie?'

And I says to him: 'These are the Tatters of England. And all the Whole and Beautiful things are no more.'

And then I sent home the girls who work for me, Mabel and Marie, and went and locked my Door to the Street and put up my Sign: *Mrs Pierpoint regrets that the Laundry be Closed today. Pray bring your Raiment tomorrow*, and I took from my shelf a flask of wine, and then I sat down beside Sir Rob upon the Linen and held him close to me and said: 'Shall we drink this, though it be ten in the morning, and let all the world go softly by and be hanged?'

And he lays his head on my breast and says: 'Rosie Pierpoint, I have always cherished you in my heart and through all my life you have given me Solace.'

I kiss his forehead and say: 'I shall not forget all the Capons and all the pots of Cream you brought me and how I always smeared the cream upon the roasted Capon, and never have any Birds tasted so fine.'

We began to drink the wine. And Sir Robert, he started to tell me how he was to journey into Switzerland and there make a fine Marriage to an honourable woman, and I said I was glad for him and glad for the fortunate lady who would be the Wife of a man so Sweet and full of laughter.

And he said: 'Alas, I cannot hear laughter in me any more, Rosie. My skull aches. My daughter is to marry, and make her way into a finer life than any I have provided and soon enough forget me. I buried my servant, Will, and England has buried the King, and all my mirth is spent.'

I could not imagine this: that Sir Robert Merivel would laugh no more. And so, to cheer him and try to hear his laughter again,

I began to remind him of all the times he and I had played the Beast together and how, once long ago, his father had come upon us, in the middle of our play, and hidden his poor face for shame in the bed Curtain, and a solemn smile did spread itself across Sir Robert's features for a trice, but then he said: 'I am weary, Mrs Pierpoint. I cannot find it in my heart or in my body to do Any Thing – even though I know that my life in Switzerland will be an Easy Life.'

And what could I say by any way of Contradiction, for did not I, that very morning, have to drag myself to my fires and, when I looked down at the cold River, had I not for a little moment envied my late husband who drowned there, long years past, trying to get a haddock from the raging water, and who sleeps now with Angels' wings folded upon him, with all his sufferings and poverty forgotten, while I toil on in the March cold?

So then I say – and I am willing to set this down too, for that I swore I would be honest in this Testament – 'Shall we but go on, as ever we did, my fine Sir, and play a little? For the door is shut and locked, and though we are Mourners we are yet alive.'

And Sir Rob took my hand and kissed it and said to me: 'Sweet Rosie, let me rest. My head is sore and my foot is swollen. Let me not move . . .'

I told him he would be more comfortable in my bed than on a pile of Laundry and that besides, 'the garments under you, as well as being torn and tattered, are most foul, Sir Rob. For people's want of money stretches out the Interval between their visits to my Wash House. They will wear a Shirt for days and weeks and, though a tablecloth be stained, keep setting it out again and again. Can you not smell the stench of sweat and grime and gravy?'

He smiled and said: 'The stink of the world has never troubled me. Even at Cambridge, when I dissected cadavers . . . Even the King when he was dying . . . Even raising Will from the Paupers' Pit . . . A Physician must learn to breathe difficult air, and that is that.'

'Nevertheless,' said I, 'let me go and prepare my bed. I will help you to it. And if your desire is only to sleep, then sleep you will and I shall be the Watcher of your dreams.'

I stirred my Coppers and mixed in a quantity of Lye and then I left Sir Robert on the wash Pile, holding the flask of wine, and I saw him take off his wig and fling it away, and then he laid his head down on the Pile and closed his eyes.

I made my bed with a clean Coverlet, and plumped the pillows and emptied my pisspot into the river, then closed my little window. I next took off my drawers, in case we might come to a lovemaking, remembering how Sir Rob was ever excited by finding me Naked under my petticoats, and liking to put his hand there and touch me. And I thought how, of all the men that I have known, my dear Sir Robert was the boldest Lover and most attentive to me, and then I thought of the 'honourable' woman in Switzerland who was to be his Wife, and I envied her and all her beautiful life remaining.

At length I returned to the Wash Room, somewhat foggy now with steam, and through the clouds of steam made my way to the Laundry heap where Sir Robert lay.

I knelt down beside him. He lay very still, asleep, and the flask of wine had fallen across his chest and spilled over his Waistcoat.

I was loath to wake him, for I knew by every sign that he was Weary, but, God forgive me, I wanted him in my bed to console me for the feelings of Death that were in the London air, so I took the flask from him and touched his face and said his name. He opened his eyes and looked at me, but his look was vacant, as though he could not see me, nor know where he lay.

'Sir Rob,' I whispered, 'let me help you up. Try to stir yourself a little and we shall go to my room and lie down together and forget the Sad Times that are come upon us.'

I put my arm under his shoulder and tried to lift him up, but the weight of him seemed, on a sudden, very great, as though there was a Stone lodged in his heart.

'Come on,' I said. 'Raise your head and your chest. Help me to help you. And then we shall, in a trice, be comfortable together under my new Coverlet.'

He managed to lift himself a little. But when he looked up at me his gaze was all bewildered, and then, on a sudden, as I had him sitting up, he gave a great Shout, which sounded almost like a clap of laughter. And there was such a wild and vibrant Echo to the Shout that I seemed to hear it carried out of my window into the air and fly westwards along the river, past the boats crowded at Southwark Steps, past the Commerce milling at Black Friars, past the gates of the Temple, and sounding on and on and on above the water, until at Whitehall it faded and was heard no more.

And he was gone in that instant of the Shout. It was his last sound on earth.

I closed his eyes and laid my head next to his, and held him to me and wept. The steam from the boiling Coppers shrouded us and made all the air around us white.

I could ardently have wished that he had not passed away so sprawled as he was upon a heap of dirty Laundry, but there I could do nothing. The World is as it chooses to be and he was one who knew it well.

MERIVEL

Rose Tremain

DISCUSSION QUESTIONS

1. What does beginning the book with "five endings" accomplish? Do you see Merivel moving toward any of these endings or working to avoid them?

2. What relation does *The Wedge*, as well as the novel itself, bear to Merivel's "Life's Work"?

3. Time, in the guise of Merivel's friend the clockmaker, is often a subject. Why do you think time is so important to Merivel? How does Merivel conceive of time?

4. Merivel says, "What moves me most in the World is seeing that which was once lost to us restored" (p. 146). What is restored to Merivel? Who else experiences restoration?

5. Merivel often thinks of his friend Pearce, judging his actions on earth. Why does Merivel need Pearce, and what does Pearce give him?

6. Thinking back, Merivel wonders, "[w]hat I had truly achieved in the world? And all that I could answer was that *I had persevered*" (p. 263). Do you agree with Merivel? Is perseverance itself an achievement?

7. What do you think makes Merivel want to save the bear? Why is he so sympathetic toward animals? Merivel often calls himself an animal. What characteristics do you think he sees as animalistic?

---

8. What do you make of Merivel's relationship with the King? How does it change over the course of the book? How does the King's death change Merivel?

9. Why do you think Merivel doesn't want to marry Louise?

10. What do you make of Merivel's relationship with his servants—Gates in particular? Do you sympathize when Cattlebury compares the servants' actions to Merivel's and his guests' at the end of the novel?

11. In the epilogue, Merivel suggests that he has lost everything. Do you think this is true and that this is why he dies? Or do you believe he dies a happier death?